ARE YER LAKIN'?

Diary of a Huddersfield Lad

By Bryn Woodworth

For my brother Alan,
sorely missed.

DIALECT

The entire book is set in Yorkshire where we talk in a strange way. For ease of reading I have avoided emphasising the local accents. A few Yorkshire phrases have crept in and these are usually tagged and explained by a note which you will find at the end of the book. I apologise for any others which have not been clarified and trust that this wont affect your understanding and appreciation of the story.

CHAPTER 1 – WHERE IT ALL STARTED

Summer 1958

It was the first day of the 1958 school holidays and the sun was shining as two boys cheerfully jogged up the middle of the quiet road on the Council estate. All the while trying their very best to pass a plastic football from one to the other. Unfortunately the ball was far too light and kept getting blown off course in the gentle breeze. The younger and smaller boy was having the greatest difficulty controlling the wayward ball. It seemed the more he tried the less it obeyed him. As he got more and more frustrated he stumbled on the stone curb and fell over.

'Ouch!' he yelled as his right knee crashed onto the rough road surface.

'Are you alright' his taller friend asked; the smirk on his face and the snigger in his voice betrayed his amusement at his smaller friend's misfortune.

As the boy started to pick himself up off the road he began to curse 'I don't know why you're laughing, it was your rotten pass that made me fall over. I told you this ball was rubbish'.

His mate held out his hand to help him to his feet and chuckled, 'Don't worry Oggy the Wilkinsons have a much better ball, you might be able to control that one without falling on your backside'.

They made their way up the road past the drab grey pebble dashed houses arranged in blocks of two and four. At number 16 they picked up the ball, opened the gate and jumped down the four steps onto the path.

Bang, bang bang, they gave the glass panel on the front door of the house a pounding.

'Thes sumdy at t'door' shouted a grizzly old man from somewhere inside the house.

'Who was that?' the smaller boy asked.

'That'll be their grandad, Wilky says he's dead miserable' came the reply.

The old man's two grandsons, who were munching away happily on their cornflakes in the kitchen, responded by hurrying to their feet and the race was on as they ran towards the door. Aiden – the older one – was the first to react and reached the door just before his younger brother Barry. He opened the door to find their two mates having a shoving match, which the smallest one seemed to be winning. 'Are yer lakin□*□' they both shouted at once and continued to push and shove for the privilege of being at the front.

'Who else's lakin'?' Aiden responded, at the same trying to fend off his younger brother who was directly behind him and desperately attempting to get a look in.

'You're the first we've asked' replied the taller one, 'but I'm pretty sure Fergy'll be coming out 'cos he said he would last night, and Sutty'll probably play as well. So with you two we'll have at least 3 a side'.

'And the Henshaws, don't forget them' added the smaller boy.

'Shut that bloody door, there's a gale blowing in 'ere' the old man shouted.

The two brothers stepped outside and closed the door.

'Take no notice of 'im, he's always grumpy in a morning. OK we'll just 'ave to finish us breakfast and then we'll be out, where shall we meet yer?' Aiden asked.

'We'll be on the circle' replied the taller one, 'can you bring your ball 'cos this one's a bit too light and it'll be flying into people's gardens every time we take a shot'.

'Aye alright. Tell yer what you might as well take it now'. Barry, the younger brother, re-opened the door, scrambled back into the house and went in search of the ball.

Whilst Barry was looking for the ball Aiden noticed the blood on his friend's knee. 'What've you done to yer knee?'

'Shut the bloody door!' came the shout again - Barry had left the door open.

'Oh bugger off grandad' mumbled Aiden.

'What was that Aiden, are you cheeking me lad?' for an old man their grandad had very good hearing.

'Err no I was just telling Barry off for leaving the door open'. He closed the door and sniggered before turning his attention back to his young friend.

'Oh its nowt' replied the smaller boy, 'I just fell over on the road, I'll put a plaster on it when I get home later'.

Barry returned with the ball. 'It should be OK now. It went flat yesterday but my dad fixed it with the hot poker'. He handed over the ball which bore the marks of several repairs which made it resemble the surface of the moon. The taller of the two boys gratefully accepted the heavier ball and the two of them ran off, passing it carefully from one to the other, this time with a little more success as they tried to imitate their new heroes. The lighter ball was discarded and left in the front garden where it eventually lodged itself under the privet hedge, where it would remain, untouched, for a few months.

The heroes the boys were imitating were in fact the football stars they had seen on the telly during the 1958 World Cup. All the boys had been enthralled by the competition, held in Sweden, and won by a Brazilian team who played the most exciting style of football they had ever seen and whose players had exotic names like Pele, Garrincha and Vava. These grainy black and white pictures were the first time any of the boys had seen a football tournament live on TV and the skills on display had inspired them to want to play like their heroes. All of the home nations, England, Scotland, Ireland and Wales, were represented at the '58 World Cup. The boys recognised many of the players taking part from the football cards that they were all collecting. These cards were supplied inside the wrapper of the 'penny bubblies' that most of the boys spent their pocket money on. There was an unofficial competition taking place to see who would be the first to complete the set of pictures. This competitive spirit would be a major driver in their football journey, a journey which for many of them would last a lifetime and play a major part in their lives.

The two mates – the small one was Terry Ogden and the taller, skinny one was Martin Kelly – continued on their way up the street to where their football pitch stood. To say the pitch was a little unusual would be an understatement. Instead of an oblong area of grass it was a just a circular area of broken concrete with a reddish, ash-like surface. This was the place where these boys and their friends had spent hours developing their skills and living their dreams – despite the locals trying to drive them off with their complaints about the ball ruining their gardens.

Not that there were many 'proper' gardens on this particular council estate to ruin. Most were an untidy mess of overgrown grass and weeds, often populated with items of discarded furniture and other household rubbish. At least the garden's had a privet hedge which acted as a barrier and often prevented the ball from going into the gardens; only the truly wayward shots would clear the hedge and land in the garden.

The soccer pitch was in fact a traffic roundabout, and, therefore, it was surrounded by a road. Fortunately in the late fifties not many cars were to be seen - most of the people who lived on this, and other similar council estates, had to rely on their legs, a bicycle or public transport to get around. As soon as they reached the circle the pair got to work on marking out the football pitch. Some large stones were piled up to mark the goal posts, more stones were used to mark the corners, and the edge of the penalty area was marked by the boys walking backwards dragging their heals in the loose surface to make the lines. How can you have corners on a circle, you might well ask? The young lads had come up with a creative solution to this problem. They would count twenty paces from each of the goalposts and a stone would be placed to act as the corner flag. If the ball went out of play on one side of the stone it would be a dead ball or corner kick, on the other side and it would be a throw in. Once the pitch had been clearly marked the two friends got in a bit of practice, with Terry in goals and Martin taking shots. Shortly after they started practising they were joined by their friends, Sutty and Fergy, who both lived in houses alongside the roundabout.

'Shall we start a game' suggested Terry, 'we can have 2 a side with a goaly-when-needed.' This arrangement involved one of the two players on each side being nominated as the goal-keeper but they were also allowed to play as a normal outfield player.

The lads had also devised some special rules to take into account the playing surface and its surroundings.

The first rule was an application of common sense, namely, no slide tackles. The broken concrete and ash had many sharp edges so only the most foolhardy of players would even attempt such a tackle. All the boys wore short trousers and consequently their legs were covered in plasters, scabs and scars; the results of falls on this unforgiving surface. These were badges of courage and didn't deter the lads in the least, but it did mean their mams had to keep a stock of plasters on standby to patch them up.

The second rule concerned the retrieval of the ball if it went into someone's garden, which it frequently did. When this happened it was agreed that the last person to touch it was responsible for getting it back. Now very few people on this estate paid any real attention to the state of their garden, but a few did. If you were unlucky enough to be the last person to touch the ball before it went into one of these smarter gardens you had a choice; either sneak in whilst no-one was looking, or do the polite thing and knock on the door and ask permission to retrieve the ball. This latter option took much longer so it was rarely applied, however if the owner caught you in their garden without permission you were likely to get a good telling off. Sutty and Fergy were in particularly vulnerable positions as they lived by the circle and were often threatened with the dreaded 'you cheeky little bugger I'll be having a word with your father about this'.

Finally play would be suspended if a vehicle was approaching and would only resume when the vehicle had passed by the roundabout. The same applied if an old lady or a mother with small children was walking across the circle.

No sooner had the four boys kicked off than the Wilkinson brothers, Aiden and Barry, arrived and were added to the teams making it now three-a-side. The boys decided to continue with 'goaly-when-needed' until more players arrived. Aiden, who was slightly older than the other boys, decided that one set of goals looked bigger than the other one. Terry objected to this criticism and replied 'How can it be? I marked one and Martin did the other one and we both counted 8 steps'.

'You daft bugger' replied Aiden ' Martin's at least four inches taller than you so his strides will be bigger than yours, it's no wonder one set is bigger than the other. Let me mark 'em both out.' That was typical of Aiden – always wanting to take control; the others didn't like it but didn't protest as Aiden was bigger than them and occasionally had a mean streak to him.

Eventually the game got under way.

The skill level of the boys left a lot to be desired, but what they lacked in skills they made up for with enthusiasm. After all they were just starting out on their footballing careers, every one of them hoping and imagining that one day they would be running out at Leeds Road in the blue and white stripes of Huddersfield Town, their home town club.

They were just about to kick off again when the Henshaw brothers, Dave and Jimmy, appeared and were added to the teams.

Terry Ogden, who had the nickname of Oggy, got in there first – 'baggy we're Town, and I'm Dennis Law.'

'OK we'll be Man United and I'm Bobby Charlton' replied Martin Kelly who resented the fact that he had been given the rather insulting nickname of 'spotty'.

The two teams were well matched and the score remained close, it was agreed that half time would take place when the first team reached five goals. Oggy's team which also included Sutty (whose real name was James Sutcliffe), Barry (also known as Baz) and Dave Henshaw were the first to reach five whilst Spotty, Aiden (known as Wilky), Fergy (real name Richard Ferguson) and Jimmy Henshaw were close behind on four. As the game progressed there were the usual arguments – any shot where the ball went close to the brick which marked the goalpost was hotly disputed and arguments about who touched it last before it went out of play were rife, but the boys usually resolved these issues fairly quickly.

It was a close game and some of the tackles were getting decidedly fierce as the second half progressed so it was no surprise when Dave Henshaw was knocked to the ground by his younger brother. Unfortunately for Dave, he landed on a particularly large and sharp piece of shale that caused a two inch long, rather deep, cut just above the knee on his right leg. As he lay on the rough ground yelling in pain his brother came over to apologise and help him to his feet. The other lads could tell that there was something wrong by the shocked look on Jimmy's face.

As they gathered round the prone figure they could see blood pouring out of the gash on poor Dave's leg. 'We'd better carry him home so his mam can sort him out' suggested Fergy.

'We can't, me mam's gone down to the shops at Fartown Bar' there was real panic in Jimmy Henshaw's voice. 'She won't be back for at least half an hour'.

'Well you'd better carry him over to our house' instructed Sutty 'me mam's in and she done a First Aid course at work. She'll know what to do with him.'

Dave Henshaw was a stocky lad so the four strongest boys were needed to lift him off the ground. Fergy and Wilky took an arm each and Barry and Martin each took a leg while Sutty ran ahead to warn his mam. It wasn't a particularly effective arrangement and Dave cried out in pain 'Put me down, I think I'd be better limping on my good leg if somebody supports me'.

The lads eventually got him into the kitchen of Sutty's house and left him in the hands of Sutty's mother. They made their way back to the circle where a dark red stain marked the spot where Dave had fallen.

The game continued and full time was declared when Oggy scored the winning goal to make the score 10-8. The highlight of the last part of the game came when Baz tripped his elder brother as he was about to shoot. Wilky was raging as he got up, dusted himself down and clipped his younger brother on the side of his head. The brothers then exchanged blows before the other boys pulled them apart. Wilky took the resulting penalty but Baz was not letting it past him and dived to his right to pull off a good save. The graze he received on his elbow was a small price to pay for preventing his brother from scoring. Wilky was not amused.

After the match the boys sat down outside the gate of Fergy's garden and discussed the game. Not surprisingly everyone was claiming the best goal or the best save and the arguments continued without agreement for a few minutes before Fergy said 'I'm off for a drink of water does anybody else want one?' Six hands shot up along with a chorus of 'I'll 'ave one'. Fergy returned a few minutes later, with water dripping down onto his scruffy old jumper with holes at the elbow, carrying a quart bottle. The label on the bottle showed that it had originally contained Ben Shaw's□*□ lemonade but now had been refilled with corporation pop (tap water). The boys jostled to have first sup and as usual Wilky commanded the first drink. The other boys watched on thirstily as he guzzled it down, before taking their turns. Each boy would carefully wipe the top of the bottle with their hand before drinking as they didn't want to catch the previous lad's germs. The fact that their hands were filthy from the football game didn't really matter and it didn't seem to do them any harm.

After about ten minutes Dave Henshaw appeared and hobbled over to the group. He was sporting a bandage above his right knee. He winced with pain as he sat down on the step by the other boys.

Jimmy was the first to speak 'How bad is it Dave?'

'What d'you care you little shit, there was no need for that!' Dave was not in a forgiving mood.

'I'm really sorry Dave, I didn't mean it – honestly it was an accident, it's not my fault you landed on a sharp stone'.

Dave mellowed a bit at this apology 'Well you need to be more careful in future, especially on that surface'.

'I'm sure he didn't mean to hurt you Dave' Fergy added calmly 'but you're both right about the surface on the circle, every time anybody falls over it's a cut – or just a graze if you're lucky'.

The conversation continued as the boys reflected on what had happened to Dave. The circle had been their pitch for a while now but as the boys learned more about the game of football and their meagre skills improved they decided that the limitations of their pitch was holding back their development not to mention the unforgiving surface.

As well as watching the world cup on TV the boys would go to Leeds Road to watch their home team who were playing in what was then called the second division. Oh how the boys longed to be able to dribble like Kevin McHale or head the ball into the net like Les Massie, make a sliding tackle like Brian Gibson or take a penalty like John Coddington. He was Huddersfield Town's burly centre half, who had a near 100 per cent record of successful penalty kicks using a technique which was based purely on intimidation. Whenever Town were awarded a penalty the lads would rush to stand directly behind the goals so they could watch him as he took a very long run at the ball whilst it sat motionless on the penalty spot, before smashing it past the helpless goalkeeper, almost breaking the net in the process. The surface of the circle just wasn't conducive to the development of any of these skills – especially the sliding tackle.

Sutty was looking worried. He had been caught during the game retrieving the ball without permission from his next door neighbour's garden and he knew that he was in for it when the neighbour would, inevitably, complain to his dad. The other boys sympathised with Sutty as they knew his dad had a short temper and was a bit liberal with his clouts□*□. Wilky made a suggestion, 'Dave's injured, Sutty's in bother with his neighbour and I'm fed up of sneaking into people's gardens as well so,' he paused for effect 'why don't we take the advice of the old bat who lives over there who keeps telling us to go and play football in the field?'

'D'you mean the ugly one, her with the big fat arse' asked Terry 'what lives over there?' He pointed to a house on the opposite side of the circle.

'Aye the one that's always moaning' responded Wilky 'miserable old cow'. Wilky and Terry had a lot in common when it came to insults. 'I'm sick of her; she always seems to pick on me as well. I vote we go and lake in the field'.

'Don't be daft Wilky' replied Baz 'the big lads play in there and they'd never let us near where they play, they'd soon kick us off'.

'I thought most of 'em had left school now and were working' chipped in Sutty.

'That's true' Fergy agreed 'I know that Len Bagshaw works on the dustbins 'cos I've seen him and I'm sure I saw Dennis Monroe walking across the circle last night in greasy overalls and his hands and face were black from summat, 'appen□*□ he's got a job an'all. Come to think of it I've not seen any of the others laking for a while now'.

Just then Sutty's mother called him for his dinner, so the boys agreed to go and get something to eat and meet in about an hour by the swings in the field. The next stage of their journey to football stardom was about to start.

CHAPTER 2 – OLD FRIENDS

November 2010

G entle organ music was playing as the small collection of mourners made their way out of the crematorium. 'Close friends and family only' the announcement in the Deaths column of the local paper had stated. The chief mourner was a grey haired man, who, along with his wife, was shaking hands with the other mourners as they left the building, accepting their mumbled condolences. A number of people were lighting up cigarettes and drawing heavily on them. The cold north easterly wind was blowing quite hard so most of the mourners were taking advantage of the shelter provided by the wall of the crematorium building.

A tall man with thinning grey hair spotted an old friend he hadn't seen for a few years and went over to him, held out his right hand and said 'How are you doing Fergy, it's been a long time' as they shook hands.

'Well if it isn't Barry Wilkinson, and if I'm not mistaken that's your Aiden over there, isn't it?' came the reply.

'Aye it is, he's come over from Jersey, especially for the funeral. Him and Val mated around for a good while over in Jersey' he paused and looked around, 'I'm pretty sure that's Terry Ogden who our Aiden is talking to, shall we go over and have a natter with them?'

The two of them made their way over to where Aiden and Terry were chatting away and exchanged handshakes.

Aiden, never one to mess about with small talk, made a suggestion 'I don't know about you lads but I'm gagging for a pint and I'm not one for these sort of dos. Besides which, it's bloody freezing. I don't really know any of the others here so why don't we nip down the road and call in that new pub opposite the golf course? Our Barry's come in his car if you lads need a lift.'

The suggestion was welcomed by the others so they made their way to shake hands with the chief mourner, who was Val's elder brother Derek, and passed on their condolences. They politely turned down Derek's invitation to the wake.

Terry had also driven to the funeral so he gave Fergy a lift, whilst Barry and Aiden made their way to the pub in Barry's car.

'It's a sad day, I never realised Val was in such a bad way' Fergy was the first to speak, as the four of them sat around the table in the brightly lit pub, 'but it's grand to meet up with you lot after all these years'.

It was a cold November day so they had chosen the table nearest to the roaring coal fire. The men were all in their early sixties, sombrely dressed as befitted the funeral which they had just left. A stranger might have mistaken the gathering for a business meeting. The men had all aged quite well. There was an uncomfortable silence for a while, as they sat there just contemplating their beer.

'Aye, well he'd been living rough on and off for a few years you know. It was bound to catch up with him eventually. The last time I saw him he looked shit' Wilky replied. 'He's been on his way down ever since that Scottish bird got her teeth into him, what fifteen – 'appen more – year ago. She was already a coke head when they met I reckon. God only knows why he took up with her. Mind you he was a bit of a layabout by then himself, couldn't hold a job down. Every time I saw him he was off his head on summat or other.'

'I heard he'd become a bit of a drifter, can't remember who told me that quite a few years ago' chipped in Barry. 'I wonder what happened to his first wife, Jane wasn't it? They had a place over in Jersey didn't they Wilky?' Barry (and everyone else) still referred to Aiden as Wilky, 'And didn't they have a kid and then move back to England, somewhere down south?'

'Aye, I never really cared for Jane – not my type – but she did keep Val in check. Lost touch with them when they went back to England, and you're right Baz, about them moving to the south coast, it was Bournemouth actually. Then a few years later and completely out of the blue he turns up at our house in Jersey, only we're away on holiday. Our Andrew answered the door and there's Taylor (Val was another one who was universally known by his surname) on the door step. He blagged his way in and asked if he could get a bed for the night. Our poor Andrew didn't know what to do. Taylor told him I'd said if he was ever in Jersey we'd put him up for a few nights, so our Andrew agreed he could stay. Bugger me but ten minutes later his foul mouthed Scottish bird turns up expecting to stay as well. Our Andrew told them when we'd be back, but the pair of them pissed off the day before we were due to get back. Taylor knew he was in for a right bollocking from me so he buggered off. Never saw or heard from him again. Then about a year ago I heard a rumour that he was back in Huddersfield. I can't say it was that much of a shock when I heard from his brother that he'd carked it', Wilky took another mouthful of beer. 'What about you lads, had any of you guys seen or heard from him?'

Terry was the only one who answered 'I bumped into him up at the infirmary. I was on my way in when somebody called out my name. He was having a fag with all the other smokers and you're right, he looked dead rough; I wouldn't have recognised him if he hadn't spoken first. When I asked him what he was doing up there he said he had lung cancer. He saw me looking at the fag in his hand and he just shrugged his shoulders and said one wouldn't make much difference.'

'Where was he living?' Fergy asked.

Terry took up the story 'From what I can gather one of his old mates from Leeds Road Con club took him in and straightened him out a bit. You know got him cleaned up, got some decent clothes on him and got him back on the straight and narrow-ish. Apparently he did clean his act up but had the occasional blip where he'd just disappear for a couple of days. I think the police picked him up a few times and put him in the cells to sober up. He must have over done it once too often and when the police went to wake him up the following morning he was dead. Heart attack the pathologist said, death by natural causes.'

'I can't help thinking we let him down, do you think we could have done anything to help him' asked Barry.

'Don't beat yourself up Baz, from what I've seen and heard he was past saving, anyway let's not talk any more about the bad times let's remember him for the good ones. Go on Baz get 'em in while I go for a piss.' Wilky handed his brother a twenty pound note and headed for the Gents.

'I see he's still bossing you about Barry, just like old times play-ing soccer in the field' smiled Terry.

'Aye well there's no point making a fuss on a day like today, just let him feel he's still the boss' replied Barry defensively, before confirming the drinks order and setting off for the bar.

'Those two were always arguing and fighting when they were lads' whispered Terry, 'I remember Barry once threw a shoe at Wilky in their house, Wilky was just by the front room door and dodged behind it just before the shoe landed. It left a shoe sized dent in the panelling of the door. When their Mam came home and saw it, Wilky grassed Baz up and he was in serious bother'. Fergy smiled just as Wilky returned.

'Well I see you two have chirped up a bit, what's so funny?' asked Wilky.

Bryn Woodworth

'Just talking about the good old days' said Fergy 'you and Baz were always at each other's throats in those days weren't you?'

'Normal brotherly love and affection, not something you two would have known - both having sisters that is. How is your Carol anyway Fergy?'

'Oh she's fine, she's divorced now with two grown up kids, really nice strapping lads, she lives up at Holmfirth, been there about 8 years I think.'

'Do you see much of her?'

'Yeh we keep in touch – probably see her every five or six weeks, you know the score, family birthdays, weddings, Christmas that sort of thing. I saw her last week actually and told her I was coming to the funeral and might be seeing some of the old Fartown mob and she said to remember her to you all'.

'Eh, do you remember that time when we held our Barry down while your Carol kissed him, he didn't half wriggle a lot but she got her kiss.'

They were all still laughing when Barry returned with the four pints on a tray.

'What's so funny?' asked Barry.

'We've done that line already' said Terry and the three of them burst into more fits of laughter.

'What?' said Barry, there was a slight pause as the laughter continued, 'what? Oh go on amuse yourselves at my expense why don't you'.

'Don't be so sensitive Baz' Wilky chided his brother, 'we were having a laugh about the time we all held you down while Fergy's sister, Carol, kissed you, do you remember?'

'Aye I do, I didn't think it was funny at the time but looking back I can see the funny side, how old were we then?'

Fergy explained 'Our Carol was about eleven so you would

have been twelve or thirteen, there weren't any girls her age on the estate so she used to tag along with us.'

'That's right, Fergy weren't you supposed to look after her in the school holidays. You were a bit nasty to her though, I think you really resented her being around didn't you' said Terry.

'I suppose I did, but thankfully it wasn't all the time, my mother used to work mornings so I got rid of her in the afternoon otherwise I would have gone mental.'

'We were a bit mean to her and made her play in goals most of the time didn't we?' added Barry.

'Anyway, changing the subject back to Taylor' said Barry 'he's the reason we're all here. What's your first memory of him?'

Fergy started, 'Well, he lived at the other end of the estate so I didn't know him at first, I remember seeing him walking across the circle a few times with his older brother but I never took much notice of him. Then one day we were laking football in the field and I saw him, he came in through the ginnel and walked past the air raid shelter to where we were playing. He had a football shirt on, it might have been a Town shirt actually, and he just said something like 'OK whose side am I on'.

'He always was a cocky little bugger wasn't he' said Wilky. 'He was quite a decent player though, and he was the only one of us who was a natural left footer.'

'Bit of a short arse though wasn't he you could barely see him when he chased after the ball when it went in the long grass,' sniggered Barry and there was a chorus of laughter. 'D'you remember how he was always diving around in the mud? Our mams always told us to try not to get too dirty but he used to get covered in mud, when we asked him how he got away with it he said they kept a bucket of cold water outside and he'd strip off in the garden and chuck his gear into the bucket, wash it through and hang it on the line. Bloody good idea, when we told me mam she threatened to make us do the same.'

Terry chipped in 'I don't think he was any smaller than the rest of us at first it's just that we grew faster than him, especially when he started smoking Woodbines – stunted his growth we all reckoned.'

'What's your excuse then Terry you were always a bit shorter than the rest of us and you never smoked did you – maybe your mam didn't feed you proper' Wilky bated him, 'or was it that 'other habit' you had.' More laughter from the friends.

Terry bit back 'There's no need to get personal Wilky, or should I mention those horrible National Health specs you wore? They were patched up with elastoplasts most of the time weren't they?' The good natured banter continued.

'Come on lads that's enough, it really is getting like old times with all this bickering,' interjected Barry. 'Taylor was in a band wasn't he, played guitar if I remember rightly. I remember him telling me once about the band meeting at his house to practice. Now his house was on the corner and from the front room window you could see all the way up the street. One of the lads was late so the others were staring out of the window, checking their watches, when one of the lads said out loud – '*Where the fuck is he?*' Taylor was so embarrassed 'cos his mam was in the room at the time. So Taylor gives his mate a nudge and nods towards the back of the room where is mum is sitting – '*what?*' says his mate, Taylor tells him to watch his language 'cos his mam's in the room, the penny finally drops and his mate says '*Oh shit - sorry Mrs Taylor*'. We never dared to swear in front of us mams and dads did we? Knew we'd get a clip round the ear 'ole for sure'.

'His mam was dead nice though wasn't she, she used to come and watch us when we played for Bradley Mills Working Mens, used to bring slices of oranges to refresh us at half time', said Wilky.

'He was quite funny though wasn't he?' Barry continued 'I remember him telling me he had tried to pick up a bird in the

Mecca dance hall in Wakefield one Saturday night. She turned him down and told him he was drunk, so, quick as a flash, Taylor says 'You're right I am drunk, and you're ugly – but I'll be sober tomorrow'. Then I think she smacked him one. What a lad!'

'He was always late though wasn't he, no matter what arrangements we made he was always the last to arrive, he used to drive you mad Wilky didn't he?' added Terry.

'I think that was part of his downfall' observed Wilky, 'he was always getting warnings at work over his poor time keeping, that's why he got sacked from Stevenson's Developments'.

There was a period of silence as they all reflected on times gone by.

Barry interrupted the silence when he produced a rather scruffy piece of paper from his jacket pocket. It was about A4 size, folded in the middle to make four smaller pages, it was yellow with age.

'What have you got there Barry' asked Fergy. Barry passed the paper to Fergy. Fergy studied it for a minute or two, smiled and passed it on to Wilky.

'Bloody hell, where did you find this Barry?' a visibly shocked Wilky asked 'have you kept it all this time? Is that your writing?'

'No I'm pretty sure Fergy was the author, isn't that right Richard?' replied Barry. 'I found it up in our loft when I was sorting through some old soccer programmes.'

'Let's have a look then' said Terry whose patience was running out. The piece of paper was duly handed over. He stared at it almost in disbelief.

The item which was causing such a reaction was in fact a homemade programme for Fartown United's first ever competitive match against Birkby in which they all featured. Barry was the goaly, Terry was on the right wing, Fergy was centre forward and Wilky was inside right.

'Oh just look at that' pointed Barry 'you've laid the team sheet out in the traditional 'W' formation, you must have copied that from the real football programmes which we all used to collect.'

'What d'you mean by the 'W' formation Barry?' asked Terry

Barry continued 'Come on Terry you must remember, it goes back to the day when we had five forwards, three half backs, two full backs and a goaly.

Terry wanted the last word 'Oh aye, I remember the theory but I don't remember us lads laking soccer quite like that'. The men smiled as they continued to sink their pints but little did they know that this relic from the past would take on a significance far greater than any of them could have imagined.

CHAPTER 3 - MOVING TO NEW PASTURES

Summer 1958

Sutty was the first to arrive and as he sat on the swing, feet dangling loosely, he started to consider the merits of the field as a new place to develop their skills and play out their imaginary cup finals and international matches.

The field itself had a gradual slope from the swings at the top to an old air-raid shelter at the bottom. It also got slightly narrower towards the bottom. It was surrounded by the, mainly scruffy, back gardens of the houses on the estate. Most of the gardens had dilapidated wooden fences to separate them from the playing field. Only a few of the gardens had a full set of railings, and even fewer had anything which resembled a garden such as flowers and bushes and - heaven forbid - a lawn. The gardens were mainly an area of overgrown grass whose main purpose seemed to be to provide a place to hang out the washing or let the owner's dog go to the toilet.

The two main entrances to the field were on either side at the top and led to a playground area which was generally referred to as 'the swings'.

The apparatus in the 'swings' were all substantial structures, built to last. Durability obviously had a higher priority than safety in those days. Mainly constructed of iron tubing on a concrete base, they had to be capable of withstanding the battering they were regularly subjected to by the kids on the estate. The cone shaped roundabout, in addition to going round and round, could be pushed in and out causing it to make a loud bang and vibrate alarmingly, this was known as 'the bumps'. Then there was a metal slide, similar in principle to the modern slides except it was much higher and lent itself to climbing up the support structure – in fact it doubled up as the equivalent of a modern day climbing frame, but was considerably more dangerous. The kids would take great pleasure in polishing the metal surface of the slide to make it run so fast that you flew off the end. The experts would land on their feet, the novices would suffer the pain and humiliation of landing on their backsides.

There was also a rocking horse with 5 seats in a row which, when pushed, moved backwards and forwards. Like the roundabout this device could be made more dangerous, and therefore more fun, if it was pushed so hard that it acted more like a bucking bronco than a rocking horse. Another lethal weapon!

The remaining piece of equipment was the swing itself. This bore no resemblance to the type of swing popular with kids nowadays. Like all the other equipment it was often pushed to its absolute limit. The swing could accommodate up to eight people and was 'worked' by a person standing at each end whilst holding onto vertical bars and leaning forward then backwards each time pushing with their feet. When used as intended it provided a gentle swinging movement for the kids who would sit astride the wooden seat and hold on to the metal handles. However, more often than not, the two people who were 'working' the swing would drive it faster and faster and thus higher and higher, the passengers would hang on to the handles for dear life as the swing went higher and higher until the entire structure shook alarmingly.

The ground surrounding the equipment was made of consolidated ash, with occasional patches of grass and an assortment of weeds. It was a very unforgiving surface if you happened to slip or fall, as bloodshed was virtually guaranteed.

The whole environment was fraught with danger and accidents were plentiful but the injuries were usually superficial; cuts and bruises rather than broken bones.

Sutty's mind was not focussed on the swings though, he was considering the potential of the grassy part where they would be playing. It was far from ideal, new grass was already pushing through the grass cuttings from when the council cut the grass a few weeks previously. The middle was just bare soil and the area at the bottom was completely overgrown. A gully had developed down the middle where the rainwater drained away.

At the very bottom of the field was the shelter, a red brick building with a flat concrete roof. The building had been an air-raid shelter in the war and had no windows, an entrance at each side led into a dark and rather spooky area which was divided into four rooms. The floor was just hardened mud and was decorated by a number of empty beer bottles, cigarette stubs and used condoms. The inside of the shelter was pitch black and a no-go area for the younger boys who would only ever go inside if they were dared to by their mates. None of the boys ever stayed in there more than a few seconds.

Just beyond the shelter was a ginnel, a narrow path which went through a gap between the houses and provided access to the field for the houses at the bottom of the estate.

Sutty was a tall lad for his ten years, and, like most of the boys his age, his light brown hair was cropped in a 'short back and sides' style and obviously hadn't made contact with a brush or comb for quite some time. As he sat on the swing and surveyed the field he couldn't help but notice that the perimeter of the field was littered with a collection of discarded household items and general rubbish thrown over the fence by the occupants of the houses.

Fergy, who was a little bit shorter but stockier than Sutty arrived a few minutes later, 'What d'yer think of it then Sutty?'

'It's a bit of a mess really, look at all that rubbish around the edges and it's got a right old dip in the middle.'

'Well we could shift all the rubbish down to the bottom and dump it where the long grass grows, and I'm sure we can put up with the dip in the middle. It's bound to be a lot softer than the circle so we can do slide tackles like Town defenders do.' He proceeded to do a mock slide tackle on his friend.

'Aye and goalies can dive about a bit' added Sutty who got into the spirit by doing an imitation dive. He really fancied himself as a future Town goalkeeper.

At that point the Wilkinsons arrived 'Is that a new dance you two were doing then?' joked Wilky. 'Seriously though what do you reckon? Looks like it needs a bit of work to me'.

'Reckon we should give it a go, let's get stuck in and try to shift some of that stuff from around the edges' suggested Sutty who was nervously shifting from foot to foot.

'You look like you need the bog Sutty, it's too far to nip back to your house when you're down here. Why don't you go for a piss up against the railings?' sneered Wilky.

'Sumdy might see me and I don't think they'd be right pleased for me to piss up against their railings'.

'Get down to the shelter then, nubdy will see you there' barked Wilky.

'I'm not goin' in there it's pitch black and dead spooky' replied Sutty.

'Just go in the entrance then yer wally, it's not too dark there and nubdy can see you' Wilky made no effort to hide his irritation.

Sutty duly trooped off to relieve himself and when he returned the boys all giggled as they saw the splashes on his legs and feet.

'What's up with you lot?' demanded Sutty.

Barry couldn't resist pointing out the splashes 'Haven't you learned how to have a slash without wetting your feet Sutty?'

'Oh that, I was so desperate when I got there me piss came out so fast that it bounced off the wall of the shelter onto me legs. I don't know why yer all laughing it could 'appen to anybody.'

The boys eventually stopped laughing and got stuck into clearing an area big enough for them to have a serious game. Their numbers were soon swelled by Terry and Martin who joined in enthusiastically. A couple of stray dogs entered the scene and one of them, a medium sized black and white mongrel, came up to Terry, who was the smallest, and started to get 'friendly' with him. The dog was standing on its hind legs, front legs resting on his thigh and then started rubbing up against his leg with its privates.

'Gerroff' squealed Terry as he tried to shake off the clearly excited dog.

'I think that dog fancies you' shouted Martin and they all started laughing at Terry's misfortune.

Terry eventually extricated his leg and aimed a wild kick at the dog with his other foot, unfortunately he missed and this air shot only caused him to fall flat on his back, to the further amusement of his pals. It got worse for poor Terry, as he put his hand down to push himself up, he felt it slide against something soft.

'Oh bloody hell I've put my hand in some dog shit now' – the boys showed their lack of sympathy by laughing even louder as Terry tried to wipe his hands clean by rubbing them against the grass.

'Steady on Oggy' shouted Barry 'there might be some more dog shit on the grass you're wiping your hands on.'

All their laughter must have attracted the attention of another boy who had been playing in his back garden which was next to the field. He climbed over the fence, walked over to the other boys and asked them what they were doing.

'We're shifting all this junk so we can have a proper game of soccer, if you must know' replied Wilky in a slightly aggressive way, which was typical of his need to assert his authority over all the younger kids.

'D-do you need any help?' the new boy had a slight stammer.

'Aye get stuck in we can use all the help we can get' said Barry in a much more friendly tone, 'do you like soccer?'

'N-not s-sure, I've never really played it proper' came the reply.

'Don't worry we're not really experts ourselves' replied Barry modestly,' you can join in the game if you like when we've finished getting rid of all this rubbish'.

The work continued as old buckets, lumps of wood, old cardboard boxes, empty bottles and even items of furniture which had passed their usefulness were found and removed.

'Hey I've just had a thought' said Fergy 'if we pile most of this stuff up we can chuck it on the bonfire and burn it all on bonfire night'. The boys agreed and carried on the work with renewed vigour.

'Hey lads come and have a look at this' shouted Wilky, 'I could do with sumdy giving us a hand with this settee'.

Terry and Martin raced over and couldn't resist jumping onto the settee from about two yards away, the settee rolled over onto its back along with the two boys who were yelling with delight.

'This is great' said Terry as he picked himself up 'it's too good to burn. We can use it to rest on at half time when we 'ave us drink of water. We're not going to chuck this away are we?'

'It whiffs a bit and it's torn but it's comfy enough, why don't we put it just behind the goals at the top' responded Martin.

The three of them attempted to drag the sofa across the bumpy surface. 'We need another pair of hands, Baz come and give us a hand with this, it needs lifting so we need one in each corner' yelled Wilky. Barry joined them and, after much grunting and groaning, the settee was transported to a place at the top of the field just behind where the goalposts would be situated.

After about half an hour the boys' enthusiasm was beginning to wain and it was decided that they should have a brief rest and then get started with a trial game of soccer.

'OK let's get the teams sorted out' said Barry, 'shall we stick with the teams we had this morning?'

'The Henshaws aren't here and what about the new lad?' asked Sutty. 'What's your name by the way?'

'It's A-Andrew'

'We could do with another player really cos we've got seven players now' added Sutty.

'I could get my little brother to p-play, if you like he's only a year younger than me and he's in the house now' Andrew offered.

'Aye OK go and get him, what's his name?'

'It's Richard' Andrew shouted as he climbed over the fence into their back garden and re-appeared with a slightly smaller boy with blond curly hair, who he introduced 'T-this is our Richard, he'll make up the numbers'.

'That's great' said Wilky 'come and join us Ricky are you any good in goals?'

'Dunno' came the reply, 'and my names Richard'.

'Well you might be Richard at home but when you're playing soccer with the big lads you'll be Ricky' asserted Wilky.

'OK' came the reply.

'Or we could call you Dick or even Dicky, how about that?'

'No Ricky will do.'

'Glad we got that settled and we'll soon find out how good you are in goals Ricky, you're on my side and your brother can be on Barry's team'. Everyone else was feeling rather sorry for the newcomer being bullied by Wilky. Wilky liked to be the big boss, thought Barry but his bark was far worse than his bite.

'Baggy we play downhill first' shouted Barry.

'No we'll do this like they do at the Town match, we'll toss for it, has anybody got a coin we can use?' ordered Wilky.

The boys rarely carried money around but nevertheless they all went through the motions of checking their pockets but there was no coin to be found. It was decided that Barry would hold a small stone in one hand and put both hands behind his back, whilst Wilky then attempted to guess which hand it was in. As it happened he got it wrong so Barry's team would have the privilege of playing downhill in the first half of the inaugural match on the new pitch.

CHAPTER 4 - THE MATCH

November 2010

'**M**y God, I remember that match, when was it?' asked Terry.

'Well the programme says it was 28th July 1959, so I would have been twelve and you lot would have been eleven' replied Wilky.

'No I was only ten, you lot are all older than me remember,' Terry smiled that same cheeky smile he had all those years ago. The men chuckled and they all fell silent for a moment as the memories of that first ever game came flooding back.

Eventually Terry spoke, 'How did we manage to arrange that match, most of us were still at junior school and Wilky you must have just finished your first year at secondary modern hadn't you?'

'Aye I had, and it was me that started it all off. There was a lad in my class who had been to Birkby junior school and, a bit like me, most of his mates were a bit younger and still at the junior school. The match was in the school holidays so, before we broke up from school, we arranged to play a proper match with them' Wilky paused and scratched his chin 'at Clayton Fields wasn't it?'

'Aye you're right it says here on the 'official programme' that the venue was indeed Clayton Fields' responded Fergy. 'It took a lot of organising from our side though didn't it? We all had to find a white shirt of some description; most of us wore the black shorts we wore for PE at school. It's a pity we didn't have cameras in them days we must have been quite a sight. You were in goals Barry, what did you wear?'

'I remember it quite clearly, I had a blue jumper which my mam had knitted, with my white shirt underneath. I swapped positions with Sutty for the second half. I think he did a bit better than me truth be told. It was the first time any of us had played on a proper, full sized pitch with full sized goals but the Birkby lot had all played for the school team so they were a lot more used to playing in their proper positions. We got a bit of a hammering if my memory serves me well.'

'I think it was about 9 – 2 wasn't it, I scored one of the goals. Who got the other one' asked Fergy.

There was a moments silence whilst three of them racked their brains for the answer. 'I can remember' said a smiling Terry 'cos it was me. Don't tell me you lot can't remember my moment of glory'.

'Oh yes Terry, I remember now, it was a bit of fluke wasn't it, their keeper slipped and you took advantage' observed Fergy 'you wouldn't shut up about it all the way home either'.

'Aye me dad gave me a shilling for scoring as well' smiled Terry, who then turned his attention to the Wilkinson brothers. 'I know this is a bit of a daft question but' he hesitated for a few seconds 'whatever happened to those rabbits of yours?'

The other men burst out laughing. 'You're not wrong there Terry, it IS a bloody weird question' joked Fergy.

'Well I know it is, but I was quite taken with those rabbits if you remember, I even asked me mam if I could have one but she wasn't having any of it. It was that bonfire night when I asked you two where the rabbits were and you just sort of clammed up and said something like *Oh we got rid of 'em*. For some reason it just flashed into my mind on the way here; I know it's a bit strange, but I always wondered what had happened to them.'

Wilky came straight to the point 'Well if you must know me grandad ate 'em'.

'Yer joking!' Terry was incredulous.

'He's winding you up Terry, you always were a bit gullible' Fergy ribbed him.

Wilky looked at Barry and nodded 'You tell 'em Baz, they might believe you'.

'OK here goes. We'd been laking soccer one afternoon after school and then me mam calls us in for tea. I said I'd just pop out to check on the rabbits and me mam steps in front of me, sort of blocking the way to the back door. I remember it like it was yesterday, she was wearing her pinny and she stood there with her arms folded and looked sort of agitated.'

''*You can't go out there Barry, I've got something to tell you*' she says. So I ask her why not? Then she says '*Cos the rabbits are dead, your grandad had to kill 'em cos there was summat wrong with 'em, they were poorly*'. Quick as a flash our Aiden jumps up and pushes past her into the back garden and sure enough the hutches are empty. I just ran upstairs, threw meself on the bed and cried me eyes out'.

Wilky took over, 'It must have been a few years later when me dad got round to telling me the full story. It was a good while after Johnny had died mind you, that the old bugger had eaten our pet rabbits. Apparently me grandad had always loved rabbit stew ever since he was a lad, and with the myxomatosis thing in the early fifties all the wild rabbits were virtually wiped out, so no rabbit stew. The miserable old git must have been licking his lips for months every time he went into the back garden and saw the rabbits, eventually he couldn't resist them any longer. And that Terry, my friend, is the top and bottom of what happened to the rabbits'.

'Unbelievable, I can understand now why you hated him so much' observed Fergy.

Their mood of nostalgia was rudely interrupted by the sound of a mobile phone with a jaunty ring tone. Barry and Fergy, who obviously had the same ring tone, reached for their phones, along with another three people who were sitting nearby in the bar.

Barry answered and Fergy put his phone away. As the name of the caller flashed on his screen Barry knew it was his wife and he suddenly remembered that he was supposed to be picking her up from the hairdressers ten minutes ago. A flustered Barry rose from the table and moved away from his friends to a quiet area of the pub to ease his embarrassment. Nevertheless they could still hear him apologising to his wife who clearly was upset about something. Barry returned to the table and explained that he would have to leave as he was late for an appointment. The other guys ribbed him a bit in a good natured way.

'I'm sorry but I've got to rush, I'ts been really great meeting you all after such a long time, it would be good to get together again sometime, can you give our Aiden your contact numbers so he can pass them on to me and then we can arrange to meet next time he's over here. Oh and email addresses would be handy, sorry got to go. Oh Wilky why don't you tell 'em about the tin of mints?'

'That's typical of our Barry always in a bloody rush' moaned Wilky.

'What about this tin of mints then Wilky, spill the beans' Terry wanted more.

'Well, Johnny was always a bit of a tight sod and sumdy bought him a tin of mints which he kept on the shelf next to his chair. He'd sit there scoffing 'em but never offered 'em round. He said they helped him with his cough. He was always coughing and now and again he'd spit the phlegm into his handkerchief.'

'Ergh' gasped Terry 'really?'

'Well it wasn't a proper handkerchief really, just a snot rag□*□ that me mother made out of an old sheet, she used to throw 'em away when he'd used 'em. Anyway one day he'd gone down to the pub and there was just me and our Baz in the house so I thought here's my chance. I went over to his tin of mints to grab one, you know, while the cats away sort of thing. But I got more than I bargained for didn't I. He'd finished all the mints, greedy bugger, and was using the tin as a spittoon. When I pulled my hand out it was dripping with the old man's spit.'

'Oh no' the other two winced with revulsion as they pictured the event in their minds.

'What did you do then Wilky?' asked Terry.

'I ran into the kitchen and washed me 'ands, what d'you think I did'.

'Did you tell your mam about it?' Terry's interrogation continued.

'I couldn't could I, after all I was up to no good wasn't I, trying to pinch his mints'.

'It just goes to prove that crime doesn't pay Wilky' observed Fergy.

'You can understand now why I never shed a tear when the old man died can't you?'

Terry checked his watch 'Aye well that was very err illuminating Wilky, but I'd better be getting off an all' said Terry 'I hadn't realised what time it was and I promised my missus I'd be home by 3 o'clock, so I'll be in her bad books as well'.

Wilky took a small note book and pencil from his pocket and asked the other two to write their phone numbers down as requested by Barry. 'You'd better add your e-mail addresses as well. I'll get our Barry to send you all our details so we can keep in touch, I'll probably be back in Huddersfield sometime next summer.'

Terry and Fergy did as instructed and Terry rose, put his coat on and said goodbye to the other two.

'I told my missus I'd ring her when I was ready' Wilky asserted 'and she'd come and pick me up, what about you Fergy?

'No wife, no problem; divorced eight years ago, been single ever since'.

'Sounds like that Bob Marley song, you know 'No woman, no cry'.

'Well it certainly makes for a simpler life, though I do get a bit fed up from time to time. I keep myself pretty busy with work an all that stuff'.

'Have you time for another pint Fergy or have you got to go?'

'Yes, why not, I got a taxi to the crem so I don't have to worry about driving home'

'Good lad, I'll tell Laura to pick us up in half an hour and we can drop you off if you like. Where are you living these days?'

'Up in Almondbury, cheers Wilky that would be great.'

Fergy returned with two pints, to find Wilky deep in thought studying the programme which Barry had left behind. 'D'you think Barry would mind if I take that programme?' Fergy asked, 'I can scan it in at work and then email it to you all once I get your addresses'.

'Can't see why not, rather you than me lad, I'm bloody rubbish at that computer stuff, I'll have to get our lass to ..' he hesitated while he searched for the right word 'reload it or whatever'.

Fergy smiled 'its download not reload, I'll upload it and attach it to an email and then you can download it and print it off, then we'll all have a copy.'

Wilky shook his head 'Aye whatever, like I said I'm not into all that computer rubbish but our lass'l sort it out, no bother. What exactly do you do anyway Fergy? I know you went into teaching but that was nigh on 40 year ago.'

The two chatted away happily until Wilky's wife Laura arrived.

'Laura I'd like you to meet my old friend Fergy, sorry Richard Ferguson, we were brought up together – or should I say dragged up together – in Fartown'.

'Pleased to meet you Richard' replied Laura, 'has the silly old bugger been boring you to tears?'

'No, not at all, but we have been reminiscing a bit, you know the good old days - stuff like that'.

'I said we'd give Fergy a lift to Almondbury – it's not really out of the way is it?'

'No problem, but sup up sharpish. You blokes might have all day to chat but, believe it or not, I've got other things to do'.

EXTRACT FROM BARRY WILKINSON'S DIARY

3rd November 2010

Went to Val Taylors Funeral at Huddersfield Crematorium, 11.00 am.

I hate funerals, but I really had to go to this one. Not because I was close to Val, I hadn't seen or spoken to him in over thirty years.

The main reason was Wilky, who had come over from Jersey, especially for the funeral and I couldn't let him go on his own. But it was more than that, it was that programme I had found in the loft when I was sorting through those old soccer and rugby programmes a couple of weeks ago. There it was, right at the top of the pile. Fartown United versus Birkby on 28th July 1959.

I just sat there in the loft and stared at it, I had to smile as I read the names on the team sheet and the characters behind the names. When Wilky called me a few days later to say that Val had died and he was coming over for the funeral, I thought there might be a possibility, just that – a possibility – of meeting some of the old gang.

Bryn Woodworth

Of course me and Aiden were the last to arrive at the crem, nearly missed the service in fact – nobody's fault, just an accident at Cooper Bridge, so we had to clog it a bit up Bradley Road just to get there on time. We sat at the back and spotted Terry and then Fergy.

We all got talking afterwards and went down to the pub on Bradley Road – Wilky's idea of course.

Terry had hardly changed, a bit of grey hair and he's put a bit of weight on but it was still easy for us to recognise him, he looks a lot like his dad. Fergy had lost most of his hair but otherwise he looked fit and well.

When I passed the programme round in the pub Terry got quite excited and so did Wilky. Fergy was just like his old self – he just calmly smiled when he read it, and he was the one who wrote it. It was a bit like old times, we had a few laughs and shared our memories of Val Taylor.

I had to rush off to pick Sandy up so I left it to Wilky to make arrangements to meet again.

CHAPTER 5 - BACK TO THE FIELD

Summer 1958

T he boys first attempt at football in their new stadium was a bit of an odd affair. The top to bottom slope turned out to be more of an advantage than first expected and Barry's team who enjoyed the advantage of the slope in the first half were 5-2 up at half time but, with the benefit of the slope in the second half, Wilky's team were the eventual winners by 10-8.

The gully down the centre also caused quite a few problems to the boys when they tried to control the ball as they dribbled down the centre of the field. The worst problem though was out on the wings and particularly in the corners where the grass was still quite long. This, together with the dried grass cuttings, seemed to engulf the ball and the boys were reduced to wildly hacking at the ball to free it from the grass's clinging grasp.

At the end of the game the boys settled around the reclaimed settee, five of them squeezed on the settee, two sat on the arms and the others sat alongside it.

'Well, what d'you think?' started Fergy.

'I thought it was a lot better at least I could dive for the ball in the goals without getting me knee cut' said Sutty who had pulled off a couple of good, diving saves which served to increase his personal opinion of his ability.

'I'm not sure' responded Oggy 'it was bloody hard work when

the ball went into the long grass'.

'Actually Oggy we could'nt see you once you went in the long grass could we lads' Wilky poked fun at Oggy and the lads all grinned.

'Don't take any notice Oggy, he was no better than the rest of us when it went in the long grass' Barry was quick to defend Oggy, especially when it was his brother who was doing the micky taking. 'There's not a lot we can do about the grass though is there?'

'Not the real grass but we could try to shift some of the dead stuff, has anybody's dad got a rake?' asked Fergy.

Andy, the new lad, was keen to please the others and chirped up 'Y-yes we've got one, I can fetch it over if you like.'

'Appen we'll have a bash at it tomorrow, I don't know about the rest of you but I'm a bit knackered' said Wilky and the rest of the lads agreed.

Whilst the conversation had been taking place Spotty and Oggy had been wriggling and pushing each other on the settee and eventually Oggy was ejected from his seat after a big push from his pal. The four remaining on the settee spread out a bit to take advantage of the extra space vacated by Oggy's involuntary departure.

'It's not fair – you're always picking on me 'cos I'm the smallest' he cried. When he didn't receive any sympathy from the other boys he decided he'd had enough for the day, and sloped off – a dejected figure – in the direction of the ginnel and towards home.

Spotty must have been feeling a bit guilty as he shouted 'Are you laking tomorrow?'

'Dunno' came the reply.

'OK I'll call for you when I've had me breakfast' Spotty called to him.

'I think you've upset him Spotty' said Sutty 'I don't think you should have laughed so much when you pushed him off the settee, do you think he'll be laking tomorrow?'

'Oh he'll be fine' replied Spotty 'we fall out regularly when we go to school but he's always fine the next day'. Spotty and Oggy both attended the local Catholic junior school, Saint Joe's, whereas most of the other boys went to Beaumont Street school. Wilky was the exception as he now attended Fartown Secondary.

'All the same I think we should all go a bit easier on him – he is a bit younger than us after all' said Sutty and the boys all agreed to be nicer to their smaller friend.

'OK, shall we all meet in here, by the settee, tomorrow morning then and we'll have a go at shifting all the dead grass' suggested Fergy. The suggestion met with general agreement and the boys set off to their homes with an optimistic air.

'Oh Andy' shouted Fergy 'don't forget to bring your dad's rake.' He turned to the other lads 'We could do with more than one so all check to see if you've got one at home and bring it along if you can.'

By the time he reached home little Terry Ogden was feeling very sorry for himself as he opened the kitchen door to find his mam busily preparing the family tea.

'What's up wi' you lad, have you fallen out with your mates then?' she enquired.

'Not all of 'em, just Spotty' he replied.

'Now who the hell's Spotty when he's at home?' Mrs Ogden turned to face him and dried her hands on her pinny.

'It's Martin, that's his nickname mam. Wilky gave it to him when he had that rash on his face last summer'.

'Well it's not a very nice name to call sumdy is it, especially when he's your best mate, no wonder he's throwing his weight about if that's what you all call him. I think you owe the lad an apology, what a dreadful name. Now how about I make you a nice glass of orange squash and then, when you've had a rest, you can help me make the tea, your sister Beryl and your dad will be home soon from work and I'm making us all a shepherd's pie, it's yer favourite. You can peel the spuds and carrots for me if you like.'

Mabel Ogden knew how to handle her son. The prospect of peeling potatoes was an offer he definitely could - and would - refuse! He quickly grabbed the glass of squash and announced 'Sorry mam the Lone Ranger is on the telly tonight and I don't want to miss it, I'm sure our Beryl will be able to help you with the tea when she gets home' as he made his way into the front room. He switched the TV on and while he waited for it to warm up he thought about what his mam had said about calling his friend Spotty. He decided that he, at least, wouldn't call his friend by that name again.

EXTRACT FROM BARRY WILKINSON'S DIARY

18th July 1958

Yippee it's here at last – summer holidays start today. No school for 6 weeks. No excuse for not keeping my diary up to date, I'm going to fill it in every night, here goes.

Played soccer in the morning on the circle. Saved a penalty from our Aiden – he was so angry. Ha ha.

Dave Henshaw got a bad cut on his leg when their Jimmy fouled him. It was bleeding like mad. Luckily Sutty's mother was able to bandage it up for him.

After the injury to Dave our Aiden said the circle is holding us back so we went to look at the field. It was full of rubbish and the grass is a bit long. We moved a lot of the rubbish and found an old settee so we put it behind the goals.

A new lad and his brother joined in. There called Andrew and Richard and then we had a game of soccer. My team lost to our Aiden's team by 10 – 8. We're gunna try to shift all the dead grass tomorrow.

◆ ◆ ◆

The following day the sun was shining again. Terry set off up the road towards Martin's house not knowing what to say to him. He didn't need to worry; Martin had already come out of the house and was stood by the garden gate. He immediately held out his right hand and mumbled 'Sorry about the settee.'

Terry perked up and as he shook hands with his friend he replied 'That's OK and I promise not to call you Spotty anymore'.

Martin suddenly remembered that they were supposed to be bringing their rakes. The two boys rushed back to collect these important implements.

A number of smaller kids were playing happily on the swings as the boys began to assemble to try to improve their football pitch.

The Wilkinson brothers were first to arrive and they brought a rake with them along with what appeared to be a homemade wheelbarrow. It was, basically, a wooden box without a top, made from old pieces of wood. It had two wheels, one either side connected by a metal axle and two handles, again one either side. The wheels and axle looked like they'd been salvaged from an old pram.

Sutty was the next to arrive 'what's that contraption you've got there?'

'It's a wheelbarrow, can't you tell. Me dad made it out of some old wood and I think he got the wheels off an old pram' replied Wilky. 'He said it would come in handy for collecting and moving the grass. Me mam uses it when she makes us go shopping with her to the co-op at Fartown Green. I'll tell you what Sutty, it's a damn sight easier than carrying them heavy shopping bags. Any road it might not look so good but it does the job. Have you brought owt?

'Nah when I asked me dad about a rake he said what would we need one for, when we never cut the grass, have you seen our back garden?'

'Why doesn't he cut the grass? Yer little brothers could play out there.'

'Me mam says its cos he's a lazy bugger, but he says he's got a bad back'.

Sutty came from quite a big family. As well as an older sister, he had two younger brothers. His mam and dad must have started their family when they were young as they were probably still only in their early thirties. His dad must have been a decent footballer in his youth and would occasionally join in their football matches on the circle to show off his skills. These exhibitions didn't last long, as he was carrying a far too much weight. After a few minutes his face would go bright red and he would be puffing and blowing and would leave the lads to finish their game without him.

Just then Martin and Terry arrived, friends once more, both carrying rakes. Wilky was adopting his foreman role as he dished out the orders, 'Well done lads. Terry you can make a start on the bottom corner over there and Martin you do the top corner, I'll carry on in my corner. Just pile it up and our Barry and Sutty can come round and collect it in the wheelbarrow and take it all down to the bottom end of the field and dump it where we don't play.'

'Aye aye captain' the two of them stood to mock attention and saluted Wilky who was in his element, organising and bossing people about.

'Dont cheek your elders' snapped Wilky, 'sooner we get this done the sooner we can get a match going'.

Andy and Richard, the new boys, were the next to show up and they were assigned the remaining corner to collect the grass using their dad's rake. Fergy, who was empty handed, was the last to appear and he joined in by helping with collecting the grass.

The boys beavered away for about half an hour but it was a slow job and soon they were getting tired and bored of all this hard work. Typically, Martin and Terry were the first to lose interest when they started kicking the ball to each other in between doing a bit of raking. Then they all took turns at sitting on the settee but eventually they decided they had done enough work and it was time to see if it had made any difference to their game.

They decided to stick with the same teams as yesterday and, after the ceremonial trying to guess which hand the stone was in (Wilky won this time), the game got under way. It was another close game and this time Barry's team won by 10-9.

The boys all agreed that moving the dead grass had helped but the length of the grass in the corners was still causing problems.

'I don't know what else we can do about the grass' sighed a frustrated Fergy.

'Appen we could ask Mr Doyle if we could borrow his what-do-you-call it?' suggested Barry.

'You mean his lawnmower?' asked Wilky who looked surprised at this suggestion.

Mr Doyle had the best garden on the whole estate, his house was one of the few houses which actually had a decent sized side garden and it was kept in immaculate condition with the aid of his lawnmower – the only one the boys had ever seen.

'He wouldn't lend it to us, he'd be afraid that we'd break it' suggested Martin.

'Well why don't we ask him, worst he can do is say no' added Terry.

After a few more minutes of debate it was agreed that an approach would be made to Mr Doyle and Terry was elected on the basis that it was his idea to ask him in the first place.

The boys gathered at the gate of Mr Doyle's house and Terry was pushed forward towards the door. Terry knocked on the door, but there was no answer, he turned to leave, but Wilky shouted 'Knock again only this time a bit harder he might be deaf'. Terry reluctantly followed the instructions and knocked again.

There was a rattling of keys and eventually the door was opened. A smartly dressed man, around 60 years old, smiled at Terry and asked him what he wanted.

Now Terry was never usually short of words or shy but he replied nervously 'Mmmr Doyle, sorry to bother you b-but can we borrow your lawnmower' there was a slight pause whilst he caught his breath, 'p-please?'

Mr Doyle was clearly taken by this curly haired little boy who was fidgeting nervously in front of him. 'But whatever would a little fellow like you want with my lawnmower?' he asked in a very pleasant way.

'Well err, you see me and my mates' he turned and pointed to the rest of the boys only to find that they had all disappeared, although he could hear them sniggering in the bushes nearby. 'We err like to play soccer and the circle is no good 'cos we keep getting cuts from the concrete and the people up there keep telling us off and and saying we should go and play in the field but the grass in the field is too long and and we need to cut it so we kind of err thought that we might be able to cut it with your lawnmower' Terry gasped for breath.

It took Mr Doyle a few seconds to take in what the little boy had said. 'Well I'd really like to help you young man, and I'm very impressed by the efforts you and your friends are making to get your game of football going but I don't think my – or anybody else's – lawnmower would be suitable'

'W-why not?' asked Terry. The boys had all broken cover now and were gathered at the gate once more and were making encouraging noises to support Terry.

'Well the last time I saw the grass in the field was when I walked my dog the other day and it's just too long and the ground too rough for any lawnmower to go over, I'm afraid.' He paused for a moment and then raised the index finger of his right hand, 'I do have something else which might be more useful but it could be quite dangerous in the wrong hands and you are so small. Do you have any bigger friends.'

'Oh yeh, me mates are all bigger and older than me, Wilky come and show Mr Doyle how big you are?' Wilky emerged from the group and walked towards Terry and Mr Doyle who were standing on the steps to the house. Wilky was indeed a few inches taller than Terry and like most of the short sighted boys on the estate wore a pair of national health free issue glasses, which in a strange way made him look slightly older than his 12 years. The frames of NHS glasses were made of dark coloured wire with round lenses. Wilky's pair also had a piece of elastoplast wrapped around the wire on the bridge of the nose to hold them together.

'What are you two called and where do you live? Asked Mr Doyle.

'Err well' Wilky hesitated 'I live over there and he lives further down the road' he pointed. Mr Doyle raised his eyebrows and waited. 'Oh and I'm Aiden Wilkinson and he's Terry Ogden mister'.

'Well come with me to my garden shed and we'll see what we can do'. The smart wooden shed was at the end of the back garden, the boys were impressed by the neat rows of vegetables and the complete lack of the type of weeds which populated their own gardens. The garden shed was as neat and tidy as the garden, with lots of fancy tools hanging on the wall arranged in rows. 'How old are you Aiden?

'I'm 12, n-nearly thirteen' he lied. It was strange how all the boys seemed to develop a stammer when they were nervous, lying or both.

'Which school do you go to'

'Fartown Secondary Modern' came the reply.

'And whose class are you in?' The gentle interrogation continued.

'I've just finished in M-mr Williams's class and I will be in Mr James's next year'.

'Ah, Tom Williams is a good friend of mine, did you like being in his class?

'Yes sir' he lied again.

The old man knew that Wilky was lying, his 'friend' Mr Williams taught first years and was very strict, and consequently was not popular with his students. He deduced from this that Aiden was probably a year younger than he claimed, nevertheless he smiled and said 'Well Aiden, I'm going to trust you with a piece of equipment that – in the wrong hands – could be quite dangerous'.

Wilky puffed his chest out with pride 'Don't worry mister you can trust me'.

Mr Doyle's eyebrows were raised again, 'Now Aiden I want you to take this tool, which is called a sickle, back home and ask your mother or father if it is OK to use it in the field. And, if it is OK with them, you can use it on the grass in the field. You can bring it back to me when you have finished with it, do you understand?' He showed him the sickle, which was a simple instrument. It had a semi-circular blade on a small wooden handle. Mr Doyle then demonstrated how to use the tool, which involved stooping down and swinging the tool to cut the grass.

He passed the sickle to Wilky and asked him to practice using it. At first Wilky was swinging the tool too far and too fast but Mr Doyle was patient and corrected his faults. 'OK Aiden off you go, and don't forget to get permission from your parents before you use it'.

The boys could hardly contain their excitement and pressed Wilky and Terry to tell them what Mr Doyle had said and what the tool was that he had given them.

'It's called a snicker, we can cut the grass with it' announced Wilky.

'I thought he said it was a sickle not a snicker' interrupted Terry who was feeling a bit put out as Wilky was taking all the credit when it was Terry himself who had been brave enough to approach the man in the first place.

'He said I was in charge of the sick-el' Wilky stared at Terry 'and I've got to get permission from me mam or dad to use it first but they're both at work so I'll ask me grandad instead. Don't worry he won't give a shit, we could chop our hands off and he wouldn't be bothered'.

The gang of boys trouped off to the Wilkinson's house, led by Wilky of course who was enjoying his moment of glory. The two brothers went inside and the other boys sat down on the steps and waited for them to return.

It seemed to the boys like ages had passed before the brothers emerged, without the sickle.

'What happened then, where is it, where's the sickle?' Terry asked anxiously.

'It's in the house, me grandad says we'll have to wait till us mam gets home and ask her, and she's working all day' announced Barry.

'Oh bugger, when does she get home Barry?' asked Martin.

'Well she works while four o'clock and then gets the bus, it depends if she's got any shopping to do, I dunno could be five before she gets home.'

'It's not even dinner time so we'll have a long wait' complained Terry.

'I've got an idea' said Wilky as he pointed his right index finger in the air theatrically. Having gained all the boys attention

Wilky paused for a while to keep them all in suspense.

'Go on then tell us what yer idea is Wilky?' the normally calm Fergy was almost pleading.

'Well me granddad's a lazy bastard and he always has a snooze after his dinner, so we could sneak in and take the sickle when he's fast asleep'.

'OK' said Barry 'but we'd have to bring it back before me mam gets home wouldn't we?'

'That won't be a problem our kid, you can distract him while I sneak in and put it back where we found it – simple'.

The rest of the boys were all in agreement with the plan Wilky had come up with and agreed that they would meet up by the swings after they had had their dinners and wait for the brothers to implement their little plan.

It was a lovely summer day as the boys assembled by the swing, fed and watered – literally, tap water was the staple drink, with real pop only enjoyed at weekends - if you were lucky!

'Just give the old man 10 minutes and he'll be snoring away' said Wilky.

'Do you think the sickle will be any good Wilky?' enquired Martin.

'It looked pretty sharp to me, the way it cut through that over grown plant when he showed us how to do it didn't it Oggy?'

'Yeh, it only took one swing and it cut straight through. That's why Mr Doyle said we'd have to be dead careful and nobody should get close when it's being used apart from the fella that's using it'.

'How long do you think it'll take' Martin continued the questioning.

'I reckon we'll have it done in an hour at the most' speculated Wilky, 'then we'll have to shift all the cuttings, but you lot can be getting on with that while I chop it down'.

'Why can't we have a turn?' asked Terry.

'You were there when old man Doyle told me he was trusting me to use it safely' bragged Wilky, who clearly had underestimated the size of the task in hand and who later would be only too pleased to let the other boys do their bit.

The other boys reluctantly accepted that they would be the labourers, restricted to collecting the cuttings, while Wilky had the glamour job of chopping the grass. After all, as Wilky pointed out, it was in a good cause – they would all be able to enjoy the benefit of an improved football pitch.

CHAPTER 6 - HOW TO
STEAL A SICKLE

Summer 1958

E ventually Barry was despatched to the house to check on the old man's snoozing. Sure enough when he quietly opened the front door and entered the small hallway he could hear the bellowing snore of his grandfather. He slipped into the front room where the old man slouched fast asleep in his chair, and performed the agreed signal that the coast was clear by closing then reopening the curtains. The noise of the curtains on the rail seemed to disturb the old man and he snorted and rubbed his nose but fortunately settled back to sleep.

As agreed in the plan, Wilky would come in by the back door to help him search for the sickle. 'I think he'll 'ave put it in the coal 'ole', whispered Wilky. The coal hole was a small closet which was accessed from a door in the kitchen and, as its name implies, it was where the family stored the coal for the fire in the front room. The boys stared inside but the sickle was nowhere to be seen, so they tried the pantry – also accessed from the kitchen, once again without success.

'He must have put it in the lobby 'ole', yet another closet but accessed from the front room, speculated Barry. 'I'll go in as quiet as I can and check if it's in there'. Barry tiptoed into the front room where granddad was snoring away, opened the lobby hole door and looked inside. 'I can't see a thing in 'ere

Aiden it's too dark' he whispered.

'I'll pass you the torch then' Aiden whispered back and duly handed him the torch which was always kept on a hook next to the back door.

Barry shone the torch into the lobby hole and sure enough there, sat on the top shelf with the handle protruding was the sickle. Barry stood on his tip toes and stretched out his hand to try to reach the top shelf but it was just out of reach. He found a box, put it in place and stood on it and - hey presto – reached the sickle. Barry pulled it out, but in his haste didn't see the small box of nails on the shelf next to the sickle which he dislodged. The sound of nails tumbling onto the wooden floor woke the old man.

'What the bloody hell's that?' shouted the old man, who was clearly startled by the unexpected noise.

Barry held his breath but Aiden came to the rescue 'It's just me grandad I came for a drink of water and I knocked summat over but it's OK - nowt's broken'.

'Well gerron out of t'house and leave me in peace yer know this is when I 'ave me nap'.

'OK grandad, sorry for waking you up' replied Aiden and he opened the back door but stayed inside, then he closed the back door with a bang to make the old man think he'd gone out.

Barry stood motionless inside the lobby hole for what seemed like an eternity before he heard the snoring return. He opened the lobby hole door, checked that the coast was clear and silently left the front room and entered the kitchen where Aiden was waiting. He proudly showed the sickle to his brother and put a finger to his lips before they quietly slipped out of the kitchen and into the fresh air of the back garden.

'What happened in there our kid? asked Aiden.

'Oh I knocked summat over, I think it might have been a box

of nails and that's what woke him up, it was a good job you had your wits about you otherwise he might have started looking around and found me in the lobby 'ole.'

'Aye well let's get back to the field and tell 'em what's happened and then we can get started on the grass.'

Barry shivered 'I was really panicking in there you know. I don't like that bloody lobby 'ole it's so dark in there and it's full of spiders, I'm sure I felt one climbing up me leg. We're gunna have a right job getting the sickle back in place before me mam get's home'.

'Don't be a wimp Baz, anyway you know me I'll always think of something'.

Barry didn't appear to be overly reassured by this statement at all, perhaps it was the fact that his brother's *think of something* usually involved Barry in some escapade where he ended up in trouble.

Wilky brandished the sickle triumphantly to the small group of waiting boys.

'That took a long time, what've you been up to?' asked Martin.

'We didn't know where he'd hidden it' responded Barry, 'and when I did eventually find it I knocked something over that woke him up. I had to stand inside the lobby 'ole in the dark for about 10 minutes till the old bugger went back to sleep. It was 'orrible, I'm sure there were spiders crawling up my leg but I couldn't move for fear of disturbing him'.

'Yeh I had to pull him out of the shit as usual' claimed Wilky 'it was my quick reaction what saved the day'.

Barry had had enough by now and pushed Wilky violently in the back causing him to drop the sickle. 'Calm down Baz you don't want to wet your pants do you' sneered Wilky.

Barry looked like he was going to bust a blood vessel and prepared to swing a punch at his older brother who had turned away. Fortunately Fergy could see what was coming and intervened by putting a friendly arm around Barry and complementing him on a job well done. This seemed to have a calming effect on Barry and they all marched into the field to start work on cutting the grass.

They decided that the work would start at the bottom corner of the field, where the grass was the longest. The boys stood around whilst Wilky made the first attempt at cutting the grass with the sickle. Unfortunately he had not really got the knack of it as he lunged at the grass with a chopping movement. After several unsuccessful lunges and amid sniggers from the rest of the group Terry made a suggestion.

'I don't think you're doing it right Wilky, Mr Doyle said you had to swing the sickle in a smooth way, not chop at it as if it were an axe'.

'OK smart arse let's see if you can do any better then' Wilky was really getting angry now.

Terry took over, made a few practice swings with the sickle, all the time trying to imitate the movement Mr Doyle had shown them. Then he bent down slightly and applied this rhythmic swinging motion to a patch of long grass and to everyone's amazement, including Terry himself, the grass was cut cleanly by the blade of the sickle.

'Oh, well done Oggy' shouted Fergy and the boys all applauded his success, all except Wilky whose moment of glory had been upstaged by the smallest boy in the gang.

Flushed with success Terry continued his rhythmic swing and the grass tumbled from the blade, whilst the other boys roared their approval and encouragement. After about 5 minutes Terry was sweating profusely from the effort in the warm summer afternoon sun. He rose from his stooping position 'It's bloody hard work though' he sighed 'how much 'ave I done?'

'Not a lot really' pointed out Fergy 'I reckon you've done about two yards wide and one and a half deep, so I reckon that's three square yards'.

'Oh bugger' said Martin 'it's going to take us forever at this rate. So much for you and your half an hour Wilky'.'

'Actually' Wilky turned to face Martin 'I said an hour, didn't I?' Wilky never liked being challenged and Martin decided not to say any more about it.

Meanwhile, Fergy, who was the brain box of the group, was doing some calculations. 'I reckon at this rate it's going to take us about eight hours!'

'You're joking' exclaimed Terry.

'Well work it out yourself' replied the boffin 'we have four corners to do, I estimate the area of long grass in each corner is about 50 square yards so that's 200 square yards in total. Are you following me?'

They all nodded though at least half of them had already lost the plot.

Fergy continued 'Terry has just done 3 square yards in about six minutes; that equates to 30 square yards per hour, round it down to 25 to allow for the occasional breather. 200 divided by 25 comes to 8, so it's going to take eight hours to cut the damn grass.'

An air of gloom descended over the boys. 'What if we all take turns, that'll speed things up' Wilky proposed.

'OK let's say we get up to 33 square yards per hour it's still going to take us six bloody hours. The problem is we have only got one sickle if we could get hold of another one – or two would be even better – with three sickles we could do it in two hours' replied Fergy.

'How about, when we get home tonight, we all ask us mams and dads if they know anybody who's got a sickle, you never know there might be one or two about' suggested Wilky, more in hope than expectation. 'Any road we're wasting time let's get on and see how much we can get done this afternoon. Me and our Barry have got to get this back into the lobby 'ole before us mam gets home from work.'

'But only one of us can cut at a time' pointed out Terry 'what are the rest of us going to do?'

Wilky's organising skills then came to the fore 'Let's split into teams of two, one does the cutting while the other collects the grass. Each team does 15 minutes, and you take turns doing the cutting. The rest of us can have a game of three goals and in and after a quarter of an hour we'll switch over and another team takes over the work. Terry and Martin you can do the first shift and then me and our Barry will take over. Andy and Ricky go next and then Fergy and Sutty finish off'.

'Only one problem nobody has a watch, I suppose we'll just have to guess when it's time to change over' pointed out Barry.

The boys attacked the challenge enthusiastically at first, but their lack of skill meant the job was very tiring for the cutter, and they ended up swapping roles every couple of minutes. As each team finished their turn they would retire to the settee for a few minutes rest before joining in the football.

As ever with these boys the cutting turned into a competition with each team claiming to have cut more than anyone else, and it was this spirit of competition that kept them motivated.

When Fergy and Sutty, the final team, had finished they surveyed the results. They estimated – or rather Fergy, who had assumed the role of expert, estimated that 35 square yards had been cut and cleared.

'Well, what do you think?' asked Martin.

'It's not exactly Wembley is it' replied Sutty as they all surveyed the uneven tufts of grass that remained.

'It'll probably flatten a bit when we start laking on it' Fergy suggested optimistically.

'If we can't get another sickle or two we're just going to have to do a bit at a time. I don't know about you but I'm knackered' said Barry 'I don't think we can do any more than an hour at a time, what d'you all reckon?'

There was general agreement to Barry's suggestion, and Fergy pointed out that even if they only did and hour a day the job would be finished in less than a week. On that sobering note the lads decided to go home for a rest before their teas.

CHAPTER 7 – THE RETURN
OF THE SICKLE

Summer 1958

As they all shuffled off to their respective homes the Wilkinson brothers faced the challenge of working out how to get the sickle back where it belonged in the lobby hole without being detected. It was obvious that they would need to get the old man out of the house altogether in order to put the sickle back.

The Wilkinson's back yard had a gentle slope from the house down to the fence at the bottom. The part of the garden nearest the house was where their two pet rabbits were housed. The rabbits shared a large hutch and Barry and Aiden were responsible for feeding and looking after them. A small area around the hutch was quite tidy, unlike the rest of the garden which was knee high in grass and weeds.

On this occasion the rabbits were to form an important part of Aiden's plan to smuggle the sickle back into its original place in the lobby hole. Barry was to enter the house by the back door and ask their grandad to come and check on the rabbits as one of them was looking ill, whilst Aiden would enter from the front door and replace the sickle on the top shelf in the lobby hole.

It was a good plan and was executed successfully, although grumpy grandad was not at all pleased about being dragged out to the garden to check on a pair of rabbits that looked perfectly well to him.

The brothers settled down to watch TV until their mother arrived home. The boys had agreed their strategy, be super nice and helpful before asking her about the sickle, so when she arrived home they jumped up and took the shopping bags from her.

'What have you two rascals been up to today then?' asked their mother who could tell by the unusual level of attention she was getting that the boys were either in trouble or wanted something.

'Oh not much, yer know, playing football with all the lads most of the day' replied Aiden who put on his most angelic face, although the national health specs he was wearing made him look slightly deranged.

'I hope you've not been upsetting any of those people up by the circle 'ave you, You've not been trampling on Mrs Watson's roses again, have you?'

'No mam, honestly. We've moved the football pitch into the field actually haven't we Barry?'

Barry backed him up with a nod.

'I thought you said the grass was too long in the field when I suggested it a few weeks ago' replied their mother as she continued to empty her shopping bags onto the kitchen table.

'Aye, well the corporation have been round and cut the grass a bit, it's still a bit long though' added Barry. 'Actually' he continued, sensing this was the moment, 'we want to cut the grass ourselves and Mr Doyle has lent us a tool to help us cut it but grandad said we would have to check it out with you first so he's put it in the lobby hole, and it will make such a difference to how long it will take and it will make the football pitch a lot better. Oh can we mam, can we, please?' he blurted the words out at machine gun speed.

Mrs Wilkinson stopped unpacking her shopping for a minute

and tried to assimilate Barry's barrage of information. 'Just a minute while I take all that in. You lads want to cut the grass in the field so you asked Mr Doyle? What's it got to do with Mr Doyle for 'eaven's sake?'

Aiden continued the story 'It's like this mam, the grass in the corners is still too long, the ball gets stuck in there so we thought we would try to cut it shorter' he spoke his words deliberately slowly and in a slightly patronising way.

'Gerron with it Aiden I haven't got all day AND I'm not stupid you know' came the reply.

'OK we asked Mr Doyle if we could borrow his lawn mower but he said it wouldn't work so he said we could borrow his sickle – you know what a sickle is don't you?'

Mrs Wilkinson sighed and nodded.

'He chose me' cos I'm the oldest, but he said we had to get your permission before we started to use it. I asked grandad but he said to wait for you or me dad to come 'ome. So what do you say, can we please mam?'

'Look, it's OK by me **IF**' she paused and raised a finger 'your dad says it's alright. He'll be home in ten minutes so ask him. Now get out of my way while I make a start on yer tea'.

The boys did as they were told and got out of their mother's way, went to the front bay window and watched out for their dad's arrival. He soon appeared, cycling towards them. He always took his bike around the back of the house so the boys ran to the back door to greet him.

Norman Wilkinson was in his early fifties and he wore an old grey rain coat over his navy blue overalls. The raincoat belt had been lost some time ago and had been replaced with a piece of string which was tied at the waist. The baggy legs of his overalls were gathered together at the ankles with a pair of bicycle clips. Like Aiden he wore a pair of national health spectacles. He smiled at his two sons as he parked his bike in its usual spot and carefully covered it with a piece of tarpaulin. 'Hiya boys had a good day?'

'Yeh dad, er we've got summat we want to ask you. Mam says it's alright by her but you have to agree as well' announced Aiden.

'Go on then' said Mr Wilkinson as he bent over and took off his bicycle clips 'ask away'.

Aiden continued 'You see this sickle' the boys had retrieved it from the lobby hole and placed it on the steps, 'we borrowed it from Mr Doyle so that we can cut the grass in the field but we have to get your permission before we can use it. Oh can we dad please?'

'Well I can see that it's very important to you, but it looks pretty sharp, how do I know you won't go chopping somebody's leg off with it, do you know how to use it?'

'Course we do, he showed us how to do it. Let me show you, dad. Barry pass it to me, and then stand well out of the way.' The last part was spoken with great emphasis and purely for his dad's sake.

Aiden took the sickle and did a small demonstration to his dad. His technique was now greatly improved from all the practice he'd had in the field that afternoon.

Norman Wilkinson spotted an opportunity. 'OK boys I'll do a deal with you, if you can cut the grass in the back garden without any accidents I'll let you use it in the field, I can't say fairer than that.'

Aiden and Barry looked at each other, Barry did a quick calculation, the over grown part of the garden was about ten yards long by about six yards wide. 'Dad that's gunna take us at least two hours, how about we do half tonight after tea and then we'll do the other half tomorrow'.

'OK boys it's a deal' Norman Wilkinson smiled and walked into the kitchen with a very smug look on his face, Mrs Wilkinson had been pestering him to do something about the grass in the back garden for weeks.

'Have you sorted them kids out Norman? I knew as soon as I got home that they were up to summat'.

'Aye it's all sorted, they're going to show me they can be trusted with the sickle after tea Nellie' he replied.

Well go and get yer hands washed and tell the kids to wash their's, tea will be ready in 5 minutes'.

Tea in Yorkshire was the main meal of the day and was akin to dinner in the rest of the country; it usually comprised a cooked meal with some form of meat, potatoes (usually mashed) and at least one vegetable. Dinner on the other hand was a lighter meal taken around 1.00 pm and was usually a sandwich or soup. Mr & Mrs Wilkinson, along with grandad, sat in the kitchen to eat their teas whilst the boys would sit in the front room watching TV with their plate sat on a buffet in front of them. The only variation to this practice was Saturday and Sunday, when dinner was the main meal of the day and they would all sit at the kitchen table together. Dinner at weekends usually included a pudding such as rice or sago. The Wilkinsons actually had a gate legged dining table in the front room but this was only ever pulled out at Christmas and, occasionally, for a special Sunday tea, when a tin of salmon would be reeled out along with tinned pears and carnation milk. A plate full of white sliced bread, covered in margarine, would be consumed with all these meals.

This particular tea passed without incident and after the pots had been cleared away the family – minus grandad - assembled in the back garden for the demonstration.

Aiden picked up the sickle and began to cut the tall grass down, after a few minutes he stopped for a breather and Barry raked up the grass cuttings.

'Where shall I put all this' Barry asked his dad.

'Just make a pile at the bottom of the garden then you can chuck it over the fence when you've finished' came the reply.

Aiden continued for a few more minutes before handing over to Barry for him to carry on the cutting. 'What do you think dad?' he quizzed his father.

'Just carry on a bit longer and then I'll decide'.

At this point in time their next door neighbour came out of her house, she was always friendly and ready to chat. 'Do you know I haven't seen anybody cutting grass with a sickle since I left the old country'. Mary was from the west coast of Ireland and spoke with a soft Irish accent. 'When the boys have finished your garden, sure they can come and do mine, I've been nagging Eric to clear a bit so the boys can play there. Now where did you get that sickle from boys?'

'Apparently they borrowed it from Mr Doyle across the road, they want to cut the grass in the field to make a football pitch' said Mr Wilkinson.

'Oh why didn't you come to me, sure I have one you could have borrowed'.

Quick as a flash Aiden was in 'Oh we do need another one. We'll get the job done in half the time if we have two'.

Mary stepped inside and reappeared with an identical sickle 'Now are you sure it's OK with your dad Aiden?' she enquired. 'I think it might need sharpening though, it hasn't been used for a while'.

Aiden took a trial swipe with the new sickle and it cut straight through the grass, he looked appealingly at his dad.

'Yes Mary, the boys have shown that they can be trusted. He turned his attention to Aiden 'If any of your other mates want to use one of them they will have to make sure their mams and dads agree, is that understood?'

'OK dad you can trust us, have we done enough now?' implored Aiden.

'Ok boys just so long as you remember to come back and finish it off tomorrow night' Norman Wilkinson spoke more in hope than expectation. Still, half the grass cut was better than none.

The two boys shot off to do the rounds of their friends with the good news and to tell them to get their parents approval. 'By tomorrow tea time we could have finished all the cutting and then we'd have a football pitch to be proud of' Aiden told them.

The two boys were smiling with satisfaction as they returned to the back door of their home, tired but pleased with their days labour.

Their dad was sat on the back step waiting for them, his pint mug of tea in his hand. 'Your mam wants a word with you two in the front room, and watch out she's on the warpath' the last part was whispered.

The boys stepped nervously into the front room to find their mother stood by the lobby hole 'Do either of you two know anything about these nails all over the floor? I've just trod on one and its gone right through the sole of my slipper.'

'N-no mam' they replied in unison.

Quick thinking Aiden carried on 'Maybe grandad knocked them off the shelf when he put the sickle in.'

Mrs Wilkinson looked at them, she wasn't entirely satisfied but decided to give them the benefit of the doubt, 'Oh alright just fetch me a brush and shovel and then you can get ready for bed'.

'Getting ready for bed' involved a quick wipe round the middle part of their faces with a damp flannel and a ten second flit around their mouths with a worn toothbrush. If their mother insisted on an inspection they would be sent back to the bathroom under instructions to 'do it proper this time'.

The brothers both heaved a sigh of relief and did a more thorough job of it than normal – they were far too tired to risk getting into their mother's bad books. The Wilkinson's house had three bedrooms and the boys had to share a bedroom with their brother, Les. He was much older than them and had been away doing his National Service in the Air Force for a couple of years. Now that Les had returned home space was limited, so the two younger boys had to share a bed. This arrangement wasn't very satisfactory as the boys would often mess about in the bed before eventually falling asleep. On this particular night they were so tired that they fell asleep straight away.

EXTRACT FROM BARRY WILKINSON'S DIARY

19th July 1958

What a day.

We cleared all the dead grass away and then had another game of soccer. It was a bit better but not much.

We decided that we needed to cut the long grass, so we got Terry to ask Mr Doyle if we could borrow his lawnmower, but he said it wouldn't work in the field. So he gave us a sickle instead but Grandad wouldn't let us use it till we had asked mam.

I sneaked in and pinched it when Grandad was asleep, I had to hide in the lobby hole cos he woke up. It was horrible. We cut some of the grass, Aiden was showing off but he didn't like it when Terry was better at it than him. It's hard work so we all took turns, then Fergy said it would take about 6 hours to do all the grass. We decided to just do an hour a day.

Then we had to put the sickle back before mam came home. Dad said we had to show him we could work it proper. He got us to cut the long grass in our garden to prove we knew how to use it.

Mary from next door saw us using the sickle and brought another one out for us to use as well. We'll be able to do the job in half the time now we have two sickles.

CHAPTER 8 - A CHALLENGE

November 2010

T rue to his word Fergy sent the email to his friends after about a week. Not surprisingly the e-mail went into everyone's junk folder and, predictably, some of the recipients were not vigilant enough to spot it.

A scanned version of the programme for Fartown United's first ever match, the one which had caused all the interest, was also attached.

The e-mail itself comprised a short message from Fergy which included the following suggestion....

'this programme has really got me thinking, how would you guys feel about trying to get as many of that team together as possible for a reunion? Have any of you come across, or have the contact details for, any of our former team mates?

Fergy went on to ask them for their views and also to suggest that if they were interested in discussing such a venture that they should all get back together to talk it over.

Barry was the first to respond, fortunately his wife had spotted Fergy's e-mail lying in the junk folder and immediately drew it to his attention. Barry was keen on the idea and added that he should be able to contact Sutty as he regularly bumped into him at the Huddersfield Giants games.

Barry knew that his brother would not have seen the e-mail as he didn't know one end of a computer from the other, so he forwarded it on from his e-mail address with the title 'READ THIS WILKY – IT'S IMPORTANT' in the hope that Wilky's wife Laura might see it. To be on the safe side he followed it up with a phone call to his brother.

EXTRACT FROM BARRY WILKINSON'S DIARY

11th November 2010

Got an email today from Fergy suggesting that we might arrange a reunion for the old Fartown United team. Sounds like a good idea to me, it would be good to meet up with some of the lads from the estate after all these years.

I wonder what our Aiden will think, it won't be easy for him to attend so he'll probably reject the idea, but who knows? He might not even see the email so I'd better give him a ring tomorrow.

Terry was the next to reply. He too was all for it but wasn't sure how they would go about it. He also said that he was still exchanging Christmas cards – after all this time – with Martin Kelly who had settled down in London after he got his degree and went into teaching. Terry and Martin had always been good friends and used to meet up when Martin came back to Huddersfield to see his mother and sister. His mother had died quite some time ago and the visits had petered out.

Wilky did eventually respond, he too thought the reunion was a great idea but, due to his location in Jersey, he pointed out that he wouldn't be able to play any part in the search for friends or the planning of the event. He suggested that the others meet up and get on with it and he would see them all the next time he was in Huddersfield. In the meantime he asked Barry to keep him updated.

EXTRACT FROM BARRY WILKINSON'S DIARY

14th November 2010

Spoke to Wilky on the phone and to my surprise he's all in favour of the reunion although he won't be able to get involved in the planning. Feel a bit guilty for doubting him.

Terry's up for it too so Fergy's going to arrange a meeting for the three of us to discuss how to make it happen

Over the next few days more e-mails were exchanged and the three of them decided to meet up. Fergy suggested, by way of a nostalgia trip, that they meet at the Stag pub on Bradford Road as it was the nearest pub to their old stamping ground. They all agreed – although Barry did voice some reservations due to the reputation the pub had for being a bit on the rough side.

In the meantime they agreed to all give some thought to how they might go about finding their former friends and bring their ideas to the meeting for discussion.

EXTRACT FROM BARRY WILKINSON'S DIARY

23rd November 2010

The meeting is on for next week – Fergy suggested the Stag on Bradford Road! Not sure that it's a good idea. Fergy suggested it cos it's the local pub to the old estate.

I told him I hadn't been in there in over 30 years – so he says all the more reason to give it a try. Keep an open mind.

We'll see.

2nd December 2010

Meeting Terry and Fergy tomorrow at the Stag. Hope it goes OK. Sandy is going to drop me off so I can have a few beers and leave the car at home.

Been studying the old team sheet and Sutty is the only one I've seen - apart from Terry, Fergy and our Aiden of course. I used to see him when I was playing for Honley and he was refereeing in the district league. I've seen him a couple of times at the Giants games.

Actually that's a lie, I forgot that I bumped into the Henshaw brothers in the Star at Folly Hall a couple of years ago.

Barry was the first to arrive. He had arranged for his wife to drop him off, ostensibly so he would be able to have a few beers but he also wasn't too keen to park his Jaguar anywhere near the pub for fear that it might get damaged or even stolen. He took a deep breath before pushing open the door. He was pleasantly surprised to see that the inside of the pub was tastefully decorated although the layout hadn't changed in the thirty years or so since his last visit. There was a nice quiet room off to the right where he thought that they would be able to sit and chat. Barry also noted to his surprise, and pleasure, that the bar had a decent selection of real ales as well as the usual collection of lagers and Guinness. There was loud music coming from a room towards the back of the pub and he could hear the cackle of people laughing and joking accompanied by the sound of pool balls kissing. The small yard at the back of the pub had been turned into a pleasant beer garden with a number of wooden picnic style tables. The area was enclosed by walls which provided privacy and some shelter from the wind and made it quite a comfortable area and offered another possibility for the meeting.

He made his way to the bar and was greeted by a very tall, man of Caribbean origin, with a big smile. 'What can I get you my man?'

'I'll take a pint of the Timothy Taylors please' replied Barry, who watched as the barman expertly pulled the beer, stopped pulling just before the glass was full and set it down on the bar.

'I'll just let that settle' said the barman, 'can I be getting you anything else?'

'No not for the moment, I'm waiting for some friends, do you serve food at all?'

'We certainly do sir' the barman passed him the menu which was encased in a well worn leather wallet, 'and there's a specials board over there. Soup of the day is tomato and I can definitely recommend the steak and ale pie, it's my wife's speciality'. He finished topping up the pint and passed it over to Barry who took a sip before taking out his wallet. 'Do you want me to open a tab for you and your friends?'

'Yeh that would be great' said Barry just as Fergy arrived. They shook hands and did the usual greetings. 'What are you having Fergy, there's quite a decent selection of real ales'.

'What's that you've got there, it looks good' replied Fergy.

'It's Timothy Taylors and it's not bad at all'.

'I'll have the same then'.

The barman was on it in a flash, 'same again gents?' As he was pulling the second pint he nodded towards the door as Terry walked in, 'is this gentleman with you guys as well?'

They turned to greet Terry 'Just in time mate, what'll you have, we're on the Taylors?'

'If it's good enough for you two then I'll have the same please' came the reply. 'Who's in the chair?'

'We've opened a tab, I thought we might have a bite to eat, here's the menu's'. Barry passed it to Terry 'the landlord's recommending the home made steak and ale pie'.

'It's a bit early to eat isn't it? Shall we sit down and have a natter for a bit then order the food about half twelve?' suggested Terry.

It was agreed and, as the sun was shining, they decided to test out the beer garden at the rear.

'There's been quite a few changes here, I don't remember a beer garden being here do you?' asked Fergy.

'When was the last time you were here then Fergy?' Barry asked. 'It must be twenty five years, maybe more since I was here, the clientele has certainly changed judging by the bunch in the back room, it used to be an old codgers place'.

'The pub's doing well to stay open if you ask me' observed

Terry 'especially when you consider how many pubs in Huddersfield have shut down'.

'That's progress for you, and I guess only the good ones survive. The Thornhill has gone and the Wagon and Horses, but I think the Harp is still open, so there's not as much competition as there used to be' added Fergy philosophically. 'Anyway enough of the small talk – let's get down to business'.

'Is this the full team then?' asked Terry 'what about Wilky isn't he coming today?'

'No he can't get away – it is a long way from Jersey to be fair' Barry replied. 'He sends his best wishes by the way'.

The three men sat down and Fergy started the discussion, 'OK lads, the reunion is what we're here for today, just kicking a few ideas around about some kind of get together for the old Fartown United team that appeared on the programme. You all got the copy of the programme I sent didn't you?'

The other two pulled out their printed copies of the programme and put them on the table. Unfortunately the wind was starting to blow and the pieces of paper were whipped off the table, as the men scrambled after them Terry suggested that a meeting outside in December was probably not such a good idea after all. They eventually captured the elusive papers and marched back inside the pub.

They quickly found a suitable table and were able to get the discussion underway. Barry pointed at the names on the team sheet 'I've been thinking about the team that played that day and there are a few more names we could add. People who for one reason or another, weren't in the team but were still a big part of our bunch, shouldn't we include them in this?' Barry's suggestion received agreeing nods from the others.

'Who did you have in mind Barry?' asked Terry.

'Well Dave Henshaw and his younger brother – oh heck what was his name' Barry gazed at the ceiling for inspiration.

'Oh yes Dave and err Jimmy Henshaw they lived on the circle near you Fergy didn't they?' prompted Terry.

'Aye they did' replied Fergy, 'Dave was the same age as me and Barry, and Jimmy was a year or so younger, we definitely should add them to the list'.

'I suppose they must have been on holiday when we had that first match but they were certainly involved for later games' Barry added. 'On the other hand a couple of the lads on the team sheet were just ringers really, you know who I mean the two lads from Cowcliffe who Wilky roped in to make up the numbers, Freddie and Brian.'

'OK' said Fergy 'we're getting into detail here but the points a good one, we need to be clear about who we really want to be part of the reunion.'

'I think we should limit it to people who lived on the estate' observed Terry.

'That seems reasonable to me' added Barry, 'what do you think Fergy?'

'Let's go through the team sheet and see who that affects' suggested Fergy who could tell he was going to have to be the 'chairman' of this little committee and he would need to work hard to keep the other two focussed on the matter in hand.

They went through the team sheet one by one and the two Cowcliffe boys were the only ones who didn't have the residence qualification. Val Taylor, who was the team's left winger obviously would not be making the reunion and one of the other players had also passed away as Barry explained.

'I was in the bar at Honley cricket club when Dennis Connor came up to me and asked me if I knew that his brother Patrick had died. He said it was very sudden. He told me that Paddy had never married but always kept himself in good shape so it was hell of a shock.'

'Did he say what he died of Barry?' Fergy asked.

'A brain aneurysm I think, he was a really grand lad wasn't he?' came the reply.

'Aye he was' agreed Terry, 'I used to see him up at the YM rugby club, you know the one up at Laund Hill, and you're right he always looked as fit as a fiddle, I was really surprised when I heard he'd died, poor bugger.'

The guys were quiet for a few minutes before Fergy dragged them back to business 'Well our original twelve is down to eight, let's make a list of the other people who we should include' continued Fergy. 'We've got the Henshaw brothers for a start. Who else should we include?'

'You two carry on while I get another round in' suggested Terry 'same again lads?' Terry set off for the bar but after he few strides he turned round and went back to the table. 'Shall I order some grub lads while I'm at the bar? I think I'm going to have the steak and ale pie but don't tell our lass, she's got me on a healthy diet at the moment'. Terry rubbed his stomach and the final sentence was whispered; presumably in case there was a spy in the room who would report the misdemeanour to Terry's wife.

'I'll have the same' said Barry.

'Make it three' added Fergy.

'So that's three pints of Taylors and three steak and ale pies please. Is this your place then?' Terry asked the barman.

'Yeh me and the wife have been here for' he paused and closed one eye as he calculated 'must be two and a half years now. Now will you be wanting your pie with chips, mash or new potatoes?'

Terry relayed the question to the other two and surprise surprise – chips were the unanimous choice.

'Just take a seat sir and I'll bring the drinks over, your food will be about ten minutes'.

By the time Terry got back to the table they had added another five names to the list and passed it to him to see if he knew any more. He studied the list and scratched his chin before asking 'What about that lad who moved in next door to me, what was his name?'

'I know who you mean, we used to call him Smee, like the character in Peter Pan didn't we', suggested Fergy.

'That's right Smee instead of Smith, or was it Smithies?' reflected Terry 'we never called him by his first name did we. He was quite a nervous kid, had a bit of a twitch didn't he?'

'Well we'll never find him if we can't remember his name will we; not with a surname like Smith or Smithies. I'll just put Smith with a question mark down for the time being.'

The landlord came over with their drinks 'And what brings you guys to this neck of the woods. Are you looking for something or someone?' He had an inquisitive expression on his face as he continued 'I know this pub had a bad reputation at one time but I've kicked all those types out of here when I took over.' Barry wasn't sure what he was on about as he was more pre-occupied with his accent which he had decided was a replica of Michael Holding's, the cricketer turned commentator.

Fortunately Terry was taking more notice and got the message 'Oh no, we're here on a nostalgia mission. Just looking back on our forgotten childhood' Terry re-assured the landlord. Then he added 'Come on, seriously, do WE look like coke heads to you?' with a look of annoyance.

'Well no to be honest you don't, but you'd be amazed how many oddballs I get in here looking for 'stuff'; we have a zero tolerance policy, it's the only way'.

'Well good for you my friend, and the best of luck with that. We all used to live up on the estate when we were kids and we started our own football team. One of our mates died a few weeks back and we met for the first time in ages at the funeral, we're just thinking about having a reunion – if we can get enough of the old gang together' explained Terry. 'We might go and have a look round the old estate after lunch, what d'you say lads?'

'Were you planning to drive up there?' asked the landlord, 'Is that your car parked round the back?'

Terry said 'If you mean the beamer yes that's my motor, is it in your way?'

'Oh no, you just need to be very careful where you park the car up there and make sure you lock it. There are some seriously bad people up there, and in a car like that you might be mistaken for a' he paused for a moment as he searched for the right word, 'character who drives a similar car to yours.'

'What sort of *character* do you mean?' Terry responded.

'Let's just say the sort you wouldn't want to mess with'.

'OK thanks for the tip off, can we leave it here it'll only take five minutes to walk up there?'

'No problem man'.

Barry wasn't paying attention, he was still in a world of his own, fascinated with the landlord's accent. He decided he must be related to Michael Holding or at least come from the same island – he sounded just like him.

The food arrived.

As they began to munch their way through the steak pie Fergy, who had been listening to the conversation intently, ribbed Terry 'So that's how you made your money, is it Terry.'

'How do you mean' came the reply.

'Well you being in the drug's business. Sounds like you've got all the vocabulary and the right sort of car'.

'Ha bloody ha, is that the best you can do?'

'Now then girls settle down and eat your dinner, it's far too good to let it go cold' ordered Barry.

Silence prevailed until they had finished their food.

'That was excellent' said Fergy, the others agreed. 'Shall we risk a walk on the wild side then?'

'I'm up for it; just as long as we stick together' joked Barry 'I take it you're in favour Terry as it was your idea in the first place?'

'We'd best settle the bill first' said Fergy as he made his way to the bar 'I'll pay this time, hopefully there will be plenty of chance for you guys to reciprocate'.

'You always did like the long words Fergy' chuckled Barry.

Fergy was slipping his wallet into his pocket as he came over to the other two. 'Listen to this guys, the landlord says he'll put on a buffet for us and reserve the back room if we want to have our reunion here.'

'Sounds like a good idea' Barry quipped and then added 'if we can find enough of them'.

The three of them said so long to the landlord and set off on the five minute walk to the estate.

CHAPTER 9 – BACK TO WORK

Summer 1958

Threw Wilkinson brothers woke early the following day, excited at the prospect of finishing cutting the grass and having a proper game of soccer. So early in fact that their dad hadn't set off for work yet. Their mam and dad worked at the same mill, dad was a wagon driver and their mam was a weaver. Dad worked full time and started work at 7.30, their mam worked slightly shorter hours, starting at nine o'clock and finishing at four. This enabled her to get the boys sorted for school, but as this was the school holidays she'd usually left the house before the boys got up; leaving them to pretty much fend for themselves under the rather remote supervision of their grandad.

Dad was just going out by the back door as they came down, the boys ran to the back door to watch him set off on his bike to work. 'Bye dad' they shouted.

'Morning lads' he responded 'you're up early. Don't forget you promised to finish off cutting the grass in the back garden today'.

'We will dad, promise' came the reply.

'We may as well have us breakfast and then get it done. None of us mates will be out till later anyway' said Wilky.

'What are you two doing up so early in the school holidays? What mischief have you got planned for today?' enquired their mother.

'Well we promised dad we'd finish cutting the grass in the back garden didn't we and then we're meeting the rest of the lads to do the grass in the field, its gunna look great int'it Aiden?' Barry replied enthusiastically.

'Well just make sure you take care with those sickles, they're very sharp and could be dangerous in the wrong hands'.

'Don't worry mam you can trust us' said Aiden reassuringly.

'Yes I know you two - that's why I'm worried' sighed Mrs Wilkinson. 'Any way I'm gunna catch the early bus and get a bit of overtime in, see you tonight, and don't forget – behave yourselves. And Aiden'

'Yes mam?'

'DON'T be cheeky to yer grandad'.

'OK mam'

The boys rushed to get their usual breakfast of cornflakes, laced with rather more sugar than the light sprinkling they were supposed to have, but no-one was there to stop them.

'OK Baz let's get stuck in. I'll do the bit on the left while you get on with the right. The lads won't be out before nine o'clock so we've got a good hour to get it done?'

'I reckon it won't take that long Aiden – 40 minutes at the most, l bet I finish before you'.

The two boys went at it hammer and tongs but soon slowed down to a more sensible pace. Sure enough it took a full hour and Wilky finished two minutes before a Barry. They were both sweating profusely.

Wilky went inside and got them both a glass of corporation pop which they drank straight down as they sat on the back step and admired their work. 'We're getting pretty good at this Baz' pronounced Wilky 'but we need to make sure the others do their share'.

'We'll get a rest in between us turns wont we, if there's six of us we'll split into two teams of three. If we do ten minutes cutting we'll then get twenty to rest' added Barry.

'Come on Baz let's go and see if anybody's there yet' said Wilky and off they went with the home made wheelbarrow containing two sickles, a rake and a full quart bottle of corporation pop, looking for all the world like two miniature farm labourers on their way to work.

'It's a good job mam and dad didn't go to have a look at the field, they would have seen how much we'd already cut' observed Barry.

'Aye we would have had a job on wriggling out of that one' laughed Wilky. 'We did a good job of persuading them though didn't we?' Their mood of self congratulation was broken by a familiar voice in the distance.

'Hi you two where did you get that other sickle from' gasped Martin who had chased after them.

'Our next door neighbour lent it us, so we should be able to get it done in half the time' explained Barry. 'Dad made us show him we could do it safely by cutting the grass in the back garden, we're getting really good at it aren't we Aiden?' Aiden nodded.

Baz lapsed into deep thought 'How long did it take us to do the back garden altogether?'

'An hour today and half an hour last night' came Wilky's reply 'why?'

Barry had a look of concentration on his face as he continued 'I'm just thinking we could rent ourselves out and make a bit of money. You know knock on a few doors and ask them if they want their grass cutting. How much do you think we could charge Aiden?'

Wilky was getting excited now 'Well the scouts charge a bob a job don't they, we could say we'd do half the garden for a bob, so we'd have a tanner each. Barry that's a great idea, if they want the whole garden doing we'd charge them double, what do you reckon?'

'We'd have to ask me mam or dad first though' Barry sounded a note of caution. 'They went mad when we went round selling bundles of firewood so we could buy that fancy gun shaped lighter from the post office on Bradford Road didn't they'.

'Aye Baz you're right, trouble was the thing we bought was rubbish, we couldn't do owt with it 'cos we'd nothing to light. It's stuck on the windowsill in our bedroom. We must have been stupid buying it in the first place and then getting bollocked by mam and dad' Wilky finished the sentence and spat on the ground for extra emphasis. Barry thought his brother seemed to be doing a lot of spitting these days for some reason but concluded that now was not a good time to point it out.

Fergy arrived 'Hiya - have you got two sickles now, that's great, shall we get started? Where did you get the second one from?'

'Mary next door to us give it us' replied Barry.

'OK, Fergy you can be in Baz's team and Spotty can work with me, we'll do ten minutes each. When the others arrive we'll add them to the teams. What's wrong with you Spotty?' Wilky was doing his organising bit again but nobody was bothered – apart from Martin who was looking pretty fed up.

'I just wish you'd stop calling me that name, I haven't got spots anymore'.

Wilky laughed, he always enjoyed winding all the other boys up but Martin was his favourite target. 'OK what would you like us to call you then Spotty?'

'Well Martin's me name what's wrong with that?'

'We've all got nicknames MAR-TIN' he emphasised the last word. 'I know, what about Tinny? The other boys laughed and joined in the fun with general agreement that henceforth Spotty was no more and Martin would be addressed as Tinny.

Martin wasn't so keen on his new name but it was better than

Spotty so he reluctantly agreed and they all made a start on the work.

Young boys can be cruel and these boys were no exception, as the work was interrupted by shouts of 'Hey Tinny what did you have for tea last night' and 'Tinny did you see the Lone Ranger last night on the telly' followed by sniggering. Martin bit his lip and did not respond and eventually they all calmed down. It was a good strategy on his part. The boys soon realised he wasn't bothered and Wilky's new nickname for him never caught on and the lads went back to calling him by his proper name.

The grass cutting was finished in just over an hour and a half. The team of workers had expanded gradually as more boys joined in.

By rotating the roles the work was completed far quicker than expected. Each boy worked flat out for five minutes and then had twenty minutes recovery time. Eventually the first game with the shortened grass got underway. Previously the boys had tried to keep the ball as close to the middle as possible to avoid getting bogged down in the long grass. The team size with the new boys had grown to five players on each side. With the grass cut short and the extra players the ball was spending more time near the edges of the pitch.

One unfortunate side effect of this expansion was that it increased the chances of the ball being accidentally booted into the gardens surrounding the pitch. The gardens down one side of the pitch were not a problem as there were large gaps in the fences and the gardens were all overgrown. Also the boys were able to easily access the gardens through the broken down fences without incurring the wrath of the residents, one of whom was the aunty of the Wilkinson brothers. The other side of the pitch was another matter and the boys were soon to incur the wrath of Claude!

The rule they had agreed when they played at the circle was

carried forward to the field, namely, if the ball went into someone's garden whoever touched the ball last had to retrieve it. The circumstances were a little different in the field however as there was no gateway by which the boys could gain easy access to the gardens to retrieve their ball. Instead they had to climb over the fence and sneak into the garden, collect the ball and then throw it back over the fence before high tailing it back into the field. If the owner of the garden was outside and saw the ball go into their garden the boys would sweetly ask if they could have their ball back and most were happy to oblige. All that is except Claude.

Now, Andy and Ricky lived next door to Claude and knew he was a grumpy old sod so the boys were already forewarned about potential trouble should the ball go into his garden. Eventually the inevitable happened, and the ball landed in his garden. Claude must have been watching the boys through the kitchen window, and immediately dashed out into the garden and picked up the ball. Barry had been the last to kick the ball so he had the responsibility of asking for it back.

'Please can we have our ball back mister?' came the polite request.

'Why do you little scruffs have to play so close to my garden? You can have it back this time but, I'm warning you, if it comes in again that'll be the last you see of your damn ball'. He threw the ball back into the field and added 'Now clear off and play at the other side of the field'.

As he turned to walk back to the door Wilky said in a stage whisper 'Why don't you bugger off you miserable sod'.

Claude turned to face the boys and his face turned bright red 'Who said that?'

No answer.

'Come on which of you scruffy little buggers said that?'

Still no answer.

'I've a good mind to report you all to the police'.

'W-what for' stammered Andy 'w-we're only p-playing f-football and this is a p-playing field'.

'Yeh that's right' came another anonymous response.

If Andy had wanted to stay anonymous he was betrayed by his stammer.

'I know that's you Andrew. I'll be having words with your father when he gets home tonight and telling him how you've been cheeking me off.'

G-g-go on then' stammered Andy 'see if I care'.

Claude eventually went back inside the house but the boys could see him watching from his kitchen window.

'Well done Andy' they all chimed and theatrically made a point of slapping him on the back in full view of the tyrant at the kitchen window.

'Will you be in bother when your dad get's home?' asked Fergy.

'N-nah he doesn't like Claude, my dad says he's so grumpy he could fall out with his sh-shadow', to which the boys all laughed.

Andy and his brother Richard had only recently joined the merry band of young footballers and the boys could tell that he was very embarrassed about his stammer, but this little example of bravery had won the other boys over and he was now a fully fledged member of the gang.

The game continued without further incident. Afterwards the boys relaxed on or around the settee and did their usual post match review; inevitably the subject of Claude's garden was raised again.

Fergy started the discussion, 'We're gunna have to be careful, I reckon the next time it goes in his garden and he sees us we won't get the ball back'.

'Can he do that, that's stealing int'it?' asked Terry.

'I dunno, it might be, but how would we get it back, would we have to report him to the police' replied Fergy.

'My dad's got a mate whose a copper.' Terry announced

'Well ask your dad to find out from his copper friend what we should do if Claude nicks us ball' it was more of an instruction from Wilky rather than a suggestion.

They all agreed that this was a good idea. 'In the meantime we'd better have a rule that says no kicking it hard or tackling near to his garden' proposed Fergy and they all agreed to this, as they trooped off to get some dinner.

'Whose laking after dinner' asked Martin and they all agreed to meet again after they had eaten.

EXTRACT FROM BARRY WILKINSON'S DIARY

20th July 1958

Got up early and finished cutting the grass in our back garden.

The lads were dead chuffed when we came into the field with two sickles and we split into teams and took turns at cutting the grass. Soon had it all finished.

Martin was complaining about our Aiden calling him spotty, I don't blame him it's a horrible name. Aiden said we'd call him Tinny instead but I think that's a daft name as well.

The pitch was a lot better and we had a good game until the ball went into Claude's garden. Terry was the last to kick it but I stuck my leg out and knocked the ball into his garden so it was my job to get it back. I asked him politely if we could have the ball back but he was ranting and raving before he would give it back. He warned us that next time he would keep it and I believe him.

Then our Aiden started cheeking him and he went mad and told us to bugger off, but Andy said he can't stop us playing cos it's a playing field. Claude knew it was Andy cos of his stammer but Andy didn't care, he says his dad doesn't like Claude anyway.

We all agreed not to kick the ball hard when we are near to Claudes garden from now on.

Over the next week or so the group expanded to a regular ten or eleven players, Val Taylor had by this time joined the group. In addition to these 'regulars' there were a few more who joined in from time to time. The boys enjoyed their games with these larger teams and even started to pass the ball from player to player instead of just putting their heads down and trying to dribble past everyone. They hadn't yet mastered the off side rule but anyone caught bug lining□*□ was called a cheat.

The matches continued without serious incidents apart from the odd shout of 'Hey watch your language boys' when the women who lived next to the field were hanging out their washing. This was usually responded to by a shout of 'Oops sorry missus'. However someone must have decided that the boys' language was getting a little bit too ripe.

The boys were happily playing one day when a policeman arrived on the scene. The local bobby was not an unusual site on the estate as it was part of his regular beat, however he normally stuck to the streets and it was unusual for him to set foot in the field.

Terry was the first to spot him and he immediately alerted the other boys 'Ey up lads there's a copper over there, better watch us language'.

The policeman stood and watched the game for a while until, eventually, the ball was hit in his direction. He stooped to pick it up, put it under his arm and casually walked over to the boys. He gestured to the boys to gather round him.

'Now then boys I've been getting some complaints about the language used during your football matches' he started.

'How d'you mean?' asked Terry.

'Swearing is what I mean sonny, swearing. Now which one of you is Wilkinson?'

Aiden and Barry half heartedly put their hands up.

The policeman turned to the older brother 'I take it you are the one called Wilky then?'

Wilky nodded, nervously stepping from foot to foot and then made a pathetic attempt at sticking his chest out.

'What is your first name young man?'

'Aiden mister, err I mean officer' he mumbled.

'Well apparently Aiden, according to my information, you are the worst offender. Now tell me where do you live?'

'Over there' Wilky pointed vaguely in the direction of his home.

'I'll be needing a bit more than that laddy, what's your address?' The policeman took his notebook and pencil out of his pocket, licked the end of the pencil and wrote down Wilky's details.

The expression on Wilky's face had turned from slightly cocky to terrified as he complied with the policeman's request.

'I'll have the names and addresses of the rest of you boys as well'.

Each boy gave his details as requested by the policeman. The sun was shining brightly but there was a very big cloud hanging over this particular group of boys.

'Right boys, I've been watching you for quite a few minutes and there are some good little footballers amongst you. I can also see that you've put a lot of effort into trying to make this stretch of overgrown scrubland into a passable football pitch, which is to your credit. So I'm going to keep these little notes which I've written down, and I'm not going to report you this time BUT..' there was a pause as the policeman scanned the terrified faces of the boys who all seemed to be holding their breath, 'if I get any more complaints about the language used in this field I will have to take the matter further' another pause 'and you all know what that will mean don't you?'

He looked at the boys and they all nodded vigorously, and he could see real fear in their eyes. As he turned away he smiled to himself at a job well done and said 'OK lads get on with your game' and with that he threw the ball over his shoulder and back to the boys.

The boys watched him stride past the swing and out of the field.

As soon as he was out of sight Martin said 'What did he mean when he said "you know what that will mean" I nodded but I don't know what he meant, do you lot'.

A few of the other boys shook their heads and then little Terry, the youngest of them, said 'I think he means we will all go to prison'. A hush fell on the lads and one or two appeared to be on the verge of tears.

Wilky tried to lift their spirits 'He can't do that, you don't get sent to prison for bloody swearing.'

'You're the worst at it Wilky, you're always swearing. If you don't stop you're gunna get us all into trouble' said his brother Barry.

'Do you think we should tell us mam's' asked Terry.

The boys remained quiet for a while until Fergy spoke, 'Look he said he isn't going to report us so we aren't in big trouble but I reckon we should tell us mam's and dad's just in case the word gets back to them,' the boys all agreed. 'Right then we all tell 'em tonight and we're all gunna have to stop swearing. Agreed?' The boys all nodded. 'Oh by the way the coppers number was 109, you'd best all tell your mams that as well.'

Barry thought to himself *'good old Fergy always a cool head in a crisis, not like my hot headed brother - thankfully.'*

The boys had no enthusiasm for a game of soccer after this episode so they all decided to go home, get some dinner and then come back afterwards. Fergy told the rest of the group that the England versus New Zealand cricket test match was on the telly and then suggested 'Why don't we have a game of cricket for a change, I've got a bat and some wickets and I'll bring a tennis ball as well'.

CHAPTER 10 - AN UNEXPECTED FRIEND

December 2010

The earlier sunshine had gone and it was a bitingly cold early December day with a hint of snow in the air as the three friends emerged from the pub onto the busy Bradford Road. As they tied their scarves around their necks, slipped on their gloves and fastened up their overcoats they took a few minutes to survey the scene, each one of them silently comparing it with the world they grew up in. It was immediately clear that the area was dominated by Asian businesses.

The old Regent dance hall was now an Asian restaurant, the Handy Corner – a small corner shop where they used to buy their penny bubblies – was now selling brightly coloured Saris and other silky material. All along Bradford Road were numerous other businesses all sporting Asian names on their shop fronts.

Terry pointed at the Asian restaurant 'Hey we had some good times in the old Regent didn't we? Course it was still a dance hall in them days wasn't it, we had never even heard of discotheques in those days.'

'I don't think the word had even reached Huddersfield then' added Barry. 'And what did they call that band they used to have, it was some Octet wasn't it, we all thought they were a bit old fashioned didn't we?'

'It was the Brian Tann Octet if I'm not mistaken and they weren't old fashioned Barry they were **traditional**' continued Fergy, the man with the memory.

'What I do remember is them playing the last waltz around half ten and anybody who hadn't pulled made one last desperate attempt at getting off with a lass. It was a bit of a scramble really. If you were lucky and succeeded you then offered to walk the lass home and tried to get a good night kiss and a date the following week' added Barry. 'Sadly I can't say I was particularly successful on that score' he reflected.

'Never mind Barry, you can't be good at everything, but Martin used to do alright didn't he?' remarked Terry.

Barry looked heavenwards as his mind travelled back 'Aye, spotty had quite a way with the girls didn't he, jammy bugger!'

The nostalgic conversation continued as the men made their way towards the old estate pointing out things which had changed and things that had remained the same. The corporation yard was still there – even though the buildings had been modernised but the brush making shop had gone. The three of them, smartly dressed white businessmen, seemed a little out of place in this particular area of the town.

As they made their way up the short hill to the estate and rounded the bend they could immediately see there had been some changes. Even before they reached the brow of the hill they could see the tops of a number of trees which appeared to be growing out of the circle – formerly a lump of concrete - where they had first started playing football. Sure enough as they reached the top they could see four mature trees planted on what appeared to be a lush grass surface. In the middle there was a large piece of smooth sandstone which had the names of the two streets which comprised the estate skilfully carved onto them.

'Bloody hell' said Terry 'that's a hell of a change from our day.'

'You're not kidding' Fergy made a silent whistle as he surveyed and took in the scene.

All the houses on the estate were built in blocks of two or four and had originally been covered in a dull grey pebble dash, much of which had fallen off, leaving large patches of bare red brick. Now they were all tastefully rendered in a light beige colour. The old wooden doors with the paint peeling off had all been replaced by modern composite doors and the previously rusty and draughty metal framed windows had now been replaced by thermally efficient, double glazed UPVC.

The three of them stood in the middle of the circle and gazed at the changed surroundings. A few of the houses had obviously been bought by the tenants under the right to buy scheme introduced by Maggie Thatcher; these were easily identified as they were the ones with smarter gardens and different doors.

One of the houses which appeared to be privately owned was Fergy's old home. There was something slightly unreal about the garden. The lawn was immaculate even in December and flowers were unseasonally growing where once there was a rough patch of overgrown grass and weeds. On closer inspection the lawn turned out to be made of artificial grass and the flowers were plastic.

'Brings back a few memories lads doesn't it' Fergy said as he pointed to the upper floor of his old house 'that was my bedroom up there, the one over the doorway'.

'Well the garden looks a lot smarter than yours did, at least from a distance. The artificial lawn looks OK but the plastic flowers are a bit tacky. I suppose it's what you'd call a low maintenance garden, and there's a flashy car parked out front' remarked Barry.

'You know what lads, I get the distinct feeling we're being watched' Terry's eyes were drawn to slight movements of curtains in a few of the houses and he gave a nervous shudder.

'Just your imagination Terry, but I suppose we do look a bit odd' Barry reassured Terry, 'let's go and have a look in the field and see what's changed in there'.

The entrance to the field had been a rough cinder track with long unruly grass and weeds at the edges next to the fences of the adjacent gardens, now it was all levelled with a smooth tarmac finish which extended into the top area of the field where the swings and roundabout had been. The three men were silent as the memories came flooding back. Terry was the first to speak 'That's where old Mr Doyle used to live, he had a lovely garden didn't he, but just look at the state of it now, it's a right mess. I'll never forget that day you all sent me up the path to ask if we could borrow his lawnmower so we could cut the grass in the field'.

'He could have sent us away but he didn't did he, he lent us the sickle and then showed you and our Aiden how to use it, he was a nice old man really' Barry smiled as he reflected on the incident.

'Not like Claude eh, what an arsehole he was' added Terry 'I'm sure it was him that reported us to the local copper'. The three men smiled and walked on into the field itself. 'We were really shitting ourselves that day when he warned us about swearing.'

The old playground had disappeared and had been replaced by a more modern, and considerably safer, set of apparatus. A child friendly rubberised surface had replaced the old, unforgiving gravel and ash covering. The playground was surrounded by metal fencing in a cheerful shade of red.

The playground though, was not what caught the friends eye, their attention was focussed on the area where their football pitch used to be.

The long grass around the edges and the bald patch in the middle with a gully running through it had all gone. They had been replaced by a fully enclosed area with a man-made surface of the kind you find on modern tennis courts. It had markings for two basket ball courts lying side by side complete with rings. Marked out and running in the opposite direction was a five a side football pitch complete with goals at either end. A group of five or six young lads were having a game of soccer and it was getting quite heated. The language was far worse than anything the boys had ever uttered.

'Bloody hell' there was a look of shock on Terry's face 'will you just take a look at that'.

'When you look back and think of the state this place was in when we first started to play soccer here' Fergy paused for a moment. 'What would we have given for something like that eh lads, it would have been totally beyond our wildest dreams'.

'Yeh' replied Terry 'but just look at all the litter there is in there, it makes me want to go in and start cleaning the place up. Kids just don't appreciate things these days.'

The three friends were so completely absorbed in the new facilities that, as they sat on the bench surveying the scene, they didn't notice that they had company.

'Well boys looky here, what have we got?' The men turned round to see a group of five youths, who were sauntering over to them. Their exaggerated swagger was intended to make them look both cool and tough but only served to make them look ridiculous.

'Oh no, looks like trouble' mumbled Terry. The three friends remained seated, as the local yobbos confronted them.

'What are you seeing here Desmond?' asked a tall black youth.

'I ain't so sure what we have here, what do you guys think?' replied a slightly lighter skinned individual.

'Are you guys looking for something for a good time maybe?' asked the first youth. 'Or maybe you've just come here snooping on us boys'.

'We're just minding our own business actually, last time I

checked that wasn't against the law' Terry replied confidently.

'Well man this is OUR territory and WE make the laws around here' chirped another of the gang, this time a white youth who looked about fourteen but already sported an array of tattoos on his neck and hands. A stud in his nose complimented the two on his left eyebrow and he had a strange plastic thing through his right ear lobe. He stepped nervously from foot to foot and seemed to have something stuck to his fingers as he continually flicked them.

'Why don't you boys go and find something useful to do and just leave us alone' suggested Terry.

'Come on lads' said Barry 'I think we've finished here'. The three of them stood up but their way was immediately blocked by the youths. 'We haven't got a quarrel with you lads just step aside and we'll pretend that nothing happened.'

One of the youths pulled out a knife and waved it in front of Barry. 'You guys will leave when we say so – gorrit?'

Barry had been an uncompromising centre half in his younger days and had earned a reputation for standing up to threats and bullies, sometimes to his own detriment, 'Now don't be silly boys this has gone far enough just let us through OK?'

Whilst all this had been going on one of the youths had been calling someone on his mobile phone.

Barry and the knife wielding youth were now a few feet apart, the youth was still waving the knife in Barry's direction. Terry and Fergy were quietly urging Barry to sit down to take the heat out of the situation. Barry wasn't inclined to follow this good advice so Terry pushed him back down onto the bench.

'For fucks sake Barry what are you playing at these guys are for real, they'd just as soon knife you as look at you' urged Fergy, who was also feeling the strain and spoke through gritted teeth.

'Well what do you two plan to do to get us out of this mess?' replied a still agitated Barry.

'I don't know but antagonising a kid with a knife is a sure fire way of getting hurt' Fergy tried to reason with him.

Barry raised his hands in mock surrender 'OK, OK I get the message, I'll let you two do the talking from here on'.

'Are you boys entertaining our guests?' everyone spun around to see a tall, gangly, Rastafarian with slightly greying hair and a rather scruffy goatee beard, who had just arrived on the scene.

'We caught these guys snooping around boss, and the grey haired guy in the middle thinks he's Tom Cruise' the one they called Desmond was pointing directly at Barry.

'So just what are you guys doing here? You don't look like the sort to go sightseeing in Fartown?' asked the Rastafarian.

Barry was sure he recognised that voice and the face did look slightly familiar, but when the Rastafarian smiled he showed a golden tooth and that's when it clicked. 'Bloody hell its Gerald isn't it, Gerald Wilson. The last time I saw you, you were in hospital after somebody knifed you up in Brackenhall?'

The Rastafarian was taken aback by this and stared at Barry for a moment, scratching his scrawny beard and squinting as he tried to recognise this man, who clearly knew him. 'That was a long time ago' he replied uncertainly.

'You don't remember me do you Gerald, I'll give you a clue – Honley football team' Barry's confidence had risen sufficiently to tease the Rastafarian. Fergy and Terry sat and stared in disbelief.

'That sure was a long time ago man' he repeated slowly and there was a further pause whilst he racked his brain and then a light shone in his eyes, 'Oh yeh I recognise you now, it's Barry, you were the captain of the second team weren't you? I can't remember your second name though, you had black curly hair in them days didn't you? He smiled a warm smile and shook hands with Barry. 'But come on guys what are you doing here, you are a long way from Honley?'

At this point he turned to the youths and spoke sharply 'What do you lads think you're doing. You been messing with my old friend Barry and his mates, get lost and do something useful while I sort this mess out'. The youths mumbled a few complaints but basically did as they were told and sloped off.

Barry responded to Gerald's question 'Well believe it or not Gerald we were all brought up here, on this estate.'

'No way man' the surprise on Gerald's face was obvious.

'Yes I lived at number 16; Terry here lived down the road'

'Number 68' interjected Terry.

Barry continued 'And Fergy here lived up by the circle, that's right boys isn't it?' The other two nodded their agreement.

'And which number did you live at by the circle?' Gerald's interest was clear.

'Number 4' came the reply.

'I don't believe it, that is where I am living man, Oh man wait till I tell me woman she won't believe it either.'

'So is that your fancy motor parked outside number 4 Gerald?' asked Barry.

'It sure is man. I am a successful business man now you know' Gerald smiled with pride, once more revealing his gold tooth.

'I've got the same model' said Terry 'what year is yours, I see you have private plates'.

'It's an 02 with the v6 engine' replied Gerald.

'Oh very nice I've got the 2000 model'.

'So what are you guys going here?'

'It's kind of a long story, but we used to play soccer in this field here, it was just a patch of rough grass in those days and we got a team together and we were thinking of trying to get all the old team members together again, you know a sort of reunion. We were just reminiscing when the local hard men arrived and started hassling us. To be honest we were warned by the landlord at the pub to be careful as the estate has a reputation for being a tough place. Looks like he was right.'

'Ah them boys are just pussycats really, they like to think they are hard men but they do what I tell them. You guys can come here any time you like, I'll put the word out and no one will be bothering you.'

'Is this your patch then Gerald?' Terry asked in his usual cheeky style.

'Well what I say goes on this estate, so yes is the answer. I really like your friends Barry.'

'Does the soccer pitch get much use these days Gerald?' asked Fergy.

'Oh yeh, we have some decent players living round here – my son plays here most evenings with his friends. A lot of the time they are playing basketball, but yeh they play a bit of soccer too.' He turned his attention to Fergy 'Tell me man when did you live in number 4?'

'My parents lived there up till the mid seventies actually, before they got one of those flats on Bradford Road, you know the ones behind the butchers shop'.

'There ain't no butchers shop on Bradford Road now man it's all Asian'.

'Oh aye – I forgot, I mean those flats near the traffic lights at Fartown Bar, on the left hand side'.

'I know where you mean, are they still living there?'

'Fraid not they died a good while back'.

'Listen lads I'd love to sit and chat about the old times but I need to get going, things to do and all that' said Terry.

'Yeh me too' said Barry.

They all got up and started making their way out of the field. 'So tell me Gerald do you ever see any of the other West Indian lads from your Honley football days, you know Bobby and Michael those guys?' asked Barry.

'No not very often; they're all settled down and married you know, kids an'all that stuff', Gerald looked dismissive of these conventional arrangements and, as they reached his house, he added 'Well it's great to see you Barry, give me your number and I'll text mine back to you. You give me a call next time you wanna come and I'll make sure you don't get hassled'.

Barry gave Gerald his number before the three men shook hands with Gerald and headed off down the hill towards the pub where Terry had left his car.

As soon as they were out of earshot from Gerald, Terry started 'Bloody hell Barry I didn't know you were a fully paid up member of the Fartown mafia, you could have told us!'

'It's just as well he is Terry, I thought we were in deep shit there for a minute' added Fergy.

'Yes it was stroke of luck really wasn't it' came the reply from a smug looking Barry. 'Gerald's business must be booming, he's obviously bought the house and that beamer must have set him back a bit'.

'What line of business is he in then?' asked Fergy.

'You must have lived a sheltered life Fergy' Barry replied with a look of mock incredulity 'let's put it this way I don't think he will be declaring it in his tax return.'

'Oh that type of business, I get it now'.

'Can I give you guys a lift anywhere?' asked Terry.

'A lift to town would be handy, I 'm supposed to be meeting Sandy there this afternoon' replied Barry.

'Yes Town for me too, I've got a few things I need to get' agreed

Fergy.

The men piled into Terry's beamer, 'Nice wheels Terry, Gerald's not the only one whose business is doing well by the looks of it' complimented Barry.

'Mustn't grumble as the saying goes' replied Terry.

'Just before we get moving can we agree what's happening next', Fergy's organising mode was back, 'How about I do a quick summary of what we've agreed today and email it to you chaps with some suggested dates for us to get back together?'

'Do you know Fergy you'd make a great secretary, I could do with somebody like you to manage my affairs' Terry sniggered.

'Bugger off you cheeky little sod' came the reply.

'You've not changed a bit have you Terry, you always were a cheeky little fella and loved a wind-up didn't you? That's why we loved you so much then - and still do. Come on get a shift or I'll be late for my missus' Barry said cheerfully.

CHAPTER 11 – CRICKET LOVELY CRICKET – A SMASH HIT

Summer 1958

Most of the boys were familiar with cricket on the telly although it seemed a bit dull to them compared with soccer. The BBC seemed to show a lot of test matches and their dad's all seemed to like watching it. They'd all played a bit, the casual sort of thing – on the beach at Filey, three small wickets with bails which kept falling off in the wind, a tennis ball and a cheap bat. Even mams and dads would join in. Mam would usually be assigned to field in the far distance, dad would insist on batting first to show off his prowess with the bat and the kids would bowl under arm and watch dad smash it all over the beach leaving their mother to chase after it. Eventually dad would declare and the boys would get a turn. Happy days.

Fergy made his way into the field determined to organise a proper game of cricket. He had his hands full, with a nearly full sized set of wickets and bails, a decent bat and two different types of ball. One was a standard tennis ball the other was a 'corky'. They all agreed to start with the tennis ball but if it proved unsuitable, and Fergy expected it might, they would revert to the corky which was much heavier and harder and wouldn't be hit as far as the tennis ball.

Terry and Martin joined him and they decided the wickets would be set up in the middle of the field. This was the area that was devoid of grass and had a gully running down the middle where the rain had drained down the field.

'OK we'll have one set of wickets here' pointed Fergy, 'Terry you get on with putting them up while I pace out the distance to the other set, it's supposed to be 22 paces.' Fergy marched down the centre of the field quietly counting out loud '19, 20, 21, 22' the last number was emphasised and Fergy turned around to see Terry hammering in the first set of wickets with the front of the bat.

'Stop that' he shouted, dropped the remaining three wickets and raced back towards Terry. 'You're not supposed to hit the wickets with the front of the bat, you'll ruin it you twerp' exclaimed Fergy.

'Oh sorry – but the ground is dead hard, how am I supposed to get the wickets to stay up' came the embarrassed reply.

'Here give it to me' said Fergy as he grabbed hold of the bat, 'this is how you do it'. He flipped the bat so the handle was at the bottom and carefully drove the wicket in with the round bit at the top of the handle.

'How was I to know, I've only ever put them in on the beach and its dead soft so you can just push 'em in' explained a rather flustered Terry.

'OK well you know now don't you' snapped Fergy.

The rest of the boys arrived. There were eight of them altogether.

'What do we do now then Fergy seeing as you are the expert?' asked Wilky who didn't care for someone else being in charge.

'Well, we will need to pick sides and decide which side bats first. You have two batsmen, one at the batting end and the other at the bowlers end. Then the other side has to bowl them out. There are three ways you can be out; bowled, when the ball hits the wicket, caught out, when someone catches the ball before it bounces, or LBW.'

'What's that last one again?' asked Terry.

'L-B-W' Fergy repeated slowly 'it stands for Leg Before Wicket and means that if the ball was going to hit the stumps but you stop it with your leg you're out. The decision is given by the umpire who is neutral'.

'What's new-tral?' responded Terry, mocking Fergy's slow and deliberate speech.

Fergy sighed and thought for a moment 'It means – oh don't bother we won't include LBW, we don't have an umpire any road.'

'Can we just gerron with it' appealed Martin 'I think we understand what it's all about Fergy. I suggest that if the ball reaches the fence it's a four, if you hit it into one of the gardens it's a six and out, AND whoever hits it into the garden has to fetch it. Are we all agreed?

There was a bit of moaning about the 'six and out' bit but they all agreed and play began. Fergy's team, including Martin, Barry and Ricky were to bowl and Wilky's team of Terry, Andy and Sutty would bat. As agreed previously the tennis ball would be used.

In fact the experiment with the tennis ball lasted all of three balls. Fergy ran in and delivered the first ball up the slight slope to Wilky who had used his captain's privilege to put himself in to bat first. The first ball hit a small stone and skewed off to the right of the wicket.

'Wide' exclaimed Wilky.

'Oh come on you saw it hit a brick and spin away' pleaded Fergy. He went on 'We need to clear all these little stones from the pitch.'

'Sh-shall I go and get a brush from our house to sweep them away?' volunteered Andy.

Play was held up whilst the brush was retrieved and used to clear the stones away, a cloud of dust rose from the bone hard surface. Fergy's next ball was a beauty, pitching just in front of Wilky who took a wild swipe at it and missed, fortunately for Wilky it bounced over the top of the wickets.

'Good ball Fergy keep 'em there' the shout of encouragement came from Barry.

Next ball up Wilky repeated his wild swing but this time connected with the ball which went, bullet like, over every one of the fielders and into the long grass at the bottom of the field. As no boundary had been declared for that end of the pitch Wilky and his batting partner, Sutty started running. As they completed each run they shouted 1, 2 and the fielders all ran towards the general area where the ball had landed. Whilst the boys searched desperately for the ball, which was buried in the long grass, they could hear the two batsmen counting 9, 10, 11.

'Stop, Stop running' pleaded Fergy we've lost the ball. At this point Wilky, Sutty and the rest of the batting team joined in the search.

'Did you see that shot though, bragged Wilky, 'nobody could have stopped it, it went like a rocket din't it?'

'Oh shut up Wilky it was just a lucky swing' came the angry response from the normally calm Fergy. 'This isn't working. Let's stop looking and try the corky instead.'

'Are we carrying on the score from when we stopped running we had got 12 I think' bragged Wilky.

'No I think we should start all over again don't you' suggested Fergy.

The batting side reluctantly agreed to this suggestion and Fergy picked up the corky ball. No-one had seen one of these before. It was a cheap imitation of a real cricket ball made from compressed cork which must have been soaked in something and then dried to give it the weight. It was much harder and heavier than the tennis ball.

The experiment with the corky ball was to last even fewer balls than the tennis ball as Wilky was about to find out to his considerable cost.

Fergy ran up as before, the greater weight of the ball seemed to enable him to deliver a much faster ball. The speed of the ball, and the fact that it didn't bounce as high as a tennis ball completely fooled Wilky. He moved his bat too late, the ball was past his bat and struck him on the middle of his bare shin with a sickening thud, a sound that was even heard by Ricky who was fielding on the boundary.

Wilky went down in a heap and wriggled in agony as the boys ran in to help him. A stream of expletives was flowing out of Wilky's mouth and there was a trickle of blood emerging from the sizeable lump on his bare leg.

'Whose fucking idea was it to play with that fucking cannonball, I think I've broken me fucking leg'.

Barry leaned over and quietly spoke to his wounded brother 'Aiden I know you're hurt but if you carry on swearing out loud somebody is going to report us to the police again and then we'll all be in trouble wont we. These kids look up to you, now's your chance to show them how tough you are.'

Wilky bit his lip, whispered a few more expletives and, with the aid of his brother got to his feet. Fergy came over and spoke, 'I'm really sorry Wilky I didn't mean to hurt you, is there anything I can do for you?'

'You can get rid of that fu-'he stopped in mid sentence 'flippin ball for a start'.

That bit of humour despite the pain he was in seemed to release the tension all the boys were feeling and they all laughed. Terry and the rest of the boys then came up to Wilky and patted him on the back.

'You took a bad one there Wilky' sympathised Terry 'can you walk?'

'Just about' said Wilky as he hobbled over to the settee with the help of his brother.

All the boys gathered around the settee. Fergy was the first to speak 'Well it looks like the corky ball is a non starter then and the tennis ball is too easy to slog into the long grass so where does that leave us?'

Martin responded 'I guess we need a ball that's harder than the tennis ball but not as hard and heavy as the corky don't we'.

Everyone agreed with Martin's summary but no-one had any suggestions to resolve the problem until ….

'I-I've g-got an idea' stammered Andy 'we have a sort of p-plastic ball, it's red and it's the size of a cricket ball, it's hard p-plastic not like the football we play with. Me d-dad bought it by mistake when we were on holiday, do you want to give it a try?'

The group agreed that anything was worth trying, so Andy went off to fetch the plastic cricket ball, 'Come and help me find it R-Richard' he shouted to his brother and they climbed the railings of their back garden and disappeared into the house.

'How's the leg Wilky?' enquired Fergy who was feeling responsible for the pain he had inflicted on Wilky.

'It feels a little bit easier' came the reply as Wilky examined the lump and cut on his leg, 'I don't think it's broken'.

'I think you'd better get something on that cut Wilky' said Barry 'let's nip back to the house and get some iodine on it and a plaster to cover it', and off they trouped.

The four who were left behind waited till the Wilkinsons were out of earshot before making any comment and,typically, it was Terry who started the conversation 'I'm glad it were him and not me, it made a hell of a thud when it hit him. I don't think I've ever heard Wilky swear as much as that, he must have been in a load of pain, he was squealing like a pig.'

'It's a good job no-one got hit in the face in't it' added Martin 'it could have made a hell of a mess'.

'You can see why the cricketers on the telly wear them great big pads now can't you' said Fergy to general agreement. 'I hope this ball that Andy went for is OK – we're knackered if it isn't'.

'Well they're coming back now so we'll soon find out' added Terry.

Andy threw the ball towards the lads with a shout of 'Catch it'. Martin was the first to react and made a pouch with his hands – just like he had seen them do on the telly – and grasped the ball. 'Ow' he squealed and shook his hands 'that stings a bit'.

The other lads laughed at his discomfort 'Nice catch Martin' complimented Terry in his usual cheeky tone.

Fergy was excited, 'Lets have a look then'. Martin tossed the ball to him and he examined it. 'It's pretty hard but not too heavy, lets try bowling it.' Fergy did a practice ball over to Terry, the ball bounced once and was caught by Terry.

'It looks good' said Terry 'you bowl it to me again Fergy but this time I'll have the bat'. Fergy complied and Terry struck the ball with the bat and it ran over the grass chased this time by Sutty. Sutty picked it up and threw it back to Fergy who caught it in the same way that Martin had but this time he absorbed the impact by withdrawing his hands a little bit after the ball was safely pouched.

'There you go Martin that's how to catch it without hurting your hands' bragged Fergy.

'Where did you learn how to do that?' asked Sutty.

'I've seen 'em on the telly, that's what they do. I've learnt a lot from watching the test match, my dad is dead keen on cricket and he showed me a few things in the back garden as well'.

At this point the Wilkinson brothers returned, Wilky was limping but was walking unaided. He was sporting a huge plaster on his damaged leg and there were still some smudges of blood further down his leg as well as a streak of iodine that nurse Barry hadn't bothered to wipe off.

Barry ran ahead of the wounded soldier 'What's the new ball like?' he asked enthusiastically.

'It's pretty good actually' came the reply from Fergy, 'I think it will be alright, are you fit enough to carry on Wilky?'

'I'm not sure if I can run, my legs still bloody sore' Wilky winced as he spoke.

Still playing the old soldier thought Barry.

'Don't worry you can have a runner, I saw them do this on the telly. You do the batting but somebody else positioned a few yards away runs for you', the ever knowledgeable Fergy replied.

'OK I'll give it a go, but let me have a few practice shots first' Wilky replied uncertainly.

So after a few practice shots the game restarted. There was a bit of confusion when the first run was scored as they only had one bat so it was agreed that the batsman would drop the bat before setting off to run. In the end they sent Andy to get another bat, it wasn't as big as the one Fergy had brought, but it was agreed that it was better than nothing.

Wilky's team managed to get to the massive total of 27 before they were all out, Fergy got two wickets and Barry and Martin got the others. Wilky, with the aid of a runner, was the top scorer with 14.

Fergy opened the batting with Martin and the score rose to 15 before Fergy was out, caught on the boundary by Terry from Andy's bowling. Next to bat was Barry and he and Martin took the score up to 25, three needed to win!

Sutty was bowling to Barry who was batting carefully and had reached a score of 8 by taking singles and the odd two. The third ball of the over sat up nicely for Barry who threw caution to the wind and had an almighty swipe at the ball. As soon as he connected with the ball he raised his hands in celebration, he knew it would be at least a four and possibly a six and out but that didn't matter to Barry as the match would be won. As he celebrated and watched, the ball arrowed its way over the fence on the leg side and his joy rapidly turned to fear. The ball was heading straight for the back door of one of the houses. The doors had two glass panels at the top, the rest of the door was made of wood. Barry spoke a silent prayer that the ball would strike the wooden part but... no such luck. Crash went the glass panel as the hard plastic ball struck it in the middle. Barry stared at the damage from his position at the wickets and then almost choked as he said 'Oh shit, what do I do now lads?' He turned to find that he was talking to no one as all the boys had disappeared from view. In fact some had run into the long grass and laid down, Andy and Ricky had hopped over the fence into their garden, followed by Martin, and a couple of others, including Terry were hiding behind the settee.

As Barry stood there wondering what to do he could hear the sound of stifled laughter coming from behind the settee. He knew it was Terry, who had quite a distinctive laugh, so he asked him 'Will you come with me Terry to explain what's happened to the people who live there?'

'No way Baz you're on your own with this one' came the giggling reply'.

As Barry made his way over to the house he thought it was strange that no-one had emerged from the house to find out what had happened. He also realised that it was in the same block as his auntie's house, two doors away in fact. He stooped to go through the dilapidated fence and made his way through the knee high grass to the damaged back door. He knocked – no reply. As he waited he saw the cricket ball had somehow bounced back off the window and was lying on the path next to the door. He picked it up and put it in his pocket. He knocked a second time but there was still no reply.

He walked along the path to his Aunty Agnes's house and knocked on the door.

His Aunt answered 'Hello Barry what are you doing here love?'

'Well' he hesitated 'I've just hit the cricket ball and it's broken the window at number 46. I've knocked on the door but there's no answer and I don't know what to do'. He sniffled a bit and wiped his nose on the sleeve of his shirt.

'Oh there won't be anybody in, they're both at work love. Come in a minute, your uncle Ray is in, I'm sure he'll be able to sort it out. Ray?' she shouted for her husband. A short, chubby man with grey stubble shuffled into the kitchen.

'What is it now Agnes?' he saw the boy 'Oh hello Barry what are you doing here, has something upset you?'

'He's hit the cricket ball and it's broken the glass in the Oldham's door. Can you make it safe Ray – they're both out at work and don't usually get home till after five'.

'Come with me Barry and we'll have a look at it' he held out a reassuring hand and walked out of the house to take a look. 'That must have been quite a hit Barry, did you think you were Don Bradman?'

'Who's that Uncle Ray?'

'Just an Australian cricketer lad, he's very good. What happened to the ball?'

'It bounced off the window, I've got it in my pocket' he took the ball out of his pocket and showed it to Uncle Ray.

'I'm going to get you a brush and shovel and I want you to clear up all the glass and put it in the dustbin while I find a piece of wood to cover the gap where the glass was, is that OK?

'Yes Uncle Ray – thank you'

Uncle Ray, who was still wearing his slippers, sidled back to his house and came out with a brush and shovel and a hammer and some pliers. 'I need to get the rest of the glass off the door before you start sweeping up Barry. It'll only take a couple of minutes'.

Barry watched on as his Uncle carefully removed the remaining glass from the window. He turned to see what his friends were up to. They were lined up by the fence watching proceedings.

'Barry!' shouted Wilky 'have you found the ball yet?'

'Yeh it's here' he threw the ball over the fence where it was caught by Martin.

'Are you going to be long?' asked Fergy.

Uncle Ray must have heard this as he shouted back 'He'll be another five minutes then you'll be able to carry on your game of cricket' as he walked back to the house to fetch some wood for the window. He came out with a piece of wood, a saw and a pencil. He measured the piece of wood against where the glass had been and marked it carefully with the pencil, then cut it down to the right size with the saw. He held it up to the space where the glass should have been.

'Perfect fit Barry', said Uncle Ray 'now you just hold it in place while I pop back for my hammer and some nails to keep it in place'. After hammering in the nails he stepped back to take a look at his workmanship, 'that should hold it until Eric can get some glass cut to size.' Uncle Ray continued 'Eric is the man who lives here and he's a plumber so he'll be able to fix it, don't you worry, but you might have to pay for the glass'.

'Oh thank you Uncle Ray'.

'I'll tell you what, why don't you come round tonight after tea with your dad and we'll sort it all out with Eric and Mary? Off you go now and join your mates. And try not to hit the ball too hard this time!'

'Thanks again Uncle Ray'.

At that very moment Mrs Oldham came around the corner

with the door key already in her hand. She stopped suddenly when she saw the damaged door. 'Oh' there was a slight pause as she moved her hand to her mouth 'what's going on here Ray?'

'It seems my nephew is a budding Don Bradman, he hit the ball for a six and unfortunately it broke the window in the door. I've just done a quick repair on it'.

'Oh is that all' Mrs Oldham gave a sigh of relief 'I thought for a moment we'd been burgled'. Barry noticed that she had a lovely Irish accent similar to his next door neighbour and she also had a lovely friendly smile. 'Eric will have it sorted in no time, don't worry young man'.

'Please tell my uncle how much it costs to fix it and I'll pay you back' Barry spoke with a nervous quiver in his voice.

'Now, are you and your friends the ones who I saw cutting the grass with the sickles?'

'Yes that's right'.

'Well I'll do a deal with you, how about you – and your friends – cut the grass in my back garden and we'll call it quits. Do we have a deal?'

'Yes Mrs Oldham – we have a deal, and...' Barry hesitated 'thank you for not being mad at me'.

'Oh run along with you.'

Barry did as he was told and went back into the field where his mates were waiting anxiously wondering what was happening about the broken window.

Uncle Ray set off back to his house and then turned around 'Be careful Mary, watch where you step, there's probably some bits of glass inside'.

'Ah to be sure there is an'all. No problem Ray I'll have this lot cleared in a jiffy. Oh and thank you for sorting this out; that nephew of yours is a grand lad isn't he?'

'Oh he has his moments as his mother will tell you, but he's a good kid at heart'.

Mrs Oldham went into the house, put the shopping bag down on the table, took off her coat and put the kettle on. She put the shopping away whilst the tea brewed and went into the front room and settled down for a relaxing cuppa.

After finishing her tea she went back into the kitchen to clear away the broken glass and, to her surprise, found a group of boys with sickles and rakes busily cutting the grass in her garden.

CHAPTER 12 - THE SEARCH BEGINS

December 2010

As Terry drove them back into the town centre snow was starting to fall as they discussed and agreed who would do what with regards to contacting the remaining members of the Fartown United team. They also agreed to meet again in a fortnight's time to see how things were going and to decide what to do next. Fergy agreed to act as coordinator and make sure that they all kept in touch.

Terry dropped them off near to the bus station and then drove off to his business to catch up on some paperwork which he had been neglecting. As he drove along he started to reflect on his, largely happy, childhood in Fartown. He remembered the characters behind the names they had been discussing. Martin Kelly his school friend, a year older than him but a soul mate throughout his youth. Their chats on the bus, their regular disagreements about whether Town were better than Fartown (the local rugby league team). Martin was always soccer first whilst Terry was a rugby man. It was great when the fixtures for the two always seemed to be Town at home one week and Fartown the next, that way they didn't need to decide on their allegiance as they could watch them both. In later years that seemed to go by the board and there were many times when they had to choose. Terry would always choose rugby whilst Martin stuck with soccer.

Terry had gone on to fulfil his dream of playing semi-professional rugby whilst Martin had gone to University down south. Although they continued to keep in touch via Christmas cards they had not seen each other in over twenty years. What would they say to each other if they did finally meet up at the reunion? No doubt they would have a lot of catching up to do.

His daydreaming came to an abrupt end when his mobile phone rang and it was back to reality as he pulled the car over, switched into business mode and took the call which was from a supplier.

After getting dropped off by Terry, Barry and Fergy walked together towards the bus station. 'Do you fancy a coffee?' Fergy asked.

'I'm supposed to be meeting the missus but I could give her a call and tell her I'll make my way home on the bus, I don't think she'll be too bothered' replied Barry.

'There's a nice Italian coffee house just over the road if you fancy it' suggested Fergy.

'Why not, I just need to give her a call' came the reply.

They crossed the road to the coffee house where Fergy went to the counter to order the coffees and Barry sat at a table near the window, where he rang his wife.

Fergy brought the coffees over and spoke 'So how do you feel about the prospect of meeting your old pals from Fartown Barry?'

'I'm not sure really' reflected Barry 'I'm pretty sure I'd like to do it, but I'm not sure how it will go. I mean, we – you,me and Terry and our Aiden – have all done pretty well, but I wouldn't want to turn it into a bragging exercise like the school reunion we went to a few years back'.

They had both been to an old school reunion where everybody seemed intent in telling everyone else how successful they had been.

'Yeh I know what you mean. But I often think back fondly to those times where we all pulled together to try and make a football pitch out of a cabbage patch.'

Barry smiled and replied 'I don't think you could have grown cabbages on the field, it was far too rough.'

'Oh I know, I just mean how simple things were, you know, all we wanted was a decent pitch to try and play football on. It sometimes felt like everyone was against us though didn't it? First of all we get kicked off the circle, then we had the run in with Claude, the incident with the copper, we certainly had our fair share of setbacks'.

'Didn't we get chased off the Tranny a couple of times as well? It wasn't as if we were doing any damage either. It sometimes felt like the world was against us; we never gave up though did we, despite all the little problems and challenges. We had to 'cos no-one was going to do it for us were they? It was all down to us. Do you remember when our Aiden saw those discarded football posts down at the back of the old ICI pitches down by the canal and suggested we could carry them up to the estate and put them up in the field?'

'Aye it seemed like a good idea at the time' laughed Fergy. 'We didn't get very far with them though did we?'

'We hadn't a clue how heavy they were going to be had we? I think there were about six or eight of us and we were going to carry both sets away at the same time, when we started to lift them we realised we'd all have to weigh in on the one set and come back for the other. They were so heavy we could only just lift them. I think we only got about five yards before we abandoned the plan altogether didn't we? They weighed a ton, what a sight we must have been, half a dozen scruffy kids struggling to lift these great things off the ground.'

'Didn't your Aiden leave a sixpence there and say something really stupid like 'fare exchange is no robbery' or something similar?'

'Yeh he did and then went back for the tanner□*□ after we abandoned the idea. Typical of our Aiden, he was always having good ideas but not many of them actually worked'.

'And what about all that money we made from cutting people's grass. It all started after you smashed the glass on the back door of your auntie's neighbour'.

'That's right we did her grass to pay for the damage to the window and then everyone else kept asking us if we'd do theirs. We were going to use the money to buy a football strip if I remember rightly, my god what plans we had. Nothing was impossible was it? What did we do with the money in the end, did we blow it on sweets from the little shop on Flint Street?'

'No, although that was Terry's preference. Actually I think we bought a new cricket set and some of those plastic cricket balls, they didn't last very long with the whacking we gave 'em'.

'Do you remember how we used to amuse ourselves while we waited for the bus up to the New College on Westgate?' asked Fergy.

'Didn't we test each other on the names of football grounds you know - Prenton Park?'

'Tranmere Rovers' Fergy replied confidently.

'Typical, I could never get one over on you back then either'.

'I could never work out why you left school after your O Levels Barry, you did really well didn't you?'

Barry thought for a moment before answering 'I think I just wanted to get away from school, all those bombastic teachers wearing gowns and all the homework. I'll be honest with you Fergy I had real difficulty adjusting from Beaumont Street where we were amongst the brightest kids to the New College where we were just one of many. For me it was a real culture shock and I had a lot of difficulty getting used to all the formality. I think I'd just had enough of all that stuff by the time

I was sixteen and I wanted to get a job. Looking back I think I missed out on the experience of going to University, and not having a degree did stop me from applying for quite a few jobs. But it all worked out OK in the end, I've done alright, got my own business and nobody tells me what to do. That is apart from Sandy, she certainly keeps me on the rails' he paused for a moment for another sip of coffee. 'How did you get on at University then Fergy, did you enjoy it?'

'I had the time of my life, I really did. I got into the football team and met loads of great lads, talented footballers too, one or two of them went on to sign professional, although none of them ever made the big time. I enjoyed the social life as well; I still keep in touch with quite a few of the lads I met at uni. Anyway changing the subject; I'm quite excited about getting the old team together, I was wondering about organising some sort of soccer match, you know - book one of the indoor pitches at the sports centre, that kind of thing, what do you think?'

'I think it's a good idea but we just don't know what sort of physical state the other lads will be in. I mean err' he hesitated 'I played soccer at Honley until my late forties but I'm certainly paying for it now, I don't think my ankles would be up to it. You and Terry look like you're in decent shape but our Aiden's carrying too much weight and he's had a couple of hip replacements so I can't see him going for it; who knows what the others will be like.'

'I guess we'll just have to ask them when we make contact with them won't we? If we could get enough for four-a-side then the others can watch if they don't want to play.'

Barry finished his coffee 'OK Fergy I've got to go but I will make a start on my hit list on Monday morning and I'll keep you and Terry informed. We'd better copy our Aiden in on any progress, as you know he doesn't like being left out.'

The snow was falling quite heavily as the two men shook

hands and said their goodbyes and went off in different directions each wondering how their search for old friends and the reunion would pan out.

EXTRACT FROM BARRY WILKINSON'S DIARY

3rd December 2010

Well what a day!

The pub was great – good landlord, good beer and good food. Not what I expected at all. He even offered to put a buffet on for us if we have the reunion there.

Terry suggested a walk up to the old estate, which turned into quite an experience.

Boy how the place has changed, the council have spent a lot of money up there, smartened it up big time. Our old football pitches are unrecognisable. The circle has been landscaped and is now covered in grass; they've even planted some trees and put up some fancy stone street signs. The field has an enclosed five a side football pitch which doubles as two basketball courts, all fenced off to stop the ball flying into people's gardens. What a difference.

We sat on a bench, a bit like our old settee really, admiring the new pitch and reminiscing. I even had a tear in my eye, overwhelmed by nostalgia.

We were so enthralled with the new pitch we didn't see some cocky youths approaching us and then threatening us. It was a bit of a close escape really until my old mate Gerald Wilson, from my Honley football days, turned up and rescued us. He just told the lads to clear off and they did as they were told – thank goodness.

We made a few plans for the reunion and we all took away a list of people to contact, I've got Sutty, the Henshaw brothers and Tony Sykes on my list. Starting to get a bit nervous.

CHAPTER 13 – THE FARTOWN YOUNG GARDENERS CLUB

Summer 1958

The boys were only half way through cutting Mrs Oldham's grass when another neighbour approached them. It was Mrs Johnson who lived three doors up from the Oldhams.

'Ee you lads are doing a reight fine job there, will you come and do mine when you've finished here?'

Wilky sniffed an opportunity 'Aye we can missus but it'll cost you two bob'.

'Oh that's a lot of money' she hesitated 'I'm just a poor widow woman you know, I haven't got a load of money to throw around.' Then she added meekly 'Will you do it for a shilling?'

Wilky the businessman replied 'Let me have a look at your garden first and we'll see what we can do'.

'OK love, come with me and I'll show it to you'. The two of them marched off to Mrs Johnson's garden. 'And what's your name then lad?' she asked.

'Aiden Wilkinson missus, I live over there' he pointed 'on t'other street'.

'So you'll be Nellie's lad then, I used to work with Nellie at Crowther and Nicks you know, in the weaving shed. Agnes must be your aunty then, she was a winder'.

Better watch what I say here thought Wilky as he surveyed the garden. All the gardens were pretty much the same size but someone, presumably the late Mr Johnson, had obviously done some work on it in days gone by. The grass was over-grown but there was a stone path down the middle which led to a shed on one side and a rather large bush on the other. The bush had some green fruit on it.

'I'll tell you what we can do Mrs Johnson, we'll cut all this grass, rake it up and dump it over the fence on that pile we have started already?'

'Yes but how much love, I can't afford two shillings, how about one and threpence?' she said hopefully.

'There's a lot of work here missus – I tell you what' he scratched his head 'we'll do it for one and sixpence, IF you let us pick them – what are they – berries on the bush. I'll bring my team of lads tomorrow morning and we'll do a reight fine job of it, how's that?'

'They're gooseberries actually and you're welcome to 'em 'cos I don't care for 'em, but don't you lads go eating them, they're fine for cooking but if you eat too many raw you'll finish up with the belly ache. OK eighteen pence it is then, I'll pay you when the works done - to my satisfaction'.

'Right then Mrs Johnson we'll be here tomorrow morning'. Wilky walked off to rejoin the labourers three doors down.

'I thought you'd have had it finished by now, have you been shirking while I've been away organising some more work for us'.

'Who elected you as foreman?' Barry challenged him 'Get stuck in here and you can tell us about the next job when we've all finished here'.

The lads carried on working but Terry was curious as to how Wilky had got on with the old lady. 'How much did you get then' he whispered.

'One and a tanner□*□' came the whispered reply.

'One and a tanner that's not bad, what are we going to spend it on?' he asked.

'We'll have to have a meeting to decide, now shut up and get on with it'.

Mrs Oldham's garden took them about an hour to complete. When the work was finished Barry knocked on the door, which was slightly open, and shouted inside 'We've finished now Mrs Oldham do you want to come and check it?'

Mrs Oldham came to the door step 'Oh you've done a grand job there lads, thank you, now would you all like a drink of orange squash, you must be thirsty after all that hard work'.

The boys quickly queued up to get their drinks. Orange squash was a real treat for many of them who normally had to settle for tap water.

'OK Wilky what's the score about the next job?' asked Fergy.

'Well there isn't as much grass to cut 'cos there's a shed and a large gooseberry bush so I said we'd do it for one and sixpence - if we could pick the gooseberries as well, and she agreed. I said we'd be there tomorrow morning. She said the gooseberries are only for cooking so all ask your mams tonight if she wants some of them and if she does bring summat to put them in.'

'Why can't we just eat 'em?' complained Terry.

'She said we'd get belly ache if we ate 'em, they must be sour or summat, I don't know' Wilky was not pleased that he was being challenged. 'Just bring a container if you want some – alright'.

All this work and talk about food was making them hungry so, as it was approaching their tea time, they all went home to eat but decided to meet after tea for another game of cricket.

EXTRACT FROM BARRY WILKINSON'S DIARY

29th July 1958

Had a close shave today.

We were just playing soccer when this copper came over and picked up the ball. He said there had been complaints about us swearing. He picked our Aiden out cos people say he's the worst for it. He is an all.

He took down all us names and addresses and warned us. He said if there's any more complaints then we know what will happen. Terry thinks we might be going to jail but our Aiden says that's rubbish.

Fergy told us to tell us mams and dads cos we're not in real trouble yet.

When we told me mam she didn't half wag her finger at out Aiden. She said that's the trouble with you Aiden you're always bloody swearing. When I said that she had just sworn she told me not to be so cheeky. She said that if there's any more complaints dad will give us the belt, but I've never seen me dad wearing a belt but I didn't dare to say owt to mam cos she was angry enough already.

We had a proper game of cricket today. Fergy brought the wickets and the bat and ball. We started with a tennis ball but our Aiden slogged it into the long grass and we couldn't find it. So then Fergy gets this really hard thing called a corky ball and our Aiden tries to slog that one an'all only he misses and it hits him on his leg. It must have hurt a lot cos our Aiden is rolling around on the floor and swearing like mad. I told him we'd all be in big trouble if he carried on swearing so he stopped but there was a big lump on his leg and it was bleeding. I had to help him back to the house so I could put some iodine on it and a plaster, he didn't half scream when I put the iodine on it.

When we got back to the field the lads had got another ball, it was sort of hard plastic and it was just right for us. We had a match and I hit a six and won the match, but I broke the glass in Mrs Oldhams door, it made a right mess and the glass was all over the place. Anyway Uncle Ray lives two doors down and he fixed it up with a piece of wood. Then Mrs Oldham came home and said if we cut her grass for her I wouldn't have to pay for the new glass. So all the lads joined in and we did a right good job, she was dead pleased and I was relieved. Mrs Oldhams husband is gunna fix the window himself.

Then another lady came and asked us if we'd do her garden an'all. Our Aiden went to have a look and said we do it for one and sixpence if we can pick all the gooseberries off her bush. We're gunna do it tomorrow.

The following morning they gathered outside Mrs Johnson's garden. The Wilkinson brothers had not arrived so the others decided to wait for them before knocking on Mrs Johnson's door. There wasn't much they could do anyway as the Wilkinson brothers had appointed themselves as custodians of the two sickles.

They discussed the cricket match they had played the previous evening. It had gone off without any incidents of note and everyone agreed that the new ball was OK for their games, unfortunately it was already showing some signs of wear and tear.

The Wilkinsons eventually arrived carrying the sickles and a metal pan.

'What's the pan for Wilky?' asked Martin.

'It's for the gooseberries, what do you think it's for?' replied Wilky. The brothers had forgotten to mention the gooseberries to their mam but brought a pan anyway so they could surprise her.

'Oh bugger' said Terry 'I'll have to nip back and get one as well, my mam said she wants some of the gooseberries to make a pie.'

The others had clearly forgotten to ask their mams about the gooseberries so the gang – minus Terry – climbed over the fence into Mrs Johnson's garden and started work. Wilky strode up to the back door and knocked on it firmly. When Mrs Johnson appeared he said 'Here we are Mrs Johnson as promised'.

'Good lads, just give me a knock when you've finished' and she turned and went back into the house.

'We'll get the grass cut first and then we can pick the gooseberries', came the instruction from Wilky.

A breathless Terry returned armed with an enormous pan. 'Couldn't you find anything smaller than that Oggy' Martin laughed.

'All the other pans were in the sink, waiting to be washed, this was the only clean 'un I could find. Anyway what'll 'old a lot'll 'old a little as my grandma always says'.

The boys got on with the job and soon all the grass was cut, they were getting pretty good at it. Whilst the rest of the boys collected all the grass cuttings together the Wilkinsons and Terry got stuck into picking the gooseberries.

As the gooseberry pickers went hell for leather on the bush which was weighed down with fruit, they noticed that Martin wasn't looking too good.

'I'm off home I've got an awful belly ache' said Martin as he trailed away in the direction of his home.

'I saw him picking some of the gooseberries when you lot weren't looking he said they were a bit sour' explained Terry.

'Serves him right then, silly bugger' Wilky wasn't big on sympathy 'I told him not to eat 'em'.

When the job was completed Wilky made his way to the door and knocked. Mrs Johnson opened the door with her purse in her hand. 'All finished is it boys?' she asked and the boys all nodded. 'Now I think we agreed on one and threpence didn't we?'

'Err no it was eighteen pence□*□, we agreed' Wilky stood his ground.

'Oh yes I do remember now, take no notice of me I'm just an old woman and my memory's not what it used to be'.

Wilky held his hand out as she took the money out of her purse and counted it out carefully. 'Thank you Mrs Johnson' he said firmly 'and don't forget to tell your friends what a good job we made of it. But please don't tell them we gave you a dis-

Bryn Woodworth

count or they'll all want one' he said to her with a wink.

'Ee that boy will go far', thought old Mrs Johnson as she watched the boys walk away. She glanced at the newly cut grass and sighed 'I hope you've been watching this Jack, those boys are helping me to keep our garden tidy as you would have wanted' as she looked up at the sky. She wiped her eyes with her apron and thought to herself 'Get inside you daft old bugger there's jobs to be done'.

Meanwhile, Martin had dragged himself back to his house hoping to slouch on the settee until his mam came home. Feeling sorry for himself and deeply regretting eating all those sour gooseberries, he made his way to the front of his house. As he walked up the path he could hear loud music coming from the house. 'Bugger' he thought to himself 'our Sheila's got her mates round'. As he opened the door he saw his sister and a few other girls jiggling around to the sound of rock and roll music.

'What you doin' home Martin?' Sheila stopped chewing gum for a moment to demand. 'I thought you were laking in't field with yer mates?'

'I don't feel so well' Martin responded meekly.

'Well me mam said I could have me mates round so you can just bugger off'.

'But I've got belly ache Sheila, I don't feel well, it must be those gooseberries I've eaten'.

'Serves you right then yer daft sod, now clear off up to yer bedroom'.

'Will you turn the music down a bit then?' he pleaded.

'No I bloody well won't, me and me mates like it loud so get lost upstairs'.

And with that he crawled up the stairs to his bedroom, making a swift detour to the lavatory on the way.

Back in the field the boys were setting up the wickets and sorting out the teams when Mrs Oldham came over to the fence and shouted across to Barry who then jogged over to her. 'I hope you don't mind Barry love' she spoke in that soft Irish accent 'but I was telling my friend Marlene about the broken window and you and your friends doing such a good job cutting my grass'.

'Well that's very kind of you Mrs Oldham' Barry blushed slightly as he replied.

'Oh you can stop all the Mrs stuff Barry just call me Mary. Anyway Marlene's husband is not very well and he hasn't been able to do anything with their garden this past two years. They live across the road, she pointed in the general direction of the opposite side of the road, 'sure the gardens are a good deal bigger than ours. She was wondering if you and your mates would go and do their garden like you did mine.' Mary could see the uncertainty in Barry's eyes, 'Oh she'll pay you boys for the work sure enough, she's not short of a bob or two Marlene isn't. So Barry, what do you think?'

'I'm going to have to ask the other lads; we've done old Mrs Johnsons this morning, so I think it will be OK. What number does she live at?'

'It's number 85 near the bottom not far from the police house, oh she'll be so pleased, can I tell you'll come around today maybe?'

'Let me just check with me mates'. Barry ran off to speak to the other lads, and then came running back. 'Yeh we'll do it, we're just going to have a game of cricket then we'll come round after dinner, just to have a look and then all being well we'll get it done straight away, will that be OK?'

'Great I'll pop over the road and tell her right now, she'll be pleased to see you, sure she will. Now don't you boys go breaking any of my windows with your cricket ball while I'm out.'

The game of cricket once again passed without incident but the boys noticed that the ball was making a slightly different noise when it was hit by the batsman and wasn't going as far as it used to. When the game finished the boys decided to give the ball a close examination and they found a very small crack on the surface of the ball.

'I reckon it's knackered, one more good hit and it'll bust open' suggested Wilky, the others agreed.

'We've got that one and sixpence from Mrs Johnson, 'appen we could buy another one. Where did you say you got it from Andy and how much did it cost?' asked Fergy.

'I'm n-not sure how much it cost, but my d-dad bought it from a toy shop in Filey. I'll ask him how much it cost t-tonight shall I?' replied Andy.

'If we're gunna do that other garden this afternoon, we won't have time for another game anyroads' observed Barry.

'We might be able to get a new ball from the post office on Bradford Road, they 'ave a lot of toys and balls and other stuff there don't they' suggested Sutty. 'Trouble is I'm not allowed to cross Bradford Road unless there's an adult with us'.

'Same here' said Fergy and the other lads all agreed that they would have to wait till their mams came home to see if the restriction could be lifted for just this once.

'Me mam finishes work at dinner time so I'll ask her' said Fergy. 'She sometimes does her shopping at the co-op next to the post office so you never know we might be able to get out this afternoon'.

'It'll have to be after we've done Mrs Oldham's friend's garden but that shouldn't take too long, we're experts at it now aren't we' bragged Wilky. 'We'll all meet outside number 83 then after dinner' it was more an instruction than a suggestion.

'85' said Barry.

'85 what?' snapped Wilky.

'85 is the number of the house where we will be working' explained Barry.

'That's what I said didn't I?' Wilky snapped again.

'No you said 83, I was just correcting you. We don't want to go to the wrong house do we?'

The two boys continued to argue as they headed for home to get their dinner, Terry and Sutty laughed at their antics. 'They're at it again, going at it hammer and tongs' sniggered Terry.

'My mam says they're like an old married couple, always arguing the toss' added Sutty,' I'm surprised they don't have more actual fights than they do'.

The ever thoughtful Fergy then added 'I hope they sort themselves out 'cos we've got a job to do after dinner haven't we and they've got the tools'.

'Ah they'll be alright, they never fall out for long' came the reassuring voice of Sutty, 'see you all outside number 83 then' he added.

'It's 85 not 83' giggled Terry.

'Oh don't start that again' the last word came from Fergy.

Sure enough the Wilkinson brothers had resolved their differences and were back to being the best of pals and the tools were safely delivered to number 85. On his way home Terry had called to see how Martin was and the news was good, he was feeling much better and would join them for the grass cutting after dinner.

Marlene Taylor looked out of the front window and saw the youths gathering at the end of her path by the front gate. 'Are you boys coming to cut the grass for me? You'd better come round the back and I'll show you what I want you to do'.

The boys filed through the gate, along the path to the back garden. The house was at the end of the block so it had a small side garden and the back garden was about 50% larger than the one they had just done for Mrs Johnson and the grass was a long tangled mess mixed with huge brown dock leaves.

'Oh bugger' whispered Terry 'this is going to take us ages'.

Mrs Taylor came out and to the boys relief said 'Look I know it's a mess and my garden is probably one of the biggest on the estate so I don't expect you to do it all in one go. If you can do the front half today that would be lovely, you see where the clothes post is, if you can get that far today that would be grand. At least I will be able to hang my washing out without getting my skirt wet' she laughed. 'You can come back tomorrow and finish it if you want to'.

The boys shuffled nervously and looked at each other, not knowing what to say. Barry remembered what Mrs Oldham had told him about Marlene not being short of money so he plucked up courage and – to the others boys surprise and relief – said 'It is a big area Mrs T-Taylor and it will be a lot of work so it will be one and sixpence for the front part and the same for the back'. He took another big breath 'We'll do the front part today and come back tomorrow to do the rest wont we lads?'

The other boys nodded.

'Oh that'll be fine, I'll get out of your way and let you get on with it then. Just give me a knock if you want a drink any time' and with that she went back into the house.

'Well done Barry, you got a good deal there' said Fergy and the other boys patted him on the back.

'Come on then the sooner we start the sooner we'll finish' Wilky was adopting his 'foreman' role again.

The boys soon realised that this garden presented a different problem to the others they had done before, and it wasn't just the size of it. The gardens that faced onto the field had only low railings and there was ample space in the areas of the field that they didn't play on to dump the dead grass. This garden however had a very high fence of at least eight feet, and beyond the fence was a steep banking leading down to a railway line, the fence was a substantial one and in good order too so there were no gaps that they could sneak through.

'We're gunna have to pile it up in the corner I reckon' said Wilky. 'You'd better tell Mrs Taylor that Barry, and make sure it's OK with her'.

Barry was beginning to regret speaking out but he made his way to the door and knocked rather timidly but Mrs Taylor heard it and came to the door straight away. 'What can I do for you, young man?' she asked him.

'Will it be alright with you Mrs Taylor' he hesitated 'if if we pile all the cut grass at the bottom of your garden in the corner?'

Mrs Taylor smiled at the boy 'Why of course you can, there's nowhere else for it to go is there'.

Barry's relief was plain to see 'OK lads you heard what she said'.

Fergy then took over 'We're gunna need to cut a pathway all the way down to the bottom of the garden first so we can carry the dead grass down there'.

The boys got stuck in and had done about a quarter of the garden when Mrs Taylor came out with a jug of squash and some glasses. The refreshments were well earned as it was a lovely warm summer's afternoon and the lads had really worked up a thirst. They thanked her and made an orderly queue for the drinks.

They decided to have a five minute break, some of the boys sat on the back door step, the rest of them sat on the floor. 'Right lads I reckon by tomorrow we should have four and sixpence in the kitty' announced Fergy 'we've already decided to buy a new cricket ball and Andy's gunna find out what the last one cost, OK Andy?'

Andy nodded.

'What else shall we spend it on besides the cricket ball?' Fergy was inviting ideas from the other boys although he already had an idea in his head for the money.

As usual Terry was the first to reply 'How about we share it out and then all go down to the little shop and spend it on spogs'. The 'Little Shop' as it was known, was at the bottom of the hill and sold groceries as well as sweets. Importantly it did not require the boys to cross the busy Bradford Road.

Spogs was a slang word for sweets. Fergy wasn't keen on that idea but he could tell some of the others were; he needed to come up with a logical reason for not blowing it all on sweets. 'Let's think about that, there's been between eight and ten of us doing the work. I think a cricket ball might cost us one and six so that leaves three bob□*□ – thirty six pence shared between ten would give us just threpence ha'penny each with a penny left over. I know you can get a few sweets for that but it does seem a bit of a waste doesn't it lads?'

'I agree with Fergy on that. It would be better to keep the money together and buy something we need' suggested Wilky.

'Such as what?' Terry was not giving up on the sweets just yet.

'Well the soccer ball isn't gunna last forever as well is it? We'll need another one of them soon' pointed out Barry backing up his brother.

'Well think on it, we haven't got the money yet, so let's get back to work' suggested Fergy who was now confident that with the Wilkinsons already on his side - and he also knew he could work on Sutty - that the money would be put to good use.

Work continued until they had cut about half of the grass and the boys decided they had had enough for one day.

'Go and give her a knock Barry and ask for't brass' urged Martin.

Barry did as he was told and Mrs Taylor handed over the money for the first day's work. 'When will you lads be back to do the rest?' she asked.

'We'll be back tomorrow morning if that's OK with you Mrs Taylor' replied Barry.

'I might not be here when you come, I've got a few errands to run tomorrow, but Jim will be in. I'll mix some squash before I leave in the morning so just knock when you are ready for a drink and Jim'll bring it out for you. He's got a bad leg so it might take him a few minutes to get to the door but don't worry he will come when you knock.'

The boys all thanked Mrs Taylor and made their way back to the playing field where they would have another game of cricket, or at least that was the plan.

In fact the worn cricket ball lasted just a few balls before Wilky's prediction came true and the crack in the surface became a full blown split. They tried playing on with it but it was useless.

'Did you ask your mam about going to't post office on Bradford Road Fergy' asked Martin.

'I did but she said she was busy this afternoon and she wouldn't let me go if there wasn't an adult with us. We might as well wait till Andy's found out what they cost from his dad tonight'.

'How about a game of soccer?' suggested Sutty. But there wasn't a lot of enthusiasm for soccer, the sun was beating down and they were all tired from their earlier exertions with Mrs Taylors grass. In the end they didn't play any games and just mooched around the settee.

Suddenly Wilky had an idea 'Have you lads seen our pet rabbits?' he asked.

'Didn't know you had any' remarked Martin 'when did you get 'em?'

'We've 'ad 'em a couple of months, mines a Dutch and our Baz's is an English. You can come and have a look at them if you like. Me grandad's in but he'll be sat inside so he won't bother us.

They like dandelion leaves so let's collect some and then you can feed 'em.' The bottom area of the field still had plenty of long grass and weeds so the dandelions were not hard to find.

'You can get'em out if you want to' offered Barry when they got to their back garden. 'We just need to put some bits of wood and netting up so they can't run away'.

The Wilkinson brothers quickly assembled a makeshift run for the pets and then they each reached in and took out their respective rabbits.

'Can we feed 'em now?' Terry was impatient as ever.

'Aye go on but be careful 'cos they might bite you, no sudden movements or else they get scared and that's when they're likely to bite' advised Wilky as he placed his rabbit, the smaller Dutch one on the ground inside the run 'and watch out for their claws they're pretty sharp'.

Barry did the same with his pet and the other boys played happily with them while Wilky and Barry cleaned out the hutches.

The happy scene continued for the rest of the afternoon and all thoughts of cutting grass and broken cricket balls were forgotten as the boys passed their time in the company of the two rabbits.

Eventually Mrs Wilkinson came home and stood on the step, 'Hey it's reight grand to see you lads playing happily with them rabbits, Aiden and Barry don't seem to bother that much with 'em these days, now that the novelties worn off', she sighed.

'I think they're great Mrs Wilkinson, I'm gunna ask me mam if I can have one' the ever enthusiastic Terry was smitten with the pets. 'Where did you gerrem from?'

'I got them from a woman I work with, love. Her lad breeds them and then sells them. D'you want me to ask if he has any more to sell?'

'Oh yes please Mrs Wilkinson, but I'll 'ave to ask me mam first'.

'Well I'm sorry lads it's tea time now so Barry and Aiden you'd better put the animals back where they belong and I think you lads had better get off home for your teas, your mother's will be wondering where you've got to' instructed Mrs Wilkinson and the boys all obediently said goodbye and went off to their own houses.

After the boys had left and the rabbits were safely tucked away Mrs Wilkinson called the boys in to wash their hands 'Make sure you do it proper now you've been laking with them rabbits and cleaning the cages out, I can smell 'em from here'.

'They're hutches mam not cages, cages are for lions and tigers these are just rabbits' corrected Barry.

'Now that's enough of your smartness our Barry, have you two got anything to tell me?'

'How d'you mean?' queried Aiden.

'Well, what have you been up to these last few days then?' the interrogation continued.

'We've just been laking cricket in't field mam that's all' protested Aiden.

'Aye I've heard about that AND the broken window!' she looked straight at Barry.

Barry looked crestfallen and said in a whisper 'Oh that'.

'Aye you might well say 'oh that' my lad'.

Wilky came to Barry's rescue 'There's nowt to worry about mam, it's all been sorted out, the windows been fixed already and Mrs Oldham wasn't mad with us'.

'Yes I heard about that from our Agnes, it's a good job your Uncle Ray was there to sort it out wasn't it?'

'Yes mam' the boys replied in harmony.

'And what about this GARDENING you've all been doing, you know I don't like you going round asking folk for jobs and taking money off 'em'.

'We haven't asked anybody they've all come to us and asked us' protested Aiden.

'Well what have you done with the brass then? I dare say you'll have spent it all on sweets haven't you' Mrs Wilkinson was determined to get to the bottom of this.

'Fergy's looking after it mam' this time Barry was doing the explaining 'and we're gunna spend it on a new cricket ball and maybe a soccer ball as well.'

'Well that's alright then, but if I hear you've been knocking on folks doors asking for work then you'll be in big trouble, do you hear me?'

'Yes mam' they both replied.

'Now get yer hands washed and then get from under me feet while I make us some tea and we'll say no more about this', and with that the boys scrubbed their hands at the kitchen sink before retreating into the relative safety of the front room and put the telly on.

'Wow that were a close shave Barry wannit?' whispered Aiden.

Barry put his finger to his lips and said nothing.

The boys had barely sat down when their mam shouted from the kitchen 'Where have all these gooseberries come from?'

Aiden rushed back into the kitchen to explain 'We picked 'em for you so you can make a pie mam'.

'Aye but where did they come from? I hope you haven't been sneaking into folks gardens and stealing 'em'.

'Course not mam, there from old Mrs Johnson's garden, she said we could pick 'em after we cut her grass'.

'Well that's alright then, I'll save 'em while weekend and then I'll make a pie, yer father doesn't care for em but yer grandad's reight fond of gooseberry pie and custard'.

When Norman Wilkinson got home from work his tea was

ready for him as usual. As he and his wife sat down to eat Nellie filled him in on what the kids had been up to.

'To be honest Nellie I don't think there's owt wrong wi' what they've been doing, if people are coming up to 'em and asking 'em to do their gardens .., well they must be doing a good job. What they spend the money on is up to them, after all they've earned it haven't they?'

'I suppose you're right, I just think they're a bit young to be working, but if they're doing it for fun I suppose it's OK.'

'As far as the broken window's concerned – well that's already been sorted with some help from Ray. I'll make sure I buy him a pint the next time I see him in the pub.'

She gave him a mucky look 'You're a bloody tight sod Norman Wilkinson you know damn well he doesn't go to the same pubs as you. Any road if these lads are playing cricket why don't you get that cricket bat out, you know the one that one of your bosses gave you when you helped him move house.'

EXTRACT FROM BARRY WILKINSON'S DIARY

30th July 1958

Cut Mrs Johnsons grass, we're getting dead good at it. She tried it on a bit, wanted us to do it for one and threepence but our Aiden made her pay the full price, well done Aiden. We picked a load of gooseberries for me mam to make a pie but Martin ate some and they gave him belly ache, serves him right, Mrs Johnson told us they were just for cooking but he didn't listen.

Mrs Oldham asked us if we'd do her friends garden as well. We had a look at it and it's a big garden so we said we'd do half today and the other half tomorrow and charge her three shillings.

The lads came round to our back garden to play with the rabbits. Terry really liked them, he even asked me mam where we got them from. He's gunna ask his mam if he can have one.

Me mam found out about the grass cutting and she was a bit annoyed but dad said it was OK as long as we don't go around knocking on folks doors asking for work, so that's OK. She were right pleased with the gooseberries we picked, gunna make a pie with them on Saturday.

The following day dawned with fine blue skies perfect for playing cricket, but the boys knew that there was work to be done first. As they raced downstairs to get their breakfast, there it was waiting for them at the bottom of the stairs. A beautiful, full size cricket bat was resting on the wall next to the front door.

'Just look at this Aiden', Barry won the race to get there first and pick up the prize. 'It feels so light' Barry tried a gentle stroke with the bat and accidentally put a small dent in the wall.

'Watch what you're doing Baz' snapped Aiden. 'I reckon that bat's a bit big for you, give it 'ere.' Aiden snatched the bat away and received a shove in the back for his troubles.

'It's for both of us yer know, it's not just for you'.

'Nah then what's all this noise boys' Mrs Wilkinson was drying her hands on her pinny as she came in from the kitchen to find out what all the commotion was about. 'Oh you found it then, I told your dad to put it out for you both.

'Where'd he gerrit from mam, it's a beauty, much better than the one Fergy has' Barry could hardly contain his excitement.

'One of his bosses gave it to him' replied Mrs Wilkinson. 'I think his lad had it when he went to private school, so it'll be a good un. Now put it down and come and get yer breakfast and no more arguing, your grandad's still in bed'.

'He was snoring away when we came down – nothing disturbs him when he's asleep, grumpy old..'

'That's enough of that Aiden, what have I told you about respecting your elders?'

Aiden put on his most angelic look 'OK mam, isn't it time you went off to work?'

'Aye right enough it is' she took her pinny off and went to the door picking up her coat on the way. 'I'll see you both tonight' she turned to face the boys and wagged her finger once more for emphasis 'and keep out of bother'.

'They rested the bat by the front door so they wouldn't forget it and went back to the kitchen to get their breakfast. I can't wait to show the bat to the other lads, they'll be dead jealous' smiled Aiden. 'I can just see me smashin' the ball all over the field with it' he gave a quick demonstration of his batting technique but in so doing accidentally tipped his bowl of cornflakes over and they were now spread liberally over the breakfast table.

As Aiden wiped up the mess Barry brought him down to earth 'Aye well, we'll need to get a ball first before any of us can do any smashing'.

CHAPTER 14 – EARLY SUCCESSES

December 2010

There was a covering of snow as Terry drove onto the drive at his house, an imposing detached house in a pleasant suburb on the outskirts of Huddersfield. It was one of the better areas of Huddersfield but by no means the poshest but it suited Terry down to the ground. It was handy for the M62 and only a ten minute drive to where his business premises were. As he got out of his car he realised that his wife Jane was home as her car was already in the garage and she had left the garage door open.

He strode into the house with an air of determination and headed straight for his 'office' which was the small bedroom at the top of the stairs. 'Hi love' he shouted as he climbed the stairs two steps at a time 'I'll be with you in a minute I just have an email I need to send while I think on'.

Five minutes later he made his way down the stairs and headed for the kitchen from where some delicious cooking smells were coming. 'That smells good. What sort of a day have you had love?' he put his arms around his wife's waist from behind and kissed her on her left ear.

She wriggled free, 'Oh Terry cut that out, not when I'm cooking you little monkey. I can tell you've had a good day. How was the reunion then? I can see that you're dying to tell me.'

He thought for a moment before answering 'It was very good actually, we all got on really well it was just like old times' he paused. 'It's a shame we haven't kept in touch more than we have. Anyway it wasn't a reunion it was just a meeting of old friends but we are thinking of having a proper reunion as it happens. I even suggested that we take a look at the old estate and the others agreed. It nearly backfired though when we were surrounded by some cocky lads – at least one of them had a knife – I think they thought we were snooping on them. Anyway they didn't like us moving in on their territory that's for sure'.

'What on earth possessed you to go up there? You're the one who's always saying that area is like the Wild West these days. What were you thinking of Terry, you could have got yourself killed' there was an air of exasperation in Jane's voice. 'How did you manage to extricate yourselves from this predicament then? Did those karate lessons you've been taking come in handy then?'

'There's no need for sarcasm Jane it was a serious situation. If it wasn't for Barry knowing one of the err' he hesitated whilst he searched for the right word 'gang leaders we could have been in deep shit.'

'And how come your 60 odd year old mate Barry is acquainted with members of the underworld?'

'It seems that Gerald – the gang leader – used to play soccer at Honley when Barry played there, that's how they met and they must have been quite pally. Barry told us later that he actually visited this Gerald guy when he was in hospital after being stabbed by a rival gang member'.

'My god Terry do you think you should be mixing with these sort of people?'

'It was quite exciting really, although I must admit I was a bit worried at one point. Barry and Fergy are dead nice guys love. I'm sure neither of them have ever been in any trouble. Anyway next time we'll be a bit more careful.'

'Next time' she spoke in shock more than anger. 'You've just had a close shave like that and you're already planning a next time. And just how do you intend to be 'more careful' exactly? Are you going to go in disguise or something, like wearing dreadlocks?'

'Hey, hey, steady on love' he raised both his hands to try to calm her down. 'I told you Barry and this Gerald guy go back a bit, well Gerald gave Barry his mobile number and told him to ring before we come next time and he'll make sure nobody bothers us. Oh, I didn't mention this, can you believe he actually lives in the same house Fergy used to live in when he was a kid. He offered to show us around but we were a bit pushed for time.'

'OK, Terry it's your life, you know what you are doing, why should I worry' she paused then smiled. 'After all you've got good life insurance haven't you?'

'Trust you, I knew it was a mistake when we took that new policy out, I'm now worth more dead than alive' he chuckled.

'Did you and your mates actually decide on anything then? Oh I forgot to ask if you'd eaten, are you hungry?'

'Yes we did make some plans, and yes I have eaten, so the answer to the third question is no, I'm not hungry but I'm sure I will be by the time tea comes round. Anyway what is that you're cooking it smells delicious'.

'It's smoked fish risotto, where did you get your lunch then?'

'In the Stag on Bradford Road, I was a bit naughty and went for the house speciality, good old steak and ale pie. It was spot on'.

'My god you actually went in the Stag – that dive. Did they ask you for your passport when you went in?'

'I must admit I had my doubts when Fergy suggested it, but the landlord seems to have sorted the place out – got rid of all the dead legs and druggies. The beer was good and the food was too. I think we might have the reunion in there actually'.

'And how are you going to get hold of all the old mates then?'

'We've each got a hit list of four people to try to contact and I've already made a start on my list. I've just sent Martin Kelly an email asking him if he wants to come along'. We know a couple of people for sure are dead but we're hoping to get nine or ten of us back together. We were thinking of maybe hiring a soccer pitch at the Sports Centre and having a game of 5 a side, if there enough takers. What do you think Jane?'

'I think you're all bloody mad now that you ask, but I think it's nice that you've got back together with some of your old mates. I'm not sure that body of yours is up to a game of football though, but as the saying goes *boys will be boys*.'

A few days later Fergy sent an email asking how everyone was doing and telling them how his search was going so far. He had already made contact with two of the people on his list and had got tentative commitment from them for a reunion. The other two were proving rather more difficult.

It was a similar situation with Terry, who had two confirmed and one provisional – his long time friend Martin Kelly. Martin, who lived in Middlesex, had replied and was very interested but not sure when he would be able to come up to Huddersfield. His mother had died quite a while ago and, although his sister still lived in Huddersfield, he hardly ever came back.

Barry had made contact with Sutty and was in the process of tracking down the Henshaw brothers. He'd also spoken to Wilky who was dead keen to come but – as with Martin – he wasn't sure when he would next be in Huddersfield.

After Fergy had received replies from the other two he sat at his computer desk and did a quick calculation. By his reckoning, including the provisional acceptances, they had probably got eight acceptances – possibly ten if Barry can confirm that Dave and Jimmy Henshaw are coming. Scheduling the reunion was going to be a bit of a nightmare though especially with

Wilky in Jersey and Martin down south. 'Not bad' he thought to himself 'onward and upward'.

He decided to make use of the internet to help him to find the remaining Fartown United players but before he could get started he had a call from his sister Carol.

'Hi Carol to what do I owe this pleasure?'

'I thought I'd better call you as you never seem to get round to ringing me these days, how are you anyway Richard?'

Fergy was feeling rather embarrassed at not ringing his sister more often 'I'm OK thanks just a bit busy at the moment, and you're right I should keep in touch more often, I'm sorry about that. Anyway how is my little sister doing?'

'I'm fine actually, so what's been keeping you so busy then? Been meeting your stockbroker and revising your overseas portfolio have you?'

'Sarcasm doesn't suit you Carol, if you must know I've had a couple of meetings with Barry Wilkinson and Terry Ogden and we are trying to sort out a bit of a reunion for the old Fartown United team, I seem to have been nominated as the co-ordinator for my sins'.

'More like you volunteered yourself if I know you Richard. You know you always like to be in control, No matter what you're involved in you like to be in charge. Anyway do I get an invite to this 'ere do? I was part of your gang wasn't I.

'Oh come on Carol do you seriously want to spend a couple of hours in the Stag pub with a load of old fogies drinking pints of bitter and reliving their glory days?'

'I dunno, could be quite interesting. Did you really say the Stag, the pub on Bradford Road? I thought that was where the underworld congregated.'

'Well you're wrong there sis, those days are gone. There's a new landlord and he's sorted the place out. Got rid of all the undesirables and he's trying his damndest to make a go of the place. Good luck to him I say, anyway its handy 'cos we're going to pay a visit to the old estate, me and the other two have already been up there to have a recky'.

'Richard, I'm speechless. You never cease to amaze me. Next thing you'll be telling me you had afternoon tea with an old lady who lives in our old house'.

'Well not exactly but I did meet the guy who lives there now and he invited me in to have a look around as it happens'.

'Oh come off it, you really are such a wind up merchant Richard, you didn't think I'd fall for that bullshit did you?'

'Well for once Carol, believe it or not, I'm not bullshitting. The three of us were sat on a bench in the field when this group of yobbos started threatening us. Barry got a bit stroppy back and one of them pulled out a knife, me and Terry had all on getting Barry to sit down.'

'My god, what happened then?'

'This is where it get's interesting Carol, the bloke who lives in our old house arrives on the scene and, you're not going to believe this but it's the gospel truth, Barry knows the guy, used to play soccer with him for Honley back in the day.'

'No way! But what did this guy have to do with these thugs then?'

'I think he must have been the gang leader, you know head honcho sort of thing. Once he recognised Barry he told the lads to bugger off basically, AND they did as they were told.'

'Are you telling me that despite the fact that you nearly got knifed you're all going back again only this time mob handed?'

'That's just about it I suppose. Barry's mate – he's called Gerald – has said he'll make sure nobody bothers us next time. We've just got to give him a bell and he'll sort it. Are you still keen to come with us?'

'Let me get back to you on that Richard. Anyway I've got to go 'cos I'm meeting my old friend Kate from school in an hour and I've got to get ready. Keep in touch Richard, and look after yourself, you're the only brother I've got and I don't want to lose you'.

'You worry too much Carol that's what I love about you' he laughed and put the phone down. Now where was I.

EXTRACT FROM BARRY WILKINSON'S DIARY

9th December 2010

It looks like the reunion is on.

I've already tracked down Sutty and he gave it the thumbs up, and I've left a message for Dave Henshaw with his wife.

Fergy says if the Henshaws confirm we'll have ten and there's still a few more to contact. We're thinking of early to mid January but it depends on when our Aiden and Martin Kelly, who have the furthest to travel, can make it.

CHAPTER 15 – THE SUMMER OF CRICKET AND OTHER NEW PASTIMES

Summer 1958

The boys duly completed the cutting of Mrs Taylor's grass and collected their well earned wages. They then made their way into the field and settled on and around their, now cherished, settee. There was usually a bit of a scramble to get there first – it was a nominally a three seater but there were usually at least four of them sat on the seat itself and another two perched on the arms. The slow coaches who were last to get there would have to sit or kneel on the grass around the settee.

Andy had questioned his dad the night before regarding the ball's origin. Unfortunately Andy was correct and it turned out that it had been bought last year on the family's annual holiday to Filey as he suspected. The good news was it only cost a shilling and the family were heading back to Filey in a week's time on holiday so it might be possible to buy some more balls there if they couldn't get any in Huddersfield.

Fergy had slightly better news for the boys as his mother had agreed that he – and a maximum of two of his friends – could accompany her on her weekly shopping visit to the co-op on Bradford Road this afternoon and they would also be allowed to go to the Post Office which was just down the road from the

Co-op. She said they could help her carry the shopping back home as she needed to stock up on fruit and veg.

'Well, what are we going to do for the rest of the day then?' asked Terry.

'Soccer?' suggested Barry

'It's too warm for soccer' came the response from a very lethargic Martin.

'I'll tell you what' Fergy was clearly excited 'I've got this present for my birthday last week, it's called Newfooty□*□, it's supposed to be played on a table top but we just need a flat surface to put the pitch down on, it's like' Fergy paused to work out how to describe it 'well it's a piece of green material which you lay down and it's got all the markings of a football pitch and some small players that you flick to hit the little ball'.

'I don't gerrit' said Terry 'how do you flick a player?'

'You use your finger like this' Fergy put his right index finger onto his right thumb and then let go.

'I still don't gerrit' moaned Terry.

'Why don't you show us what you mean?' asked Barry on behalf of the boys, who were all intrigued and wanted to find out more about this new game.

'OK come on then, come round to the back of our house and I'll get it out and show you, but you'll need to be quiet or else Mrs Fleming next door will be complaining to me mam when she gets home'. Fergy whispered the last part for emphasis even though they were a long way from the house in question.

The boys made their way out of the field and up towards the circle where the Ferguson's lived. The lads were a motley crew and were never still, with lots of pushing and shoving, kicking any loose stones and a general hubbub of noise accompanied them wherever they went. Wilky was the eldest and tallest and the only one who wore glasses. He was dressed in an old grey t-shirt, scruffy, well worn, shorts and short socks in a light brown colour which blended with a pair of scuffed sandals with a buckle fastening. He was still sporting a plaster over the injury on his leg. Terry was the youngest and smallest and he wore a brightly coloured checked short sleeved shirt with buttons, black shorts, no socks and scruffy black pumps which had small holes in the toe from repeatedly kicking the football. A grimy toe was peeping through the hole. The rest of the boys sported similarly scruffy outfits; all had scabs on their knees and elbows from the rough and tumble of sporting activities.

Most of them had unruly hair cropped in a short back and sides, some of the boys actually went to the barbers to have their hair cut, but several of the boys were subjected to home cuts by one of their parents. It wasn't difficult to spot the ones who had a home haircut, but it didn't seem to bother any of the lads. They were just a gang of ordinary boys happy to be playing out in the school holidays without any real cares to weigh them down.

Fergy's house was the second in from the end of the block of four and the back door was accessed from a shared path at the end of the block. To access Fergy's back door you had to walk directly past the neighbour's, Mrs Fleming's, back door. As they opened the gate at the end of the block Fergy put his finger to his lips to remind the boys to keep quiet. They all did as they were told until, as they came to the back corner of the block, Terry – who else – tripped on the paving stone and went down with a stifled yelp. He picked himself up and ran the few steps to get to Fergy's house only to be confronted by the frightening sight of Mrs Fleming brandishing a rolling pin.

Terry had dropped behind the other lads when he fell over and Mrs Fleming was standing between him and the others. 'Now what are you doing coming round here disturbing me with all your noise? You don't belong here. I shall have the police on you if you don't scarper now'. Mrs Fleming was in her early seventies and, although Fergy's friends didn't know it, had recently lost her husband after over 40 years of marriage, and apparently had gone a bit 'loopy' since his death.

Fergy who had been in the lead pushed his way past the other boys and spoke calmly to Mrs Fleming 'I'm sorry we disturbed you Mrs Fleming, he's my friend and he just tripped on that loose paving stone on the path. All these boys are with me and we're just going to play quietly in my back garden.'

This seemed to reassure the old lady who turned and went back to her doorstep, as she did she turned and snapped 'Well make sure you keep quiet or I'll be having words with your mother when she gets home Richard' there was a slight pause before she pointed a wizened old finger at Terry 'and you, yes you the little'n at the back you can stop sniggering you cheeky little bugger or you'll feel the back of my hand' and with that she stomped back into her house and slammed the door.

The boys were overcome with the giggles which they tried desperately to suppress but without success. Fergy was clearly worried so he put his finger to his lips again and leaned forward with an exaggerated 'Shushhhh'. He could clearly see the old bat looking out through her kitchen window. 'I knew this was a bad idea, you lot can't be trusted can you, and Terry you're the worst of the lot'.

'I-I only tripped on that loose paving over there and cracked my toe, it hurt like mad' Terry tried to sound apologetic but couldn't stop giggling.

'Well try to be quiet now I'm in enough bother already, just sit down on the step while I bring out my Newfooty game'. Off he went into the house. He returned a few minutes later and showed all the boys the box containing the game. Like all toy boxes it was brightly coloured and the front showed a number of football players in action. The sight of the bright red box only served to add to the boys' excitement and anticipation.

'Go on Fergy show us what you do then, set it up so we can see how to play it' pleaded Terry.

'We need to make a bit of space here on the paving for the pitch' Fergy opened the box and carefully took out a folded piece of green cloth which he then spread out on the paving. The other boys could barely contain their excitement as Fergy opened two smaller boxes inside the main box each one containing 10 plastic players in matching football kit. He placed the players on each side of the pitch in the formation that most real teams lined up in at the start of a game. When he took out the miniature goalkeeper he carefully inserted a metal handle into the rear of the base. He repeated the process for the other team with all the boys watching in silent awe. He then took out the goalposts, complete with nets and placed them at each end. Finally the ball was placed in the middle of the centre circle. 'There he said, what do you think lads?'

At that point Fergy's back door opened and a middle aged man holding a newspaper walked across the small open porch and went into another room.

'Who's that? whispered Martin 'and where's he going'.

'It's me Uncle Arthur, he's staying with us for a few days. He's me dad's brother and he lives in Manchester. 'That room he went into – it's the lav'.

Martin needn't have asked what the room was; it immediately became apparent as the unmistakeable sound of someone going to the toilet was followed by an unpleasant smell drifting through the open window.

The boys all squeezed their noses and started to giggle uncontrollably. Uncle Arthur seemed oblivious to the boys giggling as he continued to noisily turn the pages of his newspaper until he had concluded his 'business'. He flushed the toilet and then the door opened and Uncle Arthur re-appeared. He turned to the boys, smiled and said, without a hint of sarcasm, 'You lad's enjoying your game then?' before going back inside the house.

Fergy was really regretting bringing the boys over to his house as they all collapsed in fits of laughter punctured with imitation farts, a skill at which Terry was the undisputed champion.

'I thought you lot came here to see how to play Newfooty' snapped Fergy.

The lads did their best to adopt a straight face, all except Terry who still had the giggles.

'Well it looks great but how do we actually play with it' asked Wilky.

'Yeh show us how you do it, how do you err like flick the players then?' Terry had stopped giggling and was now bubbling with enthusiasm as he turned his attention back to the game.

Fergy proceeded to demonstrate how the game was played whilst the boys looked on in amazement. Fergy had already become quite an accomplished Newfooty player and was able to pass the ball between players and take a shot. After a few minutes of the demo he said 'Right who fancies taking me on then, first to five goals?'

'I will' shouted Terry 'can I be the red team?'

'OK Terry Red v Blue, so you can be Manchester United and I will be Everton' Fergy agreed.

Fergy played the gentleman and let Terry take the kick off. Now it must be said that controlling the small players was difficult, steering them in a certain direction with the flick of a finger does not come naturally. Getting the base of the player to make contact with the ball – the equivalent of kicking the ball in real football – was considerably more difficult.

Terry's centre forward knocked the ball forward into Fergy's half of the field and it touched one of Fergy's players. This meant that Fergy had the next play and he swiftly passed it from player to player, and before Terry knew what was happening he was picking the ball out of the net. Terry was not pleased. 'Oh come on give us a chance you've been practicing and it's the first time I've played' he pleaded with Fergy.

'OK' said Fergy 'I'll take four of my players off then you'll have four more players than me, how about that?'

'OK it's my kick off then, one nil to you' said Terry. Terry was a fast learner so this time he only tapped the ball slightly forward from the kick off and then flicked his next player as hard as he could towards the ball and by some fluke the ball ended up in Fergy's net before he had time to move his goalkeeper.

'Hey hey 1-1, how about that Fergy' Terry waved his arms triumphantly.

Fergy ever the gentleman congratulated Terry on scoring his goal and then proceeded to provide a master class of how to beat a novice who had eleven players by an expert with only seven. In truth he could have won with only three or four players.

The other boys watched the game enchanted by the skill which Fergy had developed and envious of him owning this wonderful new game.

'Where'd you get it from' asked Wilky 'and how much did it cost?'

'My mam got it for me, I think it was out of one of them catalogue things, you know where you send an order in and then they deliver it. Why are you thinking of getting one?'

'It's me birthday soon so I might get one then, it would be good to play in the winter when we can't play soccer cos it's too dark.'

'That would be good' agreed Fergy 'maybe we could set up a league, you know play each other. Have any of you lads got birthdays coming up as well?'

'Mines in September' replied Martin.

'I've just had my birthday' moaned Terry 'I'll have to wait while Christmas to get one'.

'Don't worry Terry you can still play games against the others who have got one' Fergy tried to cheer him up.

'Yeh but you'll all be able to practice and I'll still be shit won't I' the moaning continued.

'I'm going to do some jobs for me mam and save up me spending money then I'll be able to buy one meself' said a determined Sutty 'why don't you lot do the same? It won't take long will it?'

At this point Mrs Ferguson came into the kitchen and opened the back door 'Hello Richard what's all this then? Are you showing off your new game to all the lads. I bet he's been showing you how good he is hasn't he boys?'

'Yeh he's too good for us' replied Terry.

'And so he should be, him and his dad are playing on that damn thing all night. I'm sorry boys but you'll have to go now I'm going to make dinner, Richard where's our Carol you're supposed to be looking after her?'

'Oh she across the road at Mrs Knight's helping her with that new baby they've got, shall I go and fetch her for dinner?'

'Yes please Richard but pick up your game first before someone treads on it, see you later boys'.

The boys were so excited about the Newfooty game and, as they left, they were all making plans to get one as soon as possible so they could take part in the league.

Fergy put the game away and chased after them 'Who's coming with me this afternoon to see if we can get a new cricket ball? My mam said I could take two of you with me.'

Most of the boys weren't allowed off the estate so Wilky and Barry volunteered and agreed to meet back at Fergy's after dinner whilst the other boys decided to have a kick about in the field while they passed the time, in anticipation of a new cricket ball.

◆ ◆ ◆

Martin, Sutty, Andy, Terry and Ricky were going through the motions of a game of three goals and in without a great deal of enthusiasm when Ricky spotted Fergy and the Wilkinson brothers jogging into the field. Wilky – who else – was waving a small red ball above his head in his right hand.

'Have you got one?' shouted Terry.

'No' came the reply.

Terry and the rest of the footballers looked dejected as the three shoppers arrived slightly out of breath. 'What's that in yer hand then Wilky?' asked Martin

'Well we didn't get one did we lads' Wilky continued to bate the others 'we actually got two! How about that?'

'That's great how much did they cost?' asked Martin.

Fergy took up the story 'Well the chap at the Post Office said they were one and six each but we could have two for half a crown. He says he hasn't sold any for ages so he's put a couple more on one side for us for when these are worn out. Not bad heh?'

'Oh that's brilliant – let's get set up then for a game, I can't wait to try out the new ball' the ever enthusiastic Terry could never hide his excitement.

Fergy went back home to fetch the cricket tackle. At the same time Wilky disappeared without explanation and reappeared with his new cricket bat. The other boys were quite taken by this classy looking piece of equipment and were pestering Wilky to let them try it out, but he was having none of it. He was determined to be the first person to try it out, even though it was supposed to be shared with his younger brother.

When the game got under way Wilky's team batted first and, predictably, Wilky opened the batting. In previous matches

Wilky's style, if you could call it that, had been based around hitting out at every ball in the hope that some swings would connect. With the new bat in his hands he seemed to undergo a complete transformation. Instead of lashing out at every ball he adopted a safety first approach and concentrated on blocking the ball and just taking the odd single here and there. Martin, who was his batting partner at the other end watched on in amazement and at the end of the fourth over he approached Wilky for a 'tactical' discussion.

'What's up with you Wilky' he asked.

'What d'you mean' came the reply.

'Well you normally try to slog every ball but since you got that bat you just keep tapping the ball. We've been batting for four overs and we've only got five runs and I've got three from the three balls I've faced'.

'Martin lad' Wilky put his hand on Martin's shoulder in a patronising way, as if he was his dad 'don't you take any notice of the cricket on the telly?'

'How d'you mean Wilky?'

'I heard the commentator saying in the last match that the job of the openers is to see the shine off the new ball and that usually takes at least an hour and they, he pointed to the fielding team, 'have a new ball and we've only been playing for twenty minutes'.

'Yes Wilky but a test match lasts five bloody days, our matches normally take a couple of hours at the most'.

Fergy and Barry listened intently to this exchange and could hardly keep a straight face as Fergy announced 'Well you've done a good job Wilky, you've seen off the fast bowlers so we're gunna put a spinner on instead'.

Wilky stook his chest out and nodded to Martin 'See what I mean Martin, we can open up a bit now.'

Up until now no-one had tried to spin the ball on this hard, bare surface but Fergy threw the ball over to Dave Henshaw told him to be the first. He trundled slowly up to the wicket and, imitating the spinners he'd seen in the test match, lobbed the ball higher and slower than normal. This invitation was too good for Wilky to miss and he opened his shoulders and gave an almighty swing. Unfortunately he had totally misjudged the speed of the ball and had completed his shot far too soon. He totally missed the ball which proceeded on it's slow trajectory, trickling towards the stumps and, as Wilky had a second unsuccessful swipe at it, it struck the middle stump and just managed to dislodge the bails.

As the fielding side celebrated their success a dejected Wilky sloped off, threw the new bat down and flopped into the settee to watch the rest of his side's innings. Terry picked up the discarded bat and proceeded to use it to good effect as he reached his best ever score of 25 not out. Wilky looked on dejectedly as his little friend hit the ball all over the field. Not surprisingly Wilky abandoned his cautious approach and went back to his normal style of batting in the next game.

EXTRACT FROM BARRY WILKINSON'S DIARY

31st July 1958

Finished off Mrs Oldham's friends garden and got paid. We've now got four and sixpence. Terry wanted to spend it on spogs but Fergy told him we'd only get threepence each so it wasn't worth it. We decided to save the money so we can buy some more cricket balls cos the one Andy brought is cracking.

Me dad gave us a smashing new bat, he got it from one of his bosses when he helped them to move house. It's a real belter, it's dark brown, dad says that's from all the oil that's been put on it to reserve it, or summat like that. All the bosses at the mill get me dad to help them move house cos he drives the wagon, and he's always getting stuff given. Mam says they're all too tight to pay for a proper removal van but dad's not worried cos he get's paid for doing it in cash so he's got more beer money.

Fergy showed us this great new game he's got – it's called New-footy. He played Terry in a game and beat him. We're all gunna see if we can get one as well then we can all play each other and Fergy says we could set up a league, should be good fun.

Me and our Aiden went with Fergy and his mam to the post office on Bradford Road and they had some of our cricket balls. They were one and six each but our Aiden persuaded the man to sell us two for half a crown. He's dead cheeky but it saved us a tanner. He's getting quite good at bargaining with folk.

We didn't get chance to try the bat out in the morning cos the cricket ball was bust, but we did in the afternoon. I don't know what came over our Aiden he normally tries to slog every ball but with the new bat all he would do was tap the ball. Anyway Fergy tricked him by asking Dave Henshaw to bowl a spinner and our Aiden tried to whack it but missed it and was bowled out. We all laughed except for Aiden who was dead upset.

And so the boys spent the next few days of their summer holidays whacking a plastic ball around the field without any real incident until the inevitable happened; the ball landed in Claude's garden while he was pruning his roses.

Now this wasn't the first time the cricket ball had gone into his garden but it was the first time he had actually been there when it went in. On previous occasions the boys had retrieved their ball surreptitiously without being caught in the act. Claude knew they had been in his garden though, because he had seen their footprints in his meticulously maintained flower beds.

'OK you little buggers that's it, that's the last you'll see of this ball, I'm confiscating it. I know you've been trampling on my flower beds before so you wont be getting this ball back. And don't say I didn't warn you, I told you what would happen when that blasted football of yours landed on my flowers.'

The boys were at a loss at what to do. Fergy made the first move 'Excuse me Mr Langrick but please can we have our ball back?'

'No you can't young man you and your mates can pack up your cricket gear and go and play somewhere else, I'm sick of you spoiling my garden'.

Now, as it happened, the boy's merry band had been infiltrated by a girl who had approached them a few days earlier and asked if she could join in their game of cricket. The boys had taken pity on the girl, who had just moved onto the estate, and agreed to give her a trial. If she could play 'proper' cricket she'd be allowed to join in. To their great surprise she had passed the test with flying colours, batting and bowling. She even threw the ball like a boy.

Karen, as the girl was called, had watched the interplay between Claude and the boys and, without saying a word walked across to her house which was on the opposite side of the field to Claude's and went inside. The boys assumed that she had lost interest, so they were all surprised when she re-appeared a couple of minutes later with her dad. He was a tall, dark haired man wearing smart trousers and a rather snazzy cardigan, as he approached Claude's garden he could see that Claude was no longer there so he climbed over the fence and knocked on his door.

The boys – and girl – watched on as the two men had a heated conversation on the doorstep which resulted in a rather flustered Claude handing the ball over to Karen's dad and the two men shaking hands. As he climbed back over the fence he passed the ball back to Karen and said 'I think you and your friends had better move your wickets a bit further away from Mr Langrick's house, at least for the time being. It's the garden competition this weekend and the judges will be coming round so he's a bit more sensitive than usual at the moment. Do you think you can do that?'

The boys agreed and the wickets were duly moved a few yards further away from Claude's garden.

The boys quizzed Karen afterwards to find out what had been

said on the doorstep. She told them that Claude and her dad played for the same bowls team and her dad was the captain, so he just asked him to give the ball back. None of the boys really cared why he had given the ball back; they were just pleased that Karen had been playing with them when it happened and they had their precious ball back.

At the end of the cricket match the boys sat down around the settee and eventually their conversation came round to the opening match of the new football season which was in a couple of weeks time. Town would be playing Derby County and they were all looking forward to seeing their favourites run out onto the pitch at Leeds Road, but before that important event most of the lads would be going away for the annual family holiday.

For most of the boys this meant a trip to the seaside, Blackpool, Bridlington and Scarborough were the most common resorts visited by families in Huddersfield. One exception was the Chapman brothers who always went to Filey. Some families would rent a caravan, others would stay in a boarding house and some even went to Butlins or Pontins holiday camp. The Wilkinson family didn't follow the seaside rule, they went to rural Herefordshire where they stayed with a distant relative.

Not everyone could afford a family holiday and those unfortunate enough to miss out would have to pass the next two weeks at home without most of their mates and therefore unable to raise enough players for a decent game of soccer or cricket. The best that they would manage would be an occasional trip to Greenhead Park and a dip in the paddling pool. The other lads would take pity on these unfortunates and bring back sticks of rock for them to ruin their teeth on. In the case of the Wilkinsons a punnet of plums bought at the local farmers market would take the place of the sticks of rock. Fresh fruit was not something that most of the lads ever got the chance to eat, nevertheless most of them would have preferred the rock.

For the lads who didn't get a family holiday these two weeks of the summer holidays would be the least enjoyable, as the days would drag without their mates around but at least they had the new football season to look forward to.

EXTRACT FROM BARRY WILKINSON'S DIARY

3rd August 1958

Claude took our cricket ball today and wouldn't give it back. Fergy asked him nicely but he swore at us and told us to clear off.

Then Karen's dad came and he looked like he was having an argument with Claude and then Claude gave the ball back. He didn't look very happy. Karen's dad asked us to move the wickets well away from Claude's garden so we did and we made sure that we didn't hit the ball towards his garden.

On Saturday we go on holiday for two weeks. Most of the lads go to the seaside but we stay with my Aunty Kate in a place call Bromyard. It's in the country but me and our Aiden love it. All the people talk in a funny way but there's a field where we play soccer, sometimes dad joins in but he's not very good. We have to be careful where we play cos theres loads of cow muck in the field. We swim in the rivers and go fruit picking. Last year we went for a walk to this haunted church. It was really spooky, our Aiden sneaked up on me and scared me to death, he's always doing dirty tricks like that. When we get back from our holidays it will be the new soccer season and Town are at home first match.

I feel dead sorry for Martin and the Henshaws as they wont be going away on holiday this year. The Henshaws dad has been off work cos he's poorly. Martin doesn't have a dad so his mam can't afford a holiday for him and his sister. He says his mam takes them up to Greenhead Park and they watch the shows at the open air theatre and swim in the paddling pool though.

CHAPTER 16 – THE SEARCH CONTINUES

12th December 2010

Richard Ferguson was on a roll. He had six names on his list and he was determined to track them all down.

He had two names from his original list – Graham Davidson and Matthew Ransome, plus one each from Barry and Terry's lists – Gary Smithies and Tony Sykes. There were also a couple of other names which he had added to the list, lads who had played some games for Fartown United but had not been in at the start – Glyn Battye and John Robinson.

He decided to start with good old google and quickly had a hit which resulted in Matt Ransome being struck from the list. Matt had been a bit of a rebel in his younger days in Fartown and he had had quite a few brushes with the law. It was Matt who had given the other boys their first sight of a flick knife and he mated around with some decidedly dodgy characters. Despite all this he was popular with the boys. He was quite a talented player and was probably the fastest runner of all the boys. A skill which no doubt had been useful in his later life! Fergy's research quickly revealed that Matt's juvenile delinquency had turned into a career. He had a long history of crime and had spent a large proportion of his adult life as a guest of her majesty and was currently serving a long sentence for his involvement in an armed robbery in Manchester three years earlier. Fergy's thoughts drifted back to his early encounters with Matt.

Back to reality, and next up was John Robinson who it seemed was still living in the Huddersfield area judging by some facebook postings. On an impulse Fergy pulled out his telephone directory from a few years back and sure enough there were three John Robinsons listed. There was no reply on the first one he tried, the second one did answer but it turned out that John had sold the house two years previously but the new owner did have a mobile number for John which he duly gave to Fergy.

Fergy decided to give it a go. The phone rang and eventually went to voice mail, it was the default message so it was impossible to tell if it was the John Robinson he knew of old, nevertheless he left a brief message saying who he was and why he was ringing.

Fergy moved on to the next one on his list Gary Smithies, he could find nothing on google so was about to check facebook when his phone rang.

'Richard Ferguson' he answered

'Is that Fergy who lived in Fartown?'

'Yes it is, is that John?'

'Yeh John Robinson, you just left me a message didn't you? That was a bit of a surprise.'

'Yes I did, it's great to hear from you John how are you doing?'

'I'm OK thanks had a few problems with my heart last year but I'm on the road to recovery. What about you, I haven't seen you in – god I don't know how long?'

'I'm pretty good actually, sorry to hear about the heart, but it's good that you're on the mend, did you hear about Val Taylor, he died earlier this year?'

'Yeh bad do that, I would have gone to the funeral but I had an appointment to see the cardiologist on the same day'.

'It's a pity you couldn't make it the Wilkinsons were both there and Terry Ogden. That's why I'm ringing you actually, we're trying to get a bit of a reunion together you know the old Fartown United lot, we're contacting as many of the gang as possible and you were on my list'.

'Well thanks for ringing it would be nice to meet some old friends. I've bumped into a few of them from time to time when I was bowling for Marsh club, but that was a few years back, I haven't played for nearly five years now'.

Fergy thought he'd sound him out about some of the others who were on his list 'You wouldn't have come across Graham Davidson, Glyn Battye or Gary Smithies, oh and Tony Sykes by any chance have you?'

'Do you mean Graham Smithies the one who lived next to Terry Ogden?'

'Yes that'll be the one'.

'He died a good few years ago, I went to that funeral, he had a heart attack – only 51 poor bugger'.

'What a shame he always was a bit of a nervous type wasn't he? What about the others?'

'I've seen Glyn Battye a few times, in fact I've got a mobile number for him somewhere, do you want it?'

'That would be great thanks'.

'It might take a few minutes to find it – shall I text it to you?'

Yeh sure. Have you got an email address John, it would be handy when it comes to scheduling the reunion?'

'Yes I have, have you any idea when it will be Fergy?'

'I'm hoping it will be sometime early in the new year but we haven't tracked everyone down yet and some of the guys don't live locally. Wilky is in Jersey and Martin lives somewhere near London by all accounts'.

'OK then I'll dig out this number for Glyn and text it to you along with my email address then.'

'Oh by the way John, how would you feel about having a game of five a side in the sports centre as part of the reunion?'

'Definitely not for me Fergy but I'd be happy to come along and laugh at you lot, sorry I mean cheer you on'.

Fergy chuckled and then the men said their goodbyes, agreeing to keep in touch.

Fergy updated his list. 'That's two scrubbed off, one definite and another possible'.

Fergy went back to his computer and tried a few free web sites which purported to help you find missing friends. He typed in the name 'Graham Davidson', located in Huddersfield after a few seconds the system returned over 200 hits for the name none of which were located in Huddersfield. He scanned the first few pages to see if the short resumes contained anything to link them with the Graham Davidson he once knew but to no avail. 'Why did you have such a common name Graham?' he mused to himself. He tried 'Tony Sykes' expecting a similar result and he wasn't disappointed.

He decided to wait for John to send through the mobile number for Glyn Battye and leave the other two for the time being.

He did a quick mental calculation. 'That's nine confirmed and two more possible if Barry contacts the Henshaws'. He checked his email and there was a new message from Barry confirming that the Henshaws had been contacted and both of them were keen to meet up.

He decided to send an email out tomorrow to Terry and Barry to get the email addresses for the people they had contacted and then Fergy would circulate an email to everyone to find out their availability for the reunion.

'You never know' Fergy thought to himself 'someone in the gang might know how to contact Tony or Graham'.

He closed his laptop and got up to make a cup of tea when a

thought suddenly struck him 'Shit! We've not got the Chapmans on the list, how could we have forgotten Andy and Ricky. I can't believe we all forgot about them.'

He reopened his laptop and began another search for the missing brothers, his cup of tea could wait a while longer.

EXTRACT FROM BARRY WILKINSON'S DIARY

13th December 2010

Had some bad news – Aiden has been diagnosed with Prostate cancer and won't be able to come to the reunion as he's starting his treatment in mid January. Fortunately they've caught it early so the prognosis is good.

He's sick that he can't come to the reunion but I've promised to get some pictures and send them onto him.

On the positive side the Henshaw brothers have confirmed for the reunion so I think we'll have enough to make it worthwhile.

CHAPTER 17 - THE NEW FOOTBALL SEASON

Summer 1958

There were many things which generated excitement among this particular group of boys and the start of the new football season was certainly one of them. They couldn't hide their excitement as they made their way down to Leeds Road for the first match of the 1958 / 59 season. Fergy's dad was a lifelong supporter and he had taken his son to a few matches each season since he had been about seven years old. Last season he had agreed to let the other boys tag along and stand together at the ground whilst he kept a watchful eye on them. The boys had found a good vantage point where their size didn't restrict their view of the game, it was up in the top corner between the main stand and the 'cowshed', the name by which the stand at the Leeds Road end was universally known.

Mr Ferguson would escort them to the junior's entrance where they could pay the princely sum of nine pence to get into the ground where they would wait for Mr Ferguson to meet them and take them up into the main part of the stadium.

It was about a twenty minute walk from the estate to the ground. Their route involved using the old stone bridge to cross over the canal and then they would walk across the aptly named Canker Lane where the fair would come every Easter and Whitsuntide, and which, on match days, formed the main car park. Finally the group would cross the busy Leeds Road and enter via the turnstiles.

In 1958 the Huddersfied Town team was managed by Bill Shankly, who would become a legend when he later became manager of Liverpool, but the boys were still getting to know the names of the players and had little interest in who the manager was.

'Who's your favourite player?' asked Fergy.

'Les Massie 'cos he scores most of the goals' replied Barry.

'What about that young lad from Scotland, the skinny one' suggested Wilky.

'You mean Dennis Law don't you Wilky' Fergy knew all the names, 'I think he's brilliant, my dad says he'll be playing for Scotland before you know it'.

'Sandy Kenyon's my favourite' said Sutty 'I want to be a goaly like him'.

'It's Kennon not Kenyon' corrected Fergy 'did you know he's from South Africa?'

'Really? That's a long way from Huddersfield int'it' observed Terry. 'Anyhow who are we laking today?'

'Derby County' came the reply from Fergy.

'Are they any good?' asked Terry.

'OK I suppose - we drew nil nil last season' Fergy was like a walking encyclopaedia.

'Is there anything you don't know about Town Fergy?' Martin asked with more than a hint of sarcasm.

'Not much. Next question.'

Barry decided to test him further 'OK who scored for Town last year against this lot?'

Fergy studied for a minute 'Nobody I just told you it was nil nil, stupid'.

'No I mean when we beat them 4-2 at their ground' Barry had obviously been doing his homework.

Fergy's dad gave wry smile 'Looks like Barry has got you stumped there Richard'.

'Just a sec, I think it was Denis Law and Les Massie, they got two goals each'.

'Ooh you were close, Dennis Law did get two but Massie only got one, Ronnie Simpson got the other' replied Barry smugly.

'You've been doing your homework haven't you Barry?' said Mr Ferguson.

'No, actually Mr Ferguson I read it in last night's examiner in the match preview' Barry's smugness reached new heights.

'Nearly there boys, now just be careful while we cross Leeds Road then I'll see you all inside, have you all got your money ready?'

The boys all checked their money and ran off to the turnstile watched carefully by Mr Ferguson.

'I like your dad' said Barry 'he's dead nice'.

'He's OK I guess' agreed Fergy 'except when he beats me at Newfooty, he gloats'.

'What d'you mean?' asked Barry.

'He brags a lot. It's the same when we play cricket on the beach'.

There was a small queue at the junior's turnstile so Mr Ferguson was already waiting for them when they finally got into the ground.

'Are you boys going to stand in your usual spot?'

They all nodded 'OK then let's go'.

The game ended in a 1 – 1 draw, with Les Massie scoring the Town goal in front of a crowd of about 17,000. The boys were disappointed not to get the win but there was another home match coming up on Wednesday night so they had that to look forward to. In the meantime they would get some practice in and arranged to meet in the field after tea for a game of soccer.

EXTRACT FROM BARRY WILKINSON'S DIARY

23rd August 1958

First Town match of the new season versus Derby County. Mam and dad let us come back from our holidays a day early so that we can go to the match.

The match was a draw and Les Massie, my favourite player, got the goal for Town, we've got another game on Wensday against Cardiff City.

We missed Fartown's first game last week cos we were on holiday, but they are at home on Monday against Bramley, we've won one and lost two so far.

As the football season started in late August the school holidays were drawing to a close. Football still dominated the boys time but in the same way that cricket had provided some sporting variety rugby league was also interesting some – though not all – of the boys.

Terry and the Wilkinson brothers had already been to the occasional Huddersfield rugby league match, the ground where they played was in Fartown so the local team were usually referred to as Fartown in the same way that the football team were known as Town. Terry had been taken by his dad and the Wilkinsons by their grown up brother who was a keen rugby fan. The great advantage of going to watch the rugby was that entrance for young people was free and they also had a separate section for youngsters.

It seemed, at that time, that when Town were playing at home, Fartown were away and vice versa and this suited the boys as they rarely had to make a choice between their two local teams.

The fixtures for both soccer and rugby came thick and fast at the start of the season. Neither club had installed floodlights so these early weeks of the season usually included a mid-week evening kick off as well as the normal Saturday afternoon fixture. On this particular week the boys had the luxury of Town on Saturday, Fartown on Monday evening and then another Town match on the Wednesday evening – what joy. The two Town matches in one week would stretch their pocket money to it's limits, which, for most of the boys, was around two and sixpence per week.

When the boys eventually all returned to school for the Autumn term there was still enough daylight left when they got home from school to play their sports but gradually the daylight diminished until the field was too dark for sporting games.

Each weekend they would make their way to Leeds Road or Fartown to cheer on their local heroes, evenings would, as likely as not, be spent in the family home watching TV or playing games. With only two channels available the choice of TV programmes was extremely limited; kids programmes were normally shown between five and six every evening and their latest favourite was the cartoon Popeye the Sailor Man. Later evening viewing was aimed at the adults and the boys would find these programmes boring so they would resort to playing with their toys. The Wilkinson brothers had amassed an impressive collection of Dinky Toys including many war vehicles, which they would use, along with their toy soldiers, for war games behind the settee whilst mam and dad watched programmes such as What's my Line and Sunday Night at the London Palladium. Preparing for Bonfire Night would occupy them for most of October. Once November 5th had passed the excitement would start to build up towards Christmas as the prospect of new toys to play with tantalised all the boys.

This year there was one special thing on nearly everybody's

Bryn Woodworth

wish list – a Newfooty set.

CHAPTER 18 – THE REUNION, THE DATE IS SET

December 2010

Fergy eventually tracked down the younger of the Chapman brothers through Facebook. Ricky was living down on the south coast, just outside Bournemouth, where he had settled over twenty years ago. Fergy sent him a message telling him about the proposed reunion. Ricky quickly replied and explained that his brother, Andy, had taken early retirement on health grounds and was living in southern Spain. Both brothers had not enjoyed the best of health, Andy had survived two heart attacks and was very definitely living the quiet life with his wife of nearly forty years. Ricky, who had also had health issues, and his wife had left the rat race and joined the good life set. They had bought a small holding and kept a few sheep, hens and a goat and for that reason would not be able to come north for the reunion.

Fergy wished him all the best, asked to be remembered to Andy and promised to send Ricky some photos of the reunion.

Fergy took a deep breath and considered the position. By his calculations they had enough to make a go of the reunion so the next step was to establish everyone's availability.

Over the next week or so, after much sending and receiving of emails, texts and phone calls he had contacted everyone and there were ten definite and two possibles. Glyn Battye had sent his apologies but he and his wife had decided to spend the winter months in Portugal, somewhere on the Algarve.

Unfortunately Wilky would be another absentee. He had recently been diagnosed with prostate cancer and was about to start a programme of treatment which would last four weeks.

There hadn't been many takers for the idea of a five a side game at the sports centre, with only five putting their hands up so it was decided to have the reunion in mid January and the venue was to be the Stag on Bradford Road. The choice of venue caused a few raised eyebrows amongst the group, but Fergy tried to put their minds at rest and assured them that everything would be OK as they had already visited the pub and checked everything out.

He decided to give Barry a call. 'Hi Barry looks like about ten of us for the re-union on the 15th January, I thought we might pop over and see the landlord at the Stag to sort everything out, what do you say'.

'Yeh.' replied Barry 'I'm up for that when do fancy going up there? I'm OK any day next week, my diary's completely open so you choose'.

'What no work on then Barry?'

'It's always the same in December mate, nobody wants to schedule a training course just before Christmas do they? Mind you it's just as well considering the weather we've had; they reckon that it's going to be one of the worst December's on record, according to the BBC'.

'Terry is just the opposite apparently, the shop is really busy despite the weather, so he won't be able to make it. How about Tuesday lunch time then, say around 12 ish?'

'That's fine for me, are you going to give them a call just to make sure the landlord's going to be around?'

'Yeh will do, so if you don't hear anything from me I'll see you at the pub about 12ish next Tuesday and we can grab some lunch while we're at it'.

'See you then, cheers Fergy'.

Fergy immediately called the landlord and made arrangements to see him the following week.

When Barry woke up on Tuesday morning he peeped out through the curtains and the weather had lived up to the bleak forecast; high winds and sleet showers. He immediately remembered the meeting with Fergy when Sandy breezed into the bedroom.

'Come on Baz you lazy sod get moving, it's time you were up and about'.

'What makes you so cheerful on this foul morning anyway?'

'I've promised to meet our Julie in Town for coffee later and I want to have time to do a bit of Christmas shopping before I meet her and you, my dear, can be my chauffeur.'

'Ah' he paused and rubbed his grey stubble 'there might be a slight problem there. You see I've arranged to meet Fergy at the pub on Bradford Road at 12 and we'll probably have a couple of pints, you know how it is'.

'Oh Barry you didn't tell me you were out for lunch did you?'

'It just slipped my mind, I tell you what I'll come into town with you and we can do some shopping together. Then, when you go to meet your Julie, I'll go up to the bus station and get the bus on to Bradford Road and I'll make my own way home afterwards. How's that?'

'OK but get a move on – and don't forget to shave I don't want to be walking round town with you looking like an old tramp'.

'Charming!' and Barry sloped off to the bathroom to get showered and shaved chuntering to himself all the way.

'And you can stop that muttering you sound like an old washer woman'.

They decided to go to town in Sandy's car and, as usual Barry drove. Sandy was the proud owner of a Mini Cooper in midnight blue but she admitted that she preferred being a passenger to actually driving. Barry's car, on the other hand, was a six year old Jaguar XJ6 – an old man's car according to Sandy but he loved the space and comfort it provided.

As he squeezed his six foot frame into the driving seat he had his usual moan about the size of the car as he slid the seat back a few notches. 'This car's too small for a man, I'm going to do my back in one day getting into this thing'.

'Oh shut up Barry you sound more like your dad every day' Sandy smiled and pushed his shoulder 'you're still a young man Barry stop behaving like a miserable old git'.

'D'you know Sandy you're probably right, it's just on these cold winter mornings I prefer to get into the Jag, stretch out and switch on the seat warmers don't you?'

'Yes I must admit it's nice to have the luxury but I'm going to be driving home and you know I don't like driving that great big thing around town, so just shut up and get on with it old man'.

Barry smiled and off they went to do some Christmas shopping.

Sandy was in good shopping form and after an hour and a half they were loaded down with presents; mainly for their three grandchildren with a few more for their grown up son and daughter.

They had left the car in the multi storey car park above the bus station so he helped Sandy to carry the bags back to the car where they unloaded the shopping. The tiny boot on the mini was soon filled so the remaining presents went on the back seat. They made their way down the stairs to the ground floor and as they split up and went their separate ways Sandy shouted to him 'Don't forget to use your free pass now you're over 60' and laughed as she made her way out of the bus station.

Sandy had applied for the bus passes for both of them and she had used hers on numerous occasions. Barry, on the other hand, hardly ever used the bus and, for some reason even he couldn't understand, he was very self conscious about being seen on a bus. A situation which had been aggravated when on one of the few occasions he did get on the bus he was spotted by a group of his son's old school friends who recognised him and jokingly asked why he was slumming it on the bus and what had happened to the Jag.

He was in two minds whether to walk the mile or so to the pub, until he saw that a bus which went along Bradford Road was already waiting so he joined the queue. He couldn't help but notice that just about everybody else who got on the bus had a free pass of some sort. As he took his seat on the lower deck he wondered how the hell the bus company survived if nobody was actually paying and concluded that they must get a subsidy from someone for all these non-paying passengers. He made a mental note to look it up when he got home, then reprimanded himself 'That's just the sort of thing a miserable old git would be interested in' and mentally crossed it off his list in disgust.

The journey to Bradford Road only took a few minutes and Barry almost missed his stop. As he got off the bus his mind wandered back to his Huddersfield New College days when the buses used to have an open entrance and exit at the back and how the lads thought they were real dare devils jumping off the bus whilst it was still moving. They would hold onto the steel pole and jump with one foot first and the momentum of the bus would make them run as they hit the ground.

'My god what would the Health and Safety police make of that practice today' he mused as the bus drove off.

He turned his attention to crossing the busy Bradford Road. Fortunately the weather had improved by this time, the wind was still blowing but the sleet had mercifully stopped. The volume of traffic had certainly increased massively since his school days and he had to wait a few minutes before he could cross, eventually a kind motorist slowed down and flashed him. He waved politely to the driver and mumbled to himself 'Even the car drivers think I'm a doddering old git'. He was having a bad day.

He walked into the pub, 'Hi Barry' a voice came from the room next to the entrance and Barry turned to see Fergy sitting with a full pint glass in front of him. 'What're you having old man?'

'Oh don't you bloody start. If I remember rightly you're at least three months older than me' the two men smiled and shook hands. 'I'll have the same as you then young man! Is the landlord in?'

'Due back shortly apparently, gone over to the cash and carry according to the barmaid who I think might be his wife'.

They walked together to the bar where Fergy ordered Barry's pint. Barry glanced around the pub and admired the Christmas decorations and decided that they appeared to be the only people in the pub as they turned and walked back to the table. The two men sat down and took a large swig of the smooth golden liquid. 'Oh that's better' sighed Barry.

'You having a bad day then mate?'

'You could say that' he smiled. 'Sandy's been ribbing me a bit about behaving like an old man, you know the sort of stuff and then bugger me I get off the bus and this woman flashes me to cross as if I'm some doddering old man. Anyway I'm a lot better now for seeing you Fergy. What's the latest on the numbers?'

'We're up to ten definite and one probable, so it's looking good on that score. We need to work out what exactly we're going to do with them when they get here. There weren't many takers for the football so that's out, have you got any suggestions? You know, something to break the ice and get them to relax and get them talking?'

'As it happens I've been giving it quite a bit of thought. Let's start with what we don't want it to be and that's a bragging match, you know what I mean. Where do you live? What car do you drive - I've got an Aston Martin and all that sort of shit'.

'I'm with you on that score Barry but I can't see many of our old lot driving an Aston Martin'.

'You never know we haven't seen or heard from any of this lot in donkey's years, who knows what might have happened they might have won the lottery, had an inheritance or robbed a bank, who knows'.

'Yeh well the bank robber won't be coming will he? Matt Ransome is currently enjoying her majesty's hospitality' laughed Fergy.

'D'you know Fergy for some reason I was thinking about Matt last night. He was always a bit different to the rest of us wasn't he, bit of a rebel?'

'Yeh I suppose so, I had the same thoughts as you there Barry. Didn't he have a couple of younger sisters and his dad was never there. They lived in a house across the road from Terry's, near the bottom of the estate. I think he was the same age as Wilky but he was so skinny and with that gaunt face he looked much younger.'

'That's right' replied Barry 'we reckoned that he didn't get fed properly as he was always cadging□*□ food from us. We used to take pity on him and sneak bits of food out of the house to give him. I remember my mam once caught me and Aiden sneaking off with one of her home made buns, so we told her about Matt and she gave us some bread and jam for him as well as the bun. She kept doing it after that, you know, *'here take that for yer mate, the skinny one'* she would say. It didn't seem to make any difference though he was still skinny as a rake'.

'You're not wrong there Barry' Fergy smiled. 'I remember, before we got to know him, he would just stand and watch us playing soccer, he was either too proud or too shy to ask if he could play. Terry eventually broke the ice and asked him if he would like to join in. He was a decent player, not the most skilful, but he was lightening fast.'

'What about when his dad first appeared on the scene. It must have been five or six months after they'd moved into the estate. He said his dad had been working away but my dad reckoned he'd been in prison. He was a brute though, Matt would come into the field with a black eye or bruises to his face and arms when his dad was home. Fortunately for Matt, after a while, his dad would just disappear for months at a time. Probably back inside'.

'Poor sod' commented Fergy 'he never stood a chance really did he, and god knows what sort of people his dad would have introduced him too'.

'Aye I suppose we should thank our lucky stars we didn't have him for a dad, 'eh Fergy. OK back to business, I thought we might get them all here and have a pint, then have a wander up to the old estate, maybe get a couple of group photos on the circle, we could even tell the Examiner and they might do a feature, it's just the sort of thing they'd go for'.

'That's not a bad idea actually, go on, what next?'

'I thought we could ask everybody to bring any old photos they've got from the Fartown United days. Not necessarily about the match or football, maybe photos of kids playing in the field or the back yard. What do you reckon?'

'OK' Fergy hesitated 'but don't forget there weren't many cameras around in them days, so the photos might be in short supply. Have you got any?'

'We've got loads of old pictures, my mother never threw any of them away. I inherited a couple of albums and a huge biscuit tin with loads of loose pictures. There's sure to be some of us playing; the problem's going to be finding them, a bit of the old needle in a haystack syndrome. What about you?'

'Much the same as you, I tell you what I came across the other day – a picture of that holiday when a bunch of us went down to Cornwall, it was taken at Lands End. We're all stood under the signpost telling you how far away you are from all sorts of places. That's a bit later though we were 17 or 18 then weren't we?'

'Oh yes I remember that holiday, it was the first one without our parents wasn't it. Didn't you get badly sunburnt playing soccer on the beach at Woolacombe? God you were in a bad way. We all got burnt but you were much worse than the rest of us, it must have been your delicate complexion. Then didn't our Aiden knacker his A35 van when the four of them went into Newquay for a night out. All six of us had to pile into that old Ford popular of mine while his was being repaired?'

'I think you're mistaken about Newquay though Barry. We had put the tent up on a site near Lands End, it was in the middle of nowhere, so they all went into St Ives for a night out. Wilky tried to do a three point turn on those narrow streets, mounted the kerb and then split his petrol tank when the car came down off the kerb. They all had to hitch hike back to the campsite. Then there was something wrong with your motor wasn't there. I remember that one morning it wouldn't start so we had to push it on the main road to find a garage, and there was a massive queue of cars behind us tooting their horns until a guy stopped and fixed it for us'.

'Yeh it was the starter motor – it kept jamming'.

'Happy days' Fergy smiled and shook his head. 'OK let's go with the pictures idea then and hope some good ones turn up. Right – I'll send an e-mail out to everyone asking them to do some digging in the attic'.

At that point the landlord came in and his wife pointed in the direction of Fergy and Barry.

'Ah good afternoon gentlemen' he smiled and shook hands with them. 'So your little reunion is definitely on then?'

'Yeh, well it looks like it' replied Fergy.

'Which one of you is Richard then?'

'That'll be me but everyone calls me Fergy, and this is Barry. What's your name?'

'Desmond Watson is the name me mother gave me but me friends call me Dizzy. Now have you decided when you want to have the get together and how many are you expecting?'

'We're looking at mid January and preferably at the weekend so Saturday the fifteenth would be good. I've checked and Town are away that week so everyone should be available.'

'And how many of you will there be?

'Looks like about eleven maximum, will that be OK'

'I'm pretty sure we haven't got anything booked for then but I'd better check'. He turned towards the bar and shouted 'Gloria can you check the diary for the fifteenth of January?'

She quickly flicked through a desk diary situated next to the till before replying 'It's clear Dizzy do you want me to put something in?'

'These guys want to book for 11 people' he turned to Fergy 'what time do you want to start and what name shall we put down?'

'We'll go for 12.30 if that's OK and you can book it as Fartown United please'.

'OK did you get that Gloria?' He returned to face the men 'I said we'd do some sandwiches and pork pies, sausage rolls that sort of thing is that OK?'

'Yes, great, thanks' Barry took over 'but we won't be wanting the buffet until after one o'clock, as we are planning to have a walk up to the old estate and take some pictures up there'.

Dizzy looked surprised 'I didn't think you'd be going up there again after what happened last time'.

'You heard about it then?'

'Sure thing - people come to the pub, they like to talk and I'm a good listener. I heard you had a bit of a ... what shall I say... confrontation?'

'Oh it was nothing really – Barry's friend came to our rescue, isn't that right Barry?'

'You guys have got friends up there! Well you do surprise me, and I had you down as being respectable guys'.

'Actually I only have the one friend up there but it seems Gerald – my friend - had quite a bit of influence over the young lads who thought we were snooping on their territory' explained Barry.

'Are we talking about Gerald WILSON by any chance?'

'That's right – Gerald Wilson do you know him?'

'Yes I sure do, everybody knows Gerald! Let's just say he has a reputation, people do not mess with Gerald. He comes in here and he is SO polite and pleasant but I hear some stories that would make your hair curl' Dizzy looked at Fergy who was bald 'well maybe not yours. How come you know this guy Barry?'

'He used to play football for Honley at the same time as I did. He was quite a good player actually and good fun too. We all suspected he was living on the edge, so to speak, back in those days. Anyway he gave me his number and said to give him a call if we wanted to go back with the rest of the lads sometime and he would make sure we're welcome'.

'Well he's definitely the right man to know up there, I'm sure he'll keep the young lads in check. Anyway gentlemen I have a shed load of stuff to unload from the cash and carry so I'll leave you in the hands of my beautiful wife Gloria. If you're eating I recommend the Cajun chicken another one of my wife's specialities.' He checked his watch 'I suggest you get your order in soon 'cos it's going to get very lively in here in about ten minutes, we have a Christmas do for one of the local firms arriving shortly'.

He shook hands with them and made his way through to the back of the pub. Fergy and Barry ordered the chicken and another pint and returned to their seats. Sure enough the peace was shattered shortly afterwards as a group of about fifteen revellers arrived. Fortunately the party was set up for the back room so it didn't disturb them unduly although they could tell that they were having a good time. The two of them spent a pleasant hour eating, drinking and reminiscing before leaving the pub. They made a dash for the bus stop where they could shelter from the snow which was now falling.

'Isn't it strange' mused Barry 'here we are standing at the same bus stop where we used to stand every morning on our way to school all those years ago, and yet when you look around nothing much has changed – until you look closer and everything is different. The Handy Corner is still there but it's not the same shop, the Regent is still there but it's not a ballroom anymore, the old stone terrace houses are still there but somehow they're different with their colourful, painted lintels over the doors and windows. The amount of traffic has certainly changed and the people you see are definitely not the same. The buses too, they all used to be trolley buses in our school days didn't they?'

'Wow that's a bit heavy for a Tuesday afternoon Barry, I never had you down as a philosopher when we were kids. But, joking apart, I get what you're saying. What about the little old lady who used to walk up and down Bradford Road stopping and asking everybody who she passed what the time was'.

'Oh aye, we christened her Greenwich didn't we, 'cos she always wanted to know the time, we could be really cruel at times couldn't we?'

'Not as bad as our Carol, whenever she saw the old lady she went up to her and asked her what the time was before the old dear could speak. I suppose she must have been lonely, a bit sad really. But you're right it is quite strange coming back after all these years – looking back on those days when life was – I don't know – not so complicated. As long as we had a soccer ball and enough money for the Town match we were as happy as pigs in you know what weren't we?'

'Aye the highlight of the soccer season in those days was always the FA cup final. It didn't matter a jot to us which teams were playing and it wasn't just the match itself but all the build up. Grandstand used to start about 12 o'clock and we were glued to it.'

'Spot on - it was the only live football match we ever saw on telly wasn't it? Apart from the world cup that is. Match of the day hadn't even been invented then had it? Nowadays you can watch live soccer virtually every day - if you can afford a SKY contract'.

At that point the bus arrived putting an end to their nostalgia trip. On the journey into town Fergy nudged Barry as he pointed out the old post office where the plastic cricket balls had been bought all those years ago. It was now selling exotic Asian fabrics.

'We didn't half get excited about those cricket balls didn't we' Fergy sighed.

'Sure did, I can still remember that first over you bowled to our Aiden. First he whacked the tennis ball into the long grass and we couldn't find it. Then you hit him on his shin with the corky. He went down like a ton of bricks, swearing like mad. The plastic ball was just perfect for us after those two.'

They arrived at the bus station and as they left the bus Barry spoke 'Looks like we're all set for the 15th then Fergy, are you going to let Terry and all the others know?'

'Yes, will do. I'm really looking forward to it. Have a good Christmas.'

They shook hands before going their separate ways, to their

separate homes and separate lives.

EXTRACT FROM BARRY WILKINSON'S DIARY

21st December 2010

Did some Christmas shopping with Sandy before meeting Fergy at the Stag to finalise the arrangements for the reunion. Booked the pub for 15th January, looks like about ten for the reunion.

Used my new free bus pass for the first time, just one of many things today which made me feel old in fact.

Spent a pleasant hour with Fergy, planning the reunion and then a bit of nostalgia. I think it added to my feelings of getting old.

CHAPTER 19 – WINTER PASTIMES

Autumn / winter 1958

The winter months were dark and dismal. Once the clock's had gone back an hour at the end of October to the end of February it was dark by the time the boys had all got home from school but they still found plenty of ways of amusing themselves outside.

Ball games were out of the question but other games were still possible. May I, tin can squat and hide and seek were winter games which lent themselves to the dark nights. The boys would even encourage the girls to join in these pastimes. Sutty had an older sister called Karen and Fergy's sister Carol was a little bit younger but they were allowed to join in. Martin Kelly also had an older sister but she seemed to be more interested in playing different sorts of games with the older boys.

Their parents were quite happy for the kids to get out of the house on these dark evenings, provided they stayed on the estate which they felt was safe. In some ways it was a separate little world. Most of the boys had relatives who also lived on the estate. The Wilkinsons had no fewer than three aunties and two uncles on the estate, likewise Fergy and Martin Kelly had a couple and Val Taylor and the Henshaw brothers had one. House doors would remain unlocked – at least until bedtime – and people looked out for each other. A good example of the community spirit which existed on the estate would be evident when anyone on the estate died. Someone – usually a close friend or neighbour – would instigate a house to house collection for the bereaved's family and all the neighbours would partially close their curtains out of respect until the funeral had taken place. Of course there were a number of women for whom 'looking out for others' crossed over into out and out nosiness. One of the chief nosey parkers was the Wilkinson's Aunty Agnes. She was a frequent visitor to the Wilkinson's house, ostensibly to see her father, who of course was the boy's grandad. In reality she loved to stand in the bay window and observe the comings and goings on the estate from this vantage point. How Aiden and Barry chuckled to hear their aunt report to their mother on the parlous state of a neighbours washing. Lines like 'I'd be ashamed to hang those bloomers out on my washing line' or better still 'that widow seems to have a few men visiting her' were a constant source of amusement to the boys, and nothing much escaped the attention of their aunt.

By and large the kids were well behaved and stuck to the rules; they daren't do otherwise as they knew that if they did do anything wrong some eagle eyed neighbour would have seen it and report it back to their parents with unpleasant consequences.

Although the estate was relatively safe all the boys and girls had it drummed into them about the dangers of talking to strangers. Fortunately in the late fifties crime levels were quite low and the kids – both boys and girls – were trusted to play out in the relative safety of the estate.

On school nights the curfew would be 7.30 but on weekends that might be extended by an hour or so.

Winter weekends were exciting for the boys. Saturday mornings would inevitably start with a game of soccer. The level of enthusiasm would be high as it would be their first real game since the previous week-end. During the week football was played in the playground at Beaumont Street School at every break but it was a chaotic event which bore little real resemblance to football; everyone joined whichever side they thought was winning and they would all crowd around the ball in a mass of flailing legs with a great deal of pushing and shoving. The ball would progress slowly from one end of the playground to the other almost hidden in a scrum like mass of bodies, occasionally shooting out of the mass as one foot made a rare clean contact with the ball. This would be followed by a massive charge in pursuit of the ball. Woe betide the goalkeepers in this grim game as they would simply be trodden down by the mass of bodies, as the unfortunate Barry Wilkinson found out to his cost.

On this particular occasion it was afternoon playtime and he had been nominated as the goalkeeper. The playtime games of soccer were not quite as chaotic as the ones before school and at dinner time as not as many boys seemed to join in. Barry, who would have been about eight at the time, bent down on the tarmac surface to pick up the ball, but just as he did so, the boot of the biggest lad in the school was aimed at the ball and connected instead with Barry's left hand.

Barry yelled with pain and the game stopped momentarily. Elder brother Aiden must have been up to mischief in another part of the schoolyard, so Barry, accompanied by a sympathetic friend, made his way to the on duty playground teacher who was totally oblivious to the chaos around her. Barry was fighting back the tears as he showed her his injured hand. The force of the kick had split one of the nails on Barry's left hand and blood was oozing out. First aid was, unfortunately for Barry, virtually non-existent at the school so the playground teacher simply told Barry to report his injury to his form teacher when school restarted a few minutes later.

Barry didn't have to wait long as playtime was nearly over and when the bell rang he joined the queue with the other children, still clutching his injured left hand with his other hand. He went up to the teacher's desk and showed his injured hand to his form teacher. After cursory glance the teacher decided, as it was only an hour and a quarter to school finishing time, that Barry should go home immediately to allow his mother to deal with it. She sent for brother Aiden and the two of them were despatched home. Aiden, who had never been a scholar and had even run away from school a couple of times when he was in the infants, couldn't believe his luck. He was generous in his sympathy for his injured brother but also delighted at leaving school early and missing an arithmetic lesson.

Home was a twenty minute walk from school and poor Barry was in pain all the way home. When he did arrive home all his grandad would say was 'I can't do owt wi' that you'll 'ave to wait till yer mother comes home'. Aiden still couldn't believe his luck and went out in the back garden to play with the pet rabbits and left Barry to suffer on his own.

Barry was left to sit at the kitchen table staring at his wounded hand which was throbbing with pain until his mother arrived and provided some much needed sympathy, supplemented by a generous helping of tender loving care, and patched him up. She made him a cup of sweet tea – the universal cure for ailments in those days – and lo and behold he had recovered enough to go out and play with the other lads when they eventually got home from school. He wore his bandaged hand proudly and was excused having to play in goals.

Later that evening Barry tried the old wounded soldier act in an attempt to avoid going to school the following day, but his mother simply pointed out that he couldn't be so bad as he had been able to go out and play with his mates.

EXTRACT FROM BARRY WILKINSON'S DIARY

17th September 1958

I hurt my hand today at school. I was the goaly and tried to pick the ball up when big Tommy Edwards kicked my hand. It hurt a lot, I had split the nail on my left hand, it was really throbbing. They sent for our Aiden to take me home but grandad didn't do anything so I had to wait for mam coming home. She put me a bandage on it.

My mam says the nail will probably fall off in a while so I've got to keep it covered up. She was cross that the school didn't try to treat it before they sent me home and she says she's going to complain, but I hope she doesn't. I don't want to make the teachers cross.

When the Wilkinson brothers arrived at school the following morning Barry was sporting a bandaged left hand which created a great deal of interest and a quite a bit of sympathy from his school friends. Not only that but the teachers at Beaumont Street School must have been feeling a bit guilty about the lack of care they provided to the injured boy. Word had got back to the head teacher, Mr Boothroyd, who sent for Barry immediately after assembly. Normally a call to attend the headmaster's room was a signal you were in trouble but Barry – for once – had a clear conscience as he knocked on the door.

Mr Boothroyd was clearly concerned as to the boy's welfare; and well aware that his staff had not done much to alleviate his obvious pain and discomfort. He also wanted to assure himself that Barry had indeed received some treatment to his injured hand at home.

Once Barry had convinced him that his mother had dealt with his injury Mr Boothroyd sent him back to his class, although he did offer him the option of staying in the classroom at break time, an offer which Barry politely declined.

EXTRACT FROM BARRY WILKINSON'SDIARY

18th September 1958

Mr Boothroyd sent for me this morning. It's the first time I've been sent to his room. Normally it's the naughty kids who get sent and they get the cane. I knew I hadn't done anything wrong so I wasn't bothered, he just wanted to make sure my hand was OK.

◆ ◆ ◆

One of the main events during the dark autumn months was Bonfire Night. It was an event that was eagerly awaited and enthusiastically prepared for. Several weeks before the 5th November the boys would start their 'chumping' – the collection of anything burnable and pile it up to make a bonfire. Not every family had a bonfire but there were several on the estate and the rivalry to make the biggest bonfire was fierce. The chief rivals for the accolade were the Sutcliffes and the Wilkinsons. During the period from mid October to Bonfire Night itself the boys were split into two camps, the ones who were going to the Sutcliffe's bonfire and the rest who were going to the Wilkinson's. The split, by and large, was based on geography. Fergy and the Henshaws lived close by the Sutcliffes so they would be part of the team gathering chumps for the Sutcliffes bonfire. Martin Kelly and Terry Ogden, on the other hand, would align themselves with the Wilkinsons.

Norman Wilkinson drove a lorry for a local woollen mill and was usually able to supplement the boys collection of burnable materials with some old yarn skips from the mill where he worked. These skips were made of interwoven whicker and, over their considerable working life, were used to store yarn which could be very oily. Inevitably the oil from the yarn soaked into the skips to make them even more combustible. This usually meant that the Wilkinsons would have the most impressive bonfire with the biggest flames.

The Sutcliffes however definitely had the advantage when it came to fireworks as Sutty's aunty worked at Standard Fireworks, the local firework factory, and was able to obtain an enviable amount of fireworks for her nephews and nieces at a substantial discount.

In addition to these 'private' bonfires there was always a communal bonfire in the field. This was sited in the area between the playground and the football pitch. This bonfire benefitted from anyone who lived around the field simply chucking their rubbish onto this communal pile – although it wasn't always the kind of rubbish which would burn!

Friendships were temporarily suspended during the run up to Bonfire Night and stealing 'chumps' from each other was part of the fun. The boys did not consider this to be theft but rather part of the cut and thrust of their regular October activities and the practice was referred to as raiding. As November fifth approached, and the bonfires grew in size, guards would be posted every evening by the bonfires, to ensure that no-one could steal their chumps.

One year when the Wilkinson's bonfire was not very large the brothers hatched a plan.

'We've not done right well this year Baz' commented Wilky 'I've seen Sutty's bonfire and it's a lot bigger than ours. We're gunna have a weedy little fire unless we can get some more chumps'.

Barry surveyed the rather disappointing pile of wood and twigs 'Yeah your right, but we will be OK if dad get's us some skips to chuck on, like he normally does'.

'IF he gets some' emphasised Wilky 'but we've only got a week left so we might miss out this year'.

'Well what do you suggest then?' Barry demanded 'Have you got some great plan up your sleeve or what?'

'You should know me by now Baz I've always got a plan' came the conspiratorial reply. 'I think we need to go on a raiding party'.

'Don't be daft Aiden, Sutty and his brothers are keeping a close watch on their bonfire this year, we'll never be able to sneak in and pinch some of their chumps'.

'Who said anything about Sutty's bonfire, I had a bigger one in mind'. He paused for a minute to let Barry work out what he had in mind.

'If you're thinking of the bonfire in the field you're wasting your time Aiden, they've got people watching it every night'.

'I wasn't thinking about raiding it at night Baz. Look, the bonfire in the field is huge this year, they won't miss a bit if we help ourselves, especially if we do it in the morning before we go to school nobody's gunna be watching then are they? What do you say Baz, whose a genius then?'

Barry thought for a moment then smiled 'OK that could work, but when are we going to do it?'

'I thought we could do it on the morning of the fifth itself, that way even if they realise that some of their chumps have gone missing they won't have time to do owt about it will they? We'll have to get up early, get our playing out gear on then wait for dad to set off for work, sneak out and grab the chumps and bring them back to our house before mam notices we're not in bed. We'll just have to sneak back in without her noticing and put our school clothes on before we go down for breakfast. Bingo – jobs a good 'un.'

Barry had an inbuilt distrust of Aiden's plans as he had been involved in too many failures in the past which had landed them both in trouble but he had to admit that this particular plan could work.

EXTRACT FROM BARRY WILKINSON'S DIARY

28th October 1958

Our bonfire this year is looking a bit pathetic so our Aiden has come up with a plan. I don't usually like his plans cos we usually end up in bother but this one sounds good. We're gunna do a raid on the bonfire in the field on November 5th before we go to school.

The plan was agreed and when November 5th finally came around the boys executed the plan to perfection; they were just returning from their third raiding trip with the stolen chumps and were piling them onto their own bonfire when their mother opened the back door.

'W-what do you think you're doing boys, where have all those extra chumps come from?'

Barry looked sheepish but Aiden was not intimidated 'We've just raided the field's bonfire, they've got plenty left, they won't even notice mam.'

'Are you telling me you've stolen their chumps Aiden?' She looked at Barry who was visibly shrinking with shame and then at Aiden who looked far from contrite.

'No we haven't mam it's called raiding and everyone does it'.

'Well you might call it 'raiding' but in my book it's stealing so you can just put them back where you got them from'.

'But mam' started Aiden.

'No buts Aiden just take the bloody things back before I really lose my temper'.

Barry knew they were on a losing wicket so he nudged Aiden and said 'Come on Aiden we're in enough trouble we'd better do as me mam says'. So the boys trouped back into the field and were in the process of putting the chumps back on the pile when they were spotted by a woman who lived nearby as she hung out the washing.

'My word, you lads are keen aren't you, still adding to the pile on the final day and before you go to school as well, well done lads'.

Nothing more was said over breakfast, the boys had learnt that it was better to stay silent when they were in bother. What's more they hadn't returned all of the stolen chumps, just enough to satisfy their mother.

On their way to school they discussed the mornings events.

'Well my plan worked quite well didn't it Baz?' bragged Wilky.

'If you call getting caught red handed by me mam a success I suppose it was' Barry replied sarcastically.

'We finished up with more chumps didn't we, so it must have been a success'.

'Yeh well we might have got away with it if you hadn't been so bloody greedy and gone back for that third trip. That's your trouble Aiden you're greedy, you're never satisfied'.

'Better than being a little wimp like you Barry, *'Sorry mam we'll take them back"* Aiden mocked his younger brother.

Barry had had enough, he wanted to smash his brother in the face but knew from past experience that he would come out worst from any fight they had. He spotted one of his class mates and ran off to join him. Wilky took his frustration out on a stone which was lying on the pavement and gave it a hefty kick. As he admired the strength of his kick as the stone careered its way down the road, he suddenly realised it was heading in the direction of a parked van. He set off running just before the stone hit the van with a loud crack and a very large man emerged from inside the van.

'Hey come back here you little bugger' he shouted but to no avail, Wilky was well out of range.

After school finished they were back to being friends but they were both still rather subdued as they made their way home from school.

'It's gunna be a pathetic bonfire Barry, I bet if we light it at six o'clock it'll have fizzled out by seven, we'll hardly have enough time to set all the fireworks off'.

As they walked up the hill onto the estate their dad's lorry passed them and on the back there were five or six old yarn skips. The boys eyes lit up and they set off running back to their house. When they got to the house their dad had already unloaded the skips and was setting off back to work to drop the lorry off.

They ran around the back of the house and in addition to the old skips there was a big pile of old wooden planks. They ran into the house 'Where's all that wood come from Grandad?' asked Aiden.

'One of your mates – the curly haired, cheeky one – came with his dad and dropped them off about half an hour ago'.

'That'll be Oggy then' said Barry 'I knew it was a good idea to invite them to our bonfire, come on Aiden let's get out of our school clothes and get out there to stack it all up properly'.

Aiden, who had a penchant for the melodramatic, looked heavenwards, put his hands together in mock prayer and mouthed 'Thank you' before they both raced upstairs to get changed.

By half past five the boys had finished stacking the bonfire and announced that it was ready and began pestering their mum about when they could actually light it.

'You can tell your mates to come round about 6 o'clock, your dad will be home by then and he'll light it for you'.

Bonfire night at the Wilkinsons was a family affair, aunts and uncles, neighbours and friends were invited. Dad would have overall responsibility for lighting the fire and most of the fireworks and the ladies would prepare the usual bonfire night fare of parkin, baked potatoes and sausages. Not to mention the bonfire toffee – which was so hard it could break your teeth if you tried to bite it.

The boys would generally behave themselves in adult company, but on bonfire night they would take great joy in mischievously dropping the odd jumping cracker behind the legs of the ladies standing next to the wall. Oh how they loved to see these older women jumping and shrieking as the fireworks lived up to their name and crackled and jumped around their feet.

EXTRACT FROM BARRY WILKINSON'S DIARY

Bryn Woodworth

5th November 1958

Got into bother this morning, mam caught us raiding chumps from the bonfire in the field. It was our Aiden's idea and we nearly got away with it. We did three runs and got caught on the last one. Mam made us take the chumps back, she said it was stealing, which I suppose it was. We only took half of the chumps back though so it wasn't a complete waste of time.

Dad brought six old skips from work and Terry's dad got a load of old wood from his place as well so we had a decent bonfire after all.

The REAL mischief, however, would have taken place the previous night – November 4th the dreaded mischief night! Dreaded, that is, by the adults but absolutely loved by all the kids – boys and girls alike. None of this trick or treat nonsense, this was trick, trick, trick all the way. Dustbins would be tipped over, doors would be knocked on and fizzing bangers (the firework variety not the sausages) left on the doorstep to explode just as the door was opened. Treacle would be smeared on gates and door handles and eggs were thrown at windows. This was serious mischief and the kids loved it.

Bangers were the boys' favourite firework and came in various sizes starting with the most common, the penny banger, a penny ha'penny would get you a little midget and threepence would get you a cannon with a very big bang indeed. The boys would play a dangerous game which involved lighting the firework, counting up to ten and then throwing it in the air so that it would explode in mid-air. Not surprisingly many of the boys would go to school the following day sporting bandages and plasters to cover burnt fingers and hands, but like their football injuries they were seen as badges of courage rather than the symbols of carelessness or stupidity which they really were.

Their school teachers hated the period in the run up to bonfire night and would heave a sigh of relief when it had passed. Fireworks were banned everywhere in school but that didn't stop some of the boys smuggling them in and setting them off surreptitiously. This period also seemed to coincide with a great deal more fratching and scrapping□*□ in the playground.

EXTRACT FROM BARRY WILKINSON'S DIARY

4th November 1958

Mischief night. Mr Boothroyd told us all at assembly this morning that we shouldn't do any mischief. When I told our Aiden he says hes wasting his breath nobody will take any notice and for once I agree with him.

Me and Aiden have been saving a bit out of our spending money so we can buy some extra bangers. We love to light the banger, drop it on the doorstep and then knock on the door. We run like hell and hide behind the privets so we can watch what happens. Sometimes if they're slow coming to the door the banger goes off too soon and some houses don't even answer the door cos they know it mischiefers but when we get the timing right it's brilliant. They jump out of their skin and then they'll look around and swear at us.

We had a close shave tonight though. We set off a Cannon at No. 44 and this young bloke came out, he had an army uniform on. Anyway the banger goes off just as he's opening the door – perfect, he nearly jumps out of his skin. I think he could hear our Aiden giggling behind the privets so he starts walking up the path and he's swearing like mad, so we set off running and he's chasing us up the street. He would have caught us too but we ran into the field and it was pitch black so we hid. He stood there by the swings for ever so long shouting and bawling and saying what he was going to do to us if he catches us. I was a bit scared but we kept us heads down and eventually he went away. We didn't move for a while afterwards and we made sure we went out of the field by the bottom ginnel cos our Aiden said he might be waiting for us, and he was right. We walked past the entrance to the field a few minutes later and he was still waiting there but luckily he didn't recognise us.

We decided not to do any mischief at no. 44 next year.

Once bonfire night had passed, a sense of calmness seemed to take over as the kids turned their attention to Christmas which was fast approaching. It was an exciting time but one much more focussed on good behaviour rather than the mischief and aggravation associated with bonfire night. Little devils temporarily turned into little angels in order to maximise their chances of receiving the presents they were hoping to get from santa or their parents.

CHAPTER 20 – A SURPRISE
AT THE REUNION

January 2011

EXTRACT FROM BARRY WILKINSON'S DIARY

14th January 2011

Re-union day minus one. Getting excited and nervous, I just hope it goes OK and enough people turn up. Should have around ten people according to Fergy. Shame that our Aiden can't come, I think he wanted to delay the treatment but Laura wasn't having any of it! Can't blame her either – got to put your health first.

I phoned Gerald and he's put the word around to leave us in peace. He said to give him a knock when we get there so Fergy can have a look round his old house, should be fun.

The day of the reunion finally arrived. Barry and Fergy had arranged to arrive early at the pub in order to check that everything was as it should be. As they wanted to keep a clear head they ordered coffees rather than their usual beers from Gloria at the bar and sat at their usual table.

'Well Barry it's a real shame about your Aiden, I'm sure he would have enjoyed the reunion, but you can't take risks where your health is concerned'.

'I can tell you he's well pissed off about it, he would have really been in his element' replied Barry. 'He was even going to ask the hospital if they could delay starting the treatment but there was no way Laura would allow that, and to be honest I can't blame her. Are all the others still coming?'

Fergy took out his phone and checked for texts, 'No last minute cancellations so I'm expecting everyone to turn up. Tell the truth Barry now that the day has arrived I'm actually feeling quite nervous, how about you?' Fergy sipped his coffee but his eyes were firmly focussed on the pub door.

'Relax Fergy, they won't be here yet, there's another three quarters of an hour before they're due to arrive. Tell you what – why don't we have a competition to see who's first to recognise each person as they come through the door, could be quite entertaining'.

'It could be bloody embarrassing as well, let's say Martin Kelly comes through the door and one of us shouts out John Robinson or somebody else'.

'Well we'd wait for them to introduce themselves wouldn't we? The guess would be just between you and me, whispered rather than shouted out loud; just a thought, bit of fun to help us relax. By the way what shall we do about paying for the drinks, is the landlord still doing the buffet for free as he promised before?'

'Yes I've spoken to Dizzy and the food is covered, how about you and I paying for the first round of drinks, we're only expecting a maximum of eleven so it shouldn't be too expensive and most people will be on pints won't they.'

'That's a good idea – I'll just go and tell Desmond, sorry Dizzy, to put the first round on a tab and we'll sort it out at the end. Shall we all walk up to the estate after the first round of drinks?'

'That's the plan Barry, I've told everybody that's what we're going to do and no-one has raised any objections, so I'm assuming that they are all physically up to it. Did you find any old pictures to hand around?'

'I've found a few but there's none with us all on, there's one of me and our Aiden in our Newcastle Unite kit in our back yard. I HAVE got something that I'll guarantee will bring back a few memories when I pass it round.' Barry fished around in the inside pocket of his overcoat which was slung over the back of a chair and dug out a rather grubby looking booklet which was enclosed in a clear plastic wallet. 'Heh you must remember these Fergy, we all used to collect them didn't we?' He took the booklet which had the words CHIX BUBBLE GUM FOOT-BALL PICTURE ALBUM on the cover and then he flicked open the first page to reveal an album full of pictures of footballers from the late fifties and early sixties.

'Well I never, where the hell did you get that from? I'm pretty sure I had that one as well, but I don't know what happened to it, and all my other albums for that matter, I had quite a few'.

'Well I didn't get it on Amazon that's for sure. Seriously, it was up in the attic along with stacks of old footy and rugby league programmes, I came across it when I was looking for the photos. I'm thinking of flogging some of them on Ebay; apparently they fetch a few bob and they're not doing any good up in the attic are they.'

'You're right though Barry, it will bring back a few memories when you pass it around. I found a few old pictures, including this one which my dad took at a Town match'. Fergy passed an old black and white photo with several cracks where it had been folded showing five happy looking boys with overcoats and hooped – presumably blue and white - bobble hats and scarves in front of the old Leeds Road ground.

'That's me and our Aiden on the right and Martin Kelly and Terry on the left, with you in the middle, oh and look we've all got one of those wooden rattles which we used to swing to make a noise. You'd never get one of them into a football ground now; they'd be classed as an offensive weapon.'

The door swung open and Fergy whispered 'Terry Ogden'.

'Ah come on, Terry doesn't count you only saw him a few weeks ago'.

'Hi lads I'm a bit early, I thought I'd be the first to arrive. Our lass was on her way to a meeting in Bradford so I got her to drop me off. So why don't I count then?'

Barry and Fergy looked at each other and started to giggle like schoolboys.

'Oh come on fellas what's so funny?' Terry gave his friends a look of frustration. 'Is this part of the nostalgia trip taking the mick out of the little lad, just like old times?'

'Sorry Terry, we're not laughing at you' explained Barry 'we were just having a competition to recognise who everybody is when they come in and you were the first, Fergy here was claiming a point but I disallowed it 'cos its only a few weeks since we saw you. Anyway..' he looked at his watch 'I don't know about you two but I reckon it's time for a pint.'

It was ten minutes past twelve as Barry approached the bar and ordered three pints of Taylors and put them on the tab as agreed with Fergy. As he turned away from the bar the door opened and in stepped a red faced stocky man about their age.

Fergy stood up and held out his hand 'Hello John glad you could make it'.

'Wouldn't miss it for the world Richard, how are you doing?'

'Nobody calls me Richard – apart from our Carol – and she only does it to annoy me, I'm still Fergy to my mates'. Fergy turned to face Barry and wrote the number one with his finger.

Barry pointed to the bar as he shook hands with John 'Get yourself a pint John, I haven't seen you in a long time, you're looking well. The Taylors is excellent and the first one is paid for. Do you recognise Terry Ogden, your house was across the road from him wasn't it?'

John shook hands with Terry and then went up to the bar and ordered his pint and sat down with the others. 'How many are we expecting today?' he directed his question to Fergy.

'We've got eleven acceptances and no cancellations up to now, so just got enough for a soccer team, how appropriate'.

Over the next twenty minutes the remaining friends rolled up at regular intervals and hands were shaken and greetings exchanged. It was little bit uncomfortable for a while as everyone was feeling their way with people they hadn't seen in over forty years. Once the pictures and the album were circulated the atmosphere became more relaxed as jokes were shared about their scruffy youthful appearances and how much they had all changed.

Barry and Fergy were chatting happily away when a look of surprise appeared on Fergy's face. Barry, who had his back to the pub door, was taking a large gulp of his pint when Fergy said 'I thought you said that Wilky was staying in Jersey for his treatment?'

Barry almost choked on his beer as he spun round to see his brother standing there, large as life, 'What the hell are you doing here Aiden I thought you'd started chemo?'

'That's a fine way to greet your brother Baz' came the reply and the two brothers hugged each other. 'I got a call the other day from the hospital saying they were putting it back a week so I talked it over with Laura and we said 'sod it' let's get over to Huddersfield. Oh and it's radiation not chemo by the way'.

'Either way it's great to see you' enthused Barry 'but why didn't you call and tell us you were on your way you daft bugger?'

'Just thought I'd give you all a surprise' smiled Wilky.

'Well you certainly did that – anyway how come you're a bit late?'

'Blame our lass, she thought we were meeting at the Stag on Wakefield Road not Bradford Road so we were a bit late setting off. Any road I'm here now isn't anybody going to buy me a drink?'

Terry and Fergy had stood back while the Wilkinson brothers greeted each other but went over to shake hands with Wilky whilst Barry went to order a drink for their unexpected guest.

Barry came back with a pint for his brother, Wilky held out his hand but Barry pulled the drink away from him 'Now you're sure you're allowed alcohol – with the treatment and all that stuff. I don't want to get into Laura's bad books?'

'Sod that – anyway my treatment doesn't start till next week so bollocks is what I say. Cheers Barry'.

'You'll need to get it down you sharpish 'cos we're going up to the estate in a few minutes'.

No sooner had Barry uttered the words when Fergy stood up and addressed the group 'Now you've all had the email so you'll be aware that we've arranged a buffet lunch which will be served at around 1.30, but before that we're going to take a little stroll up the hill to the estate. I trust you are all up for it?'

'Are you sure this is a good idea Fergy' it was Martin Kelly 'only my sister Sheila says it's pretty dangerous up there, she says there's a lot of drug gangs and that sort of rabble. Says the local rag is full of incidents up there'.

'Ah she shouldn't believe everything she reads in the Examiner, Martin' responded Fergy 'anyway we have our own guardian angel up there don't we Barry?'

All eyes turned to Barry 'I dare say my friend Gerald will have been called many things in his time but I seriously doubt he's ever been called a guardian angel'.

The group wanted to know more and Fergy encouraged Barry to fill in the details.

'Well to cut a long story short – Terry, Fergy and meself went up to the old estate purely for nostalgia's sake and had, what shall I call it – an encounter with some young bucks who thought we shouldn't be trespassing on their 'territory'. It could have got nasty but an old football friend of mine came to our rescue. Gerald – that's his name – seems to be a bit of the lord of the manor type and he just told the boys to clear off and give us some space. I called him the other day to tell him we were coming up today and he said to give him a knock – he actually lives in Fergy's old house believe it or not'.

'So how long have you been a fully paid up member of the Huddersfield mafiosa then Barry' chimed in John Robinson 'what haven't you been telling us?'

Barry laughed and looked at his watch 'I deny everything, anyway come on lads it's now or never, we've got people to see' and he nodded at Fergy as they all got up and put their coats on. The weather outside was cold but clear and the men all wore jackets or overcoats and most had scarves and gloves as well.

Terry and Fergy led the way with the Wilkinson brothers close behind, while the rest of the old friends followed all chatting away merrily in groups of two and three. 'Looks like it's going OK chaps' commented Terry 'did you say that you'd had a word with the Examiner and they were sending up a photographer Fergy?'

'That's right Terry, he said he'd be here about one-ish which is why I wanted to get everybody moving out of there'.

As they reached the top of the hill Barry branched off from the group and went over to call on Gerald. Before he could knock on the door it opened and Gerald's gold tooth twinkled as he smiled and said 'Hey how you doin' my man, it's great to see you. So this is the old football team then?' Gerald pointed to the group of sixty something's who were admiring the new layout of the circle - their former football pitch. 'Is that one of your crowd sat in the car over there as well, he's been there about ten minutes man?'

'No I don't think so but we've got quite a good turnout, we managed to contact about fifteen and we've actually got eleven, sorry twelve, here today. Did you speak to your 'boys' Gerald? One or two of our lot are a bit nervous – the place does have a bit of a reputation after all'

'If you mean those pussycats who bothered you last time you were here, don't worry there ain't gunna be any trouble today, trust me.' Gerald smiled 'So Barry come and introduce me to your old friends'.

As they walked across to join the group on the circle a middle aged man holding an expensive looking camera got out of the driver's seat of the parked car and a smartly dressed young woman got out of the passenger seat and walked across to the crowd on the circle. The young lady spoke 'Hi which of you gentlemen is Richard Ferguson?'

'That's me' Fergy stepped forward and shook hands with the lady 'are you from the Examiner then?'

'Yes I'm Sacha Charlesworth, I'm a reporter with the Examiner and this is our photographer Jim Watson'. Fergy and Jim shook hands.

'I was expecting a photographer but not a reporter, it's hardly the social event of the year is it?'

'Believe it or not Richard it's actually just the sort of thing our readers like – old friends meeting for the first time in... How many years is it Richard?'

'It's over 50 years since the original Fartown United match but we were mates for quite a few years after that, we all kind of went our different ways in our late teens really. You know the sort of thing Uni, jobs, and families; all that boring stuff' replied Fergy.

The other men were spread out around the circle, busily taking individual and group photos, and while all this was taking place the Examiner photographer was trying manfully to get them together for a full group shot.

Eventually the photographer called over 'Sacha we're ready to do a group picture if you can spare Richard for a moment'.

'Off you go Fergy' instructed Sacha 'by the way who is the black man, I'm sure I've seen him before?'

As Fergy jogged over to the group he shouted back 'I'll tell you later'.

The group shot was duly taken and the men dispersed into small groups to stroll around their old stomping ground, cheerfully pointing out who lived where and commenting on the changes. The relaxed buzz of men talking was suddenly interrupted by the unmistakeable sound of a gun being fired, everyone froze.

Wilky had wandered off on his own and was admiring Gerald's BMW when the shot was fired. Instinctively everyone crouched down, a few seconds passed and then a second shot was heard. Chaos reigned as everyone took cover. Wilky was hiding behind the privet hedge of Gerald's house where the shots appeared to be coming from. Gerald instinctively ran back towards his house shouting his son's name 'Michael, Michael are you OK?'

As Gerald reached the gateway to his house, two teenage youths one black and one white – burst out of the house. One was carrying a hand gun and the other had a large knife in his hand. Gerald was now in front of the house alongside the crouching Wilky and blocking the way. The sensible thing to do would have been to step aside and let these lads pass, but all he could think of was his son who was inside the house – injured or even dead. Throwing caution to the wind he lurched forward towards the lad with the knife and raised his arm to throw a punch at him. As he did so the white youth didn't hesitate and stuck the knife into Gerald's body just below his ribs, stopping him in his tracks. At the same time the other one grabbed the cowering Wilky by his coat collar, pulled him to his feet and put the gun to the side of his head.

'Stand back everybody or your fucking mate's dead', no-one

was in the mood for arguing as they were all doing their best to keep hidden from view.

Gerald slumped to the floor holding his wound as blood started to ooze out onto his hands and clothes.

This was not a time for heroics and everyone stayed out of sight. The youth who had knifed Gerald ran towards a blue car which was parked a little way down the hill from the estate with its engine running. When he reached the car he opened the rear door and turned to see the where the second youth was. He was making his way to the car but at a much slower pace as he had to continually push Wilky with one hand whilst holding the gun to his head with the other. They bundled him into the back before jumping in themselves with Wilky sat in the middle. There was a third man already sitting in the driver's seat revving the engine and he wasted no time in zooming off as soon as they were all in the car. The sound of approaching sirens could be heard as the getaway car sped down the hill.

'What the fuck is he doing 'ere?' shouted the driver, a shaven headed, dark skinned youth with tattoos covering most of the left hand side of his head.

The black youth, who was still holding the gun, was in a state of high tension and shouted back 'For fucking security man - wadyer fucking think, stupid'.

The driver was also extremely agitated, 'Shit man what the fuck are we gunna do with him man, we ain't got no fucking place to keep him. You got shit for brains?' The car swerved alarmingly as the driver turned to speak, only missing an on-coming van by inches as its driver slammed on the brakes and steered away from them.

Wilky had already worked out that these lads seemed to be out of their depth so he calmly said 'You don't want to make the situation worse lads, just get a safe distance from the es-tate and chuck me out'.

The youth with the gun was getting more and more agitated and waggled the gun in Wilky's face and screamed 'Keep your fucking mouth shut'.

The driver carried on driving for a moment before banging both hands on the steering wheel and said 'He's right in't he, we's in enough shit already'. He slammed on the brakes and as the car skidded to a halt he told the lads in the back to chuck Wilky out. The youth with the gun protested but the other one jumped out and then leaned back into the car, grabbed hold of Wilky by his shoulders and dragged him out of the car and dumped him in the middle of the road before jumping back into the car. The tyres on the car screeched as the wheels spun and they shot off in the direction of Deighton.

A middle aged couple hurried over to Wilky who was getting back to his feet rather gingerly. 'Are you OK lad?' the lady asked Wilky.

'A few bumps and bruises but nowt serious thanks' replied Wilky as he brushed the debris off his coat.

'What was that all about lad, they seemed to be in a hell of a hurry?' asked the man.

'There's been a shooting up on the estate, they took me as a sort of hostage, but they didn't really know what they were doing. I need to sit down' Wilky was shaking like a leaf.

They helped him to a small wall nearby and sat him down 'Ee you're fair shaking lad and look at your hand, it's bleeding, here put this round it' the lady gave him a handkerchief which he wrapped around a large graze on the knuckles of his left hand. 'Listen lad we live just round the corner, if you're OK to walk come with us and I'll make you cup of tea while you pull yourself together'.

'I think he might need something a bit stronger than tea love' replied the man. He winked at Wilky and said 'I think a drop of brandy will do him a lot more good'.

Back at the estate, as soon as the car set off Barry ran over to Gerald who was still conscious, the knife protruding from the left hand side of his body just below his ribs. 'Don't pull the knife out Barry or I'll bleed to death, just leave it in'.

Barry took off his scarf and held it against the wound, Gerald was shaking. He took off his jacket and wrapped it around Gerald's shoulders 'Don't worry mate the ambulance will be here in a minute I can hear the sirens, just keep talking'.

Gerald smiled 'So much for me telling you everything would be quiet heh. You guys got a lot more than you bargained for didn't you. Not like when you were young?'

'I don't know we used to have our moments but you're quite right I don't recall anyone ever getting shot at or stabbed'.

'Has anyone checked on my boy inside the house? I heard two shots'.

'Shit nobody's been in there yet,' Barry looked around and shouted 'Can somebody go in the house and check if Gerald's son is OK?'

Fergy, who was standing close by, was the first to react and ran into the house where he immediately saw a black youth sitting at the bottom of the stairs, he was holding his right shoulder where he appeared to have a bullet wound, and blood was also oozing from the back of his right leg onto the stair carpet.

'Have they gone?' gasped the young man.

Fergy immediately took off his belt and pulled it as tight as he could around the top of the young man's leg, the lad winced with pain. 'Yeh, they've gone alright, but they stabbed your dad on the way out and they've taken one of our mates' Fergy responded, just as the sound of multiple vehicles, sirens howling, slammed on their breaks and doors could be heard opening and closing. 'Sounds like the police and ambulance are here'. Fergy opened the door and shouted to the ambulance crew 'There's somebody in here with multiple gunshot wounds'.

He returned to the injured boy.

'How's my dad is he OK?'

'He was talking to one of my friends so I think he's OK but he's still got the knife in him, they're treating him now'.

At this point two paramedics pushed their way through the door 'OK sir just leave it to us now, we'll deal with this' the leading paramedic instructed Fergy 'OK son where have you been hit?'

Fergy was another one who was visibly shaking as he made his way down his old path to the front gate where a group of his friends were congregating – also in various levels of shock and disbelief. Someone shouted 'What's happened in there Fergy?'

Fergy looked at his hands which were stained with blood and hesitated before speaking 'I can't believe it, I just said *There's somebody in here with multiple gunshot wounds.* It's unreal, things like that only happen in films'. He paused as his old friend Sutty gave him a hug. 'Did all that REALLY happen Sutty? Is everyone else all right?'

Sutty appeared to be one of the calmest and he replied quietly 'Just Barry's mate and the young lad you were tending to, we think they're the only casualties. We don't know what's happened to Wilky though. They threw him into the back of the getaway car. I just hope he's OK'.

'Well that was a surprise wasn't it, talk about being in the right place at the right time' the two of them turned to see the smiling face of Sacha Charlesworth accompanied by the photographer who was snapping away merrily. 'So Fergy how was the boy inside the house, is it true he had been shot?'

'Not now Sacha' came the reply 'just give us a break, we'll talk to you later I promise but not right now'.

The police were busily taping off the area around Gerald's house and pushing the onlookers back.

Sacha couldn't hide her disappointment but she reluctantly turned away and spoke to her colleague 'Come on Jim we've got work to do, I'm sure some of these locals will have plenty to say about the action' and they strode off towards the crowd of people who were milling around the circle.

CHAPTER 21 – THE NEWFOOTY
SEASON KICKS OFF

Christmas 1958

C hristmas arrived and, like kids all over the country, the Fartown contingent were looking forward to finding out if their wishes had come true and they had received the presents they had been hoping for. The boys had long since given up believing in Santa but they knew how the system worked. Make sure you do your household chores - preferably with a smile, do those little extra bits like helping your mam to unpack the shopping, going to bed when instructed and most of all - not being cheeky to your parents. Their parents knew full well what was going on and enjoyed the cooperation which was so freely given, knowing that once the Christmas season was over it would be back to business as usual. Hopefully the new toys and games would keep the boys happily occupied.

Christmas 1958 would be seen by the boys and their parents as well worth the effort. All the boys had asked Santa for a Newfooty set, some were more pleased than others.

Fergy of course already had the full set of two teams, goalposts, ball and corner flags plus the all important cloth pitch. Now it transpired that you could just buy the *basic* set which comprised two teams of players plus the goals or the *deluxe* set which came with the above plus the pitch. The full set including pitch was just over £2, whereas the standard set without the pitch was just over £1.To put these prices in context the average weekly wage in those days was £12 and 13 shillings or approximately £12.65 in new money.

Martin Kelly was the only one who was fortunate enough to get the full version, the others had to settle for the basic set. Nellie Wilkinson had created a home-made pitch made from a piece of green woven wool fabric on which a pitch had been marked using tailors chalk. Having parents who worked at a woollen mill obviously had some advantages. Dad would often arrive home with lengths of woollen cloth with minor faults some of which were used as blankets on their beds. The boys' requirement for a plain green piece of cloth was not too difficult to satisfy.

The Christmas period was also a busy time for the local soccer and rugby teams. Fartown actually played away at their local rivals Halifax on Christmas Day and then played them again at home on Boxing Day. Town had a similar home and away fixtures against Charlton on Boxing Day and the 27th. The Wilkinson brothers and Terry went to watch the rugby whilst the other lads favoured the football.

EXTRACT FROM BARRY WILKNSON'S DIARY

26th December 1958

Went to watch Fartown against Halifax but we lost 18 – 5, we lost yesterday as well by 24 – 14. At least Town won 1-0 at home to Charlton. We play them away tomorrow.

Played some more Newfooty with our Aiden, he's beating me 10 games to 8 so far.

Up to this time all the different games which the boys played had been of the outdoor type so the boys rarely, if ever, actually went inside each other's houses. However, Newfooty in the winter months was very much an indoor activity. There were three pre-requisites for a competitive game of Newfooty. The first requirement was for two players, next came a pitch and finally a flat surface where the pitch could be laid out and the game could be played.

The Wilkinson brothers had a double advantage, firstly they could play each other every night if they wanted to, and in so doing hone their skills. Their pitch was the second advantage because it was made of thick woollen material which meant that the ball and players moved slightly differently to the other, smoother, pitches of their friends. This second factor gave them a huge advantage when playing 'at home' but obviously worked against them when playing 'away' on someone else's pitch.

Games were quickly arranged and parents got used to requests to have some friends round and it wasn't long before Fergy said the time had come to set up a league. Results would be recorded and points awarded in the normal way, which at that time was two points for a win and one each for a draw. An independent referee was required at all these league games to make decisions on the inevitable points of argument which occurred during the games. The length of the game had to be a minimum of 15 minutes each way but this could be extended if both players agreed before the game started.

It soon became clear that there would only be one winner of this competition as Fergy was far better than any of the other boys. The Wilkinsons weren't far behind, mainly due to the advantages they had, but the league kept the boys busy through the darkest weeks of the winter, until the evening daylight returned and the boys could get back to playing the real thing.

Winter snow was another exciting opportunity for the boys. When fresh snow had fallen the boys would rush home from school to enjoy the normal youthful pleasures of snowballing, building a snowman and of course sledging. All the boys had sledges. The hill leading off the estate was their first choice of sledging track and, with its it's steep slope and ninety degree left hand bend half way down, it was a real tester. The boys polished and levelled the track by sliding down on their feet until the surface was ready for their sledges. It took a great deal of skill to take the bend at speed and if you misjudged it you could finish up on the road with obvious risks. Luckily the council snow plough had been round and the snow piled at the side of the road had set hard and formed a kind of crash barrier of deep snow for the wayward sledgers.

Their fun on this particular track was brought to an abrupt end the following morning, after a hard frost had made the track even slippier. The people whose houses were on the hill were not pleased when they surveyed the glassy surface they would have to cross to reach the relative safety of the road, which had been cleared of snow and had salt and sand spread on it. To overcome the danger of slipping they all had spread hot ashes to melt the ice and snow. As the boys surveyed the destruction of their version of the Cresta Run on their way to school, they resolved to try out another track when they got home from school later that day.

That evening the boys made their way to the other end of the estate where the long ginnel led down towards a cinder road way. This track was dead straight and was quite steep at the top, so it was ideal for getting some speed up. This track was quite narrow with a ditch on the left hand side with a dilapidated wooden fence, on the other side there was a more substantial metal fence. At the end of the ginnel was a flat area of compressed cinder and ash. An element of danger was also attached to this track as the occasional lorry would drive along the track on its way to the recycling plant. The fences at either side of the ginnel meant that it was impossible to see anyone coming down the track from the cinder track at the bottom. On a couple of occasions the boys had close escapes as they shot across the cinder track just before a lorry was passing. Rather than panicking after these near misses the boys would just laugh off the danger as it just added to the excitement. They did, however, realise that if they listened intently as they reached the end of the ginnel for the sound of approaching vehicles they could 'bail out' by turning their sledges and crashing into the ditch at the side.

Accidents were part of the fun of sledging, a crash into the fence or ditch at high speed could be very painful, but again these were usually accompanied by laughter mainly from the other boys who would take great joy in taking the mickey out of the ones who were stupid or clumsy enough to crash their sledges.

Typically Barry was, once again, the unlucky person, as he found a rather innovative way of injuring himself. Most of the boys had single seater wooden sledges and these were very slick, if a little unstable, on the icy snow track. The Wilkinsons' on the other hand, had a much larger two seater sledge which had a metal frame and wooden seat. The Wilkinsons soon got tired of going down two at a time as they just couldn't generate as much speed as the other boys, so they decided to take turns. The technique that all the boys used was to run stooped over the sledge positioned in front of them pushing it as fast as they could and then – at the optimum time – they would hurl themselves forward head first onto the sledge and shoot down the track lying on their stomach. The sledge was steered by putting either leg down onto the icy surface. Their launching technique was very effective but quite tricky as you had to jump forward onto the moving sledge and this often de-stabilised the sledge, causing it to tip over and eject the rider. These sort of crashes were common and the only injury they usually caused was to the fallen rider's dignity.

The Wilkinsons, now sledging individually, copied this technique on their larger sledge but still could not match the speed and therefore the thrill that the other boys were getting on their lighter, more agile sledges. All the sledges had a rope attached to the front so that you could drag them along and Norman Wilkinson had attached a longer than usual piece of rope to his sons' sledge and this was to prove Barry's downfall.

Frustrated at the lack of speed of their sledge Barry decided to give it everything when his turn arrived. He set off much further back than the others and, running as fast as he could, pushed the sledge with all his strength. When he reached the steeper part he launched himself forward to jump onto the moving sledge, unfortunately he had stepped on the long drag rope just before he jumped forward. Result? The sledge stopped dead and Barry jumped forward onto fresh air and landed on the hard, cold snow – nose first.

The other boys looked on in silent wonder at the strange phenomenon of their friend sliding down the track on his nose. Wonder quickly turned to laughter as a very embarrassed Barry eventually came to a halt, picked himself up, covered from head to foot in snow. He was well aware of the laughter as he rubbed all the snow off his clothing and went back to collect his sledge, all the while trying to retain some dignity by not showing any pain to his friends who were so amused at his misfortune.

'Are you OK our kid?' sniggered brother Aiden, who had probably been laughing the loudest at his brother's downfall. 'What's up with your nose?'

'What d'you mean' asked Barry who was very sensitive about his nose which happened to be a bit on the big side, 'what's wrong with it?'

'Well there isn't any skin on it by the looks of it, doesn't it hurt it looks really sore?' Wilky tried not to smile at his brother's discomfort.

The cold surface of the sledging track must have anaesthetised Barry's nose 'No it doesn't hurt at all actually'. Barry thrust the ropes of the sledge into his brother's hands and said 'I hate that bloody sledge, you can have it all to yourself, yer welcome to it' and trudged off to get some first aid – and, hopefully, a little sympathy – at home.

The next time the other boys saw Barry he was sporting a long strip of elastoplast from top to tip of his nose; unfortunately for Barry this was cause for even more hilarity amongst his so called friends. Barry silently repeated his vow to never to use that stupid sledge again.

EXTRACT FROM BARRY WILKINSON'S DIARY

17th January 1959

No soccer or rugby for over two weeks now, all the matches have been postponed cos of the snow and ice.

Been out sledging but our sledge is rubbish, it's too big and too heavy. The other lads have smaller wooden ones, they don't look much but they go a lot quicker than ours.

Went sledging down the ginnel and I ended up missing the sledge when I jumped onto it and landed on my nose, the lads were all laughing and pointing at my nose. I couldn't feel anything but when I got home me mam had to put a long plaster on it cos I had taken all the skin off on the ice.

31st January 1959

All the snow and ice is gone so sport is back on but Town lost to Sheffield United at home and Fartown lost to Wakefield Trinity away. It was the first match we've seen since the beginning of January so we've saved up some money but we will need it at the end of the season when they play all the games which have been postponed.

As winter moved into spring the boys played more and more football and firmly believed they were becoming accomplished players. Conversations after their matches would inevitably lead to ideas about playing a 'proper' match on a proper pitch with real goalposts.

Their regular trips to the Town match involved a twenty minutes walk to the ground on Leeds Road. The shortest route took them down the ginnel which had been their sledging track, along the cinder road and then under the railway bridge followed by the bridge over the canal and finally across the Canker Lane fairground area. Each time they took this route they could see a full sized football pitch complete with goal-posts. One day on their way back from the Town match some-one suggested that they should try out this pitch for one of their games of soccer

EXTRACT FROM BARRY WILKINSON'S DIARY

17th March 1959

Went to Town match – we beat Ipswich Town 3 – 0, so we've gone up in the league a bit from 16th to 14th. Fartown won as well 9 – 4 away at Bramley so a good weekend for my teams.

As we were walking back from the match Martin suggested we try playing on the big football pitch which we pass down by the canal. It's got proper goals and markings so we're gunna try it out tomor-row if our mams say it's alright.

The following day they met in the field as normal and agreed that the time had come to test their skills on a full sized football pitch. After getting permission from their parents, they cheerfully made their way down to the pitch, which was called the Transport field as it was the home ground for a team from the transport department of the local council. An old bus, minus the wheels, was parked at the far end of the field and had been converted into a changing facility for the players, complete with showers.

There were twelve boys and they split into two teams of six. The game started with great optimism but it soon became ap-parent that the pitch was far too big for a six a side game be-tween these small boys.

'This is rubbish' Martin suggested after a goal had finally been scored and they all trudged back to the centre circle.

Sutty who was in the goals at the other end of the field joined in 'we've been playing for ten minutes and I haven't even touched the ball yet.'

The boys gathered together for a discussion and Fergy, as usual, summed up what everyone was thinking 'It's obviously too big but its dead good to be playing on a flat pitch with no gully running down the middle and no worries about the ball going in sumdy's garden. It's nice when you pass the ball and it goes in a straight line as well'.

All the boys nodded and it was agreed that they should try just playing on one half of the field from one touch line to the other, jumpers could be put down and their normal size of goals could be set up in this way - after all the real goalposts were enormous for players of their size. The half way line on one side and the goal line on the other would serve as touch-lines.

This proved to be a good move and they all enjoyed a great game complete with slide tackles, passes and diving saves from the goalies. As they walked away after the game they decided that from now on this would be where they would play football.

'The only problem' suggested Wilky 'is it takes us about a quarter of an hour to get here and then the same again to walk back so if we're short of time we should still lake in the field'. So their trusty field was not rejected totally but whenever the lads had plenty of time the Tranny became the place to play.

EXTRACT FROM BARRY WILKINSON'S DIARY

18th March 1959

Played at the Tranny for the first time.

The pitch was far too big for us so we decided to just use one half of the pitch and play from touch line to touch line, it was a lot better.

The pitch is great, it's dead flat and great for tackling and dribbling so we're gunna use it all the time from now on.

Spring gave way to summer and the football season came to a close. The final match of the season was the FA Cup Final, which was always shown live on TV. It didn't matter which teams were involved the game was a highlight for the boys and the TV coverage started around noon and lasted all afternoon.

From this point in time football would share the boys attention and enthusiasm with cricket. The games of cricket were taken to another level due to an innovation – instigated, once again, by Fergy. His dad, who was quite a sporting chap, had shown him how real cricket teams keep the score, and in fact had bought him a scoring book. From this point onwards when the lads played cricket every ball would be recorded, along with every run scored, every wicket and catch taken. Batting and bowling averages would be calculated once a week. Being top scorer or leading wicket taker for the week was an honour every one of them wanted to achieve and led to an unfortunate incident for a certain Barry Wilkinson.

EXTRACT FROM BARRY WILKINSON'S DIARY

30th April 1959

Last match of the season, Town beat Rotherham United away 1 – 0 and finished 14th. Sheffield Wednesday are the champions and get promoted with Fulham who finished second.

Fartown's last game is tomorrow at home to Keighley and then it's the FA Cup Final on Saturday between Nottingham Forest and Luton Town, and that is the last game of the season.

We've already started playing cricket in the field and Fergy has got this book where he keeps a record of peoples scores and who is bowling. We're gunna have a competition each week to see who is the best batsman and bowler. I don't think I'll have any chance of being the best bowler as Fergy and Dave Henshaw are the best but I might have a chance of best batsman if I get enough runs.

The series of events which led to Barry's embarrassment took place on the Friday of the Whitsuntide holidays. The batting and bowling averages were to be calculated on Saturday morning. Barry had had a good week with the bat and he had been doing a bit of mental arithmetic. By his calculation he was in the lead for the coveted title of top scorer.

EXTRACT FROM BARRY WILKINSON'S DIARY

21st May 1959

We've had loads of games of cricket this week cos it's the holidays and I think I'm in the lead for best batsman. I got 17 this morning, 8 this afternoon and 12 tonight. Sutty is close to me and could beat me but as long as I score more runs than him tomorrow I'm sure I will be the best batsman when Fergy calculates the averages on Saturday. I think Dave Henshaw will be the best bowler cos he's got loads of wickets.

The weather was ideal, sunny but not too warm and a game was scheduled for the morning, another for the afternoon and the last one of the week for the evening. Barry's batting form had been good, until, that is, the fateful Friday. In the morning game he was out first ball, he had another duck in the second match in the afternoon and the final straw came in the evening game when he achieved the unwanted distinction of three ducks in the same day. This was just too much for the young man, who, after being out for the third time for nothing left the field of play in a strop, walked directly home and when his mother asked why he was home so early he deposited himself in the dark cupboard under the stairs without uttering a word and there he spent the rest of the evening. When Aiden arrived home much later he was quizzed by his mother as to why Barry was sulking in the lobby hole.

Aiden was never big on sympathy and simply replied 'The big baby's sulking 'cos he got three ducks at cricket'.

Barry remained there until hunger and the smell of toast for supper got the better of him and he reappeared as if nothing had happened. He did notice his mother discretely put her finger to her lips when Aiden started to say something, so he simply helped himself to toast and jam and settled down to watch the evening telly without any further word of explanation or recrimination.

EXTRACT FROM BARRY WILKINSON'S DIARY

22nd May 1959

I didn't win the best batsman. I got three ducks in the same day, nobody has ever done that before. Dave Henshaw bowled me out in the morning, second ball. Then I got caught out by Martin Kelly on the boundary when Fergy was the bowler. In the game after tea I was out first ball to Dave Henshaw again, I was so angry I went straight home. I didn't know what to do with myself so I hid in the lobby hole. I don't know why I did that - I don't even like it in there.

I was gunna come out but then our Aiden came home and I could hear me mam ask him what was wrong with me and he told her I was a big baby cos I had been out three times for a duck. So I decided to stay there a bit longer. Then my dad was making toast for supper and it smelt so nice and I was hungry so I came out. I think our Aiden was going to say something horrible but mam shushed him and asked me if I wanted some toast and jam for supper. I wanted to punch our Aiden but we all sat down and watched telly till bed time and then we were friends again.

Although he didn't realise it at the time (he was only ten years old after all) Barry's three ducks experience had a significant effect on him. The embarrassment of the three ducks was bad enough but he realised that walking away in a strop only made him seem more childish. He was determined to make sure that it would never happen again.

As the warm and mainly dry summer wore on and the boys started to get bored with cricket they reverted to their first love – soccer. Evenings after school would be spent playing soccer in the field, whilst the Tranny would be the location for their games at the weekend. Their skills increased slowly but steadily. One evening after school Wilky gathered everyone together to discuss a proposition that had been made to him by another boy at Fartown secondary modern. Wilky had been bragging to this lad about how good he and his mates were at soccer and the lad responded by laying down a challenge, as Wilky explained.

'This lad thinks his mates from Birkby will beat us in a proper game but I told him we were better than them' explained Wilky.

'Where would we play this game?' Martin asked.

'Good question Martin' replied Wilky 'and the answer is Clayton Fields'.

'Where's that?' asked Terry.

'I dunno exactly but its somewhere in Birkby and it's a proper pitch with goals but it's a bit smaller than the Tranny 'cos the under 11's at Birkby junior school use it. What d'you say lads are we up for it?'

Every one of them was in favour of taking up the challenge and their enthusiasm knew no bounds.

'We're gunna whip 'em' enthused Terry 'it'll be a massacre'.

Fergy, the voice of reason, chipped in 'How old are these lads though Wilky, you're the only one on our team that's twelve the rest of us are only ten or eleven'.

'He says there's three of 'em who are twelve and the rest are still at junior school, so we can have three twelve year olds as well. I've got two mates at school who want to play for us'.

'When can we play 'em Wilky?' continued Terry 'I can't wait to get stuck in'.

'Calm down Terry you're gunna wet yourself if you're not careful' Wilky was enjoying dragging the suspense out. 'Apparently Birkby junior school use the pitch on Saturday mornings and some of the lads play for them so we'll have to wait a couple of weeks till the summer holidays to have the game. It'll give us time to get some practice in and my mates from school can come and join in and get to know us all'.

'What are we gunna wear, we don't have any kit do we?' once again Fergy was ever the practical one.

Everyone looked at Wilky for a solution 'Don't all look at me' he held his hands up, 'I haven't worked that out just yet but I'm sure we can come up with summat'.

Fergy came up with an idea 'I've got a brochure with all these football kits in it, but they aren't cheap. It's in t'house, I'll go and get it if you like'.

All the boys had got a football shirt but they were nearly all different, Fergy, Martin and Val had Town shirts, the Wilkinson brothers, for some reason, had Newcastle United ones and the rest were all odds and ends.

Fergy returned with a brochure containing every style of football kit you could imagine and the boys gathered round to catch a glimpse of what was available.

They immediately started to select the type of kit they wanted to wear and, of course, each boy had his own ideas and preferences. They argued and contradicted each other's choice until Fergy noticed something that would bring them all down to earth.

He coughed as a sign that he had something important to say 'I think we may have a problem. We obviously can't decide what colours to choose but even if we could, we don't know how much the kits cost AND' he paused here for effect, 'it says there is an eight week wait for delivery'.

'What – you mean if we ordered them today' questioned Terry

'we'd have to wait for eight weeks, we'll all be back at school by then. That's no good'.

'What colours do Birkby play in Wilky?' asked Barry.

Wilky thought for a moment before responding 'Red shirts and white shorts, I think that's what he said'.

'Have we all got some black shorts, you know the ones we wear for PE at school' suggested Fergy. Everyone nodded. 'What about white shirts?'

'I've got a white shirt but it's not a proper soccer shirt' said Terry.

'Me too' added Martin.

'Hands up if you have a white shirt of any kind?' instructed Wilky. Just about everyone held up their hands.

'OK white shirts and black shorts just like England' Martin tried to sound positive.

'I think England play in dark blue shorts' corrected Fergy.

'OK like Bolton Wanderers then' came the response from Martin.

'They're blue as well, try Fulham' Fergy had that smug look on his face that said *I'm always right.*

Martin gave up 'Whoever!'

'What shall we call us selves?' asked Sutty.

'How about Fartown Rovers?' Martin suggested.

'Or we could be Fartown United, a bit like Man United, they're my favourite team' Terry was getting excited.

'I do like the sound of Fartown United' added Fergy. 'Hands up those who want Fartown United?'

About six hands shot up. 'Fartown Rovers?' Martin and Sutty raised their hands. 'Any other suggestions?' No one spoke. 'Looks like we're going with Terry's suggestion then Fartown United it is'.

'Great!' little Terry did not try to hide is enthusiasm. 'Fartown United forever!'

Even Martin, who was disappointed that his suggestion wasn't adopted, couldn't help but smile as his friend got his way.

EXTRACT FROM BARRY WILKINSON'S DIARY

18th June 1959

We're gunna have a real soccer match. Our Aiden is arranging a proper game for us against Birkby. One of his mates from school lives in Birkby and they have a team a bit like us. I think it's gunna be in the summer holidays.

Our Aiden's got a couple of mates who want to play and that's OK cos Birkby have three players who are twelve and the rest are under eleven like us. I think we'll play in white shirts and black shorts cos we all have them. We are gunna have some practice matches down at the Tranny so we can prepare for the game. We're all dead excited – especially little Terry.

CHAPTER 22 – FIVE MINUTES OF FAME

January 2011

he police had arrived at the same time as the ambulance and got to work straight away. The area around Gerald's house was already taped off as the senior officer approached Fergy's group. 'OK gentlemen can you give me a brief summary of what's happened, we have a report of a shooting and stabbing is that correct?'

Sutty took the lead 'Yeh there's a young man inside the house who's been shot and is being treated by the paramedics and as you can see the guy over there' he pointed to where Gerald was being treated 'has been stabbed. There were two of them and they got away in a blue Audi. They grabbed one of our friends and took him with them, y'know like a hostage thing?'

'A blue Audi you say, and your friend was in the car?'

'Yeh' Sutty tried to explain 'they put a gun to his head and bundled him into the back of the car, he looked terrified'.

'Did you see which way they went sir?'

'I couldn't see officer, the car went out of sight down the hill but it sure as hell sounded like he turned right onto Alder Street towards Woodhouse Hill judging by the way the engine was revving'.

'Thank you Mr ?'

'Sutcliffe, James Sutcliffe'.

'Thank you Mr Sutcliffe, stick around please I might need to speak to you later'. The policeman radioed details of the get-away car and then turned to his colleague 'Can you get all those rubberneckers back out of the way please Matt?' He turned back to Sutty 'What are you and all these people doing here anyway, you don't look like you live here? Did anyone else see what happened?'

Sutty responded 'Yeh we all did, the Examiner photographer had just taken a team photo of us all on the circle when it all kicked off. Wilky, sorry Adrian Wilkinson, the bloke they got hold of, just happened to be nearest to the house so they grabbed him and held a gun to his head and then they bundled him into the car and shot off, it was parked over there' he again pointed, this time to the place where the car had been parked.

'Team photo? Are you lot all members of a bowls club or something? Anyway did you get the registration number sir?'

'Sorry no I didn't but somebody else might have got it, it could even be in the background of one of the photos, we've all been taking loads of pictures. And, no we're not in a bowls club. The team we played for is the Fartown United football team of 1959 seeing as you ask.' Sutty made a half hearted attempt to avoid a sarcastic tone but failed.

'OK sir can you tell all your friends, sorry TEAM MATES' the officer replied with even more sarcasm 'to give your names, addresses and contact numbers to my colleague over there, we're going to be needing statements from you all'.

'Aye OK officer' Sutty waited for the officer to turn away and then clicked his heels together, placed the forefinger of his left hand between his nose and top lip, and did a mock 'sieg heil' salute before walking over to where Terry, Martin and a couple more of their friends were chatting and passed on the message.

Fergy and Barry surveyed the scene; there were three police cars, the ambulance and now several more cars were arriving

'Oh God I hope your Aiden is OK' Fergy put his arm around Barry's shoulder.

Barry tried to put on a brave face 'I should think after five minutes with our Aiden they'll be desperate to get shut of him don't you?'

'I hope you're right' Fergy tried to sound upbeat but then he shook his head and added 'those lads looked off their heads to me, like they were on something.'

'They were certainly very agitated, God knows what they are capable of. Shit why couldn't he just have just stayed in Jersey'.

Desmond from the pub stepped out of one of the cars and called out to Barry and Fergy 'Are you and your friends alright? I heard about the shooting. As soon as I heard I got Gloria to fill up some flasks with tea and coffee I thought you might need something.'

'Come on Barry, I think the lads could do with some hot sweet tea it's supposed to be good for shock - or so my dear old mother used to say' suggested Fergy.

'I think that's a good idea Dizzy, thanks' Barry called back as they all made their way over to his car. As they neared the car Sacha called out to them, they could see that she had been pushed back behind the tape by the police but that wasn't going to stop her from trying to get some info from the men.

'You go and get a drink Barry' said Fergy 'while I talk to our reporter on the spot. Oh and get me a coffee please, white no sugar, I'm not a tea drinker'.

'So Richard what did you find when you went into the house, have there been any fatalities?' she glanced at the dried blood on Fergy's hands and the cuffs of his jacket.

Fergy saw where she was looking and examined his hands, his mind flashed back to the young man bleeding on the stairs of his old house.

'Richard, Richard?' Sacha tried to get his attention.

He blinked as he came back to reality. 'Err no thank God, no fatalities, just a young lad who'd been shot twice, once in the shoulder and the other in the back of his leg. I think he must have been trying to get away up the stairs when they shot him the second time, the paramedics are treating him now.' Sacha held out a wet wipe which she had pulled out of her handbag and passed it to him.

As they were speaking the door to the house opened and the young man was carried out on a stretcher and loaded into the ambulance. The Examiner photographer was clicking away merrily and he wasn't the only one as camera phones were working overtime, no-one wanted to miss any of the action. A few minutes later Gerald, also on a stretcher, followed his son into the ambulance which then left the estate with the blue lights flashing and siren blaring.

'Do you know either of the injured people Richard?' Sacha continued.

'The older guy is Gerald Wilson, and I think the younger one is his son. The shootings took place in Gerald's house. I've met him a couple of times but Barry knows him better than me'.

Sacha's eyes lit up when she heard Gerald's name. 'Gerald Wilson, now that name definitely rings a bell and his face looks familiar too. I'll check him out when I get back to the office and see what we have on him'

'Sorry Sacha but I need to go and check that everybody's OK'.

As he turned to walk away she shouted 'The guy who was held at gunpoint and bundled into the car – what's his name. Richard what's the hostage's name?'

Rather than shout the name out loud Fergy turned and walked back before speaking quietly to Sacha 'He's Barry's brother Aiden but I'd prefer it if you didn't print his name until we know what's happened to him.'

Sacha thanked Fergy for the information and then set out to

quiz some of the locals to get a bit more background on this Gerald guy; she was convinced he'd been in the Examiner previously.

Fergy made his way back to Barry who held out a coffee. 'Persistent little bugger isn't she. Not a big fan of the old sweet tea remedy then?'

'Can't stand the drink actually! Sacha's OK, she's only doing her job I suppose. It's not every day you witness a stabbing or a shooting not to mention a kidnapping. It's a reporters dream isn't it? Bloody nightmare for us though.' Fergy paused for thought. 'Is there owt we can do about your Aiden, d'you really think they might have actually dumped him somewhere?'

'It's possible, why don't we go looking for him?' Barry responded and then added 'Maybe we can get Dizzy to drive up towards Woodhouse Hill on the off chance, he might be laying at the side of the road bleeding to death for all we know'.

'I don't think the coppers would be too pleased if we left the scene though' Fergy pointed out.

'Bollocks to the coppers Fergy, they don't seem to be doing anything about finding him do they. Anyway they're too busy getting names and addresses at the minute, we could just sneak off without them seeing us. I can't just stand around doing nothing, it's killing me'.

'OK let me have a word with Dizzy' Fergy continued the conspiracy 'I think he's finished dishing out the tea by the looks of it'.

Fergy approached Dizzy and he nodded in agreement, he waved Barry to come over and join them, and then they all jumped in to the car and quietly drove away without anyone taking any notice.

As they drove off Fergy told Dizzy to head in the direction of Woodhouse Hill and to drive at a steady pace so that they could look out for any signs of Wilky being ejected from the car. When they reached the top of Woodhouse Hill without seeing any signs of him Dizzy spun the car around and headed back down the hill and then in the direction of Fartown Bar still watching out for any signs of Wilky. The search proved fruitless so they asked Dizzy to take them back to the estate where he dropped them off and they rejoined their friends. The police had almost finished taking down the contact details of their mates so they joined the back of the queue.

While they waited Sutty approached them and asked Barry 'Was your friend Gerald OK then Barry?'

'I don't know to be honest; the knife was still in so that's a good sign apparently, he told me not to take it out or he could bleed to death. I'm sure he told me the same thing all those years ago when I went to visit him in hospital, only that time I think he drove himself all the way to the hospital on his own with the knife still in him. Can you believe that - he's a tough old bugger is our Gerald I'll give him that. Shit, I forgot about my jacket, I put my scarf over the wound and my jacket round his shoulders to keep him warm, has anyone seen it?'

'Was it a dark blue quilted one?' asked Sutty. 'Gerald had one wrapped around his shoulders when they put him into the ambulance, there was a load of blood on it.'

'Yeh that'll be mine, it's probably ruined anyway.' For the first time that afternoon Barry shivered in the cold January breeze, with all the adrenaline pumping he hadn't noticed how cold it actually was. He looked around and saw that Dizzy had resumed dishing out the hot drinks and went over to join the queue. He was the last person to be served and he immediately cupped his hands around the plastic cup to get some warmth and took a big swig of hot tea.

Desmond packed the flasks away and said 'I'm going back to the pub now. The food's all waiting for you and I've got a lovely fire going; you guys must be frozen out here all this time. Can I give any of your friends a lift down there?'

'No thanks' replied Fergy 'I think we'll walk,it might help to clear our heads a bit'.

Fergy checked with the police and eventually got the all clear from them, after explaining that they would all be down at the Stag for the next couple of hours. The friends all moved off together but before they had got very far they were intercepted by a different reporter who was joined by a film cameraman with the words SKY NEWS plastered on the side of the camera.

'Which of you guys is Richard err' the reporter looked at his notepad 'Ferguson?'

'That's me' Fergy stepped out of the group 'you guys go ahead I'll be down in a couple of minutes'.

The friends continued but Barry decided to stop and wait for Fergy, he really didn't want to leave him on his own 'You never know who might be watching and waiting for us' he thought as he nervously scanned the surrounding area.

He waited patiently whilst Fergy was interviewed live on SKY News. He was reliving every minute of the incident in his head when it suddenly occurred to Barry that this historic moment should be recorded for posterity and he sneakily took out his mobile phone and video'd Fergy being interviewed LIVE on SKY news.

After the interview had finished the two of them made their way to the pub to join the rest of the old Fartown United set. As they made their way Barry desperately sought reassurance from his friend 'I'm worried sick about our Aiden, I can't think what use he'd be to them can you?'

'No not really Barry, they didn't look like they'd have the nouse to do a kidnapping and then ask for a ransom did they, just didn't look the sort'.

'To be honest Fergy the two lads looked more scared than our

Aiden, and he was shitting himself. I just hope they see some sense and let him go. My God we certainly got more than we bargained for didn't we mate?'

'Too bloody right, I can honestly say I never expected in my wildest dreams anything like that. There was one point there when I didn't know if I was coming for the proverbial shit, shave or shampoo. Can you believe that' he paused and shook his head 'I had to run past a man who had been stabbed to get to a lad who had been shot in MY old house; and then my mate gets kidnapped. I still can't take it all in'.

'I think you need a stiff drink Fergy – and you're not the only one'.

As they entered the pub together a massive cheer went up as they were applauded by the rest of the team. Their old team mates had obviously recovered their composure, aided no doubt by a couple of welcome drinks.

Martin shouted 'What's happening about Wilky, has anyone seen him?'

Barry shook his head and nodded to Fergy to fill them in, he was clearly too emotional to speak.

Fergy gave them a brief summary of their abortive search around Fartown Bar and Woodhouse Hill and explained that the police were looking for the blue Audi so it was basically a waiting game.

After a long silent pause Terry asked 'How are the injured blokes? Are they OK?'

Barry had recovered his composure and responded 'We don't really know to be honest but the paramedics seemed to be doing a good job of patching them up before they went to hospital. I was with Gerald who'd been stabbed just below his ribs and he had lost quite a bit of blood, but the kid who stabbed him had left the knife in and that might have saved him. Fergy you went to the young lad who was shot, how was he?'

'He'd been shot in the shoulder and then another one in the back of his thigh, there was a lot of blood, I used my belt as a tourniquet on his leg, I don't think it was life threatening, but you never know. Oh and the copper asked me to ask those of you who had been taking photos to see if there are any shots where you can see the getaway car's number plate'.

Most of the guys took out their phones and browsed through the pictures they had taken but none of them had a clear shot of the number plates on the car although on a couple of them the two thugs could clearly be seen sneaking round to the back of the house where the shooting took place.

'I suppose we'd all better make sure that we don't delete any of the pictures we've taken today just in case the police want to see them, OK?' suggested Barry.

'I've got a good one of us all downing our first pint d'you think they'll want that one?' shouted Dave Henshaw.

'No I think I can safely say they won't be interested in that one but the rest of us might be Dave. Anyway I need a pint, whose round is it?'

'We've all put a tenner in the kitty' Martin pointed out 'but you guys got the first round so we'll count you as in. Just tell Gloria to put them on our tab'.

Barry quipped 'I'm impressed Martin, you always were a quick worker with the ladies, on first name terms with the landlords wife already; better watch your step though we've had enough bother for one day', to muted laughter from the assembled mob.

Barry and Fergy turned and made their way over to the bar but before they could order a drink another tremendous cheer went up. They spun around to see Wilky standing in the doorway with his arms spread, milking the applause, he had a bandage on his hand and his coat looked a bit worse for wear but otherwise he was in good shape.

As Barry ran over and hugged his brother there was a tear in his eyes. Wilky chided him 'Pull yourself together our kid, anybody would think I'd been missing for weeks'.

Barry laughed and wiped his eyes 'You daft bugger you had us worried there. What happened then, how'd you get away from the idiots?'

'Well would you believe I wrestled the gun from one of them and then put it to the head of the driver and told him to stop the car and let me go?'

All the men were incredulous and as a group exclaimed 'NO!'

Wilky smiled, paused for a second before saying 'You're right I didn't'. Everyone collapsed in fits of laughter.

Terry was still giggling when he said 'Go on Wilky how did you make your escape then?'

Wilky loved being the centre of attention and was determined to spin this out, so he paused, rather like a comedian tantalising his audience. When the laughter finally died away he confessed 'It was the drivers idea, he said I was a liability..'

Someone shouted 'He wasn't wrong there was he?' to more laughter.

Wilky continued 'He said I was a liability and they were in enough shit already, I simply agreed with him. I was a bit worried though 'cos the lad with the gun was off his head, sweating like hell and shaking like a leaf. The driver slammed the brakes on and the other lad just opened the door and pulled me out into the middle of the road and then they just shot off. That's when I cut my hand'. He held up his bandaged hand for effect.

Barry jumped in 'Where was this Aiden, we went looking for you and there was no sign of you, we went all the way to the top of Woodhouse Hill and then back to Fartown Bar'.

'Top end of Alder Street actually, there I was lying in the middle of the road. As I picked myself up this couple came over –

they must have seen the whole incident – and asked me if I was alright. To be honest I didn't know if I was coming or going, I was shaking like mad' he paused and gave a brief demonstration of a shaking hand. He glanced around the group who were literally hanging on his every word.

'Somebody get him a drink, calm his nerves' shouted Terry. Fergy who was closest to the bar ordered a double brandy and brought it over to Wilky who drank it down in one go. 'Carry on with yer tale Wilky' insisted Terry.

'They could see I was in a bad way so they took me round the corner onto Red Doles Road where they lived and, while the woman, Brenda she was called, cleaned the cut on my hand and bandaged me up Jack, her husband, poured me a large brandy'.

'So' Barry took a deep breath 'while we were all shitting ourselves wondering what had happened to you, sick with worry, you were actually sitting in a nice couple's kitchen downing large brandy's and having your wound tended! I don't believe you Aiden – why the hell didn't you ring us and tell us you were OK?'

Fergy thought to himself 'Just like the old days – at each other's throats again'.

Wilky turned to his brother and with a deadpan expression simply said 'Flat battery'.

Everybody – except Barry – burst into laughter, Fergy put his arm around Barry and whispered 'Come on Barry the old bugger's been through a lot but he's safe now don't spoil the moment'. Barry relaxed a little and his face broke into a thin smile.

'I suppose I can see the funny side, let's have that pint' Barry gave out a sigh. 'At least the lads seem to be enjoying the Wilky show'.

'Aye – but not as much as your Aiden' observed Fergy. 'It's

probably relief more than anything else Barry; you must admit it was pretty tense up there. Anyway enough of that', he turned to the barmaid 'two pints of landlord please Gloria and have one yourself'.

'Thank you but it's a bit early in the day for me, are you all ready for your lunch? All that excitement must have made you fellas hungry, shall I bring it out?'

'That would be great, thanks' replied Fergy 'I think we've earned it today.' The two of them went over to sit at the end of the table while Wilky continued to hold court at the other end. 'It'll hit him later you know Barry, he's milking the attention, lot's of adrenalin at the moment but later he'll need your support. Don't be too hard on him.'

'Aye I suppose you're right' sighed Barry. 'Anyway grubs up and I'm starving. Nothing like a shooting and stabbing to build up the appetite'.

'And a kidnapping – don't forget the kidnapping' joked Fergy.

'I've got a feeling that somebody not too far away from me won't let me forget that – EVER!'

Ten minutes later Wilky had finished his performance and had a slice of pork pie in one hand and a pint of Timothy Taylors in the other so Fergy made his way over to him. 'How are you feeling Wilky, that was a bit of a close call wasn't it?'

Wilky dropped the bravado act in response as he replied in a low voice 'Tell you the truth Fergy it was too bloody close for comfort. It's a long time since I said my prayers but I did then, I really thought ... you know' Wilky looked away from his friends for a moment whilst he composed himself.

'Hey, hey it's OK Wilky, it's all over.' Fergy tried to re-assure him and put his arm around his shoulders. 'You'll have a hell of a tale to tell your lass tonight'.

'Don't I know it – she'll be well pissed off with me. She always thought we were a bit loopy organising the reunion in the first place and having it here was the icing on the cake!'

'Well the rest of the lads seem to be enjoying it now' Fergy turned to Barry and surveyed the friends laughing and joking as they tucked into the sandwiches and pies. 'To think we were worried about how it would go. I can't believe how worried we were about being able to create the right atmosphere'.

'No problems on that score' Barry sighed 'but we might have a problem keeping them sober enough to get home in one piece by the looks of some of them'.

Desmond came over to speak to them 'Man that was a shock, one of my regulars came in and said it was all kicking off up there, police ambulance and reporters all over the place. Are all your friends OK? Is that the guy who was kidnapped?' he pointed in the direction of Wilky.

'Yeh they dumped him in the middle of the road, thank God' Fergy explained 'and we think Gerald and his son should be OK'.

'Well your little reunion certainly made an impact, you' he pointed at Fergy 'have just been on the national news'.

At that point Sacha and the photographer came into the pub and walked straight up to Fergy, she smiled as she asked 'Can I have a word with you in – in private'.

Fergy sighed 'I'm not really in the mood for any more questions Sacha, I'm absolutely knackered and I need to spend some time with my friends – I haven't seen some of these lads for over forty years'.

'No interrogation I promise, just two minutes in private, please'.

'Oh all right, let's sit in the back room it's a bit quieter in there'. Fergy stood up wearily and guided Sacha to the back room. 'OK I'm all yours – but two minutes remember'.

'Thank you Richard. I've been keeping my editor updated on today's action and he's decided that he would like us to do a feature on you and your friends, the whole Fartown Rovers thing. It's quite possible that it will get syndicated across the whole of our group of papers, including the Daily Mirror. How do you feel about that?'

Fergy let out an audible sigh and ran his hand through what was left of his hair 'I can't get my head round all this. I came in here this morning an ordinary bloke, just looking forward to meeting some old friends and now I feel like some kind of celebrity.' He thought for a few moments and Sacha, for once, kept quiet to allow him time to think things through. 'OK this feature thingy what will it involve? And by the way it's Fartown United not Rovers'.

Sacha leaned forward and explained 'We will want to do an interview with you – not now, but sometime in the next couple of days. I'll need to get all the background on Fartown err UNITED and the names of the guys who are here today. We've already got some photos from earlier but we'd like a few more of you guys here at the pub. I'd really like to get some quotes from the chap who was kidnapped by the...' she searched for the right word 'gangsters'.

'Let me have a word with the lads in general and then I'll need to have a separate word with Wilky'.

'Thank you – off you go then and talk to them, Jim and I will have a drink whilst we're waiting, all this action has given me a thirst. Come on Jim' and off they trotted to the bar.

Fergy explained the situation to the lads who all seemed quite positive about the prospect of more publicity. He made his way over to where Wilky was sitting and asked him if he would be OK to speak to Sacha about his experience.

Wilky pretended to ponder for a while before agreeing to the request.

'I think she wants a mug shot of you as well Wilky, are you OK with that?'

'Yeh, yeh OK let's get it done' and the two of them walked back to where Sacha and Jim, the photographer, were sitting and gave them the good news.

Fergy had a quiet word with Dizzy to check that he was OK for them to take the picture inside.

Dizzy thought long and hard about the suggestion. 'You know man I've worked really hard to get rid of all the riff raff that used to come in here, I'm not sure whether this sort of publicity is good or not'.

'I'll have a word with Sacha and see if we can put a positive spin on us guys choosing your pub for our reunion, in fact I'll insist on a quote from me thanking you for all your help and support. How about that?'

Dizzy scratched his small goatee beard and reflected 'Yeh OK man we'll do it, what the hell'.

Martin approached Fergy, he was holding his mobile phone which he lifted and showed to Fergy. It was a video, right from the first gunshots, which showed the two thugs leaving the house, Gerald being stabbed and Wilky being taken hostage. It even showed the getaway car driving off and although the video was very jerky you could clearly see the number plate on the car.

'The police are gunna want to see that Martin, it's dynamite. I thought you'd checked all your photos for the car's number plate.'

'I did check but I forgot that this was a video. I've only just remembered it.'

'Where were you when you took it?'

'I was in the centre of the circle just doing a video of the old estate, you know for old time's sake, when the shooting started. I crouched behind one of those stone signs in the middle and just kept pointing the phone.'

'Can you send me a copy straight away, the coppers might

want to take your phone once they see this.'

'Give me a minute I'll send it to you as an attachment to an email, it's a pretty big file'.

'Great the policeman gave me his number so once I get the file I'll ring him and tell him what we've got'.

A few minutes later Fergy's phone pinged to say an email had arrived. He gave Martin a thumbs up gesture and took out the business card he'd been given and had just started to dial the number when two uniformed policeman, along with what appeared to be a detective in plain clothes, entered the pub.

'OK gentlemen' the detective addressed the group 'we're going to need statements from you all, Constables Morgan and Ashraf here will interview you individually' he scanned the interior of the pub 'in the back room'. He pointed in the general direction of the back room 'And I would like to speak to Mr Ferguson if I may'.

The jovial fun and laughter of a few minutes earlier gave way to a quieter, more serious, mood as the men were called over one by one to give their statements. Meanwhile the detective started to get the background to the situation from Fergy, who started by pointing out Wilky who was having his picture taken by the Examiner photographer. 'He's the bloke who was kidnapped; he just walked in about ten minutes ago'.

The detective looked surprised at this and said 'I'm going to need to speak to ...' he hesitated and scanned through his notes without success 'what's his name?'

'Aiden Wilkinson, but go easy on him he's had a rough time, not to mention a couple of stiff brandy's and a pint or two'. The detective made a quick phone call to tell his colleagues to call off the search for Wilky and then continued his interrogation of Fergy.

To add to the general chaos another reporter and film crew marched into the pub and the reporter immediately asked 'Is there a Richard Ferguson here?'

Barry went over to the reporter. 'Thank you Mr Ferguson I'm Derek Turner from BBC Look North. Have you got a few minutes to give us a statement please?'

'Oh no sorry' Barry apologised, 'Fergy, that is Mr Ferguson, is a bit busy at the moment speaking to that detective over there' he pointed them out. 'I'm Barry Wilkinson, Fergy and I have organised this reunion, maybe I can help you'.

The reporter looked disappointed but obviously decided that in the absence of Mr Ferguson they would make do with this guy. He addressed the camera crew 'It's a bit noisy and crowded in here so I think we'll have to do the interview out-side. Can you guys check with the landlord to see if it's OK to film outside the pub' and they went off in search of Desmond.

The reporter pointed to a spare table away from the crowd and they made their way to it. 'So Mr Wilkinson were you a witness to the shooting and stabbing up on the estate?'

'Well the shooting took place inside one of the houses so none of us actually saw it, but we certainly heard the shots. I saw the stabbing at close hand and also my brother getting kidnapped by the two lads. What do you want to know? And please call me Barry, everybody else does'.

'So there was a kidnapping as well as the shooting and stab-bing?' the reporter looked surprised.

'Yeh, my brother Aiden but they let him go shortly after they had got away, just dumped him in the middle of the road, that's him over there' Barry pointed out his brother who was starting to look a bit worse for wear. Barry made a mental note to give Aiden's wife a call and get her down here as soon as possible.

The camera crew returned and gave the reporter the thumbs up and they made their way outside to set up for filming, while the reporter went through a few details with Barry.

The interview lasted about three minutes and covered why the guys were at the estate as well as the shooting and stabbing. When it was all finished Barry looked at his watch, to his surprise it was a quarter past three. He suddenly realised that if SKY were covering the events live then it was quite possible that some of the lad's wives or partners could have heard about it. He checked his own phone but there were no missed calls. He suggested that the rest of the group do the same and then check in to let their nearest and dearest know that they were OK.

By the time the detective had finished interviewing Fergy, Wilky was in no fit state to be interviewed. Obviously the adrenalin that had been keeping him going had worn off and had been replaced by the effects of the alcohol. Barry gave the detective a brief outline of what had happened to Wilky and promised to get his brother to call the detective tomorrow to arrange to give a detailed witness statement. Barry called Aiden's wife, Laura, and told her to come and collect Aiden as soon as possible'.

'Has the silly bugger had too much then Barry?' she asked.

'Well yes and no – listen give me a call when you get here and I'll pop out and give you the low down, I can't say any more, apart from he's OK, don't worry'.

Fortunately Laura was the type of person who took everything in her stride, not to mention the fact that Aiden had a track record of misdemeanours usually associated with alcohol consumption. Nevertheless she couldn't help thinking 'When someone says *don't worry*' that's usually a signal that you should worry'. She picked up the car keys and set off for Bradford Road.

The police finally finished taking down all the statements. Martin had shown them the video on his mobile; he'd even managed to persuade them to let him hold onto the phone on the condition that he emailed them the footage. The detective had also finished with Fergy so they all went back to their tables. Fergy was looking drained so Barry took the lead. 'When we arranged this we suggested that we would be finishing around now so some of you may need to leave soon. Unforeseen circumstances have obviously taken control of our day somewhat.'

'You can say that again' remarked Martin.

Sutty added sarcastically 'I thought you had arranged it all for our enjoyment'.

'No Sutty we can't take credit for that – it certainly was an extraordinary sequence of events, I'm just relieved that none of us were injured. Before you leave we wanted to ask if you thought it was worthwhile and if you would like to do something again, although we can't guarantee that it will be quite as exciting as this one has been'.

The reunion was deemed to be a success and there was an appetite for more. Dave Henshaw got up to speak 'I'd just like to say – and I'm sure all the other guys here will agree with me' he paused.

'It depends on what you're gunna say Dave' quipped Martin.

Dave, who was clearly half pissed, threw a 'V' sign at Martin and continued 'as I was saying before I was rudely interrupted, we've all had an amazing time and we'd like to say a big thank you to you guys' he pointed in the general direction of Terry, Fergy and Barry 'you've done us proud'. He sat down to a ripple of applause and then as an afterthought 'And I'm really looking forward to watching it all again tonight on the news' which brought a chorus of laughter.

Barry responded 'Well, thank you all for coming today, when we first had the idea we weren't sure if anybody would be interested but the turnout has been great, it's just a pity that our Aiden had to spoil it by getting himself kidnapped' more laughter 'and, thanks to Martin's recording of the action, we'll all have a record of the err..' he struggled to find the right word.

Martin helped him out with a shout of 'Wild West Show', even more laughter from the group.

When the laughter finally died down Barry added 'I'd also like to say a big thank you to Desmond and Gloria who have looked after us so well today'.

A cheer went up followed by a round of applause.

Barry continued 'But before we all leave here I would like to propose a toast to absent friends'. Glasses were raised and for a moment at least silence reigned as they reflected on the friends who had passed away.

As the men finished their drinks and started to put their jackets on Fergy suggested that they should circulate the old photos. 'Those of you who have brought some old photos can you get them scanned in and then circulate them to us all by email. If you don't have access to scanners you can leave them with me and I'll get it done. Take care on the way home we don't want any more casualties'.

Fergy made his way over to Terry and Barry who were deep in conversation. 'How are you chaps getting home?' he asked.

At that moment Barry's phone rang, it was Laura. 'Just a second chaps I need to give Laura the low down before she sees the state Wilky is in.' He rushed out to meet her and explained what had happened; as Barry had expected she took it all in her stride.

By the time Barry and Laura came into the pub Wilky was slumped in a chair – he had nodded off. Laura walked over to him and gave him a shake 'Come on bugger lugs let's get you home'.

Wilky shook himself, rubbed his eyes and generally pulled himself together, 'You won't believe what's happened to me today love'.

'Well you can tell me all about it when we get back to our Diane's, let's just get you into the car'.

Wilky stood up and turned to Barry, Fergy and Terry, shook hands with each of them and then said 'That was quite a reunion lads, I wouldn't have missed it for the world' and then strode out of the pub with his head held high, like a nineteenth century lord of the manor.

Barry scratched his head and smiled, 'He always liked to be the centre of attention didn't he? Now where were we lads?'

'Arrangements for getting home' reminded Fergy.

'Yeh, Sandy is picking me up Fergy and I've already arranged to drop Terry off at his place. Do you need a lift as well, it's no problem'.

'Thanks Barry but I think I'll pass on that. I need to clear my head a bit so I'm going to walk into town and then get the bus up to Almondbury. It's been a hell of a day'.

'One for the history books I think' observed Barry. 'I'll settle up with Dizzy then before Sandy get's here.'

Fergy shook hands with Terry and Barry and made his way out of the pub. Barry settled the bill and then they decided to wait outside in the fresh air while they waited for Sandy to come and pick them up.

Sandy pulled up outside the pub in Barry's blue Jaguar. 'I came in your car 'cos I thought you might want to give some friends a lift and it would have been a bit of a squash in my little mini'.

Barry got in the front seat whilst Terry went in the back, 'Good thinking Sandy, this is Terry"

'Hi Terry how was the old boys reunion then?' she enquired.

'Interesting' replied Barry 'wouldn't you say Terry?'

'That's one way of describing somebody getting shot, another stabbed and your Aiden having a gun stuck in his neck and dragged off' came the reply.

'Oh you've been playing silly games then. I bet that was Barry's idea; he does these sort of games on his training courses you know. He tells me it's a way of getting people to relax'.

'Sandy' Barry searched for the right words and put on his most serious voice 'we haven't been playing management games, or any games for that matter. You obviously haven't heard the news have you. There was a shooting and stabbing at the old estate and we were caught up in the middle of it. Our Aiden was held hostage at gunpoint and then kidnapped.' There was a slight pause before Barry added 'Fortunately they didn't hurt him and let him go.'

It was a good job that the car was still stationary as Sandy turned to Barry 'Tell me you're having me on Barry, you're just winding me up aren't you?'

'Fraid not love, it all actually happened. It's already been shown on SKY News. D'you remember me telling you that one of my old West Indian football friends lived on the estate?'

'You mean the dodgy one, Godfrey or something?'

'Gerald actually, but yes the same one. Well, our Aiden was standing next to him when he was stabbed AFTER his lad had been shot. They grabbed Aiden and pushed him into the get-away car and off they went'.

She spun round to face Terry in the back seat 'Are you OK Terry, I'm sorry for being sarcastic it must have been so scary for you all'.

'You're not kidding, we were all shi... err terrified' his voice quivered slightly as his mind flashed back 'but it was a lot worse for Wilky. They were only young lads and the one with the gun was shaking so much I thought he might pull the trig-ger by accident.'

'Right then we'd better get you home, does your wife know about it? She must be worried sick'.

'No, I don't think she knows, I tried calling her but it kept going to voice mail and I didn't leave a message for obvious reasons'. Terry's cheeky humour took over 'I thought a message like *High darling how are you we've just seen a stabbing, shooting and one of our mates has been kidnapped* might have upset her'.

Barry smiled 'Nice to see you've not lost your sense of humour Terry, but I can't see your missus seeing the funny side somehow'.

Sandy and Barry made sure their friend arrived home safely but turned down the offer of coming inside for a cup of coffee and left Terry to explain the recent events to his wife, Jane.

When they finally got home Barry was exhausted but he still took the time to check on how Gerald and his son were progressing in hospital. All the hospital would tell him was that both of them were 'in a stable condition'.

As Fergy made his way on foot along Bradford Road he started to count the pubs which were no longer there, starting with the Thornhill at the bottom of Honoria Street where the lads used to meet on a Sunday night to discuss their match that afternoon. Next came the Wagon and Horses, not a pub he had ever visited. Across the road was the Engine Tavern, an old man's pub which he had been in a couple of times. As Bradford Road gave way to Northgate he started to rack his brain for the name of the pub which was demolished when the inner ring road was built. He worked his way through the alphabet until the letter F – 'Fox and Grapes' he said to himself triumphantly. Next came the Fitzwilliam and finally the Broadway where they used to meet to select their Sunday League team every Thursday night. Six pubs, all closed. Dizzy at the Stag was definitely doing something right to buck the trend.

As he continued to make his way through the town centre towards the bus station his mind wandered back to the action earlier that day. How strange it was that all hell would be let loose on the exact day and the exact time that he and his friends, all former residents of the estate, were revisiting the scene of their youth. Most of the men didn't seem to have been too badly affected by the violence and general mayhem, and Wilky, bless him, seemed to have almost enjoyed his brush with danger. But deep down inside he knew that it had had an effect on himself and Barry in particular. Maybe their feelings were heightened by a sense of responsibility; they were the ones who had made the arrangements to visit the estate after all. His introspection was interrupted when he saw that his bus was about to leave it's stand at the bus station and he put all thoughts to one side as he dashed to catch the bus before it left.

CHAPTER 23 – THE BUILD UP TO THE MATCH

Summer 1959

T he boys were getting excited; the prospect of their first real football match was all they could think of. They had decided they needed to get in as much practice as possible before the big match. It was agreed that the practice should take place at their newly adopted ground, which they all called the Tranny, and would be attack versus defence but first they needed to select a team.

Most of the boys had never heard of the word democracy, nor did they understand what a committee was, but that's the approach which they fell into for selecting the team - no-one took the lead and everyone had a say. It says a lot for their sense of fair play that somehow from this chaotic process a team was selected. Wilky was the only one who knew the two extra players from his school so the lads had to take his word for the best positions for them to play in.

As Fergy wisely observed 'It's only a provisional team anyway, just so we can split into attack and defence. We'll just have to see how well everybody plays in their selected position.'

'What does pervisional mean?' Terry was the one who asked the question but quite a few of the others were also wondering what it meant.

Fergy sighed 'It means we can change it later. Look, it's like this; we've picked Val on the left wing 'cos he's the only one who has a decent left foot, but if he doesn't play well there in the practice matches but is a good tackler we might move him to err, say left back. D'you get it now Terry?'

'OK, so you've picked me at right half but if I score a hat trick in the practice I might be moved to centre forward?'

'Don't be daft' joked Martin 'there's no chance that you'll score a hat trick, you're too small and you're not quick enough'.

Martin was always goading Terry, even though they were best mates but Terry was a fiery little sod and Martin had gone too far this time, he jumped on Martins back and tried to pull him over. Martin was having none of it; he shrugged him off and wrestled him to the ground. They rolled around on the dusty floor for a couple of minutes with the other boys watching on in amusement, eventually they decided to pull the fighting friends apart.

'Calm down you two' Barry chided them 'that's a great start to our preparation for the match, what d'you call that little episode?'

'Team building' joked Sutty and the lads started to laugh. Even Martin and Terry could see the funny side and joined in the laughter.

Wilky told them to shake hands and pointed out they were both covered in dust and strands of dead grass from rolling around on the dry ground. The boys dusted themselves down as instructed and shook hands and mumbled 'sorry' to each other.

Wilky decided to take control of the situation 'Why don't we have the first practice on Saturday morning down at the Tranny and I'll make sure my mates are there. You lot who are in the defence' he looked around at the defenders 'can you wear a white shirt, it doesn't really matter about the attackers anything other than white will do. Are we all agreed?'

The suggestion got a group nod of agreement.

'Ahem' Fergy did his little cough to get attention.

'What now!' Wilky was annoyed that his little period of control had been interrupted and turned to Fergy.

'We've only got one goaly which is Barry, is he going to play for the attack or the defence, and who's going to be in goal for the other side?'

'Aye that's a good question' Wilky agreed and there was a slight pause 'it makes sense for our Baz to play for the defence – agreed?' Everyone nodded.

'Yeh but what about our side?' asked Terry, who was member of the attack team.

Wilky thought for a moment as he scoured the group for inspiration, then his eyes lit up as his they came to rest on the youngest member of the group and he responded triumphantly 'Pat Connor can play in goals for the attack that's who. He's first reserve and that'll give us six v six', he smiled smugly.

Pat was a nine year old who had recently started playing with them, he was big for his age and was a fast runner but no-one had ever seen him play in goals.

'B-but Wilky' young Patrick pleaded, 'I've never played goaly before.'

'Ah don't worry lad' Wilky replied in a condescending tone 'me and the other attackers will make sure that they never get near our goal'.

Barry, who had been selected as goaly – much to Sutty's annoyance – reassured the young lad, 'Don't worry Paddy I'll give you a few lessons after tea tonight, you'll be fine'.

Young Patrick Connor did not appear to be overly reassured by this gesture from Barry but accepted that there was nothing he could do about it.

As agreed they all assembled at the top of the ginnel at 10

o'clock on Saturday morning. Well, all except Val, who was habitually late. Fortunately his house was very close to the ginnel and Barry was despatched to rouse their missing player.

Barry suspected that Val would still be in bed so he started to knock heavily on the door. Mrs Taylor swung the door open before he had even finished knocking, she looked a little startled. 'Oh it's you Barry you had me worried there, that was a real policeman's knock'.

'Oh sorry Mrs Taylor' Barry apologised 'it's just we've arranged to meet for an important practice match at ten and Val hasn't turned up and I thought he might still be in bed'.

'You're right there Barry, Val has never been good at getting up in the morning love, he's always in trouble at school for being late you know. Just wait a minute and I'll go and wake him up' and off she went.

Barry could hear her knocking on the bedroom door and then there was a muffled conversation and Mrs Taylor returned to the back door to give Barry an update. 'He's overslept but he's getting up now and he says he will join you down at the Tranny – wherever that is – in about ten minutes. You and your mates had better go ahead love and I'll make sure he doesn't go back to sleep. I've never known anyone sleep as much as him'. She closed the door and Barry ran off to rejoin his mates and give them the news.

'Typical!' snorted Wilky when Barry gave him the news, 'we'll have to go because my mates will be down there by now, we'll just have to start without him, lazy bastard'.

Sure enough as they crossed over the canal on the approach to the Tranny they could see two lads amusing themselves by passing an imaginary football to each other while they waited for the rest of the gang to arrive.

'Are they yer mates Wilky?' asked Martin.

'Aye the one with the bushy hair is Freddy Lewis and the other one is Brian Nugent, they're both good lads and decent footballers, let's run down and meet 'em.'

As they emerged from the small bushes surrounding the pitch Freddy, the one with the bushy hair shouted across to them 'Hiya Wilky, you're late; we've been waiting ages. We thought you weren't coming'.

'We've been waiting for one of the lads, the lazy bugger was still in bed but he'll join us in a few minutes'.

Wilky reminded everybody what their positions were and the eleven players were split into two teams based on attack and defence. As agreed Barry would play in goals for the defence and young Patrick would be the goaly for the attack who would have the disadvantage of having to start the game a man short until Val arrived.

The game started and not surprisingly the defence team, with their extra man, were doing most of the attacking and the attack, minus Val, were doing most of the defending.

When the score reached three nil to the defence Wilky suggested a change. 'This isn't working out is it?' he looked around and everyone agreed. 'We're gunna have to switch one player from defence to attack until Taylor arrives'. Wilky couldn't bring himself to use Val's first name.

'I'll swap sides if you like' offered Martin. 'I can swap back when Val gets here. I'll put my jumper on top of my white shirt so I don't look like one of the defence'.

The game restarted and the defence were under pressure from the strengthened attack team. Barry was having a dream game in goals, diving this way and that to save the best shots the attack could find. Eventually the defence was breached by a shot from the normally deadly foot of Fergy which was going wide until it hit the leg of Dave Henshaw and rebounded into the goals.

After about half an hour, with the score still standing at three one to the defence, half time was declared. As the boys started to quench their thirst on the bottles of corporation pop Val appeared in the distance wearing a white shirt.

'Not only is he three quarters of an hour late he's got the wrong bloody shirt on' Wilky spat on the floor just to emphasise his annoyance. 'Somebody had better tell him to keep clear of me in the game 'cos I'd love to give him a kick up his lazy arse.

Fergy neatly pointed out the futility of that statement 'Seeing as how you're both on the same side that wouldn't be a good idea' and then changed the subject. 'Never mind all that Wilky, how do you think the practice is working out lads?'

Barry was the first to offer an opinion 'I think the defence is doing great, everybody's playing out of their skin'.

Terry was next to speak 'I'm not very happy having to play on the left hand side but I suppose Val will be playing there in the second half so can I go back onto the right hand side'.

'OK Terry' Fergy continued 'you've played well considering you're playing out of position, and yes you can move back to the right hand side in the second half'. He turned his attention to the new boys 'How about you Freddy are you happy with where you're playing and what about you Brian?'

At this point a slightly out of breath Val arrived 'Sorry I'm late lads, my mam forgot to wake me'. Barry knew this to be a lie but bit his tongue in the interest of group harmony.

'Not only are you late, Taylor but you've put the wrong bloody shirt on you stupid bugger' Wilky was getting angry again.

'I thought you said to wear a white shirt?' came the reply.

Fergy jumped in before Wilky could say anything else 'Only the defence Val, you're playing on the left wing – you know for the attack. But don't worry you can slip my jumper on top of your shirt'.

Fergy was quite stocky and about three inches taller than Val so the jumper swamped his much smaller friend's frame. Val thought about it but decided it would be unwise to complain, Wilky was already pissed off with him, nevertheless he thought he would chance his arm. 'Have I got time for a quick fag, I haven't had one yet today?'

'You lying bugger I could see a puff of smoke around you before you crossed the bridge, so the answers no!' Wilky was so angry you could almost see a puff of smoke rising from his ears. The other boys stifled a laugh as they knew it would only make Wilky worse.

The new lads witnessed this episode quietly and when it was finally over said they were happy to carry on in their allotted positions and the second half got underway.

The match was much more finely balanced with equal numbers on each side, the attack team managed to score two goals but the defence also scored a goal to make the final score four goals to three in the defence's favour.

As the boys made their way back over the canal towards the estate they did their usual unstructured review of the game. Fergy was claiming a hat trick having been the scorer of the two second half goals and attempting to claim the goal in the first half which had taken a wicked deflection before going in, but the other boys were having none of it and he had to settle for just the two.

There was general agreement that the practice match had been useful and another one was scheduled for the following Saturday morning. Wilky stressed the importance of this match as it would be their last full scale practice before the game which was taking place a week later. He turned to Val and gave him the hard word 'Make sure you are up on time next week Val or you'll find yourself dropped. Young Patrick here' he pointed to their youngest player 'is a quick runner and I'm sure he'd like to play in the big match'.

The boys had reached the bottom of the ginnel when Val made

a solemn promise to get up in time for the start of the next practice match, though few amongst the boys had any confidence that the promise would be kept.

The bottom end of the ginnel was also where the two older friends of Wilky's would branch off as they made their way along Red Doles Road towards Bradford Road and then on to Cowcliffe where they both lived.

It was early July so the soccer and rugby league seasons hadn't yet started so the boys arranged to meet in the field after dinner to have a game of cricket. As they walked through the estate the group got progressively smaller as the boys reached their individual homes. Val was first, then Terry and Patrick, followed by Martin Kelly then the Wilkinsons which just left Fergy, Sutty and the Henshaw brothers who all lived at the top of the estate around the circle.

'He's a bossy bugger in't he? Sutty commented.

'D'you mean Wilky by any chance?' responded Fergy.

'Aye I do, he gave poor Val a right going over'.

Dave Henshaw jumped in 'Yeh he did but I thought Val had it coming to him, he's always late; whenever we make arrangements he's always the last to arrive'.

'I'm with Dave on this one Sutty, I think he deserved it. Wilky only said what everyone was thinking didn't he' added Fergy. 'Anyway lads, see you all in't field later on' and they all made their way to their separate houses.

The morning football match must have used up most of the boys energy and the game of cricket was a largely lethargic affair that afternoon. There was one highlight when Barry creamed one again and it headed in exactly the same direction as the one which broke the window. It was one of those 'time stands still' moments as everyone watched the trajectory of the ball as it zoomed towards the house door. Fortunately on this occasion Barry must have hit it a little bit harder and it thumped into the wall just above the doorway releasing a hail of pebble dash from the wall as it did so.

'Bloody hell Baz' shouted Wilky who was the bowler 'I thought you'd done it again then. Anyway it's six and out so you can bugger off over to Aunt Agnes's and get a brush and shovel to clear all them pebbles that have come off the wall, before Mrs Oldham notices it.'

Barry was a relieved young man as he made his way to Aunt Agnes's and his mood improved further as he passed Terry who was fielding near to the fence 'Bloody good shot Barry' he whispered as he walked by. The fun wasn't over though. As Barry climbed the fence to retrieve the ball from the garden, the leg of his shorts got caught on the top of the railing. Barry hadn't realised this and attempted to jump down into the garden only to find that he was suspended by his shorts hooked on the railing. The sight of their friend suspended by his shorts shouting for help was hilarious to his friends who steadfastly refused to unhook him.

Barry's cries for help eventually brought his Aunt Agnes to her door, 'What on earth are you doing there our Barry, come down before you hurt yourself'.

'I cant Aunt Agnes, I'm stuck. My shorts got caught on the railings'.

'I'd better get your Uncle Ray to help you love, just wait there a minute'.

'I haven't got much option have I' Barry thought as he waited for his release.

He didn't have to wait for long, as Uncle Ray trundled over to him and lifted him high enough to free him from the railings and put him down safely on the grass. 'What were you doing Barry to get yourself stuck like that? his uncle enquired.

'I were climbing over to get the cricket ball, it just missed Mrs Oldham's door this time'.

'Well next time walk the extra ten yards down to our fence where there's no railings left, it's a lot easier, and safer by the looks of it'.

'I will Uncle Ray, promise. Can I borrow a brush and shovel please? I need to clear the mess away from Mrs Oldham's step'.

'Of course you can' replied Uncle Ray who went into the house and on his return, handed over the brush and shovel. 'Looks like you've been playing Don Bradman again Barry' he chuckled.

Barry picked up the cricket ball and put it in his pocket. The lads were shouting for him to chuck it back to them but Barry wasn't in the mood to cooperate. He carefully collected all the pebbles and put them in Aunt Agnes's bin before returning the brush and shovel. As he ducked under the fence he heaved a sigh of relief as he realised how lucky he was that the ball had landed where it did and not six inches lower down.

As he looked back at the grass in Mrs Oldham's garden he noticed that it was about knee high just like it had been the year before and the germ of an idea came into Barry's head.

As he re-entered the field a furious Wilky came over to him and pushed him backwards 'Why didn't you chuck the ball back instead of making us all wait you daft bugger?'

Barry smiled and deliberately passed the ball to Terry before pushing his brother back and replied 'Why did you lot leave me stuck on the railings?' and calmly took up his place in the field.

After the cricket match was over the boys gathered around the old settee which, not surprisingly, was starting to get a bit smelly. 'I've had an idea lads' announced Barry.

'That's not like you Baz' came the sarcastic comment from his older brother.

'Get lost Aiden, it's a serious idea'. The boys gave Barry their full attention, all that is, except Martin and Terry who were having one of their endless pushing and shoving matches. 'When you two have finished' Barry started 'you know how we made a few bob last year cutting peoples grass, well I thought maybe we could do the same this year and try to raise enough money to buy a football kit for us to wear in our matches, what d'you think?'

'We'd need to do a lot more than last year Barry, a full kit is going to cost much more than a couple of cricket balls' wise words from Fergy. 'Have you any idea how much a full kit would cost?'

'What about that thingy, you know the little booklet, you had; are there any prices in there?'

Fergy pondered for a minute 'Yeh probably, I think they're in the back of the booklet, I'll check when I go in for me tea. Anyway we don't have to buy the full set we could just get the shirts couldn't we?'

'That'll be good, can we get that one, you know the red one with the white stripe on it from the shoulder down to the bottom, I really liked that one' Terry was getting excited again.

'Well the plain shirts are the cheapest you know. You mean the one with the diagonal stripe don't you' replied Fergy in his logical way.

'We've got a problem though' interrupted Wilky 'us mam wont let us go knocking on folks doors asking to do work for 'em, she said that last year didn't she Baz?'

'Oh yeh, 'fraid so'.

'I bet she didn't say anything about other people knocking on't doors though did she?' suggested Martin.

Barry's face brightened 'Dead right she didn't'.

'Whoa boys, boys let's not get carried away' the ever logical Fergy held up his hands 'let's see how much the shirts would cost first and then we can decide what to do'.

As the boys dispersed to have their teas Terry was still mumbling on about his favourite shirt 'How much d'you think the red one with the diagram stripe will be Martin?'

Martin smiled, he loved the way Terry always got the words wrong 'It's di-ag-onal Terry'.

'OK, OK but how much do you think it will cost?'

'More than we can afford almost certainly I'm afraid, so don't get your hopes up or you'll be disappointed' and with those words of wisdom from Martin the pair of them made their way home.

After tea the boys all made their way up to the circle and gathered around Fergy's house and waited expectantly for Fergy to emerge with the information they craved.

'Bad news lads' Fergy spoke as he came out of the house 'even a set of plain red or blue shirts is going to cost a lot. The price list says 120/6d for a set off ten shirts, that's over six quid. We'd have to do forty houses and charge three shillings a time to afford them.'

Everyone looked dejected.

'How much is it for my favourite shirt?' came the inevitable question from Terry.

'I knew you'd ask me that Terry so I made a point of checking it. A set of shirts in that style would cost an extra two pounds and ten shillings, making them eight pounds ten shillings and sixpence altogether. Satisfied?'

To say the young man was gutted would be an understatement.

'Look lads' Fergy desperately wanted to lift the gloom but all he could come up with was 'don't forget it says to allow eight weeks for delivery in any case so the shirts wouldn't be here until after the summer holidays, even if we could afford to buy them – which we can't - so let's not waste any more time worrying about it'.

'Can you buy just one shirt Fergy?' Terry was not giving up.

'Not from this company Terry but if you go to Sportsgear in Town you might be able to order one from them'.

The boys had to accept Fergy's logic, clearly there was no way they were going to get the money together for a set of matching football shirts and they looked a forlorn bunch as they made their way into the field, none more so than little Terry who had set his heart on a new football shirt.

They started a game of soccer but for some reason their normal enthusiasm was conspicuous by its absence. Perhaps it was the efforts of the morning practice match, followed by a cricket match, which had sapped their energy or maybe the disappointment over the shirts, either way they played without any real conviction.

Fergy wished he had never shown them the catalogue of football shirts in the first place and at the end of the game he called all the boys together. 'Listen if we play against Birkby like we have just done we'll get murdered, we need to put the shirts out of our minds until after the game, are we all agreed?'

There was a general acceptance of the point and Wilky tried to gee them up even further 'Don't forget we had a great practice session this morning and we've another one planned for next week. We've all got a white shirt sorted for the match so no more whingeing about kit' he pointed an accusing finger at Terry 'and that includes you Terry'.

'You're right Aiden' Barry leapt to support his brother. 'How about we split into attack and defence for all the games we have between now and the big match, starting tomorrow'.

The lads brightened up a bit and made their way back to the playground and for the first time in ages forgot about football and just messed about on the swings and roundabout. As they sat together on the roundabout Martin observed 'Have you seen all these balloons sumdy's thrown away it looks like they've been having a party?'

Wilky, man of the world, laughed and pointed out that they

weren't balloons 'They're used johnnies Martin not balloons'.

'What d'you mean Wilky' Terry asked naively.

'I'll tell you when you get a bit older Terry' came the reply.

EXTRACT FROM BARRY WILKINSON'S DIARY

27th June 1959

Had our first proper practice today down at the Tranny, we played attack v defence. Pat Connor played in goals for the attack but we won 4 – 3. Val was late as usual, he was still in bed when I called for him, his mam had to wake him up. Our Aiden was so angry, especially when Val had the wrong coloured shirt on.

Our Aiden's mates are good players and fitted in to the team. We're gunna have another practice next Saturday at the Tranny.

Played cricket this afternoon and I nearly broke Mrs Oldhams window again, but just missed this time. My shorts got caught on the railings and I was hanging there and none of the lads would help me so Uncle Ray had to lift me off. So I made the lads wait till I'd finished cleaning up the pebbles before I gave them the ball. Our Aiden was angry again but I didn't care.

CHAPTER 24 – THE MORNING AFTER

January 2011

B arry woke early after spending a restless night tossing and turning. He just couldn't stop going over the events of the previous day. He knew that it was just coincidence that the shooting and subsequent stabbing took place just as their reunion was getting going, and yet despite this he still felt responsible.

After all it was Barry who had assured everyone that things would be OK just because of his relationship with Gerald; the events of the previous day had proved him spectacularly wrong. How would he have felt if his brother or one of his friends had been injured, or worse still killed, he would never have forgiven himself.

He tried to snap out of this cycle of self-blame. 'Come on Barry pull yourself together, what's done is done. They let Wilky go and none of your mates were injured be thankful for that and look forward not backwards' he kept reminding himself.

He eventually got out of bed and headed for the bathroom 'A good shower is what I need' he thought to himself and then 'A good kick up the backside more like it'.

He showered and dressed and when he walked into the kitchen he looked at the clock - it was still only seven thirty. He realised that it was too early to be ringing Aiden and he knew that the hospital wouldn't tell him anything further about the condition of Gerald and his son. He made a pot of tea and took a cup in to Sandy who was sleeping soundly. As he sat at the breakfast bar sipping his tea his mind started to clear and he decided he would wait till ten o'clock before ringing Aiden and then he would make his way up to the infirmary and see if he could visit Gerald. He took the opportunity to log down yesterday's events in his diary.

EXTRACT FROM BARRY WILKINSON'S DIARY

15th January 2011

I'm writing this the morning after the reunion. What a day!

Talk about being in the wrong place at the wrong time. We just happened to get to the old estate when a rival gang decided to attack Gerald's son. Miraculously no-one died, thank god. Gerald and his son, Michael, ended up in hospital, Gerald was stabbed and Michael shot twice.

Worse still, our Aiden only goes and get's himself kidnapped at gun point. He wasn't even supposed to be coming but his treatment had been delayed so he decided to surprise us. Luckily they let him go – I told Fergy they wouldn't be able to put up with him for long. We're all shitting ourselves wondering what's happened to him and he just saunters into the pub, large as life, and starts to milk the situation. Typical Aiden playing to the audience. He can be infuri-ating but I was so relieved to see him alive and in one piece.

Everyone who said they were coming turned up, but I didn't get much time with most of the lads as we were a bit pre-occupied, and that's putting it mildly. Think we might do another one – probably next year. I suspect there will be a few sore heads this morning.

Fartown United have certainly hit the headlines and Fergy has be-come a TV star, he was interviewed live on SKY News and I've been on Look North. Fergy had arranged for someone from the Examiner to take some pictures, but we got more than we expected when a reporter turned up with the photographer. The reporter – Sacha – must have thought it was her lucky day when it all started kicking off; I expect we'll be all over the front page of the Examiner today.

Couldn't sleep last night, every time I closed my eyes I could see Gerald getting stabbed and Wilky being kidnapped. I need to find out how Gerald and Michael are. I need to keep busy today.

Once he had finished updating his diary he reverted to his normal morning routine and opened his iPad to browse the news and check on last night's sport. To his surprise – no shock, there it was on the home page of the BBC website; a picture of someone on a stretcher being loaded into the ambulance with the caption *'Football team reunion turns into bloodbath'*.

'Oh no' he mumbled and quickly closed the iPad. His heart was racing and he took a few deep breaths, after a couple of minutes he had relaxed a bit and his curiosity started to get the better of him as he switched the iPad back on, clicked on the picture to open the article and read it.

Twelve middle aged men got more than they bargained for when they held a reunion yesterday in a suburb of Huddersfield, reports Derek Turner.

When Barry Wilkinson and his friends decided to have a reunion for their old Fartown United football team they chose to go back to their old haunts where they were brought up – nothing particularly strange about that you might think. Except the estate where they used to live now has a bit of a reputation - for violence and crime. As the group were happily posing for photographs the gang warfare, which has been simmering in this area for some time now, exploded into action with devastating effects resulting in two people being seriously injured one with a knife wound and the other with gunshot wounds. To make matters worse one of the ex-footballers was kidnapped at gun point before being released a few minutes later.

When I asked Mr Wilkinson why the group had decided to visit the estate which has such a bad reputation he shook his head and said 'Maybe we shouldn't have come but Richard, Terry and myself had been here on a recky and spoke to one of the residents who assured us we would be OK'.

When I asked him to name the resident he initially declined but when pressed agreed that it was one of the injured, Gerald Wilson, who had given him assurances of the group's safety.

Fortunately none of the old football players were injured but it is believed that Mr Wilkinson's brother, Aiden, was the person who was temporarily abducted after being used as a hostage by the gunmen and bundled into their blue Audi getaway car.

We understand that the two injured people are in fact Mr Gerald Wilson and his teenage son, Michael. Both are said to be in a serious but stable condition in Huddersfield Royal Infirmary.'

Barry shook his head 'Bloody hell, this is getting out of hand, whatever next?' he mumbled to himself. He was soon to find out as he casually opened the front room curtains and spotted an unfamiliar car parked opposite the house with two people sat inside. As soon as they saw the curtains move they jumped out of the car, one was holding what looked like a microphone and the other reached into the boot of the car and took out a video camera.

He was dumbstruck and sat down on the sofa, he put his head in his hands just as the rat-tat-tat of a knock on the front door broke the silence. He got up wearily, looked at the clock, which showed ten to eight and made his way to the door.

He had barely opened the door when there was a flash which dazzled him. He started to close the door but the female reporter almost pleaded 'Mr Wilkinson can we have a few words about the reunion yesterday'.

Barry stepped outside and quietly closed the door behind him, hoping that Sandy had not been woken up. 'OK I'll answer your questions as long as you promise to leave me alone after that'. The reporter agreed to Barry's request and introduced herself as Katey Lawson from Channel 4 News and asked him if he would object to the interview being filmed.

The interview lasted three or four minutes and covered much the same ground as the one he had given to Look North yesterday until, that is, the reporter asked him 'Are you aware that the young man who was shot was currently on police bail in connection with the supply of controlled drugs, along with three other youths from the area?'

Barry's surprise at this revelation quickly turned to anger and he curtly replied 'I'm not sure what you are implying but I've never met the young man so how would I know that?' He turned away from the camera and made his way back to the front door where he turned and said 'That's enough Katey I've given you what you wanted now keep your side of the bargain and leave me in peace.' He didn't wait for a reply as he went back into the house.

He popped his head into the bedroom and gave a sigh of relief as, by some miracle, Sandy had managed to sleep through all that and her cup of tea remained on the bedside cabinet, untouched.

He went back into the kitchen, picked up his phone and called Fergy 'Morning Fergy how are you coping this morning, have you had the reporters round as well?'

'Not this morning thank God, but I had some round last night. I'm beginning to feel like David Beckham but without the brass. Have you heard how Gerald and his lad are today?'

'I called the hospital last night but they won't tell me owt, I thought I might go up and visit him today, if they'll let me. Tell the truth Fergy – and I know this doesn't make sense – but I'm feeling really guilty about yesterday's goings on. I feel responsible for putting the lads in danger, but it's more than that. Something is telling me that I can't just sit back and let things fall apart up there and that I should try to do something about the situation. It's like what happened yesterday was fate, somehow sending me a message. I don't know - am I being stupid?'

'No, no you're not. And you're not the only one Barry; I've been thinking about it all night mate. Listen why don't we go together to visit Gerald, d'you know what time visiting is?'

'It used to be pretty much all day but I'll ring and check and then get back to you.'

'Hey what about your Aiden have you heard anything from him this morning?'

'I spoke to Laura last night she said he was OK. I'm going to call him but I thought I'd give him time to come round a bit before ringing him'.

Two hours later Barry made the drive from Honley to Almondbury, by way of the Castle Hill road, to pick Fergy up. As he pulled level with the Castle he stopped the car and took a few moments to take in the view. It was a view he had enjoyed many times. He reflected on the changes that had taken place to the landscape since he came here as a young child with his parents and his brother. He couldn't help but smile as he reminisced on how they used to race each other up the hill from the road side to the castle and Aiden would always be first to the top where he would taunt Barry about being a slowcoach. After a few, quiet moments with his thoughts he got back into the car and continued his journey to pick up Fergy.

As they made their way to Lindley to visit Gerald in the infirmary Barry gave Fergy an update on the conversation he had just had with Wilky. 'Laura answered the phone and she said he was in the shower but he was a bit 'delicate'. She said they've arranged to go and make a statement to the police later this morning. Anyway Aiden must have finished in the shower and, when he heard our conversation he took the phone off Laura. I kept it short but he said he was having flashbacks and couldn't sleep; when I suggested that he might have this post traumatic stress thingy he laughed, but I'm still worried about him. I told him that we were concerned about him and to keep in touch'.

'He's a tough old bugger is your Aiden, but that was one hell of an ordeal he went through and he's not in the best of health is he? It's hardly surprising he's up-tight. Have the press been bothering them as well?'

'Thankfully no' replied Barry 'they're staying with Laura's sister over in Mirfield so the press won't have been able to track them down; otherwise I'm sure they'd be on the doorstep. Laura's pretty sensible though, she'll look after him in any case and make sure he doesn't get too much hassle.'

The conversation dried up for a while until they arrived at the car park barrier, took their ticket and found a parking space almost straight away. 'Must be our lucky day Fergy, I usually have to hunt around for a space up here' commented Barry. They made their way into the hospital and, after checking at reception, went up to Ward 9 where Gerald was being treated.

'I'll let you do the talking Barry, you know him better than me.'

Gerald was sat up in bed reading last night's Examiner, he was surprised but pleased to see them both. 'What brings you two guys here then?'

'I've been trying to find out how you are' Barry started 'but the nurses aren't allowed to tell me as I'm not family, so we thought we'd come and check you out for ourselves'.

'Well as you can see man I'm fine and dandy, couldn't be better' he laughed.

'What about the wound then has it done much damage?' enquired Fergy.

'It seems like I am a lucky man, no major damage, the knife missed my organs. They want to keep me here for a few days just to make sure the wound heals proper like'.

'What about your lad' asked Barry 'how's he doing?'

'That's Michael over there why don't you ask him yourself, that's him with the head phones on' and Gerald pointed to the other side of the ward. They turned to see the young man who had his arm in a sling and a heavily bandaged leg was raised in a sort of sling which hung from a metal arm above the bed.

Fergy walked over to the boy's bedside and gave him a slight nudge, he looked up and then, with his good hand, took his head phones off. 'Hey man you the geezer what looked after me yesterday? The paramedics told me you might have saved my life with that tourniquet thing so thank you man' he held out his good hand and Fergy shook it.

'So how are you today Michael, pretty sore I bet?'

'I'm OK man, them Deighton boys don't get rid of me that easy'.

'You know the men that did this to you'.

'Sure man, they're pussycats really, only big men when they're carrying. Me and me mates gunna sort them out proper when I get out of here'.

Fergy was disappointed, but not surprised, at Michael's response, he had seen that type of bravado many times when dealing with difficult kids as a teacher. 'Listen, Michael, you look after yourself. You've had a lucky escape this time you might not be so lucky next time'. He turned to walk away and then hesitated before turning back to the injured young man. 'Do you play soccer Michael? I hear your dad was a good player?'

'Yeh man I'm like a striker, leading scorer for the school team – why d'you ask, and how d'you know about me dad man?'

'I don't, but my friend Barry over there' he pointed 'used to play for the same team as your dad, he said he was a good player. Anyway look after yourself, stay cool'. 'My god I'm starting to talk like these lads now' he thought as he walked back to Barry and Gerald.

'Michael tells me he is a striker in the school team is he any good?'

'He's OK but he needs some proper coaching, he's got attitude and them referees they don't like that you know. Good player - bad attitude'.

'Is he one of the lads we saw playing the first time we came to the estate, there seemed to be a few talented boys amongst them?'

'Probably but the problem is them boys ain't got no discipline – they all want to be a striker, they can dribble but when it comes to passing they are rubbish. I keep telling them that football is a team game and you have to use your brain' Gerald pointed to his head 'as well as your feet and keep your mouth shut to the referee. They won't listen to me, just say 'What do you know Gerald you is an old man' and laugh.'

Barry and Fergy exchanged glances. Barry smiled as he reminded Gerald that he was always in trouble with the referees when he played at Honley. 'Like father, like son' he suggested.

Gerald continued his rant on the youth of today in general and his son and friends in particular. 'They've got the talent you know – the skill – but they ain't got no discipline and now they've started this gang war with the Deighton mob. The school is always saying *your boy is bright but he won't apply himself and he won't respect the teachers*' he's already on a final warning, if he get's into trouble one more time – that's it - he is expelled from school. I don't know what to do with him really I don't. He's got no sense of purpose; he's just drifting towards trouble'.

'I guess it's tough for the kids these days – not like our time heh Barry?' Fergy managed to get a word in between Gerald's torrent.

'Did you boys get into trouble with the police then when you were kids?'

Barry and Fergy smiled at each other and Fergy nodded for Barry to take over the conversation 'We all got a caution from the police once'.

'What was that for man?'

'Swearing too much'.

'You're kidding me, you actually got a caution just for swearing, I can't believe it'.

'Believe it or not Gerald it's the truth; and we broke a few windows playing cricket and trampled on Claude's roses'.

'My god you guys were real hooligans weren't you' laughed Gerald. 'This team of yours Fartown Rovers'.

'United, we were Fartown United' corrected Barry.

'OK this team Fartown U-nit-ed, who was the boss man, the coach, you know who was in charge, who taught you how to play the game?'

'Nobody, we taught ourselves and we made all the decisions ourselves. We even used to cut the grass on the pitch ourselves as well; we were a team in every sense of the word. We organised all our games as well'.

Gerald gave a silent whistle 'Well maybe you could come down and show my boy and all the other lazy sods how to play as a team, give them some purpose and discipline, that's what they need'.

At this point the nurse came over 'I'm sorry Mr Wilson but the doctor is on his rounds so your friends will have to leave now'. She turned to the two men 'I'm sorry gentlemen but you'll have to go now'.

They stood up and shook hands with Gerald who said 'Think about it - you guys could really make a difference'.

The two men waved to Michael on their way out and made their way to the lift. Barry eventually spoke 'What do you think about that suggestion?'

'I think we would be biting off more than we can chew if I'm honest mate, what do you think?'

'I think you could be right, shall we go and get a coffee at the Costa downstairs'.

There was the usual queue at the counter, Barry told Fergy to grab a table while he went and ordered two lattes. Fergy pulled a copy of last night's Examiner from the shelf and browsed through it while he waited for Barry to bring over their drinks. He counted five separate reports of stabbings, attacks and muggings as well as one shooting.

Barry arrived with the drinks 'Don't tell me we're all over that as well?'

'No mate, it's last night's but it would have been printed before our incident kicked off. We'll be in tonight's you can bet on that. Even without our incident there are loads of stabbings and muggings and another shooting. Martin was right, this town is getting like the wild west, it really is'.

Barry took a large swig of his latte, wiped the froth from his lips and gave a big sigh 'The whole thing is a mess, and the worst thing is the police seem powerless to do anything about it'.

There was a lull in the conversation as the men reflected on the state of the world in general and their town in particular.

Eventually Fergy spoke 'Are you thinking what I'm thinking?'

'It all depends what you are thinking' replied Barry. 'I'm thinking that perhaps we should have a go at Gerald's suggestion. I know it won't stop violent crime in Huddersfield but we might help a few lads to stay out of trouble'.

'It's going to take a lot of effort on our part. You heard what Gerald said about the attitude of the lads didn't you. I see it a lot when I'm teaching, too many of the lads are not interested, hopeless cases if you like, but some will respond. Amongst all the failures, I've had a few successes, and that can give you a lot of satisfaction - on the odd occasion that it happens'.

Barry finished his coffee and put his cup down 'There's no need to rush into anything is there? My mind's all over the place at the minute so it's definitely not a good time to be making big decisions. Let's sleep on it for a couple of days'.

'That seems like a good idea Barry, if – and I mean if – we think it's a possibility I'd like to ask Terry what he thinks about it and whether he wants to get involved'.

'Why don't we meet up at the weekend, hopefully Terry will be available for a natter then as well. That'll give us some time to mull things over'.

'Good idea – I'll let you know when I've spoken to Terry'.

Fergy's phone started to vibrate as they got into the car. It was Sacha. Barry listened as his friend made arrangements for the in depth interview he had promised to give her. After he finished the call he gave Barry the low down. 'That was Sacha from the Examiner; did I tell you they want to do a bit of a feature on the Fartown United stuff?'

'I don't remember you mentioning it but there was an awful lot going on yesterday'.

'I've arranged to go into the Examiner office on Tuesday at 11 o'clock, why don't you come as well, it could be fun and I could do with some moral support?'

'Why not – shall we meet at the Examiner office about quarter to eleven then?'

Barry dropped his friend off and as he made his way back home he started to think about Gerald's suggestion and what they would need to do to make it happen.

And so, despite all their reservations, the men were drifting towards the possibility of setting up and running a football team for the young lads who lived in or around the estate. Fergy spoke to Terry and outlined their idea and to Fergy's surprise Terry was all for it. Terry also jumped at the chance to join them when they met up with Sacha at the Examiner office. Janice, his wife, wasn't sure it was a good idea but realised it might be good for Terry to have something to focus on besides his business.

EXTRACT FROM BARRY WILKINSON'S DIARY

16th January 2011

More media attention today. There's an article on the BBC website, based on my conversation with the reporter from Look North and I had Channel 4 news waiting outside the house so I did another interview with them. Now I know what these politicians must feel like when they've been caught having an affair and the press won't leave them alone. Fergy had them round last night as well.

Fergy and I went up the hospital to visit Gerald and his son. Both are out of danger – thank goodness. Gerald was having a real rant about the kids these days and how they needed discipline and a sense of purpose. He even suggested that Fergy and I should or- ganise a soccer team for them to get involved in. Sounds crazy but we are actually thinking about it – must be mad.

Spoke to Wilky – he's a bit shaken but he's tough, he'll get over it. He's going back to Jersey in a couple of days to start his treatment so he'll have plenty to keep him occupied.

The reporter from the Examiner wants to do a feature on the old Fartown United, so I'm going to their office on Tuesday with Fergy and Terry to talk about it.

When the three of them met at the Examiner office they chat- ted enthusiastically about how to go about setting up the new team. They were so busy talking that they didn't notice Sacha approaching them with a big smile on her face.

'Have you heard the news gentlemen?' she asked.

'What news would that be Sacha?' enquired Fergy.

'The two thugs, the ones who did the stabbing and shooting have been arrested and charged. Have the police not con- tacted any of you yet? I thought they might want you to iden- tify them?'

'Well it's good news that they have arrested them, and no we haven't been contacted as yet' replied Terry.

'It's nice to see you've all recovered from your experiences and thank you for coming into the office, I've booked a meet- ing room so we won't be disturbed. If you'd like to follow me then gents'.

A welcoming pot of tea and a flask of coffee were waiting for them in the conference room. Once they had helped themselves to refreshments Sacha switched on a small tape recorder and outlined what would happen today and how that would be developed into a feature to be run at some future date. She responded to their concerns about the content of the article by assuring them that they would see the article – in full - before it was published.

During these discussions the possibility of forming a new Fartown United was mentioned and Sacha was intrigued by the possibility, 'That would make a great storyline, when do you think you'll get started?'

'Hold on a sec Sacha' Fergy raised his hands to indicate she was getting ahead of things 'we haven't even agreed to do it yet, it's just an idea at the moment'.

'Ok guys but if, or when, you do decide can you let me know? I'm sure my editor will be interested in backing you in whatever way we can'.

Fergy smiled 'Thanks for that, I'm sure we'll need all the help we can get, I promise you'll be the first to know'.

The three of them shook hands with Sacha and as they made their way out of the building Fergy remarked 'Did you see her eyes light up when we mentioned a new team. She could definitely see the opportunity for another article there but she still managed to make it look like she was thinking of us.'

'She'll go a long way that lass, far too good for a local rag like the Examiner' added Terry. 'Mind you if we do go ahead with a new team a bit of publicity won't do any harm at all. The Examiner is part of the Trinity Mirror group so it could go national.'

'Have you heard anything from Gerald lately Barry?' Fergy asked.

'I had a text from him this morning, he seems to be on the mend, could be home by the weekend'.

'Are you guys in a hurry, have you got time for a coffee' enquired Fergy 'I've scribbled down a few points we need to get sorted before we commit ourselves to going ahead with this err... project'.

'I'm full up with coffee mate' replied Terry 'why don't we just sit here in reception and have a natter'.

Fergy went through some ideas and concerns and Barry added a few more. They decided that they would need to go through these points with Gerald before committing themselves to moving forward. Barry called Gerald on his mobile and they made arrangements to visit him at the hospital that afternoon.

The three men walked into the ward and Barry introduced Terry to Gerald and explained that they were seriously considering his suggestion of starting a new football team for the boys who lived on or near to the estate.

'That's great man, when can we get started?'

'We're not quite at that stage yet Gerald there are a few things we need to' Barry paused in his explanation 'we need to iron out'.

'What sort of things, come on man spit it out?'

Fergy took over 'We've got a list here, but don't worry it's quite short'. He started to read from the list;

- 'Membership of the team must be open to all boys within the age limit, black, white, asian whatever,
- All boys must comply fully with the coach's instructions,
- The team must be selected on merit – no favouritism, parents must respect and abide by the decisions made by the coach,
- Any boy turning up for training or matches with an

> offensive weapon will be banned from the team,
> - All drugs are banned, any player who turns up for training or matches and appears to be under the influence of drugs will be banned from the team,
> - You (he pointed to Gerald) will organise a parents committee who will support the coaching team,
> - The parents committee will take over the running of the team once it has become established,
> - Oh and finally the team must be called Fartown United.'

How does that seem to you?'

'Who will be the coach?' he asked.

Barry took over 'Fergy here will be coach he is a qualified coach and has his FA coaching badges, Terry and myself will help him out. You know my background Gerald but Terry has played rugby at professional level so he knows the sort of discipline that's required to become a professional sportsman.'

'OK man when do we get started?'

'As soon as you get out of hospital and start spreading the word' suggested a smiling Barry.

'I can start spreading the news right now. Michael I want you to call your friends and tell them we are going to have a football team' he shouted across the ward but Michael was too busy listening to his music to hear him.

Gerald picked up an orange from the fruit bowl next to his bed and was about to throw it at Michael but Terry managed to stop him. 'You can tell him later Gerald when you've got his undivided attention, an hour or two isn't going to make any difference in the general scheme of things. We'll be doing our bit to publicise it as well and we thought we might arrange a sort of trial and signing on session to see how much real interest there is'.

'Sounds real good man I can't wait to get started' Gerald's face was glowing with excitement.

A note of caution from Fergy 'There'll be a lot to organise, kit, a ground to play on, which league to join all that boring stuff will have to be sorted. One of the first things we need to do is to get the pitch on the estate cleaned and smartened up so that we can use it for training, and I'd like to get the boys involved in that, but all that can wait until you are back home. Have they told you how much longer you'll be here?'

'Maybe tomorrow or the day after they said and then I have to rest at home until I get the stitches out, Michael will have to stay in a bit longer.'

'OK just text us when you get home' added Fergy 'and we'll come round to see you and make some plans to get the show on the road'

The men shook hands with Gerald and left him with a big grin on his face.

As the three of them piled into Barry's car Terry smiled and said 'Looks like it's a goer then, I've got butterflies in my stomach - I'm not sure whether it's anticipation or fear of what we are taking on'.

'Probably a bit of both for me, it's gunna be a bit of a roller coaster I reckon chaps but you know what they say' chimed Barry.

'Go on then what do they say?' Terry looked quizzically at Barry.

'Fasten your seat belts and enjoy the ride'. They all laughed, three middle aged men getting excited about organising a football team. 'It's almost like going back to being a kid again isn't it lads?'

The men remained silent as Barry negotiated the town centre traffic, eventually the peace was broken by Fergy's phone, he looked at the number and whispered 'It's Sacha', and he put the phone on speaker mode so that they all could hear what she had to say.

'Hi Richard it's Sacha, I've been speaking to my Editor and he's really keen to find out about your plans for the new team, we might even be able to do a bit of sponsorship, you know a kit with our name on it, that sort of thing.'

'Hi Sacha that sounds interesting, we've just left the hospital after speaking to Gerald Wilson and we've agreed to take it to the next stage, sort of test the water and find out how many kids would be interested and then take it from there. We just need to wait until he get's out of hospital and starts spreading the news'.

Terry couldn't resist and broke into the old Frank Sinatra song until Fergy nudged him and put his finger to his lips.

'Have you got the other guys there with you Richard, have you lot been drinking?'

They all laughed and Barry shouted 'Not yet Sacha but I think we might call for a swift pint on the way home if you fancy joining us?'

It was Terry's turn to admonish Barry by giving him a sharp dig in the ribs.

'Sorry guys too busy I'm afraid maybe another time, but thanks for the offer. We're going to run the article in Friday's paper, I've already emailed the draft to you all. Can you check it out this evening and let me know if it's OK. If you like I could include something about you looking to start a team and want young players to come forward if they are interested in playing for you, how about that?'

The three men exchanged glances and all nodded their approval. 'Yes that's a good idea Sacha, we just need to make it clear that it's for 14 – 16 year olds who live in the area' Fergy spoke for the group. 'Will it be on the website as well?'

'Oh yes, definitely guys'.

EXTRACT FROM BARRY WILKINSON'S DIARY

18th January 2011

Had a meeting with the Examiner this morning about the feature they want to do on Fartown United, it's going out on Friday. Fergy let it slip that we are thinking of setting up a new team and Sacha – the reporter – is keen to help. She also told us that the two lads who did the shooting and stabbing have been arrested and charged so that's good news.

Went to see Gerald again to go through some concerns and he was really keen to get started. He thinks he'll be home in a couple more days and promised to start spreading the news. Terry couldn't resist breaking into song! He's just the same as he was when he was younger, enthusiastic and funny in a cheeky kind of way.

Aiden went back to Jersey today, he starts his radiation treatment on Thursday, hope it goes well.

21st January 2011

The article was in the Examiner tonight, it was quite good actually and included a few photos from the reunion as well as mentioning the possibility of forming a new team. It will be interesting to see what sort of response it generates.

The day after the article was published in the Examiner there was a steady flow of enquiries from kids and parents who all wanted more information, particularly when and where the trial session would take place. Sacha spoke to Fergy and it was decided that they would agree a date for the session and that it would take place at the Zone on St Andrews Road where they could book both pitches and where there would be ample car parking as well. Sacha ran another article confirming these details and telling interested people to just turn up on the day

Everything seemed to be happening at once. Martin's video of the shooting and stabbing had gone viral. There was even a feature on News at Ten when the reunion was shown on the short item that they sometimes run at the end of the news; the voice over went:

'When a group of sixty something ex-amateur footballers in Huddersfield decided to have a reunion they got rather more than they bargained for as this video shows. (Cue Martin's video). Now one thing has led to another and the three organisers are setting up a new football team in an attempt to get the action off the street and onto the football pitch. With a little help from their local newspaper the men have been inundated with offers of help and lots of boys – and girls – are queuing up to join the new team. Our reporter recently caught up with one of the organisers, Richard Ferguson, who explained how this all came about'.

A short interview with Fergy followed, in which he gave a summary of the background to the reunion and how the action had unfolded. The interviewer then asked about the response they had received to the idea of a new team to which he replied 'We've been pleasantly surprised really, we've had about 35 kids who are interested, nine year olds up to sixteen and seventeen year olds. Initially we are looking at setting up a team for the older boys and seeing how that goes. We're going to have an initial trial session in the half term holidays and then we plan to run some coaching sessions for the older boys with a view to entering a team into one of the local leagues next season. As regards the younger kids we will do some coaching sessions for them but we don't plan to run a team just yet. We don't want to over extend ourselves initially and the older boys are the ones we really want to work with. We've also had a lot of interest from girls and we might look into the possibility of running a girls team as well at some time in the future.'

'And what about the offers of support Richard?'

'Yes that's something we never expected. To tell the truth we're really knocked out by all the offers we've had and we're in the process of sifting through them all. Some are from private individuals and others are from companies that want to work with us. In fact I'd like to take this opportunity to thank all the people who have made these generous offers and assure them all that we will get back to them.'

The reporter signed off and the news reader added with a smile *'It's good to be able to leave you tonight with a positive story for a change, good night'.*

The three friends were certainly seeing a lot of each other and had already divided up the responsibilities. Fergy in his capacity as head coach was arranging the coaching sessions, Barry was looking into where the team would play and getting them into a league and Terry was dealing with all the sponsorship offers. Gerald had agreed to set up a committee of parents and other volunteers to help out as needed.

EXTRACT FROM BARRY WILKINSON'S DIARY

26th January 2011

We're in the news again – this time it's News at Ten. Just a three minute slot right at the end of the programme, included Martin's video of the shooting and stabbing (which has gone viral) and an interview with Fergy, he's quite the TV star! He hasn't let it go to his (bald) head though, still the solid reliable mate from all those years ago. He says he's had a few interesting e-mails from 'fans' though, including a marriage proposal. Me and Terry are quite jealous, ha ha.

The response to the Examiner article has been really good; lots of people want to know about the trial. We've decided to have it down at The Zone as we don't know how many will turn up and parking would be a problem if we had it on the estate. We've also had a lot of offers for sponsorship and support so it's all looking very positive.

Another unexpected bonus is some of our old mates, the ones who we couldn't trace, have been in contact and want to know when the next reunion will be.

Aiden has had his first week of treatment and he says he's OK, just very tired, three more weeks to go poor bugger.

We've divided up the responsibilities, I'm sorting out a league to play in and a pitch to play on. I think we'll go for the District League, as it is open age and the lads will be able to stick together for as long as they want to. Fergy is organising the training and Terry is looking after all the offers of support. Judging by the initial response I think Terry is going to be busy and might need some help, which is great news really.

Gerald is setting up the parents committee and has a few volunteers who have cleaned up the pitch on the estate and the local lads are already using it a lot more.

The initial trial took place on the first Sunday of the half term holidays, both pitches at the Zone were booked for the event to cope with the level of interest shown.

The trial turned out to be a rather chaotic affair. Barry and Terry had enlisted their wives to get everyone's details when they arrived whilst the men would organise the actual trial. A table was set up where registration took place and the young players were then divided into three age groups; 11 and under, 12 – 14 year olds and the rest. In reality it wasn't really a trial in the true sense as they had agreed beforehand that no-one would be turned away irrespective of playing ability. Terry supervised the young ones, Barry the intermediates and Fergy had the big lads. The four girls who came to the trial were all in the youngest age group. The two younger age groups shared one of the pitches whilst the older boys had a pitch to themselves. At the end of the session Fergy thanked them all for coming and told them when and where the next training session would take place.

EXTRACT FROM BARRY WILKINSON'S DIARY

20th February 2011

We had the trial today – good turnout. We had 12 under elevens, including four girls, 8 in the middle age group and 15 in the older age group. Jane and Sandy did a fantastic job in registering all the kids.

We had them doing a few warm up exercises and then let them play a few games. The two younger age groups shared a pitch playing side to side and the older boys had a full pitch. The skill level varied as you would expect but they seemed to enjoy themselves which was the main purpose. It's a shame we can't run three teams but we need to take it one step at a time and the older boys are our priority. Initially we'll only be able to run training sessions for the older boys until the clocks go forward then we should be able to include the other groups.

Gerald had been given the responsibility of organising the clearing and cleaning up of the pitch on the estate for the first training session which was scheduled for Thursday the 17th of March. Fergy went down to check the pitch the day before the session and he was pleased to see that all the rubbish had been removed and the whole area had been swept clean. He rang Gerald to thank him and Gerald explained that the residents on the estate, as well as some of the older boys, had got together to make sure that the pitch was ready for the training session.

It was a fine spring afternoon when Barry, who had agreed to help out with the coaching, picked Fergy up and they made their way together to the estate. Terry was tied up at work but planned to join them later. Barry parked his car in the entrance to the field and they started to unload the equipment for the coaching session. The two large net bags, containing twelve footballs and a number of miniature cones, which would be used to mark out various challenges during the coaching session, had all been donated by the local professional team, Huddersfield Town.

The two men were excited at the prospect of getting their project up and running but their optimism was soon to be dealt a hammer blow.

Barry was the first to notice that something wasn't quite right with the ten foot high plastic coated net fencing which surrounded the playing area. There was a group of three of four boys standing around by the pitch, one of whom was Michael who had, by now, recovered from his injuries. As soon as he saw the men he ran over to meet them, clearly uptight. 'Those fucking bastards have ruined the pitch!' he shouted.

Barry and Fergy dropped the equipment they were carrying and ran over to inspect the damage. Sure enough the plastic covered netting around the pitch had been cut and pulled down in a number of places and was hanging loosely onto the surface of the pitch. The cross bar on the goal posts at one end had been broken and the words **FARTWON ARE SHITE** had been daubed in brown paint across the playing surface.

Barry and Fergy stared at the mess, speechless.

'It's them fucking arseholes from Deighton what's done it' Michael was furious. 'Me and me mates gunna pay them back for this big time'.

'Not the most intelligent of people by the looks of it' commented Fergy.

'That's a masterpiece of understatement Fergy' Barry was astonished at how calm Fergy was.

'OK – the ignorant bastards can't even spell' replied Fergy 'how's that?'

Barry looked again at the slogan daubed on the pitch and then started to laugh, Fergy joined in whilst Michael was jumping up and down in frustration 'I don't see nothing funny, what's up with you guys?'

Barry explained 'These low lifes can't even spell Fartown right. Ignorant bastards! Don't worry Michael, we can fix all these little problems. It's a setback but we're used to dealing with setbacks aren't we Fergy?'

'Dead right Barry, FartWON United don't let little things get in the way do we?' they both laughed.

'Right, Michael go back to your house and ask your dad for some duct tape or similar' Barry went into organising mode. 'The cross bar on the goal posts can easily be fixed and we can push the fencing back so that it falls on the outside of the playing area; we can fix that later with some electrical ties and the artwork on the playing surface won't stop us playing will it.'

Whilst Barry was organising things Fergy took a few pictures with his phone of the damage to the pitch and surrounding area.

'It's annoying Barry but we can't let it stop us' Fergy looked around as he was speaking to see that there were now five or six young lads who had turned up for coaching. 'I was expecting more than this Barry, I wonder where they all are?'

'You don't think the so called gang war could have anything to do with the poor turnout do you?' asked Barry.

'It's a possibility' Fergy spoke calmly 'the rival gang are almost certainly responsible for the damage to the pitch, maybe they've been twisting a few arms, if you get my meaning'.

'Whatever happens we don't want Michael and his mates going on the warpath and getting into more bother, Gerald says he's on a final warning at school already' Barry thought for a minute. 'It's a pity our Aiden's not here he would have worked out a cunning plan by now'. The two of them burst into laughter.

Michael returned, followed by Gerald, they were carrying a roll of duct tape and a bundle of electrical ties.

'What the fuck is going on guys, somebody's gunna pay for this' Gerald hissed. 'Yesterday this place was perfect now just look at it man, it's not right'.

Barry patted Gerald on the shoulder 'No it's not right Gerald but we'll let the police sort it out. We don't want your lad and his mates going out on a revenge mission and getting themselves into trouble. That's just what these arseholes want and expect us to do. All the damage can be fixed so let's get on with it and then we can start to do some coaching, OK?'

'We can't let a bit of vandalism get in the way of what we are trying to achieve' Fergy backed up Barry's message 'our boys going out for revenge is exactly what they want, well we won't give them the satisfaction will we?' he looked Gerald in the eye.

'I suppose so' Gerald reluctantly replied 'but I am so angry I wanna sort them arseholes out meself man'.

Barry walked over to Michael and the other lads and handed the tape over to them, 'Go and fix the goal posts lads while we make a start on the fence'.

The goal posts were duly patched up and Barry and Gerald started to make some temporary repairs on the netting fence to make it safe. After a few minutes a stranger walked up, introduced himself as the father of one of the young footballers and asked if they needed any help. Over the next ten minutes they were joined by another three helpers, one of whom brought a set of ladders with him. The repairs progressed at a pace and whilst they were being undertaken Fergy got on with the task of setting up for the coaching session.

With the team of volunteers working away at repairing the netting fence Barry pulled Gerald to one side. He pointed to the small group of lads who were passing the ball to each other 'There don't seem to be as many boys as we had expected Gerald. Any idea what's happened to the other lads?'

Gerald scanned the group before calling Michael over 'What's happened to all your mates Michael? I thought they were dead keen. I can't see Danny and Ruben and what about your mate Spikey, what's happened to them?'

'I don't know old man – maybe they'll come later, just chill'.

Gerald was incensed 'Now don't you 'old man' me son, you

get on that phone of yours and find out where they are, they should have been here 20 minutes ago. Go on!'

Michael scratched his head 'OK dad, I'll give them a call and find out what's happened to them'. He took out his mobile phone and wandered off to start contacting his missing mates. Gerald and Barry couldn't hear the conversation but they could tell that something was wrong by the way that Michael was gesticulating with his arm. After a few minutes Michael walked back sheepishly to where Barry and Gerald were working.

'Well what was all that about then Michael?' demanded Gerald.

'I think somebody has been putting pressure on the guys' came the response.

'What do you mean, pressure? What sort of pressure? D'you mean they've been threatened or what?' Gerald's arms were flailing about as he got even more agitated.

'Yeh' Michael hesitated 'sort of. Somebody has been telling them it's not good for them to be part of the white man's game, that they'll be sorry they ever got involved. Y'know that sort of shit man'.

Gerald's agitation was growing into full blown anger 'White man's game! What sort of shit is that, it's a game of football for Christ's sake. What is wrong with you boys? Black men play football don't they, what about Pele the greatest footballer ever – a black man. Just 'cos my friends Barry and Fergy – and Terry – are white doesn't make it a white man's game. And your friends believe that shit?'

'Well it wasn't just that dad, some of the lads have been threatened' there was a hesitation in Michael's voice.

'Look Michael' Gerald spoke with conviction 'I want you to get on your bike and go and knock on all your friends' doors and tell them to get their arses down here. Tell them I will sort out the bastards who've been threatening them.'

'OK dad' he started to jog home to get his bike.

'And make sure you don't come back on your own' added Gerald.

Michael must have done a good job of persuading his mates as the numbers had swollen to a healthy fifteen players ten minutes later and Fergy got the session underway.

Barry went over to thank the volunteers for all their efforts, two of the four had sons who were taking part in the training session but the other two had just come over to help out. 'Have you reported the damage to the police?' asked one of the helpers, a tall white man wearing British Gas overalls who introduced himself as Carl.

'Not yet Carl' replied Barry 'we've been too busy just getting organised for the coaching session but I will be doing, rest assured.'

'Good luck with that' came the reply 'I hope you have more success than we've had. There's been loads of vandalism and quite a few break-ins round here but the coppers never do anything'.

'We're kind of hoping that getting the local lads involved with the soccer team might give them a bit more direction and purpose, something to identify with y'know. It sounds like we've ruffled a few feathers in the rival gang now; apparently a lot of the lads have received threats of violence if they get involved.'

The conversation was interrupted by the raised voice of Fergy who was really putting the boys through some tough physical exercises.

The men turned to see what was happening. 'I think you're doing a great job' one of the other helpers spoke 'I really hope it works out. I saw all the stuff in the Examiner when you had your reunion. You used to live up here didn't you? I bet it wasn't like this then was it?"

'Yeh we, that is Fergy over there myself and our other friend Terry all lived on the estate up until the late sixties. And you're right it wasn't anything like this. The field was overgrown and there was a big gulley running down the middle. We tried to make it into a football pitch, cleared all the rubbish and even cut the grass ourselves. What we would have given to have a facility like this to play on' Barry seemed to drift off into a world of his own for a moment. 'After it all kicked off at the reunion we decided to try and do our bit to help change things around here. Anyway gents thanks for the help it really is appreciated'. He shook hands with all the helpers.

The two men with lads in the football practice wandered over to watch the action on the pitch and the other two made their way home. Barry decided to make the call to the Police and moved away from the noise of the training towards where his Aunty Agnes had lived and was concentrating on dialling the number when he heard the faint sound of a ladies voice. He looked up to see an old lady stood by the fence next to the field, she was waving to him. Could that be Mrs Oldham, the lady whose window he had broken all those years ago? Judging by the garden she was standing in it might well be. He walked over to the fence.

'D'you know I thought it was you Barry, I've seen you a few times when you've been down here with your friends'.

'How lovely to see you Mrs Oldham, and how are you keeping? I hope you're not going to ask me to cut the grass' Barry joked.

'Oh no' she replied with a twinkle in her eye 'sure my grandson comes and does that now. He has one of them stringer things you know. I just wanted to tell you that I was looking out of my bedroom window last night about 10 o'clock when I heard some noises coming from the field. It was a clear night and there was a full moon, I could just make out somebody out there messing about with the football pitch.'

'Did you recognise any of them Mrs Oldham?'

'No it was too dark for that, they were all wearing them hoody things but one of them had a skeleton on the back of his hoody, and it must have been luminated because it fair stood out in the dark.'

'D'you mean it was luminous, like it reflected the light Mrs Oldham?'

'Sure that's what I said didn't I'.

'You did indeed' Barry smiled 'I was just checking that I understood what you meant. Was there anything else you remember?'

'Well I always have the windows open, y'know I like the fresh air, so I could hear a lot of shouting, that's what drew my attention to them in the first place and I'm sure I heard one of them call out the name Samson, you know like in the bible.'

'Well thank you Mrs Oldham, I'm just going to call the police and I'll make sure that the police get that information, and it's lovely to see you looking so well after all these years.'

'I'm 86 you know and I've still got all my facilities' she laughed. 'Next time you come to the field make sure you visit me and I'll make you a lovely cup of tea. My Eric will be pleased to see you as well, we don't get too many visitors these days. And no more of that Mrs Oldham stuff, I'm Mary to my friends'.

Barry smiled 'I certainly will Mary. Now you look after yourself' Barry leaned over the fence and gave her a kiss on the cheek.

Barry finally made the call to the police to report the damage to the facilities. A very helpful, young sounding, WPC took all the details down but explained that it was unlikely that they could do anything about finding the guilty parties. Barry gave her the information from Mary and she promised to check with the local bobby to see if it meant anything to him.

The coaching session was nearly over when Terry eventually joined them. Barry shook hands with his good friend 'What's happened here Barry?' Terry pointed to the damaged fencing.

'You've missed all the fun Terry' Barry replied and then went on to explain what had been happening.

Terry listened intently as Barry went through the sequence of events including the unexpected help from the local volunteers. Terry shook his head and ran his hand through his still curly mop of hair before responding 'Well we knew it wouldn't be plain sailing when we agreed to give it a go didn't we? Still, we can't let these things put us off. But it must have been upsetting seeing the mess after all the efforts some of the locals made to clean the place up'.

'Aye Terry, Gerald was absolutely fuming, but you never know some good might come out of a bad thing, wouldn't be the first time would it. Come on let's go and see how Fergy is getting on with the lads'. They walked over to the football pitch where Fergy was refereeing a five a side game. The lads were really getting stuck in and Fergy had to step in a couple of times to calm things down as two of the lads were about to start fighting. 'That's what I like to see' said Barry 'a bit of passion, we've just got to show these lads how to channel their aggression for the benefit of the team'.

Fergy had divided the session into three parts. In the first part he had them doing a series of physical challenges to work on their fitness, the second part was dedicated to skills development and finally he split them into three teams of five and they had a series of matches. The match that Barry and Terry watched was the last of these matches.

Michael and a couple of his mates were sweating heavily as they approached Fergy at the end of the session and thanked him.

'Did you enjoy the session lads?' Fergy asked them as he picked up his towel and dried the sweat from his face and neck.

'The skills and five a side games were good but we didn't like the physical fitness stuff' laughed Michael.

'Well you're going to have to get used to it lads, you can't win games if you're not fit, and we want to win games don't we?'

The lads all nodded and wandered off to join the rest of their mates.

Barry told Gerald what Mrs Oldham had seen and heard so they walked over to where Michael and the other lads were standing. Gerald asked them if they recognised anyone from the description of the hoody with the luminous skeleton on the back and the name. They all shook their heads.

The three friends decided to retire to the pub for a well earned drink, Barry invited Gerald to join them but he declined the offer, explaining that there were 'important things' he had to do.

As the three old friends sat in the Stag enjoying their first pint Fergy remarked 'Well it's been quite a busy couple of months lads since the original reunion. We really have started something haven't we?'

'Aye we've come a hell of a long way in a short time, when you think about it' commented Terry as he wiped the froth from his top lip.

Barry was about to add his four pennerth when they heard someone say 'Can I have a word with you gents?'

They turned around to see Carl, one of the men who had helped with repairing the damage to the fence. He had changed out of his overalls and had had a shave but Barry recognised him immediately. Barry replied 'Certainly pull up a chair Carl, can I get you a drink, you've earned it'. He turned to the other two and explained that Carl had helped them with the repairs.

Carl said that he already had a pint in the other room where his friends were sitting. He started 'It's about the football team actually. I just want to say that I think you guys are doing a great job and I hope you're successful'.

'Thanks Carl' replied Fergy 'that's really good of you. Now what can we do for you?'

'Well' Carl hesitated, 'it's just my nephew was asking me about err, sort of' his voice tailed off and he fiddled nervously with his coat sleeve as the three friends gave him their undivided attention. He took a deep breath and went for it 'It's just he's a white kid and I noticed that most, nearly all, of the lads who were there today were black, apart from the two Asian brothers that is'.

Barry looked at Fergy and gave him a slight nod. Fergy leaned forward and said 'I take your point Carl, but when we' he pointed to Terry and Barry, 'agreed to give the football team a try it was on the understanding that it would be open to anyone irrespective of colour or religion. We'd very much like your nephew to come down and give it a try; who knows there's probably a few more white lads wanting to join but with the same concerns as you have.'

'Right' Carl stood up 'I'll bring him down to the next session. Thanks for that, I just err y'know, didn't want him to feel out of place.' He started to walk away and then turned back to face the men 'Oh and if you need any more help with the pitch or anything just give me a shout, I live at number 26 and I'm happy to help out in any way possible.'

'Thanks for that Carl' Barry replied 'and thanks for your help today'. Carl nodded and smiled as he made his way over to sit with his friends in the other room.

No sooner had Carl left them than Gerald walked into the pub and approached them. 'Hi Gerald' Barry greeted him 'can I get you a drink?' as Barry got up to go to the bar he added 'I thought you said you had some urgent business to attend to?'

'Yeh man I did' Gerald was obviously on edge. 'That's what I wanted to talk to you guys about. Skip the drink Barry and sit down, I need to get this off my chest man'.

'OK Gerald' Barry said as he sat down again, 'you've got our undivided attention.'

'Well it's like this man' Gerald looked around the room and then leaned forward and indicated to the others to copy him. He carried on speaking in a low secretive tone. 'I think I know who your old lady heard and saw the other night'. His eyes flashed around the room again, as if to check that no-one else was listening. 'I had a feeling I had seen this guy with the luminous hoody, so I had a word with me boy and he knew this guy too. He doesn't know his name but he's seen him around'.

'But we asked Michael and his mates if they knew who it was and they said they didn't, you were there Gerald.' Barry was struggling to reconcile what Gerald was saying.

'Yeh they did' replied Gerald 'but I didn't believe 'em. I know me boy and I could tell he was lying'.

'Come on Gerald, why would the lads lie like that?' Fergy was now scratching his head.

'Man you gotta understand these boys, they think they are big men so they were gunna sort things out themselves. I could see by the look in Michael's eyes what he was up to.'

Fergy spoke firmly 'That would be the absolute worst thing they could do. We can't allow that to happen.'

'Yeh, I agree man' Gerald nodded 'but how do we stop 'em?'

'We start by telling the police who these guys are. And we need to find a way of stopping them doing it again.' Terry finally joined the conversation.

'OK Terry' responded Barry 'but that's easier said than done, how do we stop them creeping in at night and doing the same – or worse – again?'

'Well, as our good friend Wilky would say *I have a plan.*' He mimicked the way Wilky would lift his right index finger as he spoke.

'Come on – we're all ears' Barry smiled at the reference to his absent brother.

Before Terry could start to explain his plan Fergy interrupted the conversation and turned to Gerald 'Whatever happens you've got to make sure that Michael and his mates don't take the law into their own hands, understood?'

'But what am I supposed to do, lock 'em up? They don't take no notice of me man?'

'Let's hear what Terry has to say first then we'll think about how we handle Michael and his mates' suggested Barry.

'Well' Terry paused as he gathered his thoughts together after the interruption 'you know all those offers of support we got after the Examiner ran the feature on us?'

'Yeh, OK go on' Barry urged him.

'One of the companies that offered to help was a local security firm, they do alarm's and security lighting that sort of stuff. I've already had a look at their web site and it says they do lighting. I was thinking about floodlighting, y'know for training in the winter months.'

Get on with it Terry' Barry was growing frustrated as Terry seemed to be dragging it out, just like his brother used to 'we haven't got all night'.

'Calm down Barry' Terry replied, knowing full well that it would have the opposite effect on Barry. 'Maybe we could get this firm to set up a security lighting system which would be triggered by movement and maybe even attach it to a security camera'.

'That's a great idea Terry' Fergy's eyes lit up. 'So the bastards sneak in when it's dark but before they can cause any damage - on comes the light and snap goes the camera, I love it!'

'Aye Terry that was worth the wait, but I thought for a minute there I was listening to one of our Aiden's bullshit ideas'. Barry smiled and took another mouthful of beer. 'Can you get on to them first thing tomorrow?'

'Yeh, will do. I'll let you know what they say.'

Fergy took over, 'For this idea to have any chance of working we need the element of surprise, so let's keep it between ourselves for the time being, agreed?' They all nodded. He turned his attention to Gerald 'Now Gerald you need to explain to Michael and his mates that we have a plan which will stop the bastards from doing any more damage and may well catch them red handed into the bargain. Don't tell him what the plan is but make sure he knows that him and his mates could ruin everything if they try to take the law into their own hands. OK?'

Gerald smiled as he picked at his scrawny goatee and then started to laugh 'I like it boys, I really like it. Man you guys are so clever, when do we get started?'

'Like I said Gerald, I'll get onto them first thing tomorrow' Terry reassured him.

'OK guys, I gotta go, but let me know when' Gerald looked around him once more and put his left hand to the right hand side of his mouth and whispered 'the plan is in place'. And with that he walked out of the pub with his usual exaggerated swagger.

'D'you think Michael and his mates will stay out of trouble?' Barry asked the other two.

'It's anybody's guess' replied Fergy 'but I certainly hope so.' He finished his pint 'I don't know about you two but I'm knackered and sweaty so I'm off home for a shower. Let me know how you get on with the lighting company Terry, and I'll see you two next week.'

And with that Terry raised his pint and proposed a toast to Fartown United - the 2011 version.

A final word from Terry 'You know lads there's just one more thing I would like to come out of all this'.

'Go on Terry shock us' Barry goaded him.

'D'you think we could make the team shirts…'

He didn't get chance to finish as Fergy and Barry joined in 'Red shirts with a white diagonal stripe', and the three old friends roared with laughter.

EXTRACT FROM BARRY WILKINSON'S DIARY

17th March 2011

St Patrick's day but it didn't bring us any luck.

The pitch on the estate had been badly damaged overnight. Fergy had checked it the day before and it was perfect. It was a setback but we still managed to get a good training session in. Fergy really put the lads through it, I don't think many of them had done anything quite so demanding before.

Old Mrs Oldham called me over and told me she had seen some lads messing about the night before and heard the name Samson shouted. I reported it to the police but I doubt they will do anything.

Not many lads turned up at first but Gerald sent Michael off to find out why they weren't there. A number of them had been threatened.

Terry has come up with a plan for some security lighting and has a potential sponsor lined up who might do it for us, he's checking him out tomorrow. The cheeky little sod was trying to wind me up a bit by mimicking our Aiden, and it worked.

CHAPTER 25 – THE MATCH

Summer 1959

Terry could hardly sleep the night before the big game. He kept seeing himself with the ball at his feet, closing in on the goalkeeper before slipping the ball under the keepers diving body and turning to be mobbed by his team mates after scoring the winning goal in the last minute of the match.

He was up early and started putting the dubbin on his football boots. By the time his mother came downstairs she would find him in the back garden running up and down in his sparkling boots muttering something to himself. 'Na then Terry what d'you think you're gunna achieve doing that, you'll just tire your sen□*□ out. And what are you chuntering about? Anyway have you had your breakfast yet?'

'No I haven't had owt mam, I can't eat owt I'm too excited' came the reply, 'it's the first time we've ever had a proper match and I can't wait'.

'Na then Terry sit down and have some rice crispies, yer favourites. Your gunna burn your sen out at this rate. What time are you meeting your mates?'

'Nine o'clock mam, kick-offs at half ten'.

'Have you got all your kit sorted?'

'Aye it's here in me bag, I'll just tie me boot laces together and sling 'em round me neck and then I'm done'.

'Well stop fidgeting for a minute and have some breakfast, you'll be needing all the energy you can get'.

Terry settled down to eat his breakfast of snap crackle and pop and at five to nine he set out. Young Patrick Connor was waiting at the gate opposite Terry's house and they made their way together to Martin Kelly's house further up the street.

Martin was waiting for them at the door with his kit already packed, next came the Wilkinson brothers who were standing at their garden gate waiting for them. The rest of the team were already assembled at the circle, each one holding a bag of some description.

Fergy counted them in 'I've got nine here, but that includes Pat Connor so who's missing?'

'Need you ask?' responded Wilky 'it's that lazy bastard Taylor again'.

'Hang on lads' came the shout from down the street as none other than Val Taylor was sprinting up the road kit bag in hand.

'Late again Taylor' Wilky made no attempt at concealing his irritation.

'Only five minutes guys, that's not bad is it?'

'It's bloody good for you Taylor' responded Wilky 'lets get off lads we've got a fair distance to walk'.

'Does anyone know where this place is?' Terry whispered.

'Wilky seems to think he does' Martin replied and then put his hand to cover his mouth as he whispered to Terry 'but it wouldn't be the first time he's got it wrong would it?'

The boys had all got permission from their mams and dads to go to the game on the understanding that they all stuck together and Wilky, who was the eldest, was in charge. They made their way carefully across the busy Bradford Road and along Wasp Nest Road to Blacker Road, when they reached the

Spinks Nest pub they turned up Birkby Lodge Road and then made their way up a back lane which ran alongside a small stream.

'Are you sure you know the way Wilky' Barry asked his brother.

'When have I ever let you down Baz, don't you trust me?'

No-one replied but there were lots of glances between the boys as none of them knew where they were and Wilky's track record was decidedly dodgy. However, on this occasion, their older friend didn't fail them and eventually they met up with their two team mates from Cowcliffe who confirmed that the pitch was just another hundred yards away.

The boys from Birkby were already there happily passing the ball around; somehow they looked bigger than the Fartown lads even though they were roughly the same age. It could have been their smart green shirts with yellow sleeves and black shorts with matching green and yellow hooped socks; such a stark contrast to the lads from Fartown with their various forms of white shirts and a mixture of black and dark blue shorts along with a variety of different coloured socks.

Fergy turned to Wilky 'I thought you said they played in red shirts Wilky?

Wilky rarely admitted making a mistake but this time he had to admit that he had got it wrong. 'Just as well they don't clash with our white shirts' observed Fergy.

The Birkby boys' preparation for the match was being supervised by a bald headed man in a faded navy blue tracksuit that had lost a lot of its colour from the many washes it had undergone. When he saw the Fartown boys arrive he made his way over to them. Morning boys I'm Mr Blackburn, I'm a teacher at Birkby Junior school and I run the football team.' He looked around 'Is there an adult with you?'

'We don't have an adult sir' replied Wilky 'we run our own

team'.

'Well good for you boys' Mr Blackburn had a surprised look on his face. 'We're going to kick off in five minutes and we'll play 30 minutes each way, is that OK with you?'

'Yeh that's OK' agreed Wilky, 'we just need to get us boots on and then we'll need a few minutes to get warmed up'.

The referee was a young man of about sixteen years old who wore a dark tracksuit top and black shorts and he was casually tossing a leather football from hand to hand. He blew his whistle to call the captains together to the centre spot and Wilky and his Birkby counterpart shook hands. The home team captain tossed the coin and Wilky called correctly and chose to play up the slight slope in the first half.

The game itself was an anticlimax for the boys from Fartown, skills wise they seemed equal to the Birkby lads but somehow they lacked the cohesion and teamwork of their opponents. The leather football didn't help either as the Fartown boys found it a bit heavier than their usual plastic one. They held out for the first ten minutes but after the first goal went in the Birkby boys scored at regular intervals and by half time Barry had picked the ball out of the net five times.

Fergy called the team together at half time 'We're getting well beaten here lads we need to tighten up the defence a bit. After a group chat the Fartown boys decided to make a few tactical changes and these led to a much better performance in the second half. The main change involved Sutty swapping roles with Barry and going in goals. The new goalkeeper was outstanding pulling off a number of good saves and Barry's tackling and passing helped to tighten up the defence. They still lost the second half but only by a slender margin of three goals to two. The Fartown goals were scored by Fergy and Terry, who fulfilled his dream of scoring, although it was not the match winner he had hoped it would be.

After the game Mr Blackburn came over to the defeated team

'Well done boys, you put up a good show there. Do you have a pitch of your own? Perhaps we could arrange to play you again at your place.

'Oh, we don't have a proper pitch sir' Fergy replied 'just the back field on the estate and we sometimes play on the Tranny down by the canal'.

'Well keep practicing boys and well done'.

Those words of encouragement lifted the boys spirits and despite losing by eight goals to two the Fartown boys were not too downhearted. As they changed out of their boots into their normal shoes for the long walk home, Terry, who was overjoyed at scoring a goal, entertained the other lads with his account of how he scored the goal of the match by beating three defenders to get to the ball before sending the keeper the wrong way. Martin, as ever, brought him down to earth by pointing out that he was actually all on his own when the ball came to him and the goalkeeper had tripped up over his boot laces. As they made their way through Birkby and back towards the estate they exchanged highlights of the game and tried to work out how their opponents were able to score so many goals against them. They took great heart from their second half performance and on the way back to the estate they were already planning their strategy for the next game and the positions they would all play in. One thing they did decide was the purchase of a leather football was essential to their development, and they had a good idea how they would raise the money to make this happen.

There wasn't a hero's welcome awaiting them when they eventually made it back to the estate, tired and weary, but Fergy's mum and his sister Carol were waiting to greet them with a tray full of homemade buns complete with pink icing, each topped with a cherry along with lashings of corporation pop. As they downed their celebration cakes Fergy turned to the Wilkinson brothers and whispered 'We need to sort out the defence before the next match if we are going to have any chance of winning', and the Wilkinson brothers nodded in agreement.

'But who are we going to play in the next match' asked Barry.

Fergy tapped his nose with his right index finger conspiratorially and whispered 'My Dad's got irons in the fire!'

'I thought you said your dad was an engineer not a blacksmith' commented Wilky.

'It's just a turn of phrase Aiden' chuckled Barry, 'it means he's making plans for another game for us'.

'You got it Barry, but listen' he leaned forward and whispered 'Don't tell the others yet – you know what Terry's like for getting carried away'.

The Wilkinson brothers nodded and then realised there was only one bun left, which Wilky quickly grabbed.

CHAPTER 26 – EVERYONE WANTS TO HELP

March 2011

Terry was true to his word and got in touch with the boss of the local security firm who had offered to support their little project. The aptly named owner, Derek Lighthouse, was quite excited when Terry introduced himself over the phone.

'I can't say how much I admire what you and yer friends are trying to achieve up on the estate' began Mr Lighthouse 'I lived up there when I were a young lad for a couple of years and I know what a tough environment it is to grow up in'.

'How old were you when you lived there Mr Lighthouse' asked Terry.

'No need for formalities Terry, everybody calls me Dekker, y'know as in Desmond the reggae singer' he laughed at his own little joke. 'Me and me mother moved up there when I was eleven, after me dad had run off wi' another woman, the bastard. Stayed until just after me fourteenth birthday when me mother remarried and we moved up to Birchencliffe. Now then what can I do for you fellas?'

'It's a bit complicated actually' Terry hesitated slightly 'might be better if I could meet you and explain the situation.'

'When would you like to come over then, I'll be free after 3.00 today, if that's any good to yer?'

Terry had a quick look at his diary, he had a couple of things scheduled for the afternoon but they could be moved, so he accepted Derek Lighthouse's offer and made arrangements to meet him at 3.15.

To Terry's surprise Lighthouse Security Ltd, whose slightly cheesy motto was '*Shining a light on your security*', were based in a modern facility on a small industrial estate off Leeds Road. There were a few vans with the company name and motto on the side and an impressive jet black Porsche Cayenne in the parking area at the front of the building. As he walked into the small but brightly lit reception area he was greeted by a smartly dressed young blonde woman. Before he had time to speak she welcomed him 'Hi, you must be Terry, Dekker told me to expect you. He's in the stores at the moment so I'll show you into his office where you can wait. He won't be long. Can I get you something to drink Terry?'

Terry, who was slightly taken aback by the warm welcome sat down and mumbled 'Err yes coffee, white no sugar please'.

He didn't have to wait long, as the burly figure of Derek Lighthouse strode into the office a couple of minutes later. Terry stood up and they shook hands. 'Now then Terry lad what can Lighthouse Security do to help your little project? I've been following your progress with great interest in the Examiner.'

'First of all' Terry began 'thanks for making the time to see me at such short notice. I must say it's a very impressive set up you have here Mr' Derek Lighthouse raised an eyebrow, 'err sorry Dekker.'

'Aye we moved in here when the units were first built, we were the first to move in and we got a cracking deal off the landlord. Best thing we ever did; business is doing very nicely as well. Now I'm pretty sure you haven't come here to buy a burglar alarm, so what is it you want from us?'

Terry explained about the damage that had been done and how they wanted to prevent it occurring again. Derek Lighthouse listened intently as Terry outlined his idea of installing security lighting for the football pitch and he also explained how worried they were that the young lads in the team might take the law into their own hands and the disastrous effect that would have on the project.

When Terry had finished Derek Lighthouse put his finger tips together and leaned forward with his elbows on the desk. 'A few questions Terry'.

'Fire away Dekker.'

'Is there any power on site that we could hook up to?'

'Fraid not, no.'

'I expected that would be the case, but it's not a problem, we'll just have to use a solar panel, with a battery for backup. When would you need this doing?'

'Sooner the better'.

'Aye I thought you'd say that as well. Just remind me; can we get a van and trailer close up to the pitch?'

'I think there are some bollards at the entrance, but they're the movable type so I'm sure we could get the Council to take 'em down for a couple of days.'

Derek rubbed his chin and then shouted 'Siobhan can you bring me next week's schedule please?'

Two minutes later his secretary, Siobhan, appeared with a document which contained about ten pages of A4 stapled together. Derek rifled through the pages. He looked up and saw that Siobhan was waiting patiently, 'Sorry Siobhan, that's OK' and she made her way back to her desk. He appeared to be weighing up the options but eventually he smiled at Terry and said 'I think we can squeeze you in next week Terry, the work should be finished, all being well, by Friday. I'll come down tomorrow with my foreman and we'll suss it out proper like, can you or one of your pals in this 'ere project be there' he paused for a moment 'err lets see tomorrow's Saturday, Charlie – my foreman will be in the office so let's say eleven o'clock?'

'That's great Dekker, oh and one last thing. We don't want anybody to know too much about what we're doing so if anybody asks your guys what's going on can you make something up, we don't want word to get back to the arseholes who did all the damage. Element of surprise, if you see what I mean.'

'No problem Terry, I get your drift. Right then we'll see you tomorrow at eleven on the estate.'

'I might not be able to make it myself tomorrow Dekker, but I'll make sure one of my friends will be there to meet you if that's OK with you?' Terry thanked him and they shook hands before Terry made his way out of the office.

Terry was in a daze, the whole process had taken less than ten minutes. He smiled at Siobhan 'A bit of a whirlwind your boss isn't he?'

'Oh he doesn't mess about; if he wants something he just goes ahead and does it. He can be a bit challenging at times but he's got a heart of gold really. Do you still want that cup of coffee, I didn't get chance to bring it in and you look like you could use one.'

'I'd love one actually, milk no sugar please. I could do with a few minutes to gather my thoughts together and make a couple of calls, if that's OK?'

'Of course, sit yourself down over there and I'll have your coffee in a jiffy'.

Terry sat in one of the visitors' chairs and checked his diary. As he suspected he had a number of important customers coming in the following day. He rang Barry to see if he would be available to meet Dekker and his foreman. The phone went on to ansaphone so he left a message asking Barry to call him as soon as possible. Next on the list was Fergy, but he got the same response.

Siobhan came over with his coffee 'Not having a lot of success love?' she asked.

Before Terry could reply his phone rang, it was Barry 'Hi Barry thanks for calling me back'.

'No probs Terry, it sounded urgent, what can I do for you?'

'What are you doing tomorrow morning around eleven-ish?' Terry crossed his fingers and held his breath.

'Nothing much at the moment, I'm at your disposal mate, what did you have in mind?'

'Oh thank god for that' Terry heaved a sigh of relief and then went on to explain the situation to Barry, who listened carefully before responding.

'Sounds like you've done a good job there Terry. So I just turn up at the estate and meet these guys from the security company at eleven o'clock then? Do I need to do any prep, or bring anything with me?'

'No mate, just be there and answer any questions they might have, and give me a call when they've been to let me know how it went'.

'OK Terry I'll be there'.

Terry put his phone down, gave another huge sigh of relief and finished off his coffee before thanking Siobhan and making his way back to his car with a satisfied grin on his face. As he sat in the car he allowed himself a little fist pump of satisfaction.

Later that day Barry received a call from the local policeman for Fartown, who was following up on the report Barry had made. Barry explained that he would be in Fartown the following day so they arranged to meet on the estate at 10.30.

EXTRACT FROM BARRY WILKINSON'S DIARY

18th March 2011

Good news – Terry's contact on the security side is prepared to install some security lighting for us. Terry has asked me to meet him tomorrow at 11 o'clock on the estate.

Had another pleasant surprise - the local policeman has actually got back to me and I've arranged to meet him tomorrow at half ten also on the estate.

Barry was ten minutes early when he arrived at the entrance to the field, so he was pleasantly surprised to see the local policeman, accompanied by what appeared to be a plain clothes officer, there already waiting for him. The policeman approached Barry and introduced himself and his colleague, DC Whitaker. The DC took over the conversation and explained that he had a particular interest in a group of youths from Sheepridge who he believed were responsible for a spate of crimes in the surrounding area. The group were led by a particularly nasty piece of work who went by the name Salomon.

'Now I understand from the report you made Mr Wilkinson that the old lady you spoke to heard the name Samson called out, is that correct'.

'Yes that's right' replied Barry 'she thought she heard the name Samson, as in the bible, but it's quite possible that it was Salamon, they are quite similar I suppose'.

'Can you give me the lady's name and show me where she lives?' the DC asked.

The two policemen and Barry walked into the field and Barry pointed to where Mrs Oldham lived 'Her name is Mrs Oldham and that's her house over there, I think it's number 46. Will you need to interview her, she's in her eighties?'

'Not at this point sir' replied the DC 'I think we can take your word for what she said'. He studied the slightly dilapidated state of the fencing around the football pitch 'I can see you've already done some repairs to the fence, do you think they'll be back?'

'We don't really know officer' Barry replied 'but we're hoping to install some security lighting which might act as a deterrent. I'm seeing the security company in' he looked at his watch 'about half an hour actually'.

'That's a very good idea sir, in the meantime PC Robinson here will be keeping an eye on things for you, but if you hear anything further just call me on this number' and he passed his card to Barry.

As the two policemen walked away Barry made his way down to the football pitch to re-examine the damage to the fencing. The temporary repairs they had made had held up but they certainly didn't improve the overall appearance. Barry was trying to work out what they could do to improve the appearance when he heard a voice behind him 'It's a crying shame if you ask me'.

Barry spun round to see two smartly dressed men wearing turbans. 'Yes I agree' Barry replied 'I'm trying to work out how we can smarten it up'.

Two Sikh men walked up to Barry and shook hands with him 'I am Gurdip Singh and this is my brother Ajay, my boys came along to the coaching session last week and told me about the damage. We'd like to help out if we can, what do you need?'

'We really need to replace the fencing but there's no point using the same materials they'll just get damaged again, we need something more substantial really' replied Barry. 'How did you know I would be here today?'

'We have a shop on Bradford Road' Ajay took up the conversation 'and another one in Birkby and I've spoken to a number of other businessmen in the area and we are all ready to help you out in whatever way we can. PC Robinson told us he was meeting you here today so we thought we would come along and introduce ourselves.

'Thank you gentlemen that's very kind of you. Actually I'm meeting a security company in a few minutes to talk to them about some lighting, why don't you stick around and we can get some ideas from them about the various options for replacing the fencing.'

'OK – but we don't want to get in your way' replied Gurdip 'we'll just sit over there on the bench and you can call us when you're ready to talk about the fencing, we are not in hurry'.

As Barry thanked them he noticed a couple of people walk into the field wearing working trousers and dark fleecy jackets with a bright yellow logo on the chest. As they got closer he could make out the shape of a lighthouse on their jackets'.

The larger one of the two men held out his hand 'Afternoon, Derek Lighthouse at your disposal, I met your friend Terry yesterday, and you are?'

'Barry, err Barry Wilkinson, Terry sends his apologies but he had to see some important customers this morning.'

'This 'ere' Dekker pointed to his colleague 'is Charlie Rowlands, my senior foreman'. Barry and Charlie shook hands. 'Charlie is my technical wizard, there's nothing much he can't do on the security side. Now as I understand it you are thinking of installing some security lighting, am I right?'

'Yes Derek, that's about the top and bottom of it' replied Barry.

'That shouldn't be a problem, heh Charlie. It's pretty much as we expected' he looked at his foreman who simply nodded. 'Oh and it's Dekker, everyone calls me Dekker, Barry' As he surveyed the scene he asked 'They've made a right mess of the fencing haven't they, the bastards. D'you know I'd love to get me hands on these hooligans, I'd make sure they didn't do it again I tell yer.'

'Actually, while you're here, I wanted to talk to you about the fencing,' Barry saw the opportunity. 'I've got some more businessmen who are interested in supporting us. They're sitting over there' he pointed at the two brothers sitting on the bench, 'do you mind if they join us Dekker?'

'No probs, bring em over, the more the merrier' smiled Dekker.

Barry introduced everyone and they had a discussion about the options available for replacing the fencing. When the conversation got round to the cost of the fencing Dekker suggested that Barry went for a walk whilst they got down to some detailed haggling.

Barry took a seat up by the swings and observed from a distance, the conversation was animated and some serious wheeling and dealing seemed to be taking place. Eventually the men all shook hands and Dekker waved Barry to come over.

'Right Barry' Dekker began 'Charlie here will be back with some of the lads on Thursday to install the lighting. There'll be a six metre pole with a floodlight attached and it will be movement triggered, but you will have an override switch so you can switch the light on and off. My lads will make sure the light is directed down onto the pitch and the immediate surrounding area so it doesn't become a nuisance for any of the local houses. These gentlemen here and their associates have very kindly agreed to sponsor the replacement fencing, which will be 2 metres high, curved metal posts, spiked at the top and above it will be another 3 metres of netting to stop the ball flying out. How does that sound. Oh we should be able to do the fencing two weeks on Monday, providing we can get the materials by then.'

Barry's face was beaming 'That's err, that's – I'm absolutely speechless!' there was the slightest hint of a tear in Barry's eyes 'I can't thank you guys enough, it's just, just amazing'. He walked up to the brothers and shook their hands vigorously.

'We are very proud to be part of this project Mr Wilkinson' Gurdip Singh was smiling 'we all are greatly admiring the work that you and your friends are doing for the boys and for the whole area'.

'Yeh that goes for Lighthouse Security too. Now Charlie and

me have got some other people to see so we'll be back on Thursday morning. Oh I almost forgot, don't worry about the bollard at the entrance I've got a contact at the council who'll sort that out for us no problem and I'll make sure he's OK with the new fencing. Cheers now' and off the two of them went.

'Thank you guys' Barry shook hands again with the Singh brothers 'do you mind if we mention you to the Examiner, they've been following our progress for a while now and I know they will be keen to publicise your generosity, maybe even a photo when the work is done?'

Gurdip and Ajay shrugged their shoulders 'We are not in this for the publicity Mr Wilkinson' Ajay pointed out 'we just want to make a contribution to the community'.

'That's OK, whatever you say' Barry looked slightly embarrassed 'if you change your minds let me know, I just think it's nice to see different parts of the community coming together for a project like this'.

The Singh brothers agreed to think about what Barry had said and then made their way out of the field. Barry took out his mobile phone and rang Terry who answered on the first ring, 'How's it gone Barry?' Terry was desperate to hear.

Barry explained what had happened including the arrangements for the replacement fencing. Terry's reaction was similar to Barry's; he was speechless!

'Are you there Terry?' Barry asked after a prolonged silence.

'Oh yeh, just trying to get my head round it all' came the reply from the still stunned Terry.

'I know what you mean, those articles that Sacha ran in the Examiner have certainly paid dividends, everybody wants a piece of the action. There's another little piece of positive news as well.'

'I'm not sure I can take any more Barry I'm in overload already' Terry joked.

'I met with the local Policeman before your mate Dekker came'.

'Bloody hell you have been a busy boy Barry, what did he have to say?'

'Well he brought a detective with him and it seems they might have a bit of a lead on who was responsible for the damage to the pitch. D'you remember I said that Mrs Oldham heard one of them being called Samson?'

'Aye – as in the bible she said didn't she?'

'That's right, well the detective thinks it might be a local gang whose leader is called Salomon. He seems to think that Mrs Oldham may have heard the name Salomon and mistook it for Samson, I suppose they do sound quite similar.'

'You could be right Barry'.

'He – the detective – seems to think they might be back for another shot, especially if we get it all repaired, so we need to tell the lads to listen out for any whispers about another attack.'

'Maybe you should give your mate Gerald a bell' Terry suggested 'get him to brief all the lads to be on the alert'.

'Good idea Terry, I'm just going to give Fergy a ring first, he'll be chuffed as hell; then I'll take a walk up to Gerald's house and let him know what's happening'.

As soon as the call finished Barry rang Fergy and gave him the good news. As expected Fergy was delighted. Barry also explained what the police had said about the possibility of another attack but, before Fergy could reply, Barry's phone buzzed with another call waiting – it was from Gerald.

Barry told Fergy that he had another call coming in from Gerald and arranged to call him back in the evening. 'Hi Gerald I was just about to call at your house.'

'Really man, where are you?'

'I'm at the entrance to the field, are you at home?'

''Fraid not Barry, but I got something important to tell you man, what did you want me for?'

Barry gave Gerald the good news about the lighting and repairs and then he told Gerald what the police had said.

'Hey man that's what I was gunna talk to you about' explained Gerald. 'One of Michael's mates has heard that there's gunna be another attack on Thursday night. Them guys are gunna tear down ALL the fencing man this time, the whole damn lot. But don't worry Barry, me and the guys will be ready for 'em this time, we gunna give 'em a whopping, we'll beat the shit out of them, good and proper'.

'No Gerald' there was a hint of panic in Barry's voice, and he made a stop jesture with his free hand 'whatever you do don't do that, we don't want a gang war breaking out. We've got to do this by the book, just leave it with me. I'm going to call the detective and we'll work out a plan together.' The germ of an idea had flashed into Barry's head 'We might need you and your mates though. Just leave it with me Gerald and I'll get back to you, OK?'

Gerald was far from convinced but, under pressure from Barry, reluctantly agreed to let him try to sort something out with the police.

EXTRACT FROM BARRY WILKINSON'S DIARY

19th March 2011

My faith in humanity has been restored today. Not only are we going to get security lighting but a group of Asian businessmen from Bradford Road have agreed to sponsor some new, more sub-stantial fencing. Terry and Fergy were chuffed – especially Terry.

The lighting will be fitted next Thursday but we'll have to wait a bit longer for the fencing.

Met the local Bobby who brought a DC Whitaker with him. Seems they think the people who did the damage may be led by a rogue called Salomon who they have been keeping tabs on for a while. They think the gang might come back for another pop at the pitch now we've fixed up the fencing.

Later on I got a call from Gerald who told me that one of Michael's mates has heard a whisper that the gang are coming back for another crack on Thursday night so the police were right. I'm worried that Gerald and his mates will try to take the law into their own hands. I've tried to persuade him to leave it to the police but I don't think he was so keen.

I need to get back to DC Whitaker and update him. I have an idea which I need to share with them.

The following day Barry met DC Whitaker at the café on Alder Street. The detective listened intently to Barry's suggestion without interrupting him. When Barry had finished he scratched his chin as he contemplated Barry's proposition.

After a few seconds he responded, 'I like it Mr Wilkinson, I think it could just work. Are you sure about the equipment being in place before Thursday night?'

'The boss of the firm who are fitting it has said it will be done by then. He seemed pretty confident that his lads would be able to get it finished when they arrive on Thursday. I know it's a bit tight but I can't see any other options, apart from standing guard all night. What do you think?'

'OK we'll go with that plan then. I'll need to get a small team together and I'll need somebody to operate the equipment. Can I rely on you for that?'

'Sure, I'll be there and Terry will probably want to come too'.

'Right then, I need you to call me to confirm that the lights are fitted and working and we'll arrange to meet just before it comes dark.' DC Whitaker handed a business card to Barry and they shook hands. As he turned to walk away he hesitated and turned round. 'And I don't want any interference from the locals we don't want them getting under our feet or messing up the operation is that understood? Can I rely on you to keep them out of the way?'

'Yes, sure I'll do my best to make sure they keep out of the way'.

After DC Whitaker had left Barry let out a loud sigh.

'As he been giving you a hard time love?' the young lady who had served their coffee asked.

'Oh no. not really. I've just got a tricky situation to deal with and I'm not sure how I'm going to manage it.' He paused for a moment 'I'm sure I'll work something out though. Can I have another coffee please I've just got a few calls to make if that's OK?'

'No problem love, one coffee coming up and you can stay as long as you like, it's a bit quiet in here this morning'.

First on Barry's list was a call to Derek Lighthouse to brief him on the plan for catching the vandals. Dekker was all for it and offered to fit an infrared camera to the security pole to take some shots of the action. After that he updated Terry and Fergy on the developments.

He was feeling a lot more positive by the time he got up to leave the café.

'Got it all sorted then love?'

'Aye I reckon I have – thanks for the coffee'.

EXTRACT FROM BARRY WILKINSON'S DIARY

21st March 2011

I finally managed to speak to DC Whitaker and told him what Michael's friend had heard about another visit. I went to meet him

Bryn Woodworth

down at the café on Alder Street and he liked our idea for using the security lighting to catch them in the act. He's organising a small team and my job is to keep Gerald, Michael and all their mates as far away from the action as possible. Could be a tall order!

CHAPTER 27 – AFTER THE GOAL RUSH

Summer 1959

As soon as all the buns had been eaten the boys made their weary way back to their respective houses. The walk to and from Clayton Fields on top of 60 minutes of non-stop football had taken its toll.

By the time the Wilkinson brothers arrived home their dad, who normally nipped home at lunch time in the firm's wagon to get his and the lads lunch, had gone back to work. Grumpy grandad greeted them 'Where the 'ell 'ave you two been? Yer dad was worried sick. He's left you a note on't kitchen table; yer'll be in for it tonight that's for sure'. The old man seemed to take great pleasure in the prospect of the boys getting into trouble.

If grandad thought he had put the fear of god into the boys he was mistaken as Aiden confidently responded, 'We've been laking soccer, grandad. We told me mam this morning that we might be late back, she must have forgotten to tell dad' he waved his hand dismissively as he walked past grandad and into the kitchen where he picked up the scruffy piece of paper with the message from his dad on it. He turned to Barry 'He says there's fresh bread in the bin and some potted meat in the meat safe for us dinner, but I'm not hungry after them buns are you, our kid?'

'Not hungry?' Barry was shocked. That's not like you Aiden,

but then you were a bit greedy with them buns. I think you must have had at least five', Barry picked up the breadknife, took the loaf out of the bin and attempted to cut a slice of bread.

'You don't do it like that you useless bugger' Aiden snatched the knife from his younger brother and started to show him how it was done. 'You're bloody hopeless, and, I only had four buns actually! He broke off from cutting the bread and brandished the knife in his brother's direction.

'Steady on Aiden I was only joking' Barry stepped away from the danger area.

Further down the road Terry was receiving a much warmer welcome from his mother. 'Ee lad you look warn out, and look at the muck on your knees why don't I run you a nice hot bath?' Now a 'nice hot bath' was a rare luxury for the boys on this estate. Bath night was usually Sunday – before school on Monday – and most of the boys would be the third in line for the bathwater which was usually tepid by the time Mam, Dad and any older siblings had had their turns.

'But there won't be any hot water mam and I'm not having a cold one' came the reply.

'Aye well I told your dad to lay the fire this morning before he went to work, so I'll light it now and in ten minutes there'll be plenty of hot water for yer bath'. Mabel Ogden walked into the front room and knelt down to light the fire. 'Any road how did the football match go, did you win?'

Terry had a dejected expression as he replied ''Fraid not mam – we lost 8 – 2'. Then his eyes lit up as he added 'I got one of the goals though'.

'Ee yer dad'll be reight pleased that yer scored, now get them mucky clothes off and slip yer dressing gown on while the fire warms up the water for yer bath'.

Back up the road his friend Martin wasn't so lucky. His sister had left him two slices of jam bread and a note telling him she had gone round to one of friends to listen to music. 'At least I don't have to listen to all that rubbish and watch them stupid girls doing their stupid dance' he thought as he settled down on the settee and tucked into his jam bread.

Later on as the lads assembled around the smelly settee in the field the conversation returned to their unsuccessful match.

Fergy started the discussion 'Where do you think we went wrong then?'

'I reckon we struggled with the leather ball' suggested Sutty. 'It was much heavier than the plastic ones we play with wasn't it?'

Everyone agreed. 'But what can we do about it?' asked Martin. 'I bet a leather ball will cost a fortune'.

Wilky added 'Does anybody know where they sell 'em' and how much they cost?'

'Didn't the big lads have one, I'm sure I saw them playing with one a couple of years ago' suggested Terry.

'So what if they did, they're hardly gunna give it to us to lake with are they?' Dave Henshaw joined in.

'Hang on though' Wilky's index finger was raised.

Barry sighed sarcastically 'Not another of your brainwaves Aiden'.

Wilky waited till he had everybody's attention before adding 'They might not give it to us, BUT they might sell it to us and it would be a lot cheaper than buying a new one'.

'He's got a point there' Fergy agreed 'but we don't know who's got the ball do we, who did it actually belong to?'

Terry chipped in 'Tell yer what I'll ask Len Bagshaw tonight when he gets home from work, he lives across the road from us'.

'OK Terry. That's a good idea, we'll wait and see what he says.

What else went wrong this morning then, any more suggestions?' Fergy was determined to hear what everyone had to say about the game.

After a slight pause Barry spoke 'I think we should make Sutty the goaly in future. He did a lot better job than me when he went in goals'.

Sutty seemed to grow a couple of inches as he spoke 'I really enjoyed playing in goals' and after a slight pause he added, by way of an afterthought, 'and I think you did better than me in defence Barry'.

'OK then – is everybody happy if we switch the two love birds around?' Wilky wasn't going to miss an opportunity to respond sarcastically to his brother.

Fergy jumped in before Barry had time to start an argument with his brother. 'Has anybody got any more ideas or suggestions?' The group remained silent so he continued 'Well I've got a few ideas. I've been talking to me dad and he says the professional clubs don't just practice by playing matches. They do lots of special drills.'

Terry looked confused 'I thought a drill was what you use for making holes in stuff'.

'Not that sort of drill Terry. The drill I'm talking about is when you practice something to develop your skill, like err.. shooting practice'.

'How would that work then?'

'OK it's like this Terry. First of all we need a goaly. Sutty go and stand in the goals. Then we have somebody whose job it is to pass the ball in front of the goals about 15 yards out. The rest of us take turns at receiving the pass and shooting at the goals. So Martin you pick up the ball and roll it into the penalty area and I'll run in and shoot. Sutty's job is to stop it so he's getting goalkeeping practice as well. Let's give it a try'.

Martin duly rolled the ball into a space about 15 yards from the goals and Fergy ran in and took a swipe at it with his right foot. Unfortunately for Fergy the ball must have hit a bump on the ground causing it to bobble just at the exact time Fergy swung his boot. He missed the ball completely and overbalanced and fell on the floor. There was a moment of silence as the boys were shocked tat the normally skilful Fergy's air shot. Eventually Terry chirped up 'I thought you said you were going to smack the ball Fergy'. All the other boys started to laugh as Fergy picked himself up and tried to regain his dignity.

He took a deep breath and tried to stay calm as he turned to Terry 'That's what I was trying to do Terry but the ball must have hit a brick and bounced up. Let's just try it again Martin. The process was repeated and this time he connected with the ball which shot past Sutty before he had time to move.' He turned to the rest of the lads took a mock bow and said 'Right whose next?'

Shooting practice continued for a few minutes but the ball kept misbehaving with some interesting results. The uneven bounce resulted in the ball being mishit several times and shooting off in all directions. After a while Fergy called a halt and said 'This isn't working is it lads?'

'I don't think there's anything wrong with the idea Fergy' said Barry 'it's just the ground here is so rough and uneven the ball is bouncing all over the place. Why don't we try it out on the flat surface down at the Tranny?' Everyone agreed that this seemed sensible. 'Have you got any other drills in mind Fergy?'

'As it happens I have a few, like passing practice and trapping the ball. We could even do some dribbling practice, but we could do with more than one ball.'

'What am I going to do when you're all doing your drills?' pleaded Sutty.

'Don't worry Sutty' Fergy smiled as he replied. 'You can join in the passing, dribbling and trapping drills and you'll be kept pretty busy when we do the shooting practice. 'If Terry can get hold of the leather ball which the big lads used to play with we should be able to manage with that and our plastic ball, so do your best tonight Terry. Anyway that's enough of the serious stuff, who's for a game of cricket?'

The wickets were set up and an enjoyable game of cricket took place in which Terry was top scorer and Dave Henshaw, as usual, took the most wickets.

Terry agreed to watch out for Len Bagshaw coming home from work so he could ask him about the old leather ball. The lads agreed to assemble at the swings after tea to plan the next day's activities.

The Wilkinson brothers had an urgent reason for wanting to get home before their mam, they wanted to get to her before grandad told her about their late return. 'Now Baz' Wilky started, 'just let me do the talking you're no good at convincing her, leave it to the professional. Come on let's watch out for her. If we sit on the steps by the gate we won't miss her'.

A few minutes later they could see their mam crossing the circle carrying two large shopping bags. 'Come on Baz let's help her with them bags. It'll get her in a good mood.'

As the two boys each took a shopping bag Mrs Wilkinson became suspicious. 'Alright then, what have you two been up to today, you don't usually run out to meet me and carry me bags?'

'Well mam' Adrian began, 'it's like this. Do you remember that we told you this morning that we were playing a match against Birkby today?'

'Aye, right enough you did, so what?'

'Well when we got back from the match Mrs Ferguson had some homemade buns waiting for us' Aiden continued the tale.

'They were lovely mam, they had icing and a cherry on top our Aiden must have eaten' Barry's speech was interrupted by an elbow in his ribs.

'Never mind that Barry' Aiden gave him a hard stare 'they were OK but they weren't as nice as your buns mam. We had to stop and eat a couple as it would have been rude not to wouldn't it?'

'If I know you our Aiden you will have had more than a couple, any road what's the point of all this'. They had reached the house now and Mrs Wilkinson reached out for the door handle and was about to go in.

'Just a minute mam' Aiden jumped between her and the door, 'the point is by the time we got back to the house me dad had gone back to work and grandad said he was hopping mad and worried about us and we'd be in bother when he comes home tonight'.

'Is that all? Take no notice of your grandad. Your dad came down to the weaving shed when he got back to work and I told him what you had said about being a bit late back from Birkby. It's all sorted. Now clear off and stop mithering me. I need to sort out what we're having for tea'.

The boys didn't need telling twice and ran out into the back garden and had a game of catch.

CHAPTER 28 – THE TRAP IS SET

March 2011

When the foreman and his gang arrived at the field on Thursday morning the council had already been round to the estate and removed the bollard at the entrance to allow the works vans to access the field. By the time Terry arrived the security team had already unloaded their equipment, which included a mini digger. Terry approached the bloke who appeared to be in charge and introduced himself. 'Hi, I'm Terry Ogden, how's it going?'

'Pleased to meet you Terry' replied Charlie, the foreman. 'Is the other fella coming as well?'

'You mean Barry?' Terry asked. 'He's gunna try to get here this afternoon, got a spot of business to sort out this morning I believe, so you'll have to settle for me I'm afraid. Is there anything I can do to help in any way?'

'No not just yet' replied the foreman 'but we might need an extra pair of hands when it comes to assembling the pole, but that won't be for a couple of hours at least'.

'OK I think I'll nip off and get some breakfast down at the café on Alder Street then. What time do you lads take a break, I could bring some bacon butties back with me if you like?' Terry suggested.

'Give us an hour and a half and then three bacon butties would go down a treat thanks'.

'What about tea or coffee?' asked Terry.

'No need Terry, the lads have all brought flasks with them, but thanks anyway'.

Terry checked his watch, it was 8.30 'OK I'll be back about ten then with the butties. Here's my number if you need anything while I'm away.' Terry gave the foreman his business card.

By the time he returned a deep round hole had been dug and the telescopic mast was lying at the side with the light already attached. One of the team was busily wiring up what looked like a camera which was already strapped to the pole.

'Is that a camera you're attaching to the pole' Terry asked Charlie.

'Aye lad it is' the foreman smiled 'and it's a good un too. We should get some decent pictures when it's triggered, my boss Dekker wants to make sure we nail the culprits. Nothing but the best he said to me, no skimping. Wants to get the bastards he does. Are those the bacon butties then Terry?'

'Aye get 'em eaten before they go cold'.

As the workers got stuck into their butties there was plenty of banter about the previous night's football results and the local rugby team's chances of a cup run. Terry managed to overcome his normal impatience and waited until the men had all finished eating their butties before asking them how long it would take to finish the job.

Charlie rubbed his chin and checked his watch before replying 'I reckon we'll have the pole in position and the attachments assembled by lunch time, then we need to let the cement set before we can do the testing. It's rapid setting cement so when we come back from lunch we should be able to get on with the testing. That shouldn't take more than an hour or so, so we should be all done and dusted by mid afternoon all being well.'

When Barry arrived at the estate at half past one the scene

was deserted, although he could see a works van with a trailer attached to it parked next to the field. He was impressed when he saw that the pole on which the security lighting was mounted was already in position. He pulled his phone out of his pocket and called Terry.

Terry replied on the first ring 'Hi mate how's things with you, have you sorted your business stuff then?'

'Aye Terry I have' came the reply 'I'm at the field now where is everybody?'

'Oh we've just been grabbing a bite to eat while the cement sets. We're just about to set off back so we'll be there in about ten minutes.'

'Couldn't bring me a sarny by any chance could you Terry, I'm starving' Barry almost pleaded. 'I came here straight from my meeting; a sausage sandwich would go down a treat'.

'No probs my friend one sausage sandwich coming up'.

As Barry sat on the bench waiting for the lads to return with his lunch, he contemplated the arrangements he had made with DC Whitaker and later on with Gerald for dealing with tonight's expected visitors. DC Whitaker was bringing three uniformed officers with him. Barry had also spoken to Gerald who had insisted that at least eight of his friends would be there as well. But would the police allow them to get involved? There were four entrances to the field altogether, the two entrances at the bottom of the field were narrow ginnels which could easily be blocked but the entrances at the top were much wider and each would need several people to block the way out. And what if the culprits were armed?

Barry was jolted out of his deep thoughts by a shout of 'Grubs up' from a beaming Terry.

'What makes you such a happy chappy today my little friend?' joked Barry as he took his lunch from Terry. 'Cheers Terry, you're a life saver'.

'Oh it's just these guys' Terry pointed to the Lighthouse team 'they're an absolute scream. When you work on your own – like you and me Barry – you don't get the craic and general piss taking that working with your mates gives you, I'm quite jealous really. Mind you when Charlie, he pointed to the fore-man, gives them the hard word they're terrific workers, got to give them their due there. As you can see everything's in place they've just got to do the testing then it's all systems go.'

'Pleased to hear it mate, just in the nick of time. You know we're expecting visitors tonight don't you?'

'Aye and not the welcome kind either. What arrangements have you made with the police then Barry?'

Barry explained what had been organised with DC Whitaker and his team. He also explained what Gerald had said and he had arranged to meet him at seven to sort things out. 'Thing is though Terry the police won't want any civilian involvement, but Gerald and his mates seem determined to get involved. I'm not sure how to convince them to stay in the background. How are you fixed for tonight mate, any chance you could come and help me to keep Gerald and his crew under control?'

'Any chance?' Terry was quite indignant 'Wouldn't miss it for the world, apart from anything else I can't wait to see the look on those shithouses faces when the lights come on'.

Barry was a bit taken aback by Terry's gung ho tone. 'You and I Terry' Barry adopted a serious expression 'will be bystanders when this all kicks off, the police have made that abundantly clear, no heroics and they don't want Gerald and his team any-where near either.'

'OK, OK point taken Barry' Terry raised both hands in mock surrender 'I'll leave my machete at home then.'

Barry gave Terry a black look 'I wish you wouldn't joke about it Terry, it's a serious business. I just hope they don't turn up with THEIR machetes tonight.'

Terry got the message and changed to a more serious tone as he put his arm around Barry's shoulders 'I solemnly promise to do as I am told tonight my friend, what time do you want me here then?'

'Let's say 6.45 then and the rendezvous point is Gerald's back garden, well out of the way of prying eyes.' Barry looked at his watch 'Listen are you OK to stay with your new mates here until the job is finished. I don't think it needs the two of us and I've got some calls to make, if that's OK with you?'

'Yeh no worries Baz. Oh what about Fergy is he joining us tonight?' Terry shouted to Barry as he set off on his way to his car.

'He can't make it, got something on apparently' Barry turned and shouted back and then added under his breath 'Lucky bugger'. For some reason Barry was not feeling half as confident about tonight's events as his friend Terry.

That evening DC Whitaker along with two PC's and a WPC, all dressed in dark coloured clothes, arrived in two unmarked cars and made their way to the back garden of Gerald's house which was the agreed rendezvous point. Terry, Barry and Gerald along with no fewer than ten of Gerald's friends were waiting for them.

'Come in, come in officers' Gerald greeted them as they came around the corner of the end house of the block. 'I never thought I would be welcoming a group of police officers into my garden' he laughed 'but I'm so pleased to see you.'

DC Whitaker was clearly annoyed that so many people were there. He turned to Barry 'I thought I made it clear that this was a police operation and no members of the public were to be involved?'

Barry held his hands up 'It's OK DC Whitaker, I've already explained to these gentlemen that they are not to interfere in the operation and are to keep well out of the way. Most of these guys have sons who are in the soccer team and they are here, primarily to ensure their lads don't get involved'. It was, at least in part, true.

The DC didn't look convinced 'Well whatever your reason for being in the area' he scanned the men's faces and thought he recognised a few, 'anyone carrying weapons is likely to be searched and will be arrested'. A few of Gerald's friends looked rather uncomfortable at this point so DC Whitaker told them to go inside the house and get rid of any weapons before the operation starts. 'I suggest you all stay here until the operation is completed. Mr Wilkinson and Mr Ogden will be accompanying me to assist in the operation of the new lighting system.' There was a good deal of murmuring from the group of men as the police along with Terry and Barry left Gerald's back garden. Rather than go en masse and risk drawing attention to themselves they left the rendezvous point in ones and twos.

DC Whitaker and the WPC, along with Terry and Barry made their way to a shed, in the garden of the house nearest to the security lighting pole, which the police had commandeered. Charlie from Lighthouse Security had set up an infrared camera on the pole and linked it by WIFI to a monitor which was also positioned in the shed along with a remote control for the lighting. The other two PC's, were stationed on the opposite side of the field. The police were unaware that Gerald and his friends were hiding close by the four entrances to the field.

Shortly after darkness fell the sound of car doors closing could be heard along with the sound of approaching voices. The four people in the shed watched intently as the would-be vandals came into the view of the camera. 'That's him' whispered DC Whitaker as he pointed at the screen, 'that's Salomon.'

A number of the men were carrying long handled wire cutters, others were holding what looked like pliers and one person had a small axe. They quickly got stuck in to dismantling the fencing, cutting and ripping it. They seemed to be enjoying their work as they laughed and joked. Eventually DC Whitaker gave the signal and Terry switched on the security lighting. Suddenly the area was flooded with bright light. As the vandals tried to shield their eyes from the glare DC Whitaker, with the aid of a loud haler, announced 'The area is surrounded by police officers, put down your tools and raise your hands above your heads'.

At the same time the two PC's emerged from the other side of the field shining ultra bright torches in the direction of the vandals. Gerald's friends, also carrying torches, waited patiently at the four entrances to the field. The element of surprise coupled with the dazzling brightness caused total confusion amongst the vandals and it was several seconds before they realised what was going on. DC Whitaker had one target in mind and he and the WPC quickly apprehended and hand-cuffed Salomon whilst the two PC's apprehended another two gang members. The rest of the gang managed to avoid capture and ran towards their cars. Several were stopped and held by Gerald and his friends whilst the others jumped into the waiting cars and set off at great pace, totally unaware that the tyres on their cars had all been let down. The cars careered from side to side, one even smashed into a parked vehicle. The getaway cars were quickly abandoned leaving the culprits to make their escape on foot.

DC Whitaker radio'd the police van which had been parked discreetly nearby and the apprehended villains were cautioned and marched out of the field to be loaded into the van and taken away for charging. The crowd of locals who had come to watch the action hurled abuse at the men as they were loaded into the van, and cheered enthusiastically when the police van drove off.

DC Whitaker gathered his team together and complimented them on a job well done. He turned to Gerald and his friends 'I thought I made it clear that you were to keep out of the way'.

Gerald responded for the group 'We did officer but when we saw them arseholes getting away we made a few, what do you call them Barry?

'Citizens arrests?'

'Yeh citizens arrests, that's what we did, so what's the problem officer?'

DC Whitaker was pleased with his night's work. They had arrested Salomon in the middle of a criminal act, three of the people arrested were carrying knives, another two were carrying illegal drugs and that meant they could search their houses. He decided not to make an issue about the unofficial support they had received. 'OK was anyone injured?' he asked.

To which Gerald replied 'Only Delroy here he twisted his ankle when he was trying to catch one of them' he pointed to a rather overweight man who was hobbling away. 'I told you Delroy, you is too old for this kind of action'.

'Quite a few of them got away though didn't they' Terry pointed out.

'Don't worry about that Mr Ogden' the DC replied, 'we got the man we came for and with the camera footage I'm sure we can ID a few more and pull them in. All in all that's what I call a good night's work. Thank you all. I'm afraid they've ruined your fencing though'.

Barry smiled 'Don't worry about that officer they've actually done us a favour, the fencing is all being replaced so we would have had to pull it down anyway' Barry pointed out.

As the group started to disperse Barry heard his name being called by a female voice, he turned to find their old friend Sacha and her photographer smiling at him.

'Looks like another chapter in the Fartown United saga Barry, care to fill me in?'

Barry smiled 'And who better to write it than our favourite reporter. How the hell did you get here so quickly Sacha? Did somebody tip you off?'

'A reporter never discloses her sources, you should know that Barry' came the smug reply.

'OK, I'll see you down at the pub when we've cleaned up here Sacha, give us half an hour'.

'What a night heh Terry?' Barry sighed and put his arm around his friend. Barry was a relieved man.

'Fergy will be sick he missed out on all the fun. But at least we've got it all on camera.' The two of them laughed as they made their way back to the shed where the equipment was. They collected all the equipment which Dekker had lent them and loaded into Terry's car which was parked on the road nearby, then went back to look at the state of the fencing. They agreed that they would come back in the morning to re-move all the damaged fencing in preparation for the training session tomorrow night.

As they lingered by the pitch deep in thought, Barry surveyed the scene 'A bit ironic really, when you think about it'.

'How d'you mean' asked Terry.

'Didn't you notice whose garden the shed we used was in?' Barry asked his friend.

Terry thought for a minute 'Bloody hell it's Claude's isn't it. I hope he was watching. He'll be turning in his grave!' And the two of them burst out laughing.

'I'm sure the irony won't be lost on our Aiden when I tell him' suggested Barry.

'Aye there was no love lost between old Claude and Wilky that's for sure' added Terry.

EXTRACT FROM BARRY WILKINSON'S DIARY

24th March 2011

Another big day in the life of Fartown United today, the 2011 version.

Terry met the Lighthouse security guys who were installing the lighting and camera, by the time I got there most of the work was done.

I was really worried about involving Gerald and his mates in the plan so I persuaded Terry to help me manage them tonight. Actually he didn't take much persuading, he was a bit gung ho as it happened. He never changes, just like when we were kids.

The trap worked perfectly and the police got their man and a few others, it was really exciting. Terry and I watched all the action from inside a shed in Claude's old garden on the TV monitor, brilliant! Pity Fergy couldn't make it but we've got it all on video.

We managed to keep Gerald and his mates in the background until the ringleader and a few of the other gang members were apprehended. They actually did a good job by arresting more of the culprits. The DC was a bit annoyed but overall he was very pleased with the night's work so he didn't make a big deal of it.

No sooner had we got all the criminals loaded into the police van and Sacha turns up – another scoop for the Examiner. I don't know how she does it, but somebody must have tipped her off. I dare say that there will be another article in the Examiner.

CHAPTER 29 – TERRY
STRIKES LEATHER

Summer 1959

Most of the boys were sat on the swing when Terry came around the corner into the entrance to the field. He was carrying an odd shaped object in a dull grey colour. He was smiling. 'Look what I've got lads'.

'Worrisit?' Sutty enquired.

'What does it look like? It's a leather football, numbskull!'

'Why isn't it round like a normal ball then?' this time Barry was the questioner.

'Ah that's because the blather inside it is flat. Didn't you lot know that all leather balls have a blather inside 'em?'

Fergy couldn't stop giggling as Terry explained the workings of a leather ball.

'What's so funny Fergy?' demanded the indignant ball carrier.

'Nothing Terry' more giggling 'it's just' the more he tried to be serious the more he laughed. They say laughter is infectious and Fergy's hysterics had certainly spread to the other boys who by this time were all laughing although they weren't sure what they were laughing at.

Eventually Fergy composed himself and, as he put his arm around Terry and gave him a good natured squeeze, he explained. 'The inside of a leather ball is called a bladder, not a blather. I just love the way you get your words mixed up. You've done a great job there Terry, let me have a look at it.'

As Fergy examined the damaged ball Terry explained how he had obtained it. 'Well I saw Len Bagshaw coming home from work and I asked him what had happened to the ball. Now he wasn't sure but he thought Bob Knight might have it, so I went round to his house and knocked on the door'. The lads listened intently, all except Fergy who was still fiddling with the ball.

'Carry on Terry' the lads urged 'what happened next?'

'Well his mam opened the door and I asked her if Bob was in. but she says he's been called up to the Army, he stationed down Alder Street.'

Fergy broke off from his ball examining, smiled at Terry, and said 'Aldershot, Terry'.

'What d'you mean Fergy?' Terry was confused.

'The army have a base at Aldershot, it's somewhere near London I think, my cousin is down there as well'.

'I thought it was strange cos I'd never seen any army people down on Alder Street. OK, anyway I said did he take his leather football with him, and she says he wasn't allowed. I asked her if we could borrow it while he was away in err … Alder .. that place Fergy mentioned.'

'Aldershot' Fergy reminded him.

'Yeh that's the place she said'.

'Oh well done Terry' Barry patted him on the back' So do we have to give it him back when he comes home?'

'No she said it was no use to him now and then she went inside and came out with it, just like that. It was flat so she says if it's any use to us we can have it'.

'That's brilliant, can we fix it Fergy?' Barry looked hopefully towards his friend.

'I'm not sure, I think we have to undo the lace and pull the bladder out'. The lads gathered round while he removed the leather lace and opened up the leather case to pull out the rubber bladder.

'Give it here' Wilky insisted 'it's like the inner tube of a bicycle tyre'. He put the neck of the bladder to his mouth and blew into it. It started to fill, a few puffs later it was beginning to take on a spherical shape. Aiden held it to his ear. 'I thought so' he said 'it's got a puncture you can hear the air hissing as it escapes'.

Terry was getting excited, 'Can we repair it though, that's the question?'

'Yeh I think we can Terry' Wilky replied. 'I've watched our Les when he repairs the tyres for his bike. If I can find his puncture repair kit we should be able to fix it. I tell you what you lads wait here while me and Baz nip home and I'll ask me dad where he keeps the repair kit, I'm sure he'll know where to find it'.

As they made their way back to their house Terry shouted 'How long will it take Wilky?'

'Dunno, we'll be as quick as we can' and off they went.

The Wilkinsons seemed to be gone for hours and eventually the patience of the other lads ran out and they all trouped over to the Wilkinsons place to find out what was going on. Barry met them at the front door 'You've come just at the right time, I think our Aiden's fixed it. Just go round to the back door and you can watch him.

As they reached the back door Wilky had a triumphant look on his face as he was pumping up the repaired bladder using a bicycle pump. 'Whad'ya think lads, it looks OK now doesn't it?'

'How d'you know it won't go down again?' asked Terry.

'That's a very good question young Terry. Now we have pumped the bladder up a bit we'll put it in a bucket of water. If there is a leak we should see bubbles rising. Come on let's give it a try?' he looked at Barry who nipped back into the house and returned with a half full bucket of water. It was a bit heavy and in his struggle to carry it Barry spilled a bit on the step.

'Watch out our kid, you're supposed to keep the water in the bucket, not chuck it all over me.' Barry managed to stay calm despite the goading from his big brother.

'OK Aiden – bang it in the bucket' Barry encouraged him and the group of lads all held their breath as Wilky immersed the inflated bladder into the bucket. They heaved a collective sigh of relief as no bubbles could be seen. Wilky pulled the bladder out and the lads applauded.

Up to this point Wilky had been squeezing the neck of the bladder between his forefinger and thumb to stop the air escaping, with the trial successfully completed he bent the rubber neck over and tied it securely with a short leather lace.

'Oh well done Wilky' yelled Terry.

'Aye but how are you gunna get the bladder inside the leather ball Wilky?' the challenge came from Martin.

Wilky studied for a moment looking first at the bladder and then at the leather casing. He scratched his head whilst he tried to figure out the answer. All the other lads looked on in disbelief. Their precious new ball was fixed but they couldn't work out how to put it together. After what seemed like an age, but was probably only a minute, Fergy came up with the answer. 'I think you're meant to put the bladder inside the case when it's flat and THEN pump it up Wilky' he suggested.

'Oh of course' Wilky laughed 'I knew all the time I was just testing you all, to see if you could work it out for yourselves'.

A look of total disbelief appeared on Barry's face at this denial but he decided not to spoil his brother's moment of triumph, after all he had fixed the puncture all by himself, something Barry would never have managed in the proverbial month of Sundays.

Wilky untied the neck of the bladder which, as the air was released made, a noise similar to a fart and the lads all giggled. Once the bladder was fully deflated, Wilky inserted it into the leather case and the ball was pumped up without any further mishaps. All that remained was the ceremonial tying of the leather lace to seal the ball up and it was ready for play.

'OK lads let's give it a try' Wilky announced as he bounced the ball a couple of times on the path. So they all made their way into the field for what would be only their second ever game with a leather ball, not any leather ball mind you, this was THEIR leather ball.

Unfortunately by the time the boys had sorted out their teams for the match it was starting to come dark. Nevertheless the boys could not wait till morning to try out their new ball and the game commenced in the twilight. After a few minutes of play in the diminishing light Sutty's dad was calling him to come in and the boys agreed it was time to go home. Their second proper game with a real leather ball would have to wait till the morning.

It was unanimously agreed that Terry should be the custodian of the ball and he proudly carried it back to his house and it was placed in a position of prominence in the front room where he could keep his eye on it whilst watching the TV. Later as he wearily made his way to bed with the football in his hands his dad asked him if he would be sleeping with the football to which he replied 'Of course I am dad, I'm not leaving it down stairs we might get burgled and I don't want to lose it.'

EXTRACT FROM BARRY WILKINSON'S DIARY

17th July 1959

Our first ever game was a bit of a disappointment and we lost 8 – 2. It was 5 – nil at half time so me and Sutty swapped positions.

He did better than me in goals and the second half was only 3 – 2 to Birkby. It was the first time any of us had played with a proper leather ball and on a proper pitch so I don't think we did too bad and Mr Blackburn said we did well.

Fergy got our first goal and then little Terry scored, he was so happy and couldn't stop talking about it all the way home which annoyed Martin.

When we got back to the estate Fergy's mam and his sister Carol had made us some lovely buns which made us all feel better. Our Aiden was greedy as usual and must have had at least five buns.

By the time we got home dad had gone back to work, grandad said he was mad with us cos he didn't know where we were, but our Aiden told him we'd explained it all to us mam before she went to work.

We decided that we needed to get some practice in playing with a leather ball and Terry managed to scrounge the one the big lads used from Mrs Knight. It was flat but our Aiden did a good job and fixed it. By the time the ball was fixed it was too dark to play soccer so we are going to try the new ball out tomorrow.

Fergy says we need to develop our skills if we want to win our next match and I think he's right. We're going to do lots of drills on things like shooting and dribbling and passing as well as playing matches.

When the boys gathered together in the field the following morning they decided that the Tranny would be the best location to try out the new leather ball. Their old plastic ball was not discarded though as Fergy was insisting that they do some of his 'drills' before the match started and both balls would be required. Despite complaints from some of the lads Fergy had them practicing their shooting, dribbling and passing for 15 minutes before the game commenced. The weather had been warm and dry for some time and the surface of the football pitch was rock hard. The boys soon found that the new ball was much more difficult to control on the hard surface and mistakes were common. Nevertheless they persevered and gradually their skills developed and they started to control the ball more effectively.

As they wandered back to the estate some of the lads were once more complaining about the drills which Fergy had made them do. Fergy and the Wilkinsons exchanged glances and Wilky gave Fergy the nod. This was the signal to tell the lads about their next proper match. Fergy told them that his dad was arranging another match for them through a chap he worked with. The atmosphere immediately changed and the lads became much more positive about doing the drills and developing their skills.

The team they were going to play were from the Woodhouse Hill area and the match would take place at Leeds Road playing fields so at least the lads wouldn't have to walk so far this time. The game would take place on Saturday in two weeks time and Fergy's dad and his work mate would be in charge of the two teams, another workmate of theirs had agreed to referee the game.

Fergy explained 'So you see lads it's really important that we work on our skills as much as possible if we want to win this game. We've got a decent ball now, so we won't be able to use that as an excuse this time. We need to make sure that we're used to playing with a leather ball, that's why we need to do those drills'.

Wilky carried on 'We all need to spend as much time as possible practicing and improving all our skills. Like Fergy said just playing games isn't good enough. Are we all agreed?' A good deal of mumbling followed so Wilky repeated 'Are we all agreed? Hands up if you agree with spending more time on the drills'. To Wilky's relief all the lads raised their hands. 'Good, so no more complaining about the drills, got it? When do we start Fergy?'

'How about this afternoon Wilky?'

'Sounds good to me' Wilky replied.

EXTRACT FROM BARRY WILKINSON'S DIARY

18th July 1959

Went down to the Tranny for our first game with the leather ball.

Fergy made us do some practice drills before we started – I don't think Terry and Martin liked doing them but I think it's what we need.

The new ball was much more difficult to control than the plastic one but we stuck at it and were doing a lot better at the end. Dave Henshaw was complaining about the drills and so were Martin and Terry but when Fergy told them that we were going to have another match they changed their tune a bit.

Fergy's dad is arranging the game it's against a team from Wood-house Hill and we're gunna play down at Leeds Road playing fields in two weeks time. Everybody agreed that we would do half an hour of practice drills before every match we play so we can win the next game.

CHAPTER 30 – PRACTICE
MAKES PERFECT

Summer 1959

So for the next two weeks the boys did a thirty minute drill session before each match that they played. As their skills improved and the number of days to their second match reduced the boys got more and more excited.

Two days before the match Mr Ferguson suggested a practice match down at the Tranny after which the team would be selected.

In total there were 14 players available for selection. This was made up of the twelve who played in the first game plus Andy and Ricky who had been on holiday when the first match took place. All the boys were desperate to play but knew that only eleven could be picked so they all tried their hardest to impress Mr Ferguson. It was attack versus defence as before and the teams were evenly balanced. The attack team eventually ran out winners by 4 – 3.

Mr Ferguson congratulated all the players and told them that he would announce the team when they got back to the estate. The boys assembled outside the Ferguson's house which was by the circle and Mr Ferguson went into the house to write out the team which he had selected. A few minutes later he emerged and began to read out the team.

'In goals Sutty' he started and then worked his way through

the team until he reached 'left wing Val Taylor'. Eleven boys were smiling but three very definitely were not. Patrick Connor, Jimmy Henshaw and Ricky Chapman, three of the younger players had been left out of the team.

'However' Mr Ferguson continued his announcement, 'I have agreed with the Woodhouse Hill manager that we will be allowed three substitutes, so Patrick, Jimmy and Ricky will be the substitutes'.

'How d'you mean □*□substitutes Mr Ferguson' for once Terry got a long word right.

'It's like this Terry' Mr Ferguson explained 'we can swap three players during the game so, if someone is injured or tired out or not playing so well, we can bring the other lads on. That way everybody will get to take part in the match and no-one is left out. The other team will also be allowed to have three substitutes so it's fair to both sides.

Mr Ferguson had pulled off a master stroke, everybody was happy and team morale was sky high as they made their way down to Leeds Road playing fields for the game on Saturday morning.

Fartown United once more played in white shirts with black shorts and the opposition lined up in red shirts and white shorts. It was a beautiful summer's day as the teams kicked off. Woodhouse Hill took an early lead but the boys from Fartown fought back and were leading at half time by 2 – 1, their goals coming from Dave Henshaw and Wilky. Unfortunately Martin had fallen over heavily in a tackle and received a bad cut on his knee from the rock hard ground. As Mr Ferguson helped him from the pitch he told Patrick to get ready to replace the unfortunate Martin.

As Mr Ferguson surveyed the team at half time he could see that Val Taylor, who suffered from hay fever, was in a bad way and decided to replace him with Jimmy Henshaw. He decided to hold Ricky back in case there were any more injuries.

As the second half began Woodhouse Hill were piling on the pressure and eventually the pressure paid off as they drew level in a rather fortuitous way. The equaliser coming when, following a corner, a clearance from Barry struck Dave Henshaw on the back of his head and rebounded into the net. With fifteen minutes to go and the scores still locked at 2 – 2 Mr Ferguson brought Andy Chapman off and replaced him with his younger brother Ricky. It was to prove a master stroke. Woodhouse Hill seemed to be laying siege to the Fartown goals when a long Fartown clearance found it's way to Ricky on the half way line. He booted the ball forward and chased after it and, as the opposition goalkeeper came running out, the two of them kicked the ball at exactly the same time. The ball flew up in the air and dropped just behind the Woodhouse Hill goalkeeper who made a desperate attempt to catch the ball but missed and the top spin on the ball did the rest as it shot into the empty goals.

The Fartown players mobbed Ricky, but the game wasn't over – there were still 10 minutes remaining. The Woodhouse Hill players tried everything they could but they couldn't beat Sutty in the Fartown goal. Then in the dying seconds of the game Fergy sealed the game with one of his rocket shots before the referee blew for the end of the game and the Fartown celebrations began.

The Fartown players were busily congratulating each other when Mr Ferguson came over 'Well played lads, you certainly deserved that, but I must admit I was a bit worried in the second half when they were doing all that attacking. Now don't forget to go over and shake hands with the other team, they played well too.'

Later on as they started the walk back along the canal bank to their homes they relived every minute of the game. All the sliding tackles, headers and shots were recounted over and over again.

Mr Ferguson was asked to decide who was the star player but he sensibly declined, diplomatically stating that football is a team game and the whole team played well. 'Everyone, including the substitutes, played their part, it was a victory for team work' was all he would say.

As the boys made their weary way up the ginnel to the estate they agreed to meet by the swings after they had had their dinners. Martin, by this time, was hobbling badly. 'Make sure your mam cleans that cut and puts some iodine on it Martin' suggested Terry 'it looks really sore'.

'I'll be OK, don't worry about me' Martin replied bravely.

'Is everyone else OK?' Mr Ferguson asked.'How's your hay fever Val?'

Val's eyes were streaming 'I think they'd just cut the grass down at the playing fields, it's always worse when the grass has been cut. I should have brought my spray with me, but I'll be alright once I get home'.

As it was a Saturday most of the boys would have had their main meal of the day before gathering in the field and they all looked refreshed. Terry arrived alongside Martin who was sporting a large bandage around his injured knee. 'Me mam says I haven't to play soccer with my knee being cut, so I suggest we lake cricket if that's OK with you lot?'

A game of cricket was quickly organised and Martin was allocated a runner to compensate for his injured knee. The boys were still full of the euphoria of their first victory and this was reflected in the way they all batted. Wilky's team batted first and scored an impressive 62 runs which was almost twice as much as the normal scores. Fergy's team looked to be on course to beat that score until Dave Henshaw had Terry caught on the boundary and then Fergy cleaned bowled. Martin, with the aid of his runner, managed to take the score to 58 before losing his wicket to a great catch by Sutty.

As the boys gathered around the settee Fergy pointed out the total scores of the two teams was 120 runs. 'That's a lot more than we usually get isn't it?'

'We must be getting good at batting then' added Wilky, who had top scored with 25 runs.

'I know' Terry jumped in enthusiastically 'why don't we form a cricket team and play against another team. You know just like we've done at soccer'.

The boys were excited by this idea but the ever logical Fergy brought them down to earth. 'We'd need a lot of equipment, you know pads and gloves and what sort of ball would we play with?'

'We'd only need those things if we played with a real cricket ball, if we stick to the plastic ball we should be OK' Barry pointed out.

'That's true Barry but who would we play against?' responded Fergy.

'We managed to find two teams to play soccer against why don't we ask them if they want to lake us at cricket, we can play down at the playing fields' Terry took over the argument.

And so the boys of Fartown United, buoyed by their first ever win at soccer, began another chapter in their sporting careers as they made plans for their first cricket match as the FCC (Fartown Cricket Club).

EXTRACT FROM BARRY WILKINSON'S DIARY

1st August 1959

The best day ever. We got our first win today – what a match. We beat Woodhouse Hill by 4 – 2. It was a close game though. We went a goal behind but then our Aiden and Dave Henshaw scored so we were winning 2 – 1 at half time. In the second half we were defending a lot and then they equalised. Their goal was abit of a fluke, I tried to clear the ball but it hit Dave Henshaw on the back of his head and rebounded into the goal.

Mr Ferguson is a really good manager, he brought Paddy Connor and Jimmy Henshaw on at half time cos Martin was injured and Val was having a hay fever attack. Later on he brought Ricky Chapman on in place of his brother and he scored a really good goal. We were defending a lot but near the end we got a break away and Fergy smashed the ball past their goaly. When it went in we knew we were going to win as there wasn't long left. When the ref blew the whistle it was the best feeling ever.

We asked Mr Ferguson to say who our best player was, but he said we all played really well which is true. It was a good idea to have the substitutes so everybody got to play a part in the win.

We had a great game of cricket in the afternoon with lots of runs scored. Our team batted first and scored 62 runs – that's the most any team has scored, our Aiden scored 25 and I got 11. Fergy's team nearly caught us but they were all out for 58 which is a good score.

Anyway after the match we were all talking and somebody came up with the idea of us having a cricket team (I think it was Terry) and we all think it's a great idea. Fergy is going to ask his dad if his mate at work wants to get a team from Woodhouse Hill and we could play them down at Leeds Road playing fields which will be great. We're gunna call ourselves the FCC which stands for Fartown Cricket Club, can't wait.

▢*▢ Yorkshire slang for playing
▢*▢ A local manufacturer of 'fizzy pop'

□*□ Yorkshire word for smacks or being hit

□*□ Slang for perhaps

□*□ It was common practice when old bed sheets were worn out to tear them up into strips for blowing your nose on when you had a cold. They would be used once and then thrown away, a sort of forerunner of the paper tissue.

□*□ A term used when one of the players stands near to the opposition goals and waits for his team mates to kick the ball to him so he can score

□*□ Slang word for sixpence, equivalent to 2.5 new pence

□*□ A slang word for six old pence, equivalent to two and a half new pence

□*□ Another way of saying one and sixpence, often used in Yorkshire. Equivalent of 7.5p

□*□ Slang word for a shilling – 5 new pence, three bob would be 15 pence.

□*□ **Newfooty** was the fore-runner to **Subbuteo** Table Soccer, and can lay claim to being the original finger flicking table soccer game.

□*□ A Yorkshire slang word for begging

□*□ Arguing and fighting

□*□ Yorkshire slang meaning self

□*□ Substitutes were first used in the Football League on 21 August 1965 when Keith Peacock of Charlton Athletic came on in the 11th minute of their game against Bolton Wanderers.

Printed in Great Britain
by Amazon

30328882R00209